BOYS OF WINTER

SHERIDAN ANNE

Sheridan Anne
Deviant: Boys of Winter #3

Copyright © 2021 Sheridan Anne
All rights reserved
First Published in 2021
Anne, Sheridan
Deviant: Boys of Winter #3

Cover Design: Sheridan Anne
Photographer: Korabkova
Editing: Heather Fox
Editing & Formatting: Sheridan Anne

DEVIANT

To all those beautiful women in happy relationships who are dreaming about letting four sexy AF dudes rail you until you pass out ...

I got you.

1

Howling tears through the silence as pressure slams down over my waist.

Familiar hands pull at me, tearing at my clothes, slipping under my head, and wrapping tightly around me as bodies fly into my side. The boys' knees press into my ribs, my shoulders, my thighs, getting as close as possible and jostling me around.

The howling continues.

My eyes flutter open and everything is blurry, but before I can make out the shapes before me, it all goes dark again.

"WINTER. FUCK. Baby, open your eyes."

King? Cruz? Maybe it was Grayson. I don't know. I'm too tired.

Too sore.

"GET THAT FUCKING DOG OUT OF HERE."

The voice inside my head is telling me to scream as the sharp burning tears through me, spreading and throbbing until I can't remember my own damn name.

"Winter. Open your goddamn eyes." The voice comes out in a strangled, pissed-off demand that's filled with pain and emotion, and just like that, I know it's King. His voice comes from above my head, and his arms are wrapped tightly around me, distracting me from the burning pain shooting through my abdomen.

My body feels heavy and just the thought of trying to get up is exhausting. I just want to sleep. Why won't they let me sleep?

"Winter, I swear to fucking God, if you don't open your eyes right fucking now, you and I are going to have problems."

A heavy groan pulls from deep within me, but I have no idea if they can even hear me. All I know is that if King keeps yelling at me to open my damn eyes, I'm going to stab him with a fork right through his dick.

A hand presses against my thigh, squeezing tight. "Come on, Winter. You can't pass out yet. Just stay with us until we can get you to the hospital," Cruz murmurs to my right, the panic in his tone almost enough to shatter every little piece of me. "I swear, once you're there, I'll even knock you out myself if you want."

My head lolls in King's hand and a pained breath slips from between my lips. "Stop being so dramatic," I tell them, my voice coming out in a shaky whisper as a bark sounds right beside my face.

"I'm fine."

I hear a scoff from my left, and without needing to look up, I know it's Grayson. Before I can berate him for his balls of steel to scoff at me while I'm mid bleeding out, he presses harder against my wound and my eyes finally find the strength to fly open. Though they don't just fly open, they bulge right out of my fucking head. "HOLY MOTHER OF FUCK. THAT HURTS," I yell as I thrash under the boys' hold. The agony is so much more than I can bear. "GO SUCK A GIANT DICK, YOU FUCKING TWATBURGER. IT HURTS. STOP. PLEASE STOP."

My screams quickly turn into heaving sobs as the pain becomes all too much. Too intense ... too threatening. "I have to put pressure on it," Grayson tells me in his no-bullshit tone, though his distress is coming through loud and clear. He doesn't want to hurt me any more than necessary, but he's going to fucking do it if it means saving my stupid ass, no matter what it costs himself to do it. "You're not bleeding out on me today."

Cruz and King hold me tight, keeping me still as I try to fight against them, but my energy is quickly wearing thin. I feel the darkness coming back and it scares the shit out of me. "No," I cry. "Stop. It hurts."

"Man the fuck up, Ellie," Grayson tells me, his tone both deeper and darker. "I'd prefer you screaming and hating me than lying dead in your parents' garage. What would your father say if you just gave up? You're fighting this whether you want to or not."

My gaze swivels to find Grayson's determined stare as the tears fall from my eyes. He's right. I have to fight this. I never got a chance to know my father, but from what I've learned, he'd be pretty fucking pissed if I gave up and let them win.

Dynasty is mine and they'll never take it from me. Fuck, I don't even care that I want nothing to do with it, but I'll do everything it takes to make sure Dynasty doesn't fall into the hands of the people who would use it to destroy everything good in the world. My grandfather had a vision in mind when he founded Dynasty, and over the years, that vision has turned to shit. I'd sell my fucking soul just to make it what it once was, and I'd do it with a fucking smile on my face if it means ridding Dynasty of fuckfaces like my mother, Preston Scardoni, and every asshole who stands against me.

I have to survive.

I won't let that bitch get away with this. I have to find her, and when I do, I'm going to fucking kill her, no matter how hard or how painful it's going to be. I refuse to see that woman as my mother. She's just a cold, hard bitch who deserves every bit of my wrath.

I seek out Grayson's hard stare. "Can't kill me that easily."

I try to reach for Grayson, but the movement only sends a searing hot ache shooting through my abdomen, making the blood flood out over his hands. "Fuck," I curse, sucking in a sharp breath as I fear the worst.

Cruz reaches across me and grabs my arm before pressing it over my chest and keeping it locked in place. "Don't move, baby," he mutters, meeting my stare with an equally panicked one, the fear strong in his tone. "The ambulance is coming. Just keep talking shit for a few more minutes. We've got you."

I take slow, deep breaths, trying to focus on King's soft, caressing touches while zoning out of the harsh, forceful ones coming from Grayson. They're a complete contrast to one another, yet so perfectly matched to their personalities.

My gaze flashes up to King as the tears flow freely down my face. "I don't want to die."

"You're not fucking dying," he grunts, his jaw clenched with eyes as dark as night.

Cruz's hand slips into mine and he laces our fingers as he moves in closer, keeping his face right where I can see it. "What do you need to keep those pretty eyes open?" he questions, desperately trying to keep me distracted from my harsh new reality. "I can find that video of Gray jerking off and yelling 'YAHTZEE.' Just name it. Anything."

"The fuck?" Grayson grunts, his head whipping up as he presses down even harder, his eyes quickly flashing back to mine.

A small smile pulls at the side of my mouth, and for just a second, I'm grateful that I have the energy to smile. If I'm going to die here today, then I want them to remember me smiling. They already have so much pain and hurt to deal with, especially King after only just losing his father last night. I can't even imagine what this would do to them. Fuck, I haven't even had a proper chance to make things right with Carver. The ball was supposed to be our shot at mending the burning bridge between us, and instead of mending bridges, all we got was an exploding staircase and smoke inhalation.

What kind of fucked-up world have I been brought into? Maybe I was better off in the foster system, but then I would have missed out on meeting these guys, and I'm man enough to admit that meeting the Kings of Ravenwood Heights has honestly been the best thing to have ever happened to me.

"You still …" I cringe, sucking in a hard breath as I look back up at Cruz. "You still have the 'YAHTZEE' video?"

Cruz gives me a dazzling smile that stretches right across his face, though his eyes don't sparkle the way they usually do. My heart aches, but his smile still manages to ease something within me. "Of course, I do," he tells me. "I've got a whole folder on each of these bastards filled with bullshit blackmail to use against them, but it's the shit I've got on you that keeps me up at night."

Cruz winks, and for just a second, warmth spreads through me, but when the heaviness starts weighing on my eyelids again, all I feel is cold.

King's thumb moves back and forth over my cheek. "Come on, Winter. You're going to be fine," he says, almost like a chant before snapping his head up and looking across the garage. "Where's that fucking ambulance?"

His question is met with silence, and I can't help following his eye line to find Carver standing by the door, the gun dropped at his feet, and a look of unbelievable, gut-wrenching fear plastered across his beautiful face.

His dark eyes roam over my body as though he's never seen anything so terrifying in his life, and as they finally scan up past the blood pouring over Grayson's hands, and he finds my gaze staring right back at his, he breaks.

An all-consuming guilt floods his dark eyes and devastation pours through me, watching as he falls to his knees, unable to come to terms with what he's done. "Carver," I whisper, desperately wishing I had the energy to run to him, to crash into his warm arms and tell him that everything is going to be alright.

The look in his eyes … fuck. He looks as though he just killed the love of his life. "Carver … I …"

He falls forward, his head dropping into his hands. "I missed," he whispers in disbelief, his voice so soft and filled with an unbelievable guilt that tears right through my chest, grabbing hold of my heart and squeezing it until it shatters into a million pieces.

Pain tears through me, but not from the bullet that's lodged somewhere deep inside of my stomach. Tears fill my eyes as I watch the guilt completely consume him, desperately wishing I could take it away, but how? What the hell can I do for him now? He's right. He shot me. He raised his gun, and in a moment of panic, he squeezed the trigger and the bullet sailed straight through my stomach.

The great Dante Carver let his desperation claim him, and because of that, he missed his mark.

That split decision to squeeze the trigger is going to haunt him for the rest of his life and there's not a damn thing I can say or do that will take that pain away. I'll never have the words to ease his guilt, it's something he'll have to work out all on his own.

It was nothing but a horrendous accident. That bullet was meant for the woman who stood behind me with a knife pressed hard against my throat.

My twisted as fuck, dimwitted, bitch of a mother.

No wonder I'm so fucked up.

What did I do to deserve a mother who has a hard-on for trying to kill her daughter? Though, I guess the apple doesn't fall far from the tree because I certainly have a fondness for slitting throats, and I just now discovered what a kick I'd get out of slitting hers.

Fuck. I hate that bitch.

Knowing I won't get anywhere with Carver, I shift my gaze back up to King's before glancing out the open garage to where the door lay in a crumpled mess on my long-ass driveway. "She ... she got away," I whisper, my words coming in slower and slower. "I ... I should have ... done something. I could have ..."

"Shhhhh," King rumbles. "I promise you, babe. She may have gotten away for now, but I won't fucking rest until I've fucked that bitch up. You did perfectly. You did everything you could do. She just has a gift for escaping, but not anymore. We know who she is now, and she better watch her back. We will hunt her down like the fucking dog that she is."

I let out a heavy sigh and nod as the pain starts to fade to a distant hum. "Good," I murmur, letting the heaviness of my eyelids win the battle. Maybe if the boys have my back and take her out for me, maybe I won't have to. Maybe I can just let go now. "I ... I can't hold on anymore."

My eyes close and Cruz instantly squeezes my leg in a panic, his grip tight enough to bruise. "Not today, babe. Wake up, let me see those pretty eyes."

"Mmmm. I'm awake."

Cruz gives me a gentle shake as we hear the ambulance wailing in the distance. "Winter? Fuck, Winter. Wake up. You're not dying on me, hold on a minute longer. The ambulance is nearly here. I have too much to tell you. Come on, I fucking love you, you can't go now. OPEN YOUR GODDAMN EYES, BABE. FIGHT IT. YOU'RE NOT GIVING UP YET. FIGHT FOR FUCKS SAKE."

I nod, as my body grows heavy and Grayson starts pressing harder, but it's fine. I don't feel it now.

I just feel darkness. A hollowness that spreads through my body and takes all the pain away.

I get to be with my dad.

"FUCK, WE'RE LOSING HER," Grayson roars, his usual cool, calm, and collected tone now completely gone and replaced with nothing but sheer terror, pain, and guilt. "HAVE YOUR FUCKING PITY PARTY LATER, CARVER. GET THE FUCK OVER HERE AND HELP BEFORE SHE BLEEDS OUT."

I feel King flinch by my head, his anger rolling off him in waves as he presses his fingers to the side of my neck, checking for a pulse. "If she fucking dies, I swear to God, I'll make you relive it every fucking day for the rest of your miserable life."

My head lolls in King's lap and as I let the darkness finally claim me, a soft, broken cry breaks through, and that one anguish-filled sob is all I take with me as I say a silent goodbye to what could have been an amazing life.

"Move," a harsh voice tears through the silence before my body is rocked and the pain comes shooting back with a ferocious anger, sending life soaring back into me in a big way.

A loud gasp comes tearing out of me as my eyes fly open to find unfamiliar faces hovering around me. I'm picked up and my body is immediately dropped back down onto a hard surface, my back flat against a table.

"Come on," the voice cuts through the pain. "Go, go, go."

My eyes widen in fear. Where am I? Where are the boys? Where are they taking me?

The people start pushing me and I grab at their hands as the searing pain calls for me to pass out again. "Stop. STOP. DON'T TOUCH ME," I scream, the wild panic tearing through my chest as I fight against their hold, thrashing and pulling. Where are the boys? "Carver? CARVER?"

I hear a loud grunt before his face appears hovering above me, his hand wrapped tightly in mine before he holds me down, keeping me still. "I'm here," Carver soothes, squeezing my hand until it hurts as he moves with me. "You're fine. These are the paramedics. You need to let them help you."

"No, no, no," I fret, trying to pull myself up off the table. "Don't let them take me. I don't want to go. Don't leave me."

"No one is leaving you," Carver says, holding me tighter and making it impossible to move. "I'll be with you the whole time, okay? Now, lay still before you make it worse."

Tears well in my eyes and I nod, quickly glancing around to find King and Cruz walking with the paramedics as Grayson remains behind, sitting on the garage floor with my blood soaking through his clothes, staring after me as though he'll never see me again.

My heart aches for him, but he's strong, and he's suffered through a lot worse than dealing with a little bit of blood. Only this time his heart is involved, and from experience, when the heart is involved, that usually means things are beyond fucked up.

Carver reaches out, wiping the tears off the side of my face as we hit the back of the ambulance. The gurney rocks, forcing a sharp breath through my clenched jaw, and as I look up and meet Carver's pained stare, I see nothing but guilt shining brightly in his eyes.

The gurney rolls into the back of the ambulance and I hold back my screams as Carver gets right in with me, crouching beside the gurney so his face is right by mine as the paramedics do their thing. Something presses down over my face as the back doors of the ambulance slam shut, closing me off to King, Cruz, and Grayson, but something tells me that they won't be far behind.

The ambulance takes off as Carver squeezes my hand, keeping my attention on him. "You're going to make it," he tells me. "You have to fucking make it."

I shake my head, letting the tears fall free. "I'm dying. I can't … I'm not going to make it."

"Don't you fucking say that," he roars at me, squeezing my hand so much tighter, so tight that I feel my knuckles pressing together. "You're going to fucking fight because if you don't, if you fucking die, it's going to destroy Cruz. It's going to kill King, and it'll fucking wreck Gray, and I won't let you do that to them. Fight for them."

A tear falls and lands right on our hands between our faces. "And what about you?"

"If you fucking die on me, Winter," he says, his gaze boring into mine. "I'll never forgive you— because we're not done yet. There's still so much more that we need to do together, so much that we haven't even had the chance to start yet, and fuck it, I want it all. You're stronger than this. You can fight it."

"The four of you keep putting me on a pedestal, but I'm not that strong."

"You are, Winter. You're a fucking Ravenwood, and I know this is all on me, and I'll fucking live with it for the rest of my life, but you're not dying today. You have too much left to do."

Pressure comes down on my abdomen and I clench my jaw as the pain continues to rock through me. "I'm scared," I tell him, hating the words as they come out of my mouth. I've always prided myself on being strong, always strived to push myself harder, and I've done everything I possibly can to hide my weaknesses, but Carver sees through it. He's been able to see my vulnerabilities since the day I first met him. He knows me better than I know myself. He's the reason I was able to survive in the beginning.

"I know," he murmurs as the paramedics step in beside him and take my arm to start an IV. Hopefully, they'll get some pain relief pulsing through my system. "But you're not as fucking terrified as I am. If I lose you ..."

Carver lets the words fall away, but I don't need him to finish them. I know exactly what he's saying because I feel it too. The idea of one of the guys being taken away from me is the most painful thought that I've ever had, and right now, all four of them are fearing that exact thing.

Carver is right. I have to fight this. I have to make it because if I don't, the boys will be shattered and I refuse to do that to them.

I have too much to do in this world. Too many battles to win.

My eyelids grow heavy and I wonder what the fuck the paramedic put into my IV, but I don't get a chance to ask as my world quickly begins to fall away. "Sleep, Winter," Carver tells me, keeping my hand tucked safely between his. "Just make sure you come back to me. This isn't the end, not yet."

2

The soft, rhythmic beep of my heart monitor sounds through my room as consciousness comes back to me, telling me that somehow, I made it. I defied all the odds, and for some reason unknown to me, I've been granted the chance to live another day.

My eyes peel open and the fogginess inside my head quickly sets in, bringing on a migraine that makes me desperate for the darkness again.

It was peaceful in the darkness. It was quiet and I didn't have to think about anything. Nothing existed but me. There were no dickheads trying to kill me, no evil mothers trying to take me out, no bastards trying to drown me in my pool or shoot me in the woods.

I was safe in the darkness.

"Fucking hell, babe," I hear Cruz sighing from beside me just as his warm hand curls around mine. The relief is evident in his tone and completely overwhelms me with the best kind of warmth. "You scared me for a while. Are you good? What do you need? Should I call your doctor?"

"Jesus," King grunts from my other side, his tone flat, forceful, and exhausted. "Give her a fucking chance to wake up. She just got out of surgery."

"She's been out for over eight hours," Cruz snaps back. "She's just fucking with us now. I'm done waiting. I need to check that she's alright."

"She'll wake when she's fucking ready to wake," Grayson's booming voice calls through the room, coming from the end of the bed.

My face scrunches as the sound of their conversation thunders against my aching head, feeding my migraine and reminding me just how human I really am. I'm nothing special. I'm not Superwoman. Though these guys would disagree. For some insane reason that I haven't figured out yet, they think the sun shines out of my ass, and for that, I'm thankful. They make me feel things I never thought I'd be capable of feeling, and it's so much more than I ever dreamed for myself.

"Would you all shut up? My head is fucking killing me."

"Shit," Cruz rushes out with a small gasp, practically launching off the seat beside my bed to get even closer, looking right at my face to see my eyes open just a slither. "You're awake?"

"Barely," I grumble, my lips stretching into a grimace as every word that comes out makes me feel as though I'm slamming my head against a brick wall. I feel King move in closer on my left, probably just as desperate as Cruz to make sure that I'm truly alright.

Cruz moves right into my line of sight, blocking out a disheveled Grayson at the end of the bed. His beautiful green eyes shine with a million truths, telling me everything that he's refusing to say out loud, and damn it, it fucking kills me. He's been through hell and back over the past few hours, I'm sure they all have, but Cruz … Cruz is the one who feels it deep in his gut. The worst would have sat on his mind until the moment I woke, and those horrendous thoughts will stay with him for years to come.

"How are you feeling?" he asks, making my heart break as he focuses every bit of his attention on me, showing me just how much he truly cares. "Do you need a drink? Water? The nurse? Whatever you need, babe, I'm here."

Cruz watches me for a second, his hand gently squeezing mine, but how am I supposed to tell him that what I really need is silence? I wouldn't dare. He can ask me every question under the sun, and I'll accept all of them with a worsening migraine. At least the pain is a constant reminder that my heart is still beating—unless this is some twisted version of hell.

"I just …" I try to swallow over the dryness of my throat. "Water. Nurse."

"You got it, babe," Cruz says reaching around and pressing the call button on a little remote attached to the side of my bed.

King grabs a bottle of water and lifts it to my lips. I take a quick sip, and as he pulls it away, he focuses on my eyes. "Better? Do you need more?"

My gaze shifts over King's handsome face, taking in his haunted eyes and renewed hope. King has been through the worst kind of hell. It was only yesterday that he lost his father, and now he has to deal with this. I wish so desperately that I could take that pain away.

I gently shake my head. "I'm okay now," I whisper as I slowly scan the room to meet Grayson's stare, only to find it filled with demons. The things he's had to do over the last few hours … fuck. I can't even imagine what that would feel like. Having my blood flooding over his hands and not being able to help me would have seriously screwed with his head, but Grayson is stronger than I ever knew. Today will haunt him, but he'll hold it together and not let it show.

Grayson's stormy eyes bore into mine, and he holds my gaze for just a second longer than necessary, telling me so much with his silent stare.

I shift my gaze up to the shadow hovering in the doorway and instantly get hit with Carver's shattered stare. There's no other way to put it—he looks like shit. Carver's chin that's usually raised with power is down, his eyes that usually shine with strength are broken, and his heart that is usually locked so far away that not even he knows what it wants is sitting out on his sleeve for the world to see.

He blames himself for this. He was strong for me in the ambulance and gave me exactly what I needed to keep myself fighting, but now …

now he's nothing but a broken man completely overwhelmed by guilt.

I have to fix this, but how? Telling him that I don't blame him is going to do nothing. He'll listen to me, but he won't hear me. Carver is just like me. He's a stubborn asshole who listens only to himself, and right now, he's determined to believe that he's responsible for nearly killing me. He doesn't give a shit that there was a crazy woman standing behind me with a knife to my throat, he doesn't care that had he not made a move, she would have slit my throat with one quick flick of her wrist, and he doesn't care that this is all on her. To him, all that matters is that it was his bullet that put me in this bed.

The urge to get up and go to him pulses through me and I try to sit up, only King and Cruz are there, shoving my shoulders back to the bed. "Whoa, baby, don't fucking move," Cruz orders. "You're going to tear open your stitches."

Stitches? Fuck me. How have I not even considered the hole in my abdomen right now? All that mattered was the boys, but Cruz is right. If I'm not careful, I could seriously fuck myself up again.

Not being able to handle the intensity of Carver's stare, I look back to Cruz then flick my gaze between the three hovering around my bed. "Don't get me wrong," I murmur, my head pounding with every word, "any girl would be lucky to wake up with four guys fussing over her, but who ... who are you?"

Cruz's eyes bug out of his head and snap to King, whose jaw drops, panic instantly spreading over his face. Grayson just narrows his eyes as Carver steps deeper into the room, watching me closer.

"What?" King breathes. "You ... you don't remember us?"

Cruz looks back at me, swallowing hard. "It's me," Cruz insists in a soft, encouraging tone, adding his other hand to our already held ones and squeezing it tighter, almost as though he hopes that just his touch will help to bring the memories back. "Please tell me you remember … I … I."

A grin pulls at the side of my mouth as my eyes begin to sparkle with laughter. I don't even get a word out before King tears his hand out of mine and flops back into his seat. "She's fucking with us," he announces, keeping his hard stare on mine as I hear Cruz let out a sigh of relief. "That's a dangerous fucking game you're playing."

"Chill out," I tell King, wishing I could manifest that bottle of water into my hands again. "The mood in here was going to kill me faster than any bullet could. Everyone needs to lighten up. I'm fine."

"You're not fine," Grayson growls from the end of the bed. "You got shot, and you nearly bled out beneath me. You're not about to sit there and shrug it off as though it doesn't matter. We nearly fucking lost you today."

"But you didn't," I insist, thankful as King reaches out and grabs the bottle of water, hearing the raspiness in my voice. "Do you really think I would have given up and left you all behind like that? We've been through so much, losing now isn't an option. We have too much left to do, and besides, if someone is going to kill me, they're going to have to try a shitload harder than that."

The boys groan at the thought of our enemies attempting harder than what they already have. We've been through the impossible together, and honestly, I don't know how much worse it can get. Fuck,

I don't know if we can physically survive any worse. We just suffered through a whole freaking ballroom blowing up. Though after the list of bullshit attacks we've made it through, surely my enemies can see that I'm not going down without a fight—none of us are.

Cruz groans and steals my attention from Grayson. "I hate how fucking blasé you're being about this. You nearly fucking died. We almost lost you, and fuck babe, I know you like to pretend that you don't fucking care, but we do. If you had died today … shit. I can't even …"

"Stop," I tell him, tugging on his hand to make him come closer. He does just that, and I pull him right in until my lips are brushing over his. "I'm not going anywhere," I whisper, pulling back just a bit and staring into his gorgeous green eyes.

Cruz holds my stare for a second before finally nodding and dropping back into his seat.

I look around the room, scanning quickly past Carver's intense stare. "Trust me," I murmur into the room. "I do care. I care so much that it freaking hurts. You guys are quickly becoming my world that I can't even bear the thought of being without you, but I can't linger on it. I can't linger on what happened today because I will crumble, and I can't do that because we still have so much to worry about. I let her get away. We had my mother right there and I should have done something more to get to her, but I froze. She put that fucking knife to my throat and I just … froze."

"Don't do that," King demands. "Had you made even the smallest move—she would have ended you. You did exactly what you were supposed to do."

I shake my head. "I could have looked around when I got out of my hiding spot, or fuck, I should have just stayed hidden in the fucking pantry."

"That's on me," Cruz says, his tone dropping as his gaze falls to our hands. "I was the one who told you it was clear. I gave you a false hope that you were safe and I have to live with that for the rest of my life. I should have stayed back to protect you while the guys swept the house."

"Stop," Grayson says, sitting forward in his chair. "Everyone blaming themselves for shit isn't helping us get anywhere. None of us are at fault here, especially not you, Carver, but right now, Ellie is our main focus. We need her to get better. We can come up with a plan to get to London later."

"I told you, I'm fine," I snap at him, knowing damn well that the boys will sneak out of here and work out a plan without me, leaving me out of the loop and in the dark, all under the pretense of trying to keep me safe. "The longer we wait, the more time she has to devise her next plan of attack. We need to get her now. We can't just sit here for God knows how long, turning a blind eye until I get better. We have to make a move. What if it's you guys she goes for next? I couldn't bear that."

King shakes his head. "She won't go for us," he insists. "It's a waste of time. She gains nothing by doing that except by taking away part of your protection. We're good."

"But—"

A nurse pushes past Carver and all conversation falls away. She meets his heavy, intense stare as she goes, and in that split moment, I feel sorry for her. I've been on the receiving end of that stare more times than I can count and it's not easy, add the self-hatred that's pulsing through his veins, and that stare might as well be lethal.

"Ahh …" the nurse starts, looking flustered as she weaves through the room and makes her way toward my bed. She scoops my chart off the end and quickly glances over it before raising her head and meeting my stare. "How are you feeling, Elodie?"

"It's Winter."

Her brows furrow and she looks at me strangely before quickly glancing at the guys just to make sure she heard me correctly. "I'm sorry?"

"My name," I tell her, wondering how the hell to explain this to an outsider. "Elodie is my legal name. I go by Winter."

"Oh, um … sure," she says, grabbing her pen and making a note of it in my chart, then dropping it back into place at the end of my bed. She walks around to my side and checks over a bunch of things that I can't even begin to understand the purpose of. "I'm Rachel, I'll be looking after you today, so anything you need, just press the button and I'll be here."

I nod, not down for small talk.

"Have you only just woken up?" she asks, reaching for the blankets and slowly peeling them back. "I just need to check your stitches. Would you prefer I clear the room first?"

I don't even bother looking up at the guys, I know exactly what would happen if this innocent nurse attempted to kick them out, and for her health and wellbeing, I shake my head. "No, it's fine," I tell her, raising my head just a bit to see what she sees.

"Alright," she continues. "I'm just going to raise your gown."

She gets to work and peels my gown up my body until it's all bunched under my tits and my black panties are on display for everyone to see, but with the thick bandages across my stomach, it's as though my panties don't even exist.

Rachel pulls at the tape and I close my eyes at the feel of her poking around. "You good?" King murmurs.

I clench my jaw and nod as he squeezes my hand. "Yeah, just hurts."

"I know, I'm sorry," Rachel says. "It'll be over in just a second and then we'll see about upping that pain relief."

I try to breathe through the pain, and as I do, I slowly peel my eyes open again and look down to see the mess my abdomen is currently in. "Holy fuck," I breathe, taking in the dark bruising and wicked stitches.

"Don't panic," Rachel tells me. "It looks worse than it is, but unfortunately, the bruising is only going to get darker over the next few days. You are one hell of a lucky girl, Winter."

I scoff. "Lying in a hospital bed with a bullet wound is your version of lucky?"

Rachel presses her lips into a tight line, and I watch as she visibly attempts not to roll her eyes at my comment. "What I mean is that you're lucky that it wasn't any worse. The bullet grazed your left kidney and shot right out through the back without catching anything else.

You got lucky. You had exploratory surgery to find the bleed, which your surgeon was able to locate and mend quickly. It's nothing that a few weeks of bed rest and some pain medication won't fix. So, for the most part, you're going to be just fine."

I can't help but look up at Carver, knowing damn well that he's been listening carefully to the trauma my body has just suffered through. There's not a doubt in my mind that he's hating on himself even more. The guilt inside this room is astronomical, and right now, it's all coming from him. But in this very moment with Rachel still in the room, there's not a damn thing I can do about it.

I turn back to Rachel, avoiding the shifty stares of the boys around me, knowing exactly why I was just looking at Carver. "For the most part?" I ask her, not quite sure how I feel about the few weeks of bed rest.

Rachel nods as she replaces the bandages. "Yes, you will be left with a small scar, but being shot is not something that happens every day, so I'm sure you will also have the emotional scars that go along with it."

"Oh, umm … yeah, I guess. I'll be fine though."

"I'm sure you will," she tells me in a tone that reminds me of a mother berating her misbehaved child. "But if you find yourself struggling, just let me know, and I can arrange for someone to come and talk with you."

I bite down on my lip and glance away, hating the idea of having to discuss my issues with a trained professional. I get it. Therapy has been a big help for some people, even lifesaving in some cases, but for me, the idea of unpacking all my emotional trauma on a stranger and being expected to sort it all out just scares the shit out of me.

"Uhh, thanks. I'll let you know," I tell her, both of us already knowing that this is the last we'll ever talk about it.

Rachel nods and pulls my gown back down before fixing my blankets back up over my chest. She steps back and we all watch as she fiddles around with my IV, hopefully giving me a good fix of morphine to get me as high as a kite.

After a minute, Rachel is done and excuses herself from the room, avoiding Carver as she walks past him. Four sets of eyes stare back at me, each one of them filled with something entirely different and impossible to decipher. Though, one thing I know to be true, the next few weeks are bound to be interesting.

3

"A few weeks on bed rest, huh?" King smirks, leaning back in his chair and struggling not to laugh at the thought of me doing it without complaint. "How the hell are you going to survive?"

"You know damn well that I won't," I tell him, my gaze still flicking back to Carver's. "I'll give you one week of bed rest and one week on the couch. That's it."

Cruz laughs. "It's not a fucking negotiation. You're having four weeks of bed rest."

"Get fucked. She said a few weeks. That's two."

"No," Cruz continues. "A couple is *two*. A few is *three*, but I added an extra week for good measure because I know that during those three weeks, you're going to do something stupid to fuck up all of your stitches."

"You don't know that."

"I do, which is why we've already talked to your doctor about it and he's agreed that four weeks is where it's at."

"Don't bullshit me. You have not talked to my doctor."

The twisted grin that stretches across Grayson's face is enough to tell me exactly what I don't want to know. "Want to make a bet?" Grayson chuckles, his usual dark and broody self nowhere to be found. "That doctor barely got a chance to sit down before these fuckers were hounding him. Trust me, if you didn't have school and graduation to get through, they would have pushed for eight weeks."

I gape at him, hardly able to believe what I'm hearing, but I shouldn't be surprised. This is King and Cruz we're talking about. I should have expected that they weren't just going to sit here and watch me sleep for eight hours.

I let out a sigh and look back at the boys who sit on either side of me. "This conversation isn't over."

"It is," Carver snaps from the back of the room. "You're fucking kidding yourself if you think your body will heal after just two weeks of bed rest. You need four as an absolute minimum, six to be perfectly safe. Not to mention, just because the time ticks by, doesn't mean that the pain is just magically going to disappear. For months, every time you bend over, or if you twist funny, you'll feel it and it will ache."

My lips press together as I meet Carver's pissed-off stare. He looks right at me and the desperation pulsing through his eyes is nearly enough to shatter every piece of my soul. So instead of commenting on his need to keep me locked in my bedroom for the rest of my life, I look back at the boys. "Would you guys give us a minute? I think it's time that Carver and I have a little talk."

King's brow arches as he looks back at Carver while Cruz's hand flinches in mine. "You sure?" he asks. "You don't have to do this now. You only just got out of surgery. Give it a few hours. Days. You can talk when you've both had a chance to come to terms with what's going on."

"I'm fine," I tell Cruz. "Seriously. I just need to talk to Carver for a minute. You guys can just sit outside. You don't even need to shut the door."

Cruz's lips pull into a tight line, but he nods and pulls himself up from the chair, letting our hands fall apart in the middle. He watches me a second longer before finally walking away, but he doesn't leave the room without grabbing Carver by the front of his shirt and slamming him up against the wall. "If anything happens to her while we're gone, I'll fucking end you."

Carver grabs Cruz, and in a flash, their positions are reversed and my precious Cruz is pressed up against the wall that Carver was only just occupying. "If anything happens to her ever again, I'll happily let you."

Well, fuck. That escalated quickly.

I watch in silence as the boys continue to stare one another down, both of them heated and ready to blow—and not in a good way.

Grayson steps in beside Cruz and grips his arm, tugging him out of Carver's hold. "Come on, bro. He's not going to hurt her."

"How do you know that?" Cruz scoffs, delivering one hell of a low blow as he glares at Carver. "*You fucking missed.* Eighteen years I've known you and not once have you ever missed."

Carver's gaze swivels back to mine with that same devastating guilt, and I know just by looking at him that he's innocent. He may be an incredible shot, but he's also human, and there's not a single piece of me that believes otherwise, but I get where Cruz is coming from. He needs to yell, he needs to scream and punch something, the same way that I do when the world becomes too much, and unfortunately for Carver, Cruz is taking it out on him.

Grayson pulls Cruz out the door but not before glancing back at me. I catch his stare and a million messages pass between us before he completely disappears out of sight. King follows them out, and soon enough, it's just me and Carver with one hell of an elephant taking up the majority of space in the room.

I hold Carver's stare, hating the silence as my hand slowly slides across the bed. I grab the little remote and press the button at the bottom, and just like that, the bed slowly begins to rise, though not just the back part—the whole fucking thing.

"Shit," I grumble under my breath, pressing the next button only to have the gears jump into reverse and start lowering me back down. "Fucking hell. How do I make this thing sit up?"

Carver's brow raises as he continues to watch me making an ass of myself, but I ignore him, intent on getting comfortable. I finally find the right button and press it for only a second, sitting up just enough so that I don't have to strain my neck to see him properly. To be completely honest, I'd like to sit up a shitload more, but I'm terrified of making matters worse, and knowing my luck, it'd probably hurt like a bitch.

Once I get myself sorted out, my gaze falls back on his suspicious stare, probably assuming that I got him all alone in here to rip him to shreds, and judging by the way he's been looking at me since I woke up, he'd probably welcome it.

"So," I start, a stupid grin pulling up the corner of my lips. "Do you come here often?"

Carver just stares, but the longer I watch him with my grin becoming ridiculously wide, he can't help but break. A laugh bubbles out of his chest, and for just a second, I see the guy that I'm quickly realizing I don't want to live without. "You're a fucking idiot," he laughs as the tension completely disappears out of the room. "Are you serious right now? Out of everything that needs to be said, you want to hit me with shitty pick-up lines?"

I shrug my shoulders, really starting to feel the pain fading away as my mind starts to get foggy once again. "It made you smile," I admit. "And if I'm perfectly honest, I think that's my favorite thing about you."

His eyes narrow as his strong arms cross over his chest, his brow arched. "Really?" he questions in disbelief, not flattered by my comment in the least. He sees right through me in the way that only Carver can.

I shake my head. "Nope. I lied," I say with a soft, breathy laugh. "My all-time favorite thing is when you throw me up against a wall and fuck me until I scream."

"The fuck are you talking about? I've never fucked you."

"I know," I grin, bringing my hand up and pointing toward my temple. "But I dreamed about it one night, and now I have a vision of it living rent-free in here, and fuck, it's the best thing I've ever experienced."

Carver rolls his eyes, and while I see him desperately trying to pretend that everything is alright, I see the pain hiding within his gaze.

Letting out a sigh, I throw the blanket back and pat the space beside me. "Come here," I tell him, knowing there's a chance that he's going to push me away, but considering the events that led up to this particular moment, I have a good chance of getting what I want out of him.

Carver narrows his gaze, studying the empty space beside me with caution. "No."

"Yes."

He pushes off the back wall and strides toward the end of my bed, propping both hands against the hard plastic and leaning into it. "Why?"

I fix him with a heavy stare, making sure he hears me loud and clear. "Because since the second I woke up, you've been looking at me as though you can't believe I'm actually here. Now come and sit your stubborn ass next to me and wrap your arms around me, just like you used to when the nightmares would haunt me."

He shakes his head. "No, don't be doing me any favors," he says. "Cruz was right. *I missed.* I fucked up and you're in that fucking bed because of me. I don't deserve to sit there and hold you like nothing happened, and you shouldn't want me to."

"Don't tell me what I should and shouldn't want. I'm not doing you any favors, Carver. I need this just as much as you do."

He just stares at me, swallowing over the lump in his throat.

"Please," I whisper. "Just stop hating on yourself for two minutes and give me this. I swear, I won't ask anything of you ever again. I just … I need you here with me."

I watch as the stubborn resolve in his eyes begins to break, and then finally he pushes off the end of the bed, making his way around to my side. He effortlessly slides onto the edge of the bed, somehow managing to pull me into his arms without a hint of pain. "I don't want you to ever feel like you can't ask something of me," he rumbles as my head falls to his chest. "No matter what, Winter, I am always here."

Tears instantly well in my eyes as the feeling of home washes over me. Everything is so right with Carver. He and I … it would be everything, but we're so far apart. It's as though we exist on different sides of the world. Fire and ice. Except for in this one precious moment.

I miss this. I miss him. I miss sneaking through his bedroom door and sliding into his warm arms. I miss his chest pressing up against my back and his arm curling around my waist, holding me tight and making me feel as though nothing could ever break me. With Carver, I'm safe. With Carver, I have it all, but without him, I'm lost.

I raise my head and meet his eyes. "Why can't we make this work?"

"You know why," he murmurs, his hand so gentle on my waist with his thumb rubbing back and forth over my hospital gown.

I let out a sigh and drop my head back to his strong chest, knowing that in his arms, nothing could go wrong. Nothing ever goes wrong when I have him beside me, you know, except for all the times that it does.

"I shot you," he tells me, his voice far away and filled with agony, making me raise my gaze to meet his once again. "No matter what happens between us, no matter how desperately I want to make you mine, I can't. Not now. You're not safe with me."

"You see, that's just the thing," I tell him, "with you, I feel safer than I've ever felt before. I don't want you to pull away from me any more than what you already have."

"I'm sorry, Winter, but I can't. Look how much I've already hurt you. When you're around me, I'm off my game. All I can think about is keeping you safe, and then when the time comes, I fuck it up. You almost died today because my head wasn't in the fucking game. That's on me."

I shake my head, letting the tears fall from my eyes. "I don't see it that way."

Carver presses his lips into a tight line and slips his hand around the side of my face, his thumb brushing over my cheek as his fingers curl around the back of my neck. His thumb wipes away the tears and I instantly lean into his touch. "There's no other way to see it, Winter. I'm not good for you. Stick with the boys. They'll treat you right and give you everything that I can't."

"You know," I whisper, raising my chin just an inch and putting my face right in front of his, "self-loathing doesn't suit you."

"Well, that's too bad, because something tells me that it'll be sticking around for a while."

"I don't want you racked with guilt over this," I demand, my tone becoming more insistent. "It was an accident. Even heroes make mistakes."

Carver lets out a sigh and drops his forehead to rest against mine. "That's where you have it wrong," he murmurs, his fingers tightening on the back of my neck. "I'm no hero."

I bring my hand up and curl it around the back of his neck as best I can, refusing to allow him to pull away, because let's face it; this is Carver, and that's his favorite move. "You are to me," I whisper, raising my chin just a little more so that as I talk, my lips gently brush against his like butterfly wings softly moving over the petal of a beautiful flower. "You've always been my hero, even when I can't stand to be in the same room as you. Right from the beginning, you've been there saving my ass time and time again. Every day that I get to wake up and see your face is another day that you and the boys have blessed me with. If it weren't for the four of you, I would have been dead and buried a long time ago, and I'm going to remind you of that every single day until you can finally see what I see."

"And what's that?"

"That you, Dante Carver, are the most frustrating, obnoxious, and arrogant asshole that I have ever met, but you're also the most loyal, strong, and extraordinary man that I've ever had the pleasure of knowing. You would lay your life down for me, and I see that every time I look at you."

"That's a nice picture you're painting, but that's not me. I'm a killer. These hands have killed more men than you can count. They nearly killed you."

"Don't try and tell me that I'm wrong, Carver," I say, moving in just a little closer so our lips touch with a little more than just a gentle brush. "I know what I see, and if you'd let me, I'd fall madly in love with you."

Carver's eyes soften, and just like that, he captures my lips in his and kisses me softly. His lips are filled with passion and need, but not a need for my body, a need for everything else that I am, and damn it, I'd give it to him if he'd just let me.

His fingers run through my hair, and reading my body, he holds me tighter, keeping me still while knowing damn well that I'd do anything in my power to roll on top of him and kiss him deeper.

His kiss is everything I needed, except unlike the others I've received from him, this one is lacking life. What used to be so full of burning flames, is now just a raw sizzle. It's lacking the desire and urgency, and I realize that while we both so desperately want each other, things will never be the same between us, not while Carver is so full of guilt.

Everything shatters inside of me and this realization kills me faster than his bullet ever could.

I pull away, and as I look up into his broken stare, I see that he's come to the same realization that I have. Carver and I will never be together.

"I'm sorry," he whispers, his heart falling out of his chest in broken, little pieces. "If I could go back …"

"I know," I tell him, dropping my head back to his warm, strong chest and allowing his arms to fall back around me. "I know."

4

"**W**INTER? WHERE THE FUCK IS YOUR DELICIOUS ASS?" Ember's voice travels from one end of the ward right to the other, and judging by the scowl resting upon Nurse Rachel's face, she disapproves.

I cringe, knowing this is going to result in one less Jell-O for me today. Rachel and I have come to an agreement over the last two days. If she gets me all the Jello-O and ice cream that she can get her hands on, then I'll happily participate in all her frequent checks. Hell, half the time I even do it with a smile on my face.

"WINTER, BABY. TALK TO ME."

I look back at Grayson who shakes his head, knowing damn well that I was only seconds from yelling back at her. "She'll figure it out eventually," he tells me. "There's only so many doors she can barge her way through."

"Good point," I grumble, watching as Rachel double checks my chart and hangs it back on the end of my bed before curiously eyeing Grayson. There have been four separate occasions over the past two days where she has stormed into my room only to find me snuggled in bed with a different guy. The first time she walked in to find me and Carver together, she was pissed, especially considering that I'd only been awake after surgery for maybe a half-hour. Since then, she's stopped fighting it and has just told the boys to be careful, but it wasn't necessary. The boys are more careful with me than she is.

I hear Ember's thundering footsteps grow closer and laugh as she throws open a door. "Oops, fuck," she grunts. "Sorry."

The door is slammed once again only for us to hear the very next door being barged open. Rachel glares daggers at me. "If she pisses off my patients, you and I are going to have a problem."

"It's fine," I grin. "Ember has one of those adorable faces that you just can't get mad at."

"Trust me, no one is that adorable," she mutters under her breath, coming around and strapping the blood pressure monitor around my upper arm to do her thing.

I sink back into my bed and can't help but laugh as the next door is thrown open, directly across from my room, knowing exactly what she's going to find in there.

"Winter?" she calls into the room. "Shit, sorry wrong ro—WHOA.

Hello, there. My name is Nurse Ember, can I offer you a sponge bath?"

The unbelievably sexy guy across the hall laughs, clearly finding her just as amusing as I do. "Sorry," he says, the smitten laughter in his tone more than adorable. "I've already had my sponge bath today. I'll take your number though."

Oooh, damn. He's smooth.

"No shit," Ember says, making me laugh as I imagine the way she'd be gaping at him with her mouth hanging open. "Really? I didn't think that line would actually work."

"Sure as fuck did," he tells her. "I'm Corey."

"And I'm free on Saturday night."

"Perfect. I'll be out of here on Friday."

"Nice. Wait," she says, her voice still somehow travelling right through the ward despite her talking at a normal tone, at least a normal tone by Ember's standards. "You're like … not a part of some secret society and intent on murdering my best friend and using me to do it, right?"

"Wow," Corey responds as I bite down on my lip, desperately trying not to laugh as she perfectly describes her twisted ex, Jacob Scardoni. "That was oddly specific."

"Well a girl can never be too sure, you know what I mean? Guys are either serial killers, rapists or just trying to get in my pants."

Corey laughs. "I'm not going to lie, the thought of getting in your pants sounds pretty fucking great to me, but I'm a gentleman, I promise. You know … unless you don't want me to be."

I glance up at Grayson who's busily playing on his phone. "You can do background checks, right?"

He holds up the phone. "Already on it."

Rachel looks between us, her brows furrowed and clearly wondering how the hell Grayson is capable of doing background checks on her patients.

"So, your number?" Corey continues.

There's a short silence before Ember's voice is lowered. "Where's your phone? I'm Ember by the way. My friend, Winter, is in here somewhere. You haven't seen her, have you? Hot as fuck with an attitude, probably giving the nurses a hard time."

"Oh, yeah, I know the one," he says, the amusement loud and clear in his tone. "You're talking about the chick with all the dudes, right?"

"Sounds like my girl."

"She's in the room directly across the hall."

"Thanks," she says in a chirpy tone. "I uhh … I guess I'll see you Saturday."

"I guess so."

There's a long silence, but when Ember's pretty face doesn't show up in my doorway, I let out a groan. "EMBER, STOP HOOKING UP WITH THE PATIENTS AND GET YOUR ASS IN HERE."

"WAIT," a guy from down the hall calls out. "THAT HOT, LOST CHICK IS HOOKING UP WITH PATIENTS? CAN I BE NEXT?"

A long, familiar groan from across the hall sounds out before I hear a door closing. Two seconds later, Ember's flushed face appears in the doorway staring back at me. "Seriously? Did you really have to ruin that for me? I was two seconds away from screwing the guy up against the bathroom door."

Rachel clears her throat beside me, and Ember twists around, her face dropping in horror. "I swear, I'm not a whore," she rushes out.

Rachel just rolls her eyes and walks out the door, pointing toward the small mini fridge that Cruz brought in here late last night. "There's Jello-O and ice cream in there," she tells Ember. "I have a feeling there will be none left by the time I'm kicking you out tonight."

I can't help but laugh. I think Rachel and I are going to get along just great.

The door closes behind her and Ember steps up to the end of my bed. "Seriously?" she grunts, her face a complete mask of disappointment. "You went and got yourself shot? Do you have absolutely no awareness of self-preservation?"

Grayson chokes back a laugh, keeping his eyes down at his phone to avoid my wrath. I glare at Ember, while also needing her carefree comments more than she could ever know. "Really? You think I went and did this on purpose. I mean, does 'hey Carver, I've been dying to know what it feels like to get shot. Show me what you can do with that gun,' sound like something I'd say?"

Ember laughs and walks around to the side of my bed, dropping into King's favorite spot on my right. "I mean, there's no telling when it comes to you. You've always been a little fucked up in the head."

"Screw you."

"No thanks, I have a new guy to screw on Saturday night."

"You're not going out with him," I tell her, grinning at the disbelief crossing her face. "At least until we get a background check done on the guy. We don't need a repeat of last time."

"I was so close to tearing you to shreds just now," she says, leaning back in the chair and propping her feet on the edge of my bed. "But you're right. This world is already too fucked up to have to worry about new players in the game."

"Tell me about it."

"So, what's the latest? Cruz said something about your mom, but like … she's dead right? I mean, I don't intend on being insensitive or anything, but I kinda thought that was a cold, hard fact." She laughs to herself before her eyes go wide. "No pun intended."

The door barges open and King, Cruz, and Carver come striding in, somehow making the massive room feel tiny and cramped. "We all thought she was dead," King says, beating Cruz to the seat on my left, and leaving the boys to squish onto the couch beside Grayson.

I look to Cruz, knowing he'll be the easiest to break. "So, what's the plan? We need to somehow figure out where my mother is and find the motherfucker who set off a bomb during the ball."

"Not to mention, some fuckwit head of Dynasty is responsible for the cyanide attack."

Cruz shakes his head as King, Carver, and Grayson all look at each other with shifty eyes that makes me suspicious as fuck. "Babe, we're not discussing this," Cruz insists. "We can work out the plan and figure out all the bullshit in a few weeks. Until then, all we're doing is waiting for your guts to heal. There's no reason to put you at risk. It's too dangerous."

I shake my head. "Spill. What the fuck is going on?"

"What do you mean?" King questions. "Nothing is going on."

"I'm not fucking stupid. I know when you guys are planning something, and right now, you're planning it without me, and if I find out that you guys are making a move without taking me along for the ride, I'm going to be pissed."

Grayson scoffs. "Sorry, babe. I really wish we could tell you that we had a plan, but when the fuck would we have had a chance to come up with one? We've been here with you since you came barging in here on a fucking gurney."

I press my lips into a hard line. I guess he has a good point, though that doesn't make me any less suspicious. These guys are shady bastards at the best of times. "You know where she is, don't you?"

The boys' shifty eyes start all over again and I realize that I've hit the nail on the head. They know exactly where to find London Ravenwood, or at least, they have a good idea where to find her. Cruz lets out a sigh and King groans, knowing that his best friend is about to break. "We think she's been staying in your parents' manor home in the mountains."

I shake my head. "No, that's not right. It burned down when Royston killed my father."

Carver leans back in his chair. "Dynasty wasn't going to allow their home to remain in ruins like that. Your father built that from the ground up. He was very proud, so Dynasty rebuilt it about a year after the fire."

"No shit," I breathe, slicing my gaze toward the back wall as I think it over. "So, technically that's mine too?"

Grayson shakes his head. "Well, up until your mother showed up, we thought it was, but seeing as though she never actually died, that means—"

"I've technically not inherited anything," I say, cutting him off and finishing his sentence. "So, my home … I … I don't have a home."

Grayson nods. "Technically, yes, but you can't look at it that way. It's your home and it's going to stay that way. She's not been here and I doubt she's going to go storming through your front door and demand the place back. She's been in hiding and she risks too much by showing herself now. Fuck, from where I'm standing, she's looking pretty fucking guilty where your father's death is concerned."

I narrow my eyes at him in curiosity. "You really think?"

Grayson shrugs his shoulder. "I don't know, that's just a theory. I could be way off."

I nod, seeing exactly where he's coming from. Royston told us she was there the night my father was killed. He told me how she was asleep in bed right beside him and she screamed as Royston slit his throat, but what if that was a lie? Royston wasn't exactly an honest man. What if he was working with my mother, and together, they conspired against my father?

No. I don't want to go there. It's too much to think about. Cruz was right. No matter how much I want to go out there and kick her ass, I can't do anything until my body is healed. I'm a liability like this.

I turn my gaze to Carver. "Do you think she's in the manor home?"

He slowly nods. "I do," he says firmly. "We're going to go down there and check it out, but not before you're out of the hospital and back at my place. We can't leave you here with no protection."

"Whoa, slow down, cowboy," I say, throwing my hands up to cut him off before he says something even more ridiculous. "There's a lot to unpack there."

"Like what?" he grunts as King sits forward, watching me closely.

"First off, you guys aren't going to the manor home without me. I'm coming whether you like it or not. And secondly, you're insane if you think I'm moving back into your place. Haven't we already learned that the five of us living in close proximity is a bad idea?"

Carver scoffs. "Tough shit. I don't give a fuck that you're the leader of Dynasty and what you say goes. Not anymore. Your safety comes first, and right now, you're not safe in your place. How many times have people been able to sneak onto the property? Your fucking mother got in there without alerting a single one of us, and do I need to remind you what happened in the pool? From now on, you're staying right where we can keep an eye on you, and I don't give a shit if you like it or not."

I let out a sigh, and as King reaches out and takes my hand, I look across at him to find his eyes shimmering with helplessness. "Please, Winter. Don't fight us on this. We've had too many close calls with you. I know you love having your independence and putting on this big show about not needing anybody but do this for us. We need you there with us. We need to know that you're safe."

I groan, and just as I'm about to respond, Ember sits forward, pulling her feet off the edge of the bed and meeting my stare. "Don't hate me for this, but I think the boys are right. You need to be somewhere that you're safe. I mean, can you imagine if someone actually got through and killed you? Dynasty would be up shit creek, the boys will be a mess, and the world will be a really shitty place without you. If I could protect you half as well as they could, I'd keep you locked in my closet, but I can't. It won't even be that long. The boys will find the threat and deal with it. Once it's gone, you can move back to your own place and rebuild it without all of your mother's shit."

"But—"

"No," she says, her tone firm and filled with authority. "You know that I'm right. You're just too stubborn and pigheaded to admit it."

My face scrunches in distaste, hating that she's right, and hating even more the feeling of being ganged up against, but there's no denying it. They're all a hundred percent right. My home isn't safe and I'd be a fucking idiot to keep living there while there are still so many threats against me. "Fine," I grumble. "I'll move into Carver's place, but Lady Dante is coming with me."

Cruz, King, and Grayson all sigh while Carver just sits still, more than happy to mask his emotions, but what's new? I wouldn't expect anything less from Carver. "Thank fuck," Cruz says, tipping his head back against the couch and showing just how much the idea of me staying in my home was weighing on his shoulders.

"Wait," I say, making all their gazes snap back to mine. "I just have one condition."

Grayson's eyes narrow to slits. "What?" he asks cautiously.

"I'm coming with you when you go to find London."

Carver shakes his head. "No, absolutely not. You're staying home where you're safe. I thought we'd been over this."

"That's just the thing," I snap back at him, hating how dismissive he can be. It's as though he has a magical gift for getting under my skin. "Where does it leave me if you guys all piss off to the mountains and there's another attack? You're leaving me vulnerable. So, which is it? You can't have it both ways. The whole reason you want me in your place is to keep me safe and keep me close. So, do you want me safe or should I just risk my life by staying behind with no protection? Besides, this is the home my father was murdered in. I have the right to go and see it. I'll stay in the car until you clear it if I have to, but I'm coming and you can't stop me."

The guys look around one another, their shifty eyes seriously getting on my nerves, but the hard set of Carver's jaw tells me that I'm just as much working his nerves as they are mine.

King sighs, seeing that I have them backed into a corner. "We'll talk about it later," he tells me. "Let's just focus on getting you out of here, and once we're home, we can work out the details there."

I nod, knowing that's the best I'm going to get out of them.

"Good," King says. "Now, can we talk about how Cruz still has the 'YAHTZEE' video?"

Grayson scoffs, his tone dark and deadly, and clearly pissed about the whole situation. "How about we talk about how Cruz screamed that he loved Ellie while she was bleeding out?" he says, throwing him right under the bus.

Cruz's eyes bug out of his head as his sharp gaze slices back to mine. "I … uhh … fuck," he stumbles out as I try to think back to my time lying in my own blood on the garage floor. The whole thing is blurry, and over the past two days, I've only been able to remember little snippets of it.

"You, umm … you said that you love me?" I murmur, keeping my stare locked on Cruz's as I recall that only yesterday morning, sitting in this very hospital, King had admitted something very similar while talking with his little sister.

Ember clears her throat and gets to her feet. "I think I hear Corey calling my name," she says, refusing to meet my eyes before she high-tails it out of the room.

King, Grayson, and Carver follow her out, and before I know it, it's just Cruz and me with nothing but a world of tension sitting between us. "I didn't mean for it to come out like that," he tells me. "I was in a panic and terrified that I was going to lose you. I didn't want you to go without knowing, but you have to know that's not how I ever intended on telling you. In fact, I wasn't planning on telling you for a long fucking time."

My brows furrow as I watch him. "Why not?"

"Because, baby, you're not fucking ready to hear those words, as much as you think you are, you're not. I can see it in your eyes now. You're freaking out, but you don't need to. I'm not going to force it in your face and demand some bullshit response out of you."

I watch him carefully. "Are you sure?" I ask, hating how easily he can read me and see the terror on my face. But the terror isn't there because he loves me. I fucking love that. The terror comes from that deep, dark part of me that's never been loved. I don't know how to love and I sure as fuck don't know what it means to be loved in return.

Cruz stands up and walks toward me, leaning over me with a hand on either side of my hips, being as careful as he possibly can not to jostle me around. "All you need to know," he tells me, his voice dropping low as his mesmerizing green eyes bore into mine and hold every bit of my attention, keeping me captivated, "is that every fucking word of it is true. I love you, and I have for a while now. I'm all in where you're concerned, but I don't expect anything in return. I'm not hanging around, pining to hear you say it back because I know you're not there yet. I know you feel something for me, and I know that scares the shit out of you, but when you're ready, you'll come to me. You already give me everything I need, and that's more than enough. I've told you before, and I'll tell you a million times more if you need me to. Just getting a piece of you is more than I could ever ask for."

My hand curls up around the back of his neck and I pull him in close, holding him right in front of me as his forehead drops to mine. "Have I ever told you how fucking incredible I think you are?" I whisper, refusing to take my eyes away from his. "You completely captured me from the day I first met you, and I don't ever want to let you go."

Cruz moves in closer, and just like that, his lips come down on mine and he kisses deeply, making every little emotion that lives deep within me, swirl around and bubble right to the surface. I hold him tight and as his lips gently move against mine, I feel my world sliding right into place.

Even if I didn't have the other guys, I know that a life with Cruz would still make me the happiest girl who ever lived. What more could a girl want? He's absolutely perfect with those mesmerizing green eyes and his flawless, cocky smirk. But when it comes to Cruz Danforth, it's his heart that gets me. It's so incredibly pure. It's as though his light evens out my darkness.

Cruz slowly pulls away, and as his eyes come back to mine, a soft, adoring smile pulls at his lips and makes his eyes light up like the Fourth of July. "I can't wait to get you home and healed," he tells me, making excitement burn deep within me. "Then I can truly show you what it means to be loved by me."

"Well, fuck me," I breathe, knowing that no other woman on this green earth could ever be so lucky.

Cruz winks, making everything flutter deep in my stomach. "That's the plan," he tells me, his voice rumbling low through the private room. He climbs onto my bed beside me and pulls me into his warm, inviting arms and as my head rests against his wide chest, I realize that no matter what, I will never let him go.

5

The warm water rushes over my head and I let out a low groan. There's nothing better than having a nice warm shower after being locked up in the hospital for a week. Nothing could get better than this. Though, if I'm honest, showering in my own shower back at home would be preferable, but I get it. I'll be the princess locked in Carver's tower until the boys deem it safe for me to walk the streets without being shot at.

I guess they have a fair point, but the second I'm free of my binds and the threats are gone, I'm riding up and down the street on my Ducati, in nothing but my birthday suit while waving my ass around and daring all the fuckwits to come for me. I can only imagine what the boys would think about that, but there's not a damn thing they can do about it.

I rinse the shampoo from my hair and sink back against the cool tiles. This week has been hard. Who knew that getting shot would take so much out of a person? Just getting up to shower is exhausting, but this is only the start. Today is a massive day, and I'm sure that by the end, I'm going to crumble into a ball and sleep for the rest of the year.

A sigh pulls from deep within me as I tilt my head back against the tiles and close my eyes, rejoicing in the rare moment that I have to myself. The boys haven't been overbearing or anything like that, but they sure as fuck meant it when they said they wanted to keep a close eye on me. I'm not complaining though, for the most part, when we're all getting along, I absolutely adore their company.

Knowing the time is ticking all too fast, I turn off the taps and carefully reach out for my towel. Everything is still so sore. Every stretch, every movement, every little sneeze and cough tears through me. I'm starting to admit to myself that maybe I do need more than just two weeks of bed rest. Once again, the boys were right.

Stepping out of the shower, I pull my towel around me and gently dry myself off, hating how slowly I have to do each little task. I used to rush through things like this, but those days are gone. At least, for now.

A sheet of wet hair frames my pale face, and I cringe to myself thinking about how long it will take to do my hair and makeup.

Dropping the towel on the bathroom floor, I glance up to find my naked reflection staring back at me. I let out a broken sigh. This isn't me at all. The bullet hole has properly closed up and is looking a million times better, but the bruising around my abdomen is still nasty.

"Winter?" Carver calls from my bedroom. "Where are you? You need to start getting ready."

"Bathroom," I tell him, not bothering to scramble for the towel at my feet. He'll be here long before I can get it up around me, and there's no point telling him to stay back because he won't, not until he's got eyes on me and can physically make sure that I'm still breathing. Hell, what does it matter anyway? It's not like he's never seen my tits and ass before. A guy like Carver would have seen more than his fair share of naked women. This is nothing new.

He appears in the bathroom door a second later and pauses, looking in and taking in my reflection through the mirror. I watch him back, my eyes scanning over the fitted black suit that makes him look like the man you don't want to bring home to Daddy.

"Fuck," he breathes, his eyes glued to my stomach.

I watch as everything inside of him breaks. He's been doing better the last few days. I've been trying to keep it from him, acting strong every time he walks into a room, and not allowing him to see the bandages, but this right here, this shit is confronting as hell.

My heart shatters watching the devastating emotions crossing his face, and just like that, he falls to his knees on the bathroom floor.

"Carver," I whisper, hating how much this whole situation is fucking with his head. He used to be the one who would be strong for me. I was the vulnerable one; I was the one who needed him to keep the monsters away, but the tables have turned and I've somehow become his saving grace. I turn and walk to him, dropping my hands to his chin and forcing his eyes up to meet mine. "I'm okay. I'm safe."

He shakes his head, his hands coming to my hips before he tilts his head into my waist and holds me there. "You're not okay."

My hands fall around his neck, my fingers gently roaming through his hair as I lower myself down, throwing caution to the wind and letting the pain consume me.

Carver's grief is so much more important.

I fall into his lap and he holds me tight. "I'll never be able to make it up to you," he tells me, his head dropping into the curve of my neck as the guilt completely overwhelms him. "How will I ever make this right?"

"I. Don't. Blame. You," I tell him, sounding like a broken record. This isn't the first time he's broken down over the past week. It's always in my room and always when we're alone. I'm his safe haven, the one place he can let it all go, and while I love that he feels that he can be vulnerable with me, it's also one hell of a dangerous game. I'm becoming way too attached to Dante Carver, and I fear that I'm only going to hurt myself. "Had you not taken that shot, she would have killed me. You did what you had to do. She pushed me right in the line of your shot, and I fell. This is on her, and the only way for us to make this right, is by taking away her power. She's nobody, and when we're through with her, we're going to make sure that she knows that."

His fingers move over my shoulder, rubbing back and forth as he holds me close. "I nearly lost you."

"I was never going anywhere," I whisper. "Do you really think I would have left this earth without somehow convincing you to a gang bang? Yeah right."

Carver draws in a deep breath before slowly raising his head and allowing me to see the agony deep within his eyes, but for the most part, my stupid attempt at a joke has given him the strength to hold himself together. "Come on," he says, pulling back just a bit. "Let me help you get ready."

I watch him for a short moment, neither of us moving off the bathroom floor as my wet hair drips all over his expensive suit. "Are you good?"

Carver's eyes soften and he nods. "Yeah," he rumbles. "Good."

I lean in and gently brush my lips over his. "Good, because you're going to have to help me up."

A small smile pulls at his lips, and in an incredible show of strength, Carver lifts us both off the bathroom floor, and he does it without even the slightest bit of pain tearing through me. He walks with me straight out of the bathroom, and as he is placing me down on my bed, King, Cruz, and Grayson stride through the door.

Cruz holds the black dress and heels he'd swiped from my closet back home, while Grayson holds all of my bandages and painkillers, more than ready to keep me safe. I'm surprised he didn't bring an industrial-sized roll of bubble wrap. That would have been more effective.

King though, he's just here because today of all days, he could really use the company.

Today, Dynasty buries Tobias King.

Grayson instantly strides across the room to bandage me up, while Cruz studies my dress, trying to work out how the fuck to get it on me without making me curse his name. King makes his way into the bathroom and grabs my hairbrush, blow-dryer, and makeup, while Carver just watches, completely out of his comfort zone.

Within half an hour, the boys have got me dressed and ready, and as Grayson carries me down the stairs, too afraid that I'll trip, Carver subtly reminds me that the rest of Dynasty hasn't been informed of London's temporary state of … aliveness? And as it is, we'll be keeping that one on the down-low until we can get in for a full council meeting. Hell, perhaps we shouldn't tell them at all. If they knew just how screwed up I am right now, they could see it as a sign of weakness and use it against me.

Who am I kidding? They all saw the ambulance screeching out of my driveway. With Dynasty's technology, it would have taken less than two seconds for them to figure out that I was the latest victim of a gunshot wound.

We get to the car and I scoot in beside King, glancing up into his warm, ocean eyes and slipping my fingers between his. "You know, you don't have to be strong today," I whisper into the silent car, trying to keep our conversation private, but in close proximity, I know they all hear.

"Thanks," King tells me, looping our hands over my shoulder and pulling me in closer as his fingers trace the lines and curves of my brass knuckles. "But if anything, being strong is more important now than ever before."

I let out a sigh, knowing that he's right. King is now the head of his family, and along with that comes a shitload of ridiculously high expectations. There's an unsaid demand of being stronger, wiser, and fiercer than his father before him. Nothing less will be tolerated by the other heads of Dynasty.

We drive for twenty minutes, the car in dead silence, and before I know it, we're pulling up to a massive cathedral. I gape out the window, staring up at the incredible building that until now, I didn't even know was here. "Shit," I breathe. "This place is massive."

"Wait until you see inside," King grumbles. "This was my father's favorite place on earth."

My brows furrow as I meet King's stare. "Oh?" I ask. "I, uhh … I didn't realize that he was religious."

"He wasn't," King says with a soft chuckle. "But he would come here to seek peace and guidance. I don't know, I think maybe it was a combination of things, but whenever the world was falling to pieces around him, he would come here and just sit in the pews for a few hours until he got clarity."

I nod and look back at the massive cathedral, watching as people dressed in black suits and dresses begin flooding through the front doors of the impressive building. King pushes his door open and climbs out before turning back and helping me.

Once I'm balanced on my feet, his arm instantly slips through mine, holding me discreetly. To the outside world, it would look as though he's just using me for comfort, but in reality, he's holding me as tight as fucking possible to make sure that I don't fall and tear my internal stitches.

As a group, the five of us slowly walk to the impressive entrance of the cathedral, but as we go to step over the threshold and enter the building, King pulls away from me, and Cruz instantly takes his place. "I need to stay out here," King mutters, seeing the confusion stretched across my face.

I nod, and just like that, it's the last I see of King as we walk through the doors and find our seats.

It's gloomy as fuck in here.

I guess for the most part, it would be beautiful with its high, open ceilings, large windows, and jaw-dropping architecture, but all the sadness pulsing through the room and the soft, grievous music changes the entire ambiance.

Why did it have to be Tobias? He was the closest thing I had to a father.

We take our seats, and Cruz instantly slides in beside me, keeping his arm curled around my waist so that I don't have to press myself up against the hard back of the pew. I look around, and as I take it all in, I'm struck by the fact that Royston Carver didn't get something like this. He was an important player in this fucked up game, so where was his grand funeral?

I glance at Carver on my other side and ignore the way his leg presses up against mine, knowing that if I focus on it for too long, I won't be able to resist reaching out and pulling him closer. Just that brief moment with him in my bathroom this morning wasn't enough— it will never be enough.

"What?" he grumbles, his voice low as he keeps his stare straight ahead, refusing to look down and meet my stare.

My tongue rolls over my lip as I realize that bringing this up with him could potentially be a bad move, but now that he knows there's something on my mind, he won't be able to let it go. I let out a shaky breath. "Why didn't your father get a grand funeral?"

I notice Grayson flinch ever so slightly at my question. My gaze slices up to his to find him glancing between Carver and me, unsure how this is going to play out.

Carver tenses and I watch as his jaw clenches, making it clear that the topic of his father's death is not something he particularly wishes to discuss, but why? He's talked about him before, he's openly admitted to how much he hated him, so why does it give him such a hard time? Is he still trying to process and deal with the betrayal that he suffered at his father's hands?

Grayson leans forward, properly meeting my stare. "When a member of Dynasty is disgraced for actions taken against our organization, they are stripped of the benefits that come along with the territory. Royston was not given a grand funeral, just as Preston Scardoni won't. However, their families are allowed the opportunity to bury their loved one in private."

My gaze flicks back to Carver. "Did you?" I whisper, sliding my hand out to brush against his knee.

Carver moves his leg away from mine. "No," he mutters, keeping his stare straight ahead and his face a complete mask. "My family went away. They never got the opportunity. His body wasn't claimed for burial, so Dynasty cremated him and disposed of his ashes. He's not my fucking problem anymore."

Guilt sits heavily in my chest as I sit back and lean closer into Cruz.

Well, fuck. Why did I let that one little piece of information claw its way inside my chest and burn my dark heart into ashes? Why should I give a shit that Carver never got a chance to say goodbye to his father? That man murdered mine. He deserved what was coming for him, but Carver? Shit.

The soft music lowers, and the thoughts of Carver and his father instantly leave my mind. Mr. Danforth steps up in front of the congregation, looking out at the crowded bodies and slowly scanning the room. As he does, I can't help but follow his gaze.

Mr. Danforth stops on the front row, and I peer around Cruz to find King's mother and his little brother and sister, Cody and Caitlin. The kids look absolutely devastated, and to be honest, with the injuries Caitlin sustained during the sham of a ball, I'm surprised she's here. Perhaps she received special permission to attend, either way, she looks like today is the worst day of her life. In fact, that goes for both her brother and her mother.

"Thank you all for being here to celebrate the life of the late Tobias King. His death was a tragedy, one we will all feel for many years to come," Cruz's father says, pressing his lips into a hard line. He takes a deep breath—as if standing up in front of Tobias' friends and family is one of the hardest things he'll ever have to do. Then without wasting a single second, he lifts both of his hands. "Please let us stand as one and rise."

Without hesitation, everybody in the room raises to their feet, and the soft, grievous music changes to something equally as chilling and heartbreaking. Every eye in the room fills with unshed tears.

Every head turns to the grand entrance of the cathedral, and as I peer through the bodies blocking my view, I find King standing among seven other men, all of which are heads of Dynasty, carrying Tobias' casket.

My heart sinks as I imagine the horrendous weight now resting on King's shoulders, but just as he had said in the car—he has no choice but to be strong. For his mother, for his brother and sister, and for the rest of Dynasty looking in and watching his every move, waiting to find his weaknesses. They won't find any though, not when it comes to King.

The walk from the entrance of the cathedral to the front of the church seems to go on forever, and as King passes us, I can't help but meet his stare. To me, he looks broken, but to the outside world, he looks like the only person in this impressive building who has his shit together.

The men take the casket to the very front and place it down on the table that has been patiently awaiting Tobias' arrival.

King hesitates at the front of the church. He looks back toward me sitting among his friends before glancing at his mother. Realizing that now is more important than ever to make an impression, he walks to his mother's side and drops down next to her.

The ceremony is lovely and exactly what I had hoped for Tobias. Taking a page out of King's book, I try my hardest to hold my composure for the people around me. For the most part, I think it works. That is until Tobias' wife takes a stand behind the dais and looks out at the crowd of bodies, all watching her with tear-stained eyes.

She clears her throat and unfolds a stack of papers before lying them on the dais before her. Her hands shake and everything inside of me breaks.

This isn't a position she thought that she'd be in quite so soon. She would have been hoping for at least another thirty years with her husband by her side. At least, if I were married and deeply in love with a guy, I'd want to have the rest of my life with him ... hell, *or them.*

King's mom takes a shaky breath and quickly glances at her children, scanning over their faces and desperately searching for the strength to say what she needs to say. A single tear falls from her eye and drops to her papers. She follows it down and stares for just a moment before scooping the papers into her shaky hands. "Thank you all for being here today," she starts, her voice already breaking. "Tobias would have been so grateful for all the love and support you've shown to us in this difficult time. He ... he was quite a man, and so it is with a heavy heart that we must say goodbye to him today."

Sobs tear through the cathedral and all eyes turn to Caitlin sitting in the front row beside her big brother. King instantly puts his arm around her, holding her tight to his chest and desperately trying to make this day just a little bit easier for his baby sister.

King's mom goes to continue, but her gaze sweeps back to her daughter and her resolve breaks. "I ... I first met Tob—" Deep, heaving sobs pull from within her as she falls forward and catches herself against the dais. Her head tilts forward, trying to mask her face from the crowd of bodies watching her breakdown.

King instantly pushes his little sister into his brother's arm and stands. He straightens his suit, fastens the button, and holds his chin high. I watch as he walks over to his mother and gently pulls her into his arms. King positions himself in front of the dais, and in an incredible show of strength, he looks out to his father's final guests and picks up exactly where his mother left off. "I first met Tobias in school. I was twelve and he was the popular jock who I never thought I'd be good enough for. I instantly hated him. If someone had told me back then that Tobias King would be the love of my life, my husband, and the father of my children, I would have called them a liar. Tobias King changed my life."

And just like that, the tears fall down my cheeks and splash against my legs, staining my dress as King goes on, his voice hypnotic and soothing as he tells his mother's story, giving her the strength to be able to say her final goodbye.

6

Sixteen sets of eyes watch me as I slowly make my way around the massive round table. Pain tears through me. I'm not ready for this. After Tobias' funeral earlier in the day, and the massive wake that went on well into the night, I should have told them to reschedule this shit for tomorrow morning, but instead, I agreed.

I need to be in bed. I need to rest my body and make sure that I'm not overdoing it. Fuck that, I know damn well that I'm overdoing it right now, but I wasn't about to let this meeting go on without me. I can only imagine what kind of bullshit they would agree on.

It was only a week ago that I was shot. My body isn't ready for all of this, and as much as I hate to admit it, the boys were right. I need a few more weeks to properly heal, and only then will I be able to rise back up and be the motherfucking bitch who all these bastards fear.

Both King and Carver stood at the door, one on either side of me, insisting that they help me to my seat, but I refused to look weak in front of this crowd. They sure as fuck didn't like it, but I sent their asses in before me. Now they're watching me walk through the big room with scowls torn across their faces. I can only imagine what they're thinking and I'd bet anything that the word 'stubborn' is flashing through both of their heads.

I only get halfway around the massive table before my body begins to scream. My abdomen is throbbing and my willpower is quickly dwindling, but I don't dare let it show. My face remains a complete mask in my need to always be strong. But fuck, I'd give anything for a painkiller right now.

My gaze flicks across the table to where Carver sits. He's always been able to see right through me. He knows what I'm thinking, what I'm feeling, and judging by the way his fingers are gripped to the edge of the table with white knuckles, I'd dare say that he's more than aware of the bullshit I'm suffering through.

Seeing his resolve quickly fading, I discreetly shake my head, knowing damn well that this bastard is about to fly out of his seat, pick me up caveman-style, and deliver me to the front of the room, but I won't stand for it. I'll break down afterward, but until then, I'm going to stand before these assholes with my head held high. Nothing will stop me, not even a shot through the gut. Hell, if Jacob and Preston's attacks couldn't bring me down, and my own mother's bullshit wasn't going to stop me, then this meeting is nothing but a walk in the park.

I make my way to my seat, and as I slowly lower myself into it, I bite the inside of my cheek, keeping myself from screaming out in agony. I taste the blood inside my mouth, and instead of allowing it to cripple me, I use it to motivate me. "Alright," I say, leaning back in my chair and making a show of how well I've been doing since they all watched me get taken away by the ambulance. "What was so important that it couldn't wait until morning?"

I glance around the room, skimming straight past King and Carver, still not being used to seeing them sitting at this table, but when nobody responds, I turn to Earnest Brooks who sits directly to my right. "Can you give me a little something to work with here?" I ask him, knowing that had Tobias still been here, he would have been the first to speak up and get this shit underway.

Earnest nods while letting out a deep sigh, not liking being the one that I call on. "Michael Harding," he says, nodding across the table to the man in question. "He's asked us all here tonight to discuss a few things and work out how Tobias' death is going to impact us as an organization."

I try not to groan too loudly as I glance across the table at Harding. "So, what Earnest is telling me is that we're all here in the dead of night to discuss something that could have been discussed in the morning?"

Michael shakes his head, looking at me in disgust. "Always so quick to dismiss the importance of what we do here."

In a flash, Carver pushes back out of his seat, his momentum sending it flying behind him until it's crushing into the wall of the council chamber. His hand winds around Harding's throat. "Instead of insulting our leader, why don't you get the fuck on with what you have to say?"

"Watch it, boy," Harding growls, not fazed by the tightening hand around his throat. "If I didn't have such respect for your father, I would have put you down years ago."

"That's a big claim," Carver says. "Am I to assume that you were in league with my father?"

Harding's gaze snaps right back to mine as if only just now remembering that he's in a room full of people who would happily end his life if the next words out of his mouth were the wrong ones. "I didn't say anything of the sort," he demands, his tone loud and heard right across the room. "Dante Carver is putting thoughts in your head, trying to diminish my credibility for his own gain. He should be reported."

I scoff. "You destroyed your own credibility just by sitting on the left-hand side of the table, but more so, do I need to remind you that only a week ago, after spending the night saving our people, you sat in my living room and happily pointed the finger at everyone else except yourself?"

"I had nothing to do with that attack," he roars, pushing Carver away from him and standing, leaning forward onto his knuckles and sending a sharp, lethal glare my way. "I buried my own fucking brother just yesterday. How dare you suggest that I was at fault."

"Tell me, Harding, at what point since entering this room did the words 'you're responsible for the attack' come out of my mouth? I simply pointed out how quick you are to blame the men around you, and in my experience, the ones who like to point fingers are the ones who will happily stab you in the back."

"You don't know what you're talking about. You've been here for two seconds and already, you think you have every one of us figured out."

I laugh. "Trust me, it wasn't hard. You're pretty fucking transparent, but that's not what we're here to discuss. Isn't the whole purpose of this council to have sixteen heads all working together for the greater good of our organization? We're supposed to be a well-oiled machine, but I see nothing but a bunch of children swinging their dicks and hoping for a little recognition." I look between Michael and Carver. "Both of you sit your stubborn asses down so we can peacefully discuss the topics which brought us here. It's been a long day, hell, it's been a long fucking month. So, can we please just get through one meeting without the world imploding around us?"

"Sounds like a good fucking idea to me," King grumbles under his breath.

I can't help but glance his way, and when I find his blue eyes locked on mine and the smirk stretched across his face, something clenches deep within me. He's had a beyond shitty day, but I'm not going to lie, his courage and strength have really surprised me. Don't get me wrong, I always knew he was strong, but something has changed within him over the last week. He's gone from being a broody, no shits given kind of boy, to a fucking relentless, strong, inspiring man.

King winks, and it's his one silent message letting me know that he's doing alright, but his wink tells me so much more. It's him also letting me know that he thinks I'm doing alright. He thinks I can handle this, and he thinks I'm strong enough to face the firing squad and come out on top.

I hate that after the day he's had, he's the one giving me encouragement to be able to keep going. It should be the other way around. I should be the one holding him up, but he just can't help it. Since the moment I first met him, he's been looking out for me, keeping me safe, and making sure I always have the tools to kick some ass.

With King's silent encouragement, I turn back just in time to watch as Carver walks back across the room to find his discarded seat, and Harding reluctantly drops his ass back into his. They both look like schoolboys who've had their asses handed to them in front of their entire class. But on second thought, isn't that exactly what happened?

"Right," I say, keeping my gaze on Harding. "Why don't you start again and tell me why the hell we're here, and this time, let's see if you can do it without insulting me or any of the men around you."

Harding narrows his eyes on me, and with his tail tucked between his legs, he lets out a shallow sigh. "I'm not sure if you are aware, but since your return in Ravenwood Heights, you've been drawing a significant amount of attention to yourself from the Ravenwood Heights police department. They've had their eye on you since your DNA was found at the crime scene of your foster parent's murder."

I roll my eyes. "Well, I hate to be the bearer of bad news, but that's bound to happen when people are constantly trying to kill me.

I mean," I say, flicking my gaze around the left-hand side of the table. "If some people weren't so adamant about taking me out, we probably wouldn't have this issue."

Mr. Danforth stands and meets my stare. "This is certainly not the time to start pointing fingers," he says, reprimanding me as though I was one of his misbehaved sons. "This is serious."

"Are you suggesting that the attacks on my life are not serious?" I question, watching him through a narrowed and pissed-off stare. His lips pull into a tight line as he holds my stare, relentless just like his son. When I refuse to back down, he finally drops back into his seat, but he's right. I can focus on the topic of my attacks later. One issue at a time.

I let out a sigh and look back at Harding. "I was cleared of Kurt's murder. The papers disappeared and the issue was put to rest."

"Yes, the physical proof was gone and your name was cleared," he says. "But what about the officers who ran your case? What about the memories that circle their minds? You may technically be off the hook, but they have been watching you very closely. After the explosion at Sam Delacourt's home, the disappearance of Jacob Scardoni, and now your face front and center at the ballroom explosion, they've been asking questions—and a lot of them. They've been snooping around, and soon enough, they're going to come across something they shouldn't."

My brows furrow as I flick my gaze to Carver and then to King before sending it across to the very few people around this table that I can trust. "So, what am I supposed to do? It's not like I could avoid the cops seeing me when I came out of that tunnel. They saw us all."

"Exactly," Harding continues. *"They saw us all.* Every one of us are now at risk of exposure. Dynasty is at risk. The whole building exploded and countless first responders rushed in to save what they could, and therefore, our underground world is at risk of exposure. How long do you think it is before they realize the ballroom wasn't the only underground building we've created?"

I run my hand over my face and lean onto the table, propping myself up on my elbows as I consider everything Harding has said, and honestly, I should have seen this coming. There were countless firemen, police, and paramedics there that night. They saw every one of us, they saw our world, and who we are.

Harding is right. We're all at risk.

I glance back up, looking at some of the older men in the room. "Dynasty has been kept secret for many years, surely something like this has happened before, or we've been close to exposure. How did you handle it then? What am I supposed to do to make this go away?"

Carver meets my eye across the table as he shakes his head. "You're not going to approve of how we've handled exposure in the past," he warns me. "It's not an option."

I nod, reading him loud and clear. In the past, when a threat from the outside world presented itself, Dynasty eliminated it before it could become a problem, and in other words, that means Dynasty is responsible for murdering innocent men and women. Carver is right; I don't approve of that plan. We need something better. Dynasty needs to be better.

"The risk is too great," Harlen Beckett says. "Yes, in the past we have simply eliminated the threat, however, there are too many witnesses. We cannot draw that kind of attention to ourselves. Elimination is not an option."

"So, what do we do?" Matthew Montgomery questions.

"Rebuild," Mr. Danforth suggests. "We all have homes outside of Ravenwood Heights. We disperse. We abandon Ravenwood Heights and keep quiet for a few years while we build a new foundation. We have all the contingency plans in place and the finances to fund it. We could be out of here by tomorrow."

I shake my head. "No. This is my home," I tell them. "This is where my father is buried and where our history originated. Rebuilding is not an option."

"But—"

"I said no," I snap at Mr. Danforth. "Because of Dynasty, I was ripped away from my family. I've spent eighteen years without a home, and now that I've got one, I'm sure as hell not about to give it up."

King meets my eye. "We're at risk, Winter. We can't just sit back and do nothing. This is our whole world, our families."

"Trust me, I'm more than aware of that, which is exactly why we should be fighting to protect it rather than allowing the outside world to trample us. We stay and we fight for what is ours. There have been rumors going around town about Dynasty for years. You've laughed them off, and that's exactly what we will continue to do. If you get questioned, you tell them that they're crazy and reading into the rumors. If asked about the underground ballroom, you tell them that we stumbled upon it years ago and that we kept it quiet for our own benefit. If the city wants to claim the ballroom as their own, let them. What is one loss in the grand scheme of things?"

"Plausible deniability," Carver mutters. "If we don't admit to anything, they won't have anything."

King leans forward, and I watch as the thoughts circle his mind. "Are you sure?" he asks me. "So much could go wrong."

"I'm not giving up my home," I insist. "If it gets too much, everyone else is welcome to take their families and vacate as you were before I arrived in Ravenwood Heights. We have the best technology in the world. We can run this organization no matter where everyone is in the world. We can regroup once the speculation dies down. All I'm saying is that I'm not running. This is my home and this is where I'll stay."

King nods, watching me carefully to make sure that I'm making the right decision for me. Hell, he couldn't give a shit what everyone else does as long as I am safe.

"Alright," I say, quickly scanning around the table again. "So what now? Is this one of those things we all need to vote on?"

Earnest clears his throat beside me. "No, I believe not," he says. "This is more of a personal matter for each of us to decide with our own families in private. You've stated that you do not wish to abandon Ravenwood Heights and we will respect that. Can I suggest another meeting in a few days where we can all share our plans moving forward?"

Sebastian Whitman scoffs from across the table. "Oh, please," he says. "If our leader wishes to stay in Ravenwood Heights and fight for our organization, then we all should. Now is the time to stand as one, not run away scared."

Carver nods. "I agree. If Elodie is putting her neck on the line to save Dynasty, to ensure that it continues to flourish, then we should all follow her lead. I vote that all families stay and fight for what we've built."

"I second this," King says, raising his hand.

One by one, hands begin to rise around the table, and before I know it, all seventeen hands are held proudly. "Good, I guess that's sorted out," I grumble, realizing that the last half an hour was more than a waste of time. What did we really discuss? That we're all staying in Ravenwood Heights and keeping Dynasty on the low just as we were before? Fuck me. And to think that I could have been curled up in bed with Grayson's head lost between my legs. "Is that it for the night? Can I actually go home?"

"There's just one more issue to deal with," Harding says, quickly flicking his gaze toward King. "There's the matter of Tobias King and his role within Dynasty."

My brows furrow as I watch King straightening in his seat. "How do you mean?" I ask Harding.

"He was your father's right-hand man, and that role continued after your father's untimely death. Because of this, he was more involved in the day-to-day business of Dynasty than the rest of us. So, we need to know that those duties are still being taken care of."

I lean back in my chair, meeting Harding's stare. "So, you're telling me that after burying the man today, your most important question is who is going to file his paperwork?"

Harding slices his gaze around the room, unsure of where I'm going with this. "I uhh … well, yes. He had an important role which ensured the day-to-day business ran smoothly."

"Oh, of course," I say with a breathy laugh, having to pause for a second as the pain in my abdomen gets too uncomfortable. "And here I thought the most important question was who's responsible for killing him."

Harding's eyes bug out of his head, but only for a second before he composes himself. As he goes to respond, I hold up my hand, having more than enough of this conversation. "Earnest came to me three days ago and we discussed Tobias's role in detail, and if you had bothered to check your emails, you would have seen that the matter was already resolved. His son, Hunter King, will step into his father's shoes, just as Tobias had always planned and trained him to do. So, thank you for again wasting my night. Now, if that is everything, you may all be excused to finish your night with your families."

Not wanting tonight to drag on any longer, the men around me stand and exit the council chamber, probably feeling that tonight's meeting was just as much of a colossal waste of their time as it was for me. The room quickly clears out and as the last man walks out of the council chamber, leaving just me, King, and Carver behind, my whole world crumbles, and I finally allow the pain to consume me.

I fall off the side of my chair, hitting the ground with a hard thud, and within moments, King and Carver are by my sides. King scoops me into his warm, capable arms and holds me tight as I desperately will myself to hold it together for just a little while longer.

I just need to survive for five more minutes before King can slide me into my bed and dose me up on painkillers. "You're going to be alright," King murmurs, dropping a kiss to my forehead. "I'll have you home in no time."

And just like that, the boys sneak my ass out of there, managing to bypass the other fourteen heads of Dynasty who are slowly making their way out of the underground world.

Within minutes, I'm lying across the backseat of Carver's Escalade as he careens down the road toward his home. King's arms are still curled around me, and before I know it, the car is skidding to a stop at the top of Carver's driveway.

I cringe with the jumpy movements, but knowing that my painkillers are calling my name on the other side of the door makes everything so much better. So, when Carver races round to open the back passenger door, I all but jump out at him, desperate to get inside.

A sharp, howling laugh tears out of me as Cruz squishes in beside me on Carver's massive couch. His arm drapes around my shoulder as his hand holds his phone up between us. "No way," I squeal, seeing the video playing on his phone.

I take the phone right out of Cruz's hand and can't help but glance across the room at Grayson, who up until a second ago was minding his own damn business, but from the twisted grin that stretches across my face, I think he knows exactly what I'm seeing.

"God, no," Grayson says, his face draining of all color as he looks at Cruz. "If that's what I think it is, you're going to fucking die."

I can't help but drop my gaze back to the phone, and as I do, I press the volume button on the side and listen as the sweet sound of Grayson's groan travels through the room.

I instantly clench my thighs. What is it about Grayson that gets me so worked up?

My gaze travels over the video of Grayson. He wears nothing but a pair of grey sweatpants that show off every little line and curve of his monster cock. His shirt is nowhere to be found, and that magnificent tattoo is well and truly on display for the world to see. Though, in this video, it only has half as much detail as it does now.

Grayson's eyes are right on the camera, and despite knowing that he made this video for some other girl, I can't help but feel as though he's staring right into my soul.

His hand roams over his body, and as it slowly travels down and palms his cock over his sweatpants, everything south of the border comes alive. I see every outline; I see the way his cock hardens beneath his touch and the small metal ball at the top of his piercing. He hasn't even lost his pants and already, it's one of the most erotic things I've ever seen.

I bite down on my lip, chewing at it as I glance up over the phone to find Grayson's heated, intense eyes on mine. He likes me watching him like this. It's getting him hard just as it's getting me wet. It's been way too long since the boys have touched me. Well, mostly. They sneak into my bed at night and disappear beneath the sheets, but they've been gentle with me, and while they've been giving me exactly what I *need,* they've refused to give me what I *want.*

Another soft groan cuts through the room, and I can't resist tearing my stare off Grayson's and looking back down at the phone. I watch as his hand disappears inside his sweatpants and fists his hard cock, and once again, my thighs clench, desperately trying to relieve the ache that pulses between my legs.

His sweatpants restrict his movement, and as he grows frustrated with them, he pushes them down over his hips, freeing his pierced monster cock.

My mouth waters, but it's nothing compared to when he roams his tight fist up and down, teasing me.

It's mesmerizing, and I find myself watching the entire show as Cruz laughs next to me, completely oblivious to the sexual trauma he's unknowingly thrown upon me. I glance up, my tongue rolling over my bottom lip as I meet Grayson's heavy stare.

He gets it, and he fucking wants it.

The little red line at the bottom of the video tells me that there's only thirty seconds left, but I don't need that little line to know how close he is to finishing. I can read his body almost as well as I can read mine. There's the way his abs are clenched, his jaw locked, and his fist tightening. His movements speed up, needing it hard and fast as his soft groans and growls get deeper and more demanding.

It'll only be a second now.

His hand tightens on his cock, and as I watch his thumb circling over his tip, I feel the excitement pulsing through me, growing stronger and wilder. I need to see him come more than I need to breathe.

My thumb presses down on the volume button, muting the video just as Grayson comes hard, sending spurts of cum shooting out past the camera. My breath comes in sharp, desperate pants, and as I look up at Grayson, I feel that wild need tearing through me.

I can't wait. I have to have him.

Cruz groans beside me, completely unaware of the way that Grayson's stare has me captivated. "What the hell?" he laughs. "Why'd you turn it down? You missed the best part."

"Really?" I ask, sweeping my heated gaze across to Cruz and grinning at the way his eyes widen when he realizes just how turned on I am. I lean into him and hover my lips right in front of his as I look back across the room at Grayson. "Because if you asked me, I'd say that I saw so much more than just the best parts."

Cruz tries to capture my lips in his, but I slowly pull away and shake my head, pressing my body against his in the process. "Nuh-uh," I murmur. "You don't get to touch."

"What?" he groans, the disappointment thick in his tone as I straddle his lap and grind my pussy against him. He grabs my waist and holds on tight as I feel Grayson's stare hitting the side of my face.

"You've been a very bad boy, Cruz Danforth," I scold, keeping my tone low and seductive. "You came in here with the intention of getting even and embarrassing Grayson, but it didn't work, and now because of that, I'm going to go over there and fuck your best friend until I scream and you're going to sit here and watch with your dick in your hand, desperately wishing it was me."

I peel myself off of Cruz's lap and smile at the way he tries to hold onto me for as long as he can. I turn to face Grayson and walk toward him, but as I go, Cruz grumbles behind me. "He had it coming. He spilled that I was in love with you. If anything, he should be the one sitting back to watch."

I grin, looking over my shoulder as I walk away from him. "Don't forget that you told me first. You can't blame him for that. So, take your pick, Danforth. You can either walk away or you can watch, but either way, I'm about to get naked, sink onto Grayson's cock and ride him until the sun comes up."

I turn back to Grayson, and as I do, I find him more than ready. His eyes are burning with lust, and as he leans back into the couch, I see the hard outline of his cock through the same grey sweatpants that he'd worn in the video.

Fuck me. What is it about the sweatpants?

His knees are open and I'm struck by just how big he is, and not just the good stuff. Everything about him is big. He's got to be well over 6'3, and compared to me, he's a freaking giant. There's just something about a big guy that screams 'fierce protector.' Add the muscles and the smolder, and I'm a fucking goner.

I step up in front of him, putting myself right between his open knees, but before I get the chance to strip naked for him, he reaches out and takes my hips. Grayson pulls me in closer, and with him leaned back in his favorite couch, I have no choice but to climb up onto his lap and straddle him.

Grayson instantly pulls me in and I fall into him, but he holds me tight, not allowing me the chance to get hurt. His lips meet my neck and quickly work their way down over my collarbone as his hand comes up and slips up the front of my white cropped tank to find me braless and desperate for his touch.

His head dips and his mouth closes over my nipple, sucking it over the fabric of my tank and making it see-through. His hand curls around my breast beneath my tank, and I push into him, needing so much more.

His other hand gently brushes over the bandages at my waist. "Are you sure?" he murmurs, his voice vibrating around my nipple and sending electric currents shooting right through to my core. "I don't want to hurt you."

"You're not capable of hurting me," I whisper, groaning deeper as his lips circle back around my nipple. "I trust you."

Grayson pulls back, raising his chin to meet my gaze. He holds my stare for a short moment, silently questioning if I'm talking shit just to get what I want or if I truly mean what I say, and judging by the way his stare softens and his fingers tighten on my body, he knows that every word is as raw and honest as it gets.

A proud as fuck grin pulls at the side of his mouth, and in true Grayson fashion, not a word is said about it, just the silent acknowledgment between us is more than enough.

Without hesitation, Grayson drops his lips back to my nipple, and I grind down against him, needing so much more. My fingers rake into his hair, fisting around his dark locks and holding him right where I want him. My back arches and Cruz's soft groan from behind me only has me arching even more, thrusting my ass back and showing off every little curve of my body.

I look back over my shoulder and watch the way Cruz focuses on me, scanning his gaze over my body and eating it up, the desire in his eyes proof of how badly he wishes I'd let him touch me.

Grayson's arm winds around my waist, and as he pulls me in closer, he presses up against me, letting me feel just how ready he is. "You know," I mutter as my head tips back, my eyes closing with the intensity of my desire and pleasure consuming me. "I'm going to need you to make another one of those videos, but just for me. I want your eyes staring right down the camera, and instead of those low groans, I want to hear my name on your lips. Give me that, and I swear, I'll go to bed watching you every fucking night for the rest of my life."

Grayson's eyes come back to mine, full of desire and promise. "You liked that?" he grumbles, his voice low and seductive.

I nod. "I didn't just like it, I fucking needed it."

A cocky as fuck smirk pulls at his lips, but before I allow him a chance to gloat about just how much I need him, I crush my lips back to his and all conversation ceases. Grayson's hands roam over my body as his tongue pushes into my mouth.

I groan into him, pressing my tits against his strong chest and grinding my pussy against his cock.

How was I so stupid to have waited so long for this? I should have thrown myself at Grayson the very second I met him. Though, I guess I was busy throwing myself at King and Cruz every chance I got.

Grayson's hand slips into the back of my sweatpants and he grabs hold of my ass, giving it a firm squeeze and rocking me forward over his cock once again.

A needy pant pulls from deep within me and the desperation

becomes all too much.

As if sensing the urgency pulsing through my body, Grayson curls his strong arm around my waist, and in the same second, he lifts me up while tearing my sweatpants and thong down my legs with his other hand.

I'm lowered back onto his lap and just as my thighs rest back against his, my hand comes down between us. I dive into the front of his sweatpants and instantly curl my fingers around his hard cock while watching the look of pure satisfaction tearing across his face.

I've never seen such a perfect sight.

My hand works up and down his velvety skin, my thumb roaming over his tip and passing over his piercing, making him silently beg for more. He raises his hips and lifts us both up from the couch as his sweatpants disappear out of sight.

Cruz's low groans tear through the room and as Grayson adjusts his hold around my waist and brings me down over his cock, Cruz's groans only grow more desperate.

I'm lowered onto him and the walls of my pussy are stretched around his monster cock, the cold metal from his piercing rubbing along the inside of my cunt. "Holy fuck," I moan, tipping my head back and closing my eyes as the pleasure instantly overwhelms me.

It's been too long. I've missed his touch so desperately. From now on, I'll definitely try to avoid being shot again. I couldn't possibly put myself through the torture of not being touched by my boys for so long. It sucked, like really fucking sucked.

Feeling Cruz's eyes boring into my back, I look over my shoulder and meet his burning stare. The poor guy, he can barely hold on. The desire pulsing through his eyes is nearly enough to have me going back on my word and inviting him to join, but I won't dare, not when he came in here with the intention to embarrass Grayson. He's been a bad, bad boy and I'll make sure that he knows it, though I'm not one to hold a grudge. I'll be sure to make it up to him later.

Cruz silently pleads, giving me the best puppy-dog eyes I've ever seen, but he should know me better than that. If he wants me to break—puppy dog eyes aren't the way to go about it. Now, if he tempted me with chocolates and ice cream; that would be a different story.

Needing to feel every inch of Grayson, I rise myself up and arch my back as best as I can while sticking out my ass and showing off my curves, and only when Cruz has the perfect view of Grayson's cock buried deep inside my pussy do I start riding him.

Slowly working my way up and down, groaning with the undeniable pleasure. I feel my wetness coating Grayson's cock and know for damn sure that Cruz can see it, and knowing Cruz, he fucking loves it. He lives for it.

Grayson's fingers tighten on my waist, as his lips come down on my neck, working over my sensitive skin and making me feel like an addict on her best high. I move slow and while usually with Grayson, it's all hard and fast, this pace is definitely proving some advantages.

I feel his piercing dragging up and down, teasing and taunting me with the promise of just how good it's going to get. It's sensual, intense and everything I've been needing since the moment my mother's knife pressed against my neck.

"Fuckkkkk," Cruz moans from across the room. "Slower."

My eyes light with excitement, and I instantly slow my pace, making Grayson's fingers tighten even harder. His fingertips dig into the skin of my waist as I rise over the length of his thick cock and, ever so slowly, clench my pussy as I come back down, feeling him deep inside me.

Grayson sucks in a sharp breath through his clenched jaw, his head tipping back onto the back of the couch. "Fuck, Ellie. You're killing me."

A grin pulls across my lips as my eyes sparkle with mirth. "Oh yeah?"

We hear the familiar sound of the front door opening, and knowing that it's King, not one of us bothers to stop or cover up. Hell, if Cruz gets to watch, why can't he?

Hearing him walking through the house, I continue grinding up and down Grayson's mammoth cock, groaning with each movement as I look out toward the entrance of the living room, only it's not just King who stops in the walkway, Carver is right there beside him, and the second his eyes come to me and drop to my body, desire pulses through them.

King's eyes burn with excitement as a thrilling smile sweeps across his handsomely rugged face. He takes a step deeper into the living room and props his shoulder against the wall as his tongue rolls over his plump lips.

Carver, on the other hand, stays right where he is. His eyes burn with a fierce jealousy, but fuck, he's not giving any signs that he's about to bail. He wants to watch, and for him, I want to put on a crowd-pleasing show. Not to make him realize what he's been missing out on all this time, but just because I want him to feel as good as I do.

I rock my hips and continue to grind over Grayson while my eyes bore into Carver's. Grayson's lips drop back to my nipple, and I suck in a sharp breath, the sensual intensity from my slow movements already too much for me to handle, but damn it, I'm down for the challenge.

Carver doesn't take his eyes off my body, roaming them over my curves, taking in the way my body moves and always … always coming back to my eyes with a raw emotion that sinks straight through to my heart.

King watches for a second, seeing the desperation on Grayson's face and knowing that if I keep going the way that I'm going and refuse to let up, this show will be over soon. He pushes off the wall and strides toward me, the hunger pulsing in his eyes. "So much for waiting until she was healed," he grumbles, stepping in behind me and brushing his fingertip down my spine. A welcomed rush of shivers sailing over my skin.

"What can I say?" Grayson mutters, clenching his jaw and speaking through his teeth. "She fights dirty."

A soft laugh rumbles through King's chest as he leans in behind me and presses his lips to my neck in a soft, lingering kiss. "Well, what do you say? Are you intent on making Cruz sit back and watch with his dick in his hand or are you open to … assistance?"

A wicked grin lifts the corner of my lips as I pause, giving Grayson a brief moment to collect himself. I glance around the room, taking in the desire in King's eyes, the intense need in Cruz's, the raw pleasure in Grayson's and then finally, the hardening caution, jealousy, and intense want in Carver's.

"I'll tell you what," I murmur for all of them to hear as I keep my gaze focused on Carver as he adjusts his hardening cock in the front of his jeans. "This can be a team project, but I have only one condition."

King moves in even closer, thinking that he's about to get his dick wet. "And what's that?" he rumbles, his voice deep and thick with desire.

I bite down on my lip and it's as though Carver already knows what I'm about to say before the words even come out of my mouth. "That all players do their part."

Cruz groans, knowing the chances of Carver giving in are slim. King straightens behind me, his fingers tightening on my skin as all eyes fall toward Carver.

I watch as he thinks it over, and the fact that he hasn't already run for the hills speaks volumes. His gaze sweeps over my body, and the desire pulsing out of his stormy eyes is nearly enough to have me sprinting across the room and throwing myself into his arms.

He remains still, and the seconds pass like a lead weight pressing down over my shoulders.

It's intense. It's raw. *It's Carver.*

His eyes slowly drift back up to mine, and as they finally meet, his tongue rolls along his bottom lip and I can practically see the wild, racing thoughts swarming his mind. "What's it going to be?" I whisper, unsure why I suddenly feel so damn nervous.

Carver's gaze flicks around the room, meeting his friends' intense stares before finally coming back to mine. He pushes off the wall and takes a cautious step into the room. "I'll make a deal with you," he tells me, making my back stiffen and my heart begin to race. "I'll—"

A loud bang sounds through the lower portion of the house, followed by a terrified grunt that has each of us quickly glancing round and within a heartbeat, King, Cruz, and Carver have forgotten about what the fuck was about to go down in this room and are sprinting through the house as Grayson all but throws me off him and grabs his sweatpants.

My heart races for an all-new reason, and before Grayson can throw the bullshit 'stay hidden' instructions my way, I'm racing after him with my tank and sweatpants in my hands.

8

My feet pound against the hard, marble tiles of Carver's home as I go screeching into the kitchen with my tank pulled halfway over my head and my ass hanging out of my sweats, desperately attempting to yank them into place.

This isn't exactly how I planned the afternoon to go, but what can I say? I love a bit of adrenaline, and if I get it by finding some asshole sneaking around Carver's home or by getting off on a monster cock, it's all the same to me. As long as I reach that high, I'm one hell of a happy camper.

I come barreling through the kitchen only to find a wall of muscle standing before me. I hit the brakes and catch myself on Carver's arm as it shoots out to keep me from falling forward.

I groan under my breath, but don't miss how King glances my way, scanning his blue eyes over my face before dropping them down my body and making sure that I'm alright. After all, running through the house at a million miles per hour barely two weeks after getting shot isn't something that comes highly recommended.

King focuses back on the man who has somehow made his way out of Carver's holding cell beneath his father's old office.

Preston Scardoni.

The pain in my ass that just never seems to go away. Until now.

The fucker had conspired against my parents and for the past eighteen years has conspired against me. I'm done. For a long time, I didn't even know that I was running from a threat. I was just running because what the fuck else did I have to do to occupy my time? Dynasty was always watching me from the sidelines, always keeping me safe in their twisted, screwed up way. But I'm not running anymore.

Preston Scardoni is the reason for so much pain and devastation over the past few months since I arrived in Ravenwood Heights. He and his son went above and beyond to make my life a living hell. I've had assassins drop in to wish me a happy birthday, I've had Jacob weasel his way into my best friend's life and break her heart, and a second attack ... well, almost a second attack. We sprung that motherfucker before he got the chance to end his call. Jacob lost his life that night and ever since this bastard has been held in Carver's underground cell.

There's also the question of the attack my bitch of a mother orchestrated against me. A man came onto my property and drowned me in my own damn pool, and my gut tells me that she didn't do it alone. Someone is responsible for giving her access to the gate, which means that same someone knew that she was alive and didn't mutter a single word. My gut tells me that person was Preston Scardoni, though I'm starting to realize that things are never so black and white in this world. There's a whole grey section that's screwed me over every step of the way.

The only issue is that no matter how long we hold Preston down there, or how hard the punches are, he refuses to break.

Preston knows more than he's letting on, and I need to know what he knows. I need to get inside his head and find the answer to the questions that have plagued me for months.

I need to know who is working against me so I can keep myself safe, so I can keep the boys safe, and the rest of the goddamn world. If Dynasty were to fall into the hands of those assholes, we'd all be fucked.

I can't let them win. I won't.

Fuck, my whole attitude on this Dynasty bullshit has changed so much since first finding out about it. I would have done anything to burn it to the ground, but now ... now I want to protect it. I want to rebuild it in the image that both my father and grandfather envisioned. I want to make it great again, I want to rid it of corruption and stick it to all the dickwads who didn't think I could do it.

I squeeze my way between the boys, shouldering past them despite the way they hold themselves so rigid, making it so much harder for me. They don't want me here. They want to cover me in bubble wrap and protect me from shit like this, but I won't stand for it. Preston is here because of me and I will see this through.

He lies in a crumpled heap on the kitchen floor, and judging by the trail of smeared blood behind him, I'd dare say the fucker has crawled his ass out here. I have to give it to the guy, he did well to get this far, but unfortunately for him, this is the end of the road. He'll be going straight back to his shithole dungeon until I get what I need. Only then will we take pity on him and end his miserable existence.

Preston looks up at the four boys with fear in his bloodshot eyes and I can't help but take a second to drag my gaze over his body. He's barely recognizable. The boys have had him hidden away for nearly three weeks and he looks like complete shit.

His body is battered and bruised, his skin barely holding on his thin frame. He must have lost at least forty pounds, yet the sneer on his face and the way he spits as he meets my stare tells me that he still has a shitload of fight left in him. What can I say? It seems that Dynasty breeds them strong.

A pissed-off stare settles across Carver's face as he decides that he's going to take point on this one. "Well, well," he mutters, dropping his gaze to the long trail of blood that he's no doubt going to be responsible for cleaning up. "It seems you've made a mess of my home."

"This isn't your home," Preston spits. "How dare you stand there and pretend this is all yours when it was stolen right out of the hands of your father. You're a fraud. You don't deserve a seat at the fucking table." Scardoni cuts himself off, desperate to catch his breath before continuing. "Royston was a leader, he exuded power. He was exactly what Dynasty needed. You'll never size up to what he was. You're just a punk kid with a chip on his shoulder. You, Dante Carver, are nothing—a spoiled little brat with a weak right hook and daddy issues."

Carver instantly steps into Preston and tears him up by the scruff of his shirt before his right hook sails around in a perfect arch and slams across Preston's face. The momentum of Carver's punch has Preston's face violently twisting around, and not a second later, we hear the familiar sound of a tooth flying right into the cabinetry of Carver's million-dollar kitchen.

Preston is released and his body crumples right back to the ground. "How's that for weak?" Carver mutters under his breath, instantly stepping back into line, but keeping his wide shoulder in front of mine, and adding one more obstacle between me and Scardoni.

King smirks at the sight, and I can't help but like how much the violence gets him off. King has a dark side and it's fucking terrifying, but for the most part, he has a kind, genuine heart and that's all that should matter. It's Carver and Grayson I need to worry about. Those two would raise hell just for something to do on a boring Sunday afternoon.

Preston sprawls across the kitchen floor, smearing his blood further and making Grayson's face pull into a disgusted leer. "Really, man?" Grayson grumbles. "There's blood all over the fucking kitchen."

Carver just shrugs, bouncing his shoulder while keeping his hard stare on Scardoni. "This could all be over," he tempts him. "Just tell me what I need to know and I might even let you say goodbye to your wife before I put a bullet through your brain."

I bite my tongue knowing damn well that Carver's lying. He has absolutely no intention of letting him speak to his wife. After all, a desperate man would say anything to save himself.

Preston reaches up and grips the side of the counter and with a loud, pained grunt, pulls himself up. He leans against the counter, dripping blood all over it and making my stomach churn. How the hell am I supposed to dish up my ice cream on that counter ever again?

Preston flicks his stare to me, his eyes narrowed and full of venom before slicing his gaze around the boys and finishing on Carver. "Do it. Fucking kill me now. I'll never talk," he says, turning that monstrous stare back at me. "Your little whore deserves what's coming for her. She'll never rule over this great organization. She's going to fucking die like the pig that she is."

I clench my jaw as my hands ball into tight fists, so tight that the brass knuckles over my fingers dig into my skin and cut deep, drawing blood. I go to step toward him when Cruz's hand falls to my shoulder, squeezing tight and holding me back.

My stare snaps up to Cruz's fiery one, and I hold it for a moment until he finally releases me and takes a step back, knowing that I have to handle this myself. After all, it wouldn't be fair of me to allow the boys to continue handling my shit for me. At some point I'm going to have to stand on my own two feet and prove that this is where I belong.

I take a step toward Preston and he watches me as though I'm some kind of rabid animal, someone non-human and not worthy of respect. It instantly grinds on my nerves. If anyone around here isn't worthy, it's him.

"That's all you've got, huh? You're barely holding on. You've been here for nearly three weeks and all you've got is a shitty 'whore' comment? Well guess what? I am a whore. I'm a whore and I fucking love it. I'm living my best life, getting dicked anytime I want—night or day, three-way, four-way, solo. You name it, I get whatever the fuck I want while you're sitting here rotting away, and guess what? No one is coming for you. They all know where you are, Preston. The whole organization sat across from Carver and accepted that you were going to die and not a damn one spoke out to save your miserable life. Who's the fucking loser in this situation? Who's the pathetic piece of shit? I can tell you that it's not me," I sneer, leaning in and letting him see the spite and deadly venom in my eyes. "You're a joke. You're the lowest of the lows, and I get to sleep soundly at night knowing that you will never take a step outside of this house again. Your ass is mine and I will take pleasure in ending you."

Preston pushes up from the counter, putting himself right in front of me. "Then do it," he growls, twisting his face into an ugly sneer and making the boys flinch behind me. "Kill me. Prove that you have what it takes. Put those pretty little hands around my throat and squeeze. DO IT. KILL ME."

I narrow my eyes and the fucker just laughs. "Yeah, that's what I thought," he says, almost looking disappointed that I haven't ended his miserable life just yet. "You haven't got it. You're weak. You're forever going to live in Dynasty's shadow, just like your pathetic father. You'll never be good enough."

My fist tightens and I feel my warm blood seeping between my fingers as my anger radiates out of me. "Don't tempt me," I spit through my teeth, barely holding on.

Preston scoffs as a wicked grin pulls up the corner of his lips, showing off the blood that coats what few teeth he has left. "Do it. What are you waiting for? Kill me. Take Dante's gun out of the back of his jeans and put a bullet right through my skull. I know you want to."

I laugh, raising my chin as I feel Carver stepping closer into my back with his fingertip just barely grazing my waist, somehow giving me the strength not to back down. "Tell me who you're working with and I'll happily end your pathetic life. Hell, I might even enjoy it."

A cocky smirk twists across his face, thinking that he has the upper hand in this twisted game, thinking that I won't kill him without getting what I need. "And if I don't?"

I stare straight into his eyes, letting the seriousness take over as he sees just how fucking desperate I am. "I'm going to drag your ass back downstairs and you and I are going to make a nice little movie. I'm going to hit record and then with the blunt razor that I'm going to take out of the back of my bathroom drawer, I'm going to hack off every single one of your fingers while listening to the sweet poetic sound of your screams. But beware, I've never done it before, and I have a feeling that slicing through bone isn't going to be easy … it might take a little while."

Carver's fingers tighten on my waist and I step out of his hold, wanting to stand on my own two feet, especially now as Preston watches me. Nothing is more important at this very moment than proving that I am the leader of Dynasty. I make the calls. No one else.

"I don't really know much about human anatomy, but I don't think that's going to kill you," I explain, watching as his face begins to drain of all color. "You might pass out for a while, but I can wait. I have nothing but time, seeing as though I'm going to be living a long life as the leader of Dynasty. Don't worry though, once you're gone, I'm going to turn it around and undo everything that you have ever put your filthy paws on."

"You're all talk," Preston scoffs.

I just smile and walk across the kitchen, scooping a spoon out of the sink and studying it closely, spinning it between my fingers. "Maybe I'm a little messed up, but I've always wondered what it would be like to gouge out someone's eyes," I mutter, turning to Grayson. "Could he survive that?"

Grayson just shrugs his shoulders. "Not sure. I've never done it."

I turn back to Preston and place the spoon down on the counter right before him and watch as his gaze sweeps over the innocent utensil, now seeing it as much more than just a spoon. "You see, here's the deal, Preston," I say, leaning onto the counter and meeting him eye to eye. "This whole time, you've been here thinking that you had the upper hand, that if you just keep your mouth shut, you might be able to walk away from this, but you're wrong. Yes, I need to know what you know, but you're not the only way I can get it."

Preston's eyes narrow and true fear begins sweeping through his gaze. "What the fuck is that supposed to mean?"

"It means that once I finish gouging your eyes out and brutally ending your life, I'm going to take my special little movie and visit your wife," I whisper, leaning closer and allowing him to see just how screwed up I really am. "I wonder how quickly she's going to talk when I tell her that in order to get you back, all she has to do is spill all your dirty little secrets? Little does she know that there would be nothing left to save." I let out a heavy breath. "Damn. If only there were a way to save her from that agony. The blood, the sounds you make, that's going to haunt her for the rest of her life."

Preston straightens and nervously flicks his eyes around the room, realizing just how fucked he really is. He takes a step back and then another until his back slams against the opposite counter by the stove, once again leaving a trail of blood behind him.

The boys begin moving in, slowly stalking him as we each watch his eyes growing wider with desperation, until they come back to mine. "Joke's on you," he tells me, quickly whipping around and grabbing the meat cleaver out of the knife block.

The boys run.

"My wife is a fucking whore just like you," Preston rushes out with a sickening gleam in his eyes. "She doesn't know shit."

Then in one lightning-fast move, Preston brings his hand down in a rapid arc and slices a viciously deep cut straight across his throat just moments before the boys reach him.

I scream as blood spurts across the room and with a smile on his deranged face, Preston Scardoni collapses to the ground and joins Royston Carver, Sam Delacourt, and his bastard of a son in hell.

9

*C*ruz's stare settles on the side of my face as Carver drives through the streets of Ravenwood Heights, dragging my ass back to school despite my endless protests.

It's been three weeks since getting shot, and since having to spend an entire night helping the boys scrub bloodstains from the grout, pretending my stomach wasn't turning, I've been in a mood. A fucking shitty mood.

Preston Scardoni is dead, and now we're all out of options. I pushed him too far—showed him my crazy too soon. I told him exactly what I planned to do, and maybe I exaggerated a bit, but regardless, I handed my game plan to him on a silver platter. Instead of sitting back and allowing me to play out my twisted little game, he took himself out of the picture. He was the last hand I had to play, and now I've got nothing.

Fucking nothing.

There are still too many questions I need answered.

Who was Royston working with? Who has been hiding my mother? Who was conspiring with Preston to kill me? And who the fuck killed Tobias King under my roof and under all of our noses?

Still feeling Cruz's stare, I turn toward him and narrow my eyes, hating how fucking bitchy I feel today. "What?" I snap, only to watch his stare harden and instantly feel like shit about it. I let out a sigh and press my lips into a tight line. "Sorry, I didn't mean that."

Cruz just nods, always so quick to shrug off my moods when they come up to bite us all in the ass. He scoots back in his seat, leaning his head back and keeping his curious stare on me. "The other day when you were describing to Scardoni exactly what you were going to do to him …"

Cruz pauses and I narrow my eyes. "Spit it out, Cruz."

His lips press into a hard line, and after releasing a soft sigh, he finally lets out whatever has been plaguing his beautiful mind. "What you said about the video and torturing his wife with it; that was some dark shit, Winter. I was expecting some fucked-up, twisted things to come out of your mouth, but I'm not gonna lie, what did come out of your mouth … that fucking shook me, babe."

My lips press into a hard line and I reach across the backseat to grip his big hand. It curls around mine as though it was made for me.

I quickly glance up only to notice both King and Grayson watching intently, making it obvious that the same thing has also been on their minds. "I know, I'm sorry, but I was desperate," I tell them, now sensing Carver watching me through the rearview mirror. "I said what I had to say to get a reaction out of him, and I was hoping that he would cave and talk. I pushed him too far, and because of what I did, we don't have the answers we need."

I turn to King. "I'm sorry," I say, fighting the tears and forcing myself to remain strong. "I know you were hoping that Preston might have gotten us one step closer to whoever killed your dad."

King stretches his arm around my shoulder and pulls me into his warm, inviting chest. "Don't stress about it, babe. We'll find who killed my dad, but that's not what we're asking you right now. We don't care that Scardoni is dead and it puts us five steps backwards. Fuck, babe, I can't tell you how badly I wanted to end him myself. Every time I went down there to get answers, he'd just fucking smirk at me ... shit. I've imagined all the ways I could have killed him, and it would have been sweet."

"King," Grayson grunts, wanting to keep him on track.

King sighs and pulls me in a little closer as Cruz's thumb roams back and forth over my knuckles. "His death is not your fault. He took his own life—that's not on you. What we care about is just how fucking dark you were willing to go to get what you wanted. That wasn't you, babe. That was some fucking dark shit ... and well, are you good?"

I let out a breath and relax deeper into his side, loving the boys' concern, but it's not warranted. "Look guys, I know that I've been through a bunch of shit that no teenage girl should ever have to face, but I'm fine. I had absolutely no intention of bringing his wife into it. I don't think I've officially met her yet, and even though she looks like a bitch and probably knows something we don't, I have morals. I know they're hard to see sometimes and, fuck, I even question them myself, but they're there. There are lines that not even I would cross. I had no intention of torturing her with that video. Hell, there wasn't even going to be a video. I mean, I know I'm new to this whole … killing people thing, but I think hacking someone's fingers off with a blunt blade and gouging out eyes with spoons is a little … beyond my expertise. That seems more like a Carver move."

Carver narrows his eyes, hating the jab, but he deserved it. He was an ass this morning, and instead of having my back when I insisted that I didn't need to go back to school, he stood by his boys and forced me into the back of the car. Apparently, my education is somewhat important to them, and seeing as though there's only a few weeks of school left, they've decided that now's the time for me to focus on it.

So much for them all being on board the 'stay home healing until I die of boredom' train. It seems that we've all switched roles, which makes me wonder if something must have happened. The boys aren't known for easily changing their minds about shit. I usually have to beg and plead to get them to do anything.

Grayson lets out a loud, relieved sigh, his cheeks blowing out in the process as I notice Carver's gaze returning to the road. "So, you weren't about to go down the torture road?"

"Don't get me wrong, I would have still brutally killed him, but no,

I wasn't going to torture him or his wife. I just wanted to scare him, and apparently, it worked a little too well."

Cruz squeezes my hand. "Okay," he murmurs, waiting until my gaze swivels back to his. "You'd tell us, right? If you were heading down that path?"

I watch Cruz for a silent, drawn-out moment, focusing on the intense concern in his eyes. "What's going on Cruz?" I question, sitting up a little straighter and pulling out of King's arms. "Why are you so worried about this?"

"Because there's a fine line between someone who kills out of obligation and someone who does it out of need, and right now, you've got me worried that you're toeing that line. And fuck babe, once you cross to that side, it's really fucking hard to come back."

I watch him for a second longer, and I can't help but wonder if he's speaking from experience or if there's something more that Cruz and I need to speak about in private. His eyes harden, silently telling me that it's not up for discussion. So instead, I swing my stare toward the front seat of the Escalade, flicking it between Carver and Grayson. "You mean, like them?" I ask Cruz, slicing my gaze back to his, knowing that while he might be talking about his own experience, that the two alphaholes in the front seat are the perfect example of men who have crossed that line and never came back. "Would that really be so bad?"

Carver's hands tighten on the steering wheel, his knuckles turning white. "Don't be fucking stupid, Winter. You don't know what you're talking about," he grumbles through the Escalade as he pulls into the school parking lot, instantly darkening the mood inside the car. "This life is fucking heavy. I'm constantly in a world filled with darkness. There's no light here, no calm from the demons living inside my head. I don't want that for you, and you sure as fuck shouldn't want that for yourself. The thoughts inside my head … fuck, Winter. If you even got a glimpse of what it's like to fall off the edge, you'd be running for your fucking life."

Silence falls throughout the cab and I'm left with way too many thoughts, but when Carver brings the car to a stop in his usual spot, a sense of dread fills me and all the heavy thoughts fade to the back. I don't want to be here. Don't get me wrong, spending the day with Ember is never a bad thing, but sitting in a class and doing schoolwork in order to graduate while someone out there is plotting my death just seems like a colossal waste of time.

I should be out there trying to catch the slimy bastards, trying to save my life and give the boys peace of mind that I can walk the street without someone jumping out to attack me.

The whole situation is absurd. Why did I have to be the heir to a society who gets off on death, corruption, power, and secrets? Fuck me. I must have done something terrible in another life.

Is it so much to ask to be able to live an easy, happy life with the four boys?

"Come on," King says, swinging his door open and climbing out of the Escalade, wanting to get out of the dark, gloomy mood that consumes the car. "Let's get this over and done with so I can get you back home where it's safe."

I roll my eyes and pull my hand out of Cruz's while he opens his door and jumps out without a backward glance. "Why don't you just take me back home where it's safe now? We can spend the day naked in bed," I comment, hoping the idea is enticing enough to ditch Carver and his mood, steal his car, and drive my ass back home where I can spend the day consumed by the sweetest type of pleasure.

King groans as I scoot out behind him, knowing damn well that it was a long shot. He takes my hand and helps me down from the Escalade, not trusting me to jump—probably assuming that I'll either fall and wind myself or somehow get shot, blown-up, or kidnapped in the process. After all, getting screwed over by the world seems to be my specialty.

I safely get my ass to the ground, and I don't miss how Carver watches my every single movement. It's been three weeks, and he's still torn up about the whole shooting me thing. He puts on a good act for everyone else, but I see the regret in his eyes, and every time I do, it tears me up inside. I wish I could take away his pain, but he's intent on letting it consume him.

King takes my hand and leads me around the front of the car as the boys fall in beside us. It's almost as if they've created some kind of protective shield around me. "Geez, would it hurt you to give us a little smile?" King teases. "It's just school. It's not like we're sending you here to be tortured."

"Aren't you?" I grumble.

"Sorry, Ellie," Grayson says. "I had a meeting with principal Torsney a few days ago to discuss your options, and it's not looking good. There are only a few weeks of school left, and if you don't show up and catch up on the work, you're going to fail. You've gotten this far, and after going through so many schools, is failing really an option for you?"

I let out a sigh, knowing he's right. Ravenwood Heights is my eighteenth school. I went from home to home, suffering a new way at each one, but I toughed it out. I stuck with it because I was intent on making something of myself after graduation. I never got a chance to figure out what that was going to be, but if I give up now, if I allow myself to fail, it will have all been for nothing.

"So, was online learning not an option?" I ask, glancing back at Grayson, just as everyone else does. "Couldn't Principal Torsney have organized something with the teachers to have them email me the work? That's what happened when I had to have time off in middle school after my appendix burst."

Grayson's face goes blank, and I watch as his jaw clenches. "Fuck. I didn't even think about that," he mutters under his breath, looking pissed at himself for now having me here out in the open at school when I could have been home safe all along. "I'll talk to him. I'm sure I could … persuade him to make the right decision."

I roll my eyes as Cruz looks over at me. "Is that what you really want though? To be sitting in bed with your computer all day instead of in a classroom around your friends? This is the last few weeks of school. You won't get this opportunity again unless you want to do the whole college thing."

My brows furrow. College? Fuck, I've always wanted to go to college, but over the past few months it's been the furthest thing from my mind. I haven't applied anywhere or even know what I want to study, but how? Going to college doesn't exactly seem like something that I have the time or ability to do anymore.

I shake my head, dropping my gaze to the ground. "For as long as I can remember, college has been the ultimate goal. If I could have miraculously gotten myself through high school and made it to college, then I know that I would have been alright. I would have been able to break free from the foster system and build myself a proper life, but … I just don't know anymore. I don't really think college is an option for me now. Besides, do I really need it anymore? It's not like I'm going to have a chance at having a career, not with Dynasty bearing down on me. That is my job now."

King squeezes my hand. "You can't think about it like that. Dynasty doesn't rule you. You rule it, so if you want to go to college, you go to college."

"But there's too much to do. I wouldn't have time for college."

Carver shakes his head. "Delegate, Winter. Just because you're the leader, doesn't mean you have to give a hundred percent of yourself to it. Hire an assistant to overlook everything. You still have a life and no one expects you to stop living it. If you want to go to college, then we'll make it happen."

"Just like that, huh?" I scoff, rolling my eyes at his arrogant confidence. "Getting me into a good college is a little different than enrolling me in your high school. Besides, what's going to happen? Are you going to follow me around campus all day, making sure I don't get a papercut?"

Cruz laughs. "We got you off murder charges, didn't we?" he says with a wink as a cocky smirk lifts the corner of his lips and shows off his perfectly straight teeth. Heat floods my stomach and sends an intense desire slamming through me, and for a second, I have to remind myself that throwing Cruz up against a wall in a school is inappropriate. Though, it wouldn't be the first time that I forgot my manners in school.

Fuck me. Maybe Scardoni was onto something. Maybe I am a whore. Oh well, I may be a whore, but I'm only a whore for my men. No one else will ever get the pleasure of seeing me like that, not as long as they hold my heart captive.

Seeing my reaction to his wicked charm, Cruz's smirk stretches wider across his face. "You have a point, though," he continues. "You're hot as fuck, and while most people would understand us following you around campus like a bad smell, your professors probably won't find it as … endearing."

"Endearing is really the word you want to use for it? Right," I laugh.

Cruz rolls his eyes as Gray grumbles from behind me. "He's right. We won't be able to protect you on a college campus the way we can here. Not unless we enroll as students ourselves."

Horror stretches over King's face, and it becomes abundantly clear that college was never a part of his big plan. "You're kidding, right?" he questions, glancing around at his friends, but when none of them respond, he kicks his foot in the dirt. "Fuck. Okay. If it means keeping her safe, I'll do it. But I'm picking bullshit classes."

"Or …" Carver says, looking up ahead at the school. "We can just wait until the threats pass and start applying to colleges when we know she's going to be safe. Besides, maybe a few extra months will give her the time she needs to figure out what the fuck she actually wants to study when she gets there."

My brows raise. He has a point … a really good point.

Who would have known that Carver has a brain floating around inside that big head of his? With all that testosterone, his ego, and his bad attitude, I figured his brain had given up a long time ago.

King squeezes my hand. "I know we're supposed to be hating on Carver right now, but there's no denying that the guy has a point. A fucking good one. I think he's right. We should wait until all the bullshit is dealt with and then we can talk about college, but if you really insist on not waiting, we'll figure out a way."

"I, umm… I hate to admit it, but for the first time since meeting you guys, I think that I actually agree with Carver. Don't get me wrong, I'm sure I would have loved having you assholes following me from class to class every minute of every day. It would have been fan-fucking-tastic, but I'm not going to learn shit if I'm worried about accidentally sitting on an explosive every time I sit down, so yeah … we'll wait."

Carver looks back at me, his eyes wide as confusion flickers through his gaze. "You're not going to fight me on this?" I shake my head and his brows raise. "You sure? You're actually agreeing with me about something?"

I give him a blank stare. "Keep questioning me about it and I might just change my mind."

Carver rolls his eyes, and just as we all look back toward the school, we find a pissed-off Sara Benson charging right for me. "Fucking hell," I mutter under my breath, dreading whatever the fuck she feels the need to say.

The last time I saw her, she'd stormed through my front door looking for a fight. I introduced my brass knuckles to her pretty face when she got too close, and damn it was fun. When I kissed her at that stupid party, getting under Carver's skin was my only thought. But he wasn't the only one affected. Apparently, she wanted more than a taste, and girls like Sara Benson aren't used to rejection.

"YOU," she roars, making sure to get the attention of every student around us. Even Ember's eyes dart up from where she waits for me by the gate.

Carver takes a discreet step to the left, putting himself directly between Sara and me, pulling her up short. "That's close enough," he demands in a way that has her swallowing back fear, his tone sending a wave of desire pulsing through me.

Sara blanches for a moment, captivated by his lethal stare before blinking three times in rapid succession. She looks between Carver and me for a few drawn-out seconds before finding her nerve and keeping her stare on mine.

I can't help but notice the soft bruising around her jaw in the perfect shape of the brass knuckles that sit upon my fingers. God, punching her in the face was good. It was nearly as good as the high I get from having Grayson, King, and Cruz inside me all at the same time. She completely deserved it though. Who the hell did she think she was storming onto my property and talking shit like that? Though, to be completely honest, up until this very moment, I'd completely forgotten that it even happened.

I bite the inside of my cheek, forcing myself to keep control, fighting the wide smile that desperately wants to sit across my lips. "Is there something you need?" I ask, stepping closer to Carver and shuffling to his right, refusing to allow him to block me in as though I can't handle my own problems.

Sara anxiously looks at the boys before coming back to me with her chin raised, feigning confidence. I'm not going to lie, she definitely gets credit for having the balls to stand here like this. Most girls who get hit with that deadly stare of Carver's would have already backed down. "Do you really think that you can just fuck off for weeks, then come back here as though nothing ever happened?"

I groan. "What the fuck are you even talking about?" I ask, figuring that if she wants to fuck with my morning that I have every right to fuck with hers.

She looks at me as though I'm crazy. "You fucking punched me. I should have had you arrested."

"You trespassed onto my property and forced your way into my home, plus you were aggressive, but you know what?" I say, bringing my fingers to my chin and pretending to be deep in thought. "I really don't know what you're talking about. I remember you storming into my house and practically begging to get me naked, but punching you? Why are you lying about what really happened? Are you embarrassed about it? Maybe you hit your head when you fell."

Sara's eyes go wide and I hold back the laugh that threatens to spill out of my mouth. "What? I … No. You're fucking with me. I know what happened. You punched me. I've had your stupid, cheap rings bruised into my face for three fucking weeks and you're not going to get away with it. Do you have any idea how much money my daddy had to fork out for the plastic surgeon to fix my face?"

"You're confused," I insist, staring right into her eyes and watching how her pupils dilate. "You were yelling. You were upset that I didn't want to get with you and then you just passed out and cut yourself against the foyer table. The boys even went with you in the ambulance to make sure that you were alright."

Sara shakes her head, looking between the boys, knowing damn well they didn't ride with her. But now she's questioning her memory, and that's all that matters. "You're lying," she seethes. "You're nothing but a lying, dirty … slut."

I shrug my shoulders. The last time she called me a slut, she ended up with my fist in her face, so I guess she isn't one who learns from her mistakes, but today, I simply just don't have the energy to deal with her.

I step into her and watch as she sucks in a breath. "What do you want from me?" I question, lowering my voice as Grayson flinches, moving in closer. "I've already made it clear that I'm not about to get on my knees and eat your pussy, and I've already made it clear what happens when you get in my face and start talking shit, so what do you want? Why are you here fucking with my morning?"

Sara clenches her jaw, and as she watches me and sees the anger pulsing within my eyes, she begins to panic. Her eyes flick between the boys and me, and if I were to listen hard enough, I bet that I could hear the thoughts inside her head, scrambling to figure out what the hell to say.

Sara swallows hard, but as she sees the other students watching, a fake confidence settles over her. But she can't fool me. I see the fear shining right through her false bravado. "You used me. You have the whole fucking school thinking that I'm hot for you when it's clear that you're the one who wants to fuck, but unfortunately for you, I'm not into bitches who sell themselves. You're fucking trash, and it's clear by the way these guys hang off you that you're fucking all of them, but what for? Are you making a little cash?" she laughs, eyeing me up and down with disgust. "They must all be fucked in the head, because God knows that I'd never pay for *that*."

A howling laugh bubbles out of me. "Are you serious? This is the best you've got?"

Sara's eyes narrow and she tosses her hair over shoulder, making her look more plastic than her nose. "This is the end of the road for you. You're not going to get away with it. I'm going to expose you to everyone, and when I do, you're done."

A grin pulls at my lips as I lean into her and lower my voice to a deathly whisper. "A war is not something that you want with me," I warn her. "But now that you've gone and declared yourself in front of all these people, you've left me with absolutely no choice but to destroy you. So, thank you. This is going to be the most fun that I've had in years."

Sara clenches her jaw and looks around our small group as the crowded students watch on with wide eyes, and seeing Sara beginning to fumble, the whispers start.

Sara huffs, her nostrils flaring wide and just when I think she's about to stomp her foot and start to cry, she turns and storms away, her hips swaying and her loud, frustrated cry following behind her.

Yeah, this really is going to be fun.

10

My phone chimes with an incoming text, and without thinking, I reach across and scoop it off the armrest of the couch, more than happy to take a break from all the bullshit schoolwork that I need to catch up on.

My eyes drop to the phone, and it's not until I see Ember's name on the screen that I glance up across Carver's living room to find her staring back at me with a ridiculous smirk stretched over her pretty face, her schoolwork long forgotten.

My brows furrow and I drop my gaze back to my phone, swiping my thumb across the screen to bring up her text. Within seconds, a loud, howling laugh tears out of me as I scan over her words.

Ember - You eat big, sludgy, diarrhea turds for breakfast.

My gaze snaps back to her smug face, seeing the challenge flashing in her eyes. Grayson and King look between us, forgetting about Sam's ledger sitting on Grayson's lap. I'm sure they're wondering what the fuck is going on, but when we don't offer to share, they get back to scrolling through their phones.

I instantly get to work.

Winter - You eat bitches like Sara for breakfast and you fucking love it, you dirty whore.

Ember - Jesus. It's a joke, not a dick. Don't take it so hard.

Winter - Can't help it. Hard is the only way I like my dicks.

Ember snickers across the room, and I can't help but look up at her with a stupid grin stretched wide across my face. Grayson and King still watch us, but it's clear that they've moved way past asking us what the fuck is going on.

Carver strides into the room with a packet of chips, and as he drops down beside me on the couch and snatches the ledger off Grayson's lap, I take the chips and tear them open as another text comes through.

Ember - Speaking of … you're not really going to go to war with Sara, right? Don't you already have too much on your plate? I mean, do you recall the whole getting shot thing and all the attacks? They're hardly a distant memory.

Winter - You don't think that I could take her?

Ember - I think taking her is exactly what she wants out of you.

Ember - FYI - I heard a rumor that her clit runs a little to the

left so when you're on your knees eating her pussy, make sure you're hitting it right!

I roll my eyes and glance up at Ember. "Really?" I grunt, giving her a blank stare as she snickers to herself and buries her head back in her phone.

Ember - Okay. Seriously? I think you'd whoop her bitch ass and make her regret ever looking your way. Don't hate on me, but I just don't think a war is something you need right now.

I scan over her text while feeling Carver's stare on the side of my face. "What's going on?" he questions, trying to peer at the screen of my phone and read what little of our conversation that he can see. I tilt my phone away and focus my glare on him. "You good there? You don't see me trying to read your texts."

Carver narrows his eyes without even a hint of guilt at being caught out. He simply shrugs his shoulders. "I get my answers anyway I can," he says unapologetically.

I let out a sigh and nod toward Ember. "If you really must know, Ember just got her period. She's on a heavy flow and now she can't move because she's worried that she's just painted your good couch red with her pussy."

Carver's eyes bug out of his head and he whips his gaze to Ember who sits across the room looking horrified and embarrassed. "Fuck you," she screeches at me, grabbing a cushion and launching it at my face as she stands up and turns around, showing everyone that I'm full of shit.

As she drops back down into her spot, she looks back at Carver who appears more than relieved about the state of his couch. "I was actually in the middle of trying to explain why I think starting some bullshit war with Sara is a fucking stupid idea, but now she's probably going to go ahead with it, just to spite you for trying to read her messages."

Carver scoffs. "I wouldn't put it past her," he says as he swivels his gaze to me. "But she's fucking right. Any other time, I'd be more than happy to sit back and watch you start some bullshit war with the people who have wronged you, but not now. There's too much going on."

"I agree," King says from across the room. "Save the war for after we figure out who the fuck blew up the staircase at the ball. We can't afford to get distracted by this bullshit when your life is at risk. Sara is nothing but a thorn in your side. She's not important."

I roll my eyes and drop my phone back to the armrest of the couch. "If you assholes had spared me a second to even reply to Ember's text, you would already know that I had absolutely no intention of going to war with her in the first place."

Ember's face scrunches in confusion. "Huh?"

I shake my head. "I don't have time for that shit, not with all the schoolwork I need to catch up on and my bitch of a mother still on the loose. Besides, Sara is probably pacing her bedroom right now, terrified and fretting about what I might do to her and that fear is going to continue until the very last day of school. Every time I look her way, she's going to wonder if that's when I'm going to strike, and that's more than enough to make me feel all warm and fuzzy inside."

Ember gives me a blank stare. "You are ... fuck. I don't even know what you are, but something isn't right inside your head."

I smile wide. "Why, thank you," I tell her, more than in love with her dazzling compliment.

Ember rolls her eyes as Carver just shakes his head, not even a little bit surprised by our bullshit. He grabs the packet of chips back, and as his hand digs into the packet, his gaze drops to the thick ledger.

The guys have all but studied every page of this ledger over the past few weeks, familiarizing themselves with every victim who was stolen from their families. I don't doubt that Dynasty is going to rescue them, it's more a question of how we're going to make it happen and when. But we will find a way. I won't give up on them. It's too important.

Cruz barges his way into the room and all eyes fall to him as he storms right up to the coffee table, and with a pissed-off grunt, slams a roll of toilet paper down right in the center, nearly knocking over the glass of ice water that Grayson keeps refilling for me. "We need to talk," Cruz spits, glaring around the room and meeting each of our stares with a horrifically lethal one of his own, and making Ember squirm in her seat. "Who the fuck thought that it was alright to buy the cheap two-ply? My finger just went straight through it and I fingered my own fucking asshole."

Loud, heaving laughs pull from both Ember and me as the boys just stare at Cruz, equally as horrified as he is. They're probably imagining just how awful that would really be, but I guess now he knows what it's like. "How far did you puncture that thing?" I ask, tears of laughter rolling down my cheeks as my abdomen starts to ache. "Did you just pierce the surface or get right through to the ring of fire?"

Cruz just stares at me as my white, fluffy ball of death comes bounding into the living room and jumps up on the couch between me and Carver. I scoop up Lady Dante while keeping my questioning stare on Cruz until he lets out a heavy sigh and drops onto the single couch opposite me. "I think I just lost my virginity," he mutters. "I feel violated."

Ember grins and I glance over at her just in time to watch her amused gaze meet Cruz's. She winks and her grin only triples in size. "It felt good, right?"

Cruz just leans forward and drops his head into his hands. "Too soon. Way too fucking soon."

King lets out a low breath while eyeing the offending toilet paper innocently sitting on the coffee table in the center of the room. "It's alright, man," he says in a supportive, but hesitant tone as he slowly nods his head. "We've all been there."

Cruz glances up to meet King's stare, and as they look at each other for a long moment, their mutual misery creates a strong, unbreakable bond between them, tethering them together as violated ass-brothers for all eternity.

I smother a laugh, desperately trying to regain control of myself. "You know, if you add a bit of lube and don't be so forceful with your … prodding, I think you'll both really get into it. You know guys have a g-spot in their asses, right?"

Grayson looks away. "Please tell me that we are not seriously discussing this."

I shrug my shoulders. "Well, you guys are always 'prodding' my ass, so it's only fair that we get to talk about all of yours."

Carver drops his attention back to the ledger, putting on a show of being extremely interested in what's inside. "Consider my ass out of this conversation."

I grin, figuring that while we're on the topic, what better way to fuck with them? "So ... you know, I've actually been meaning to talk to you guys about this whole ass thing."

Every single one of their heads snap up with nothing but sheer horror across their faces. Now, I know they've all claimed that they'd do absolutely anything for me, but I have a feeling that they draw the line if it means their asses getting involved.

Cruz violently shakes his head. "No. Absolutely not. Whatever it is, the answer is no. My ass has suffered enough. Just the shock of my finger penetrating my ... no. I can't. I'm going to need at least a week to recover."

Ember leans back in her chair, her eyes dropping to Cruz's hands. "I mean, those fingers of yours sure are thick."

Cruz glares back at her. "Don't you have a new boyfriend that you could be bugging right now?"

"I sure do," she grins wide, more than up for talking about Corey every little chance she gets. "And for the record, he's confident enough in his masculinity to admit that he fucking loves it when I shove my finger in his ass."

King swallows hard, looking at Ember as though she's speaking another language. "I really could have done without that piece of information. Next time you want to play with your man's ass, keep that shit to yourself."

"You sure?" she teases. "I could teach Winter a few tricks that would have you guys worshipping at my feet."

"Alright," Cruz says, looking across at Carver. "This conversation is over. Pass me that ledger. I was working on something."

Carver instantly tosses the ledger across the room and Cruz collects it in his capable hands and treats it as though it's liquid gold, and he's right to. This ledger is the one clue we have that could lead us back to hundreds of girls who are all scared and desperately needing to come home. This ledger is everything, and to lose it would be a crime.

While all the guys like to spend hours scanning through the pages of this ledger, Cruz spends, by far, the most amount of time agonizing over it. We quickly worked out that many of the names written in the ledger were fake, and so Cruz has made it his personal mission to figure out each and every one of them. We should have known that it wasn't going to be that easy.

He has a notebook that he uses, trying to make connections between the girls on the ledger and the profiles listed on the missing persons websites. Honestly, I think he's doing an incredible job. We can't confirm anything without seeing what these girls actually look like, and we wouldn't dare contact their parents and give hope when there's a possibility that we could be wrong.

Cruz has managed to match at least ten missing persons profiles of girls who were stolen near the Mexican border nearly three years ago to entries in the ledger, and judging by the way he drops everything that he's doing, forgets about his ass issues, and focuses on the papers before him, he might be about to match another.

Cruz gets agitated and gets up from the couch, taking his notebook and the ledger with him as he storms out of the room. We all watch him go, knowing that he'll be heading for his laptop that's been sitting open on the dining table for the past few weeks.

Hating that look on his face, I get up and walk out behind him, following through the kitchen and out to the dining room table. He doesn't bother sitting, just slams the notebook down and presses the spacebar on his laptop to bring it out of sleep mode.

Cruz braces himself against the table and hangs his head. As my hand drops to his shoulder, I can't help but glance over the box of jewelry and mementos that's been sitting right next to Cruz's laptop since the day we blew up Sam Delacourt's house.

This box has been acting as motivation, and it's doing a damn good job. Every little bracelet, every pin, shoelace, ring, or hair clip is something that Sam took off his victims—trophies of his. There are hundreds of things in this box, and I have every intention of returning each little piece to its original owner once we save them and bring them back home.

Dwelling on the box is only going to send me into an intense depression, so instead, I focus on Cruz. "What's the matter? Can I help?"

He shakes his head. "I don't know," he says, pulling his head back up and looking directly at the missing persons notice on his screen. A gorgeous six-year-old girl, Maddison Atwell, went missing from her bedroom in the middle of the night nearly two years ago. He points down at the ledger, showing me the entry for a five-year-old girl who was sold around the same time. "It's just this girl. The ages don't match up, but my gut is telling me that this is her. This is Maddison. It's just … I can't be wrong, not about this. It's too important."

I reach down to the ledger and flip through the pages. "Are you sure? Are there any other entries for kids this young around the same time?"

Cruz shakes his head. "No, this is it. She's the only one. All the other details match. She was sold within fifty miles of where Maddison went missing, and the sale date was less than a month later. It's just the age."

"This girl in here was only five. It's possible that Sam got her age wrong. He's a scary guy, and for a little kid, he would have been absolutely terrifying. I doubt that she was going out of her way to tell him how old she was. He could have just guessed. No one was going to question him."

"I know," Cruz groans, spinning around to lean against the table. He can't keep staring at the image of Maddison Atwell on his laptop when he knows that right now, all he can do to help her is match her name to a listing in a fucked-up ledger. "But what if we somehow save this girl and we bring her back only to find it isn't her? What am I supposed to tell her parents then?"

"That's not going to happen," I tell him, letting out a breath and putting myself right in front of Cruz. My fingers catch on his belt as I step in close. "I know it's hard, and you want to reunite every one of those victims with their families, but you need to remember that we're not doing this for the parent's sake, this is for the child who's spent years living in fear. We focus on saving the victims listed in this ledger, and only once we've done that, do we find their parents and reunite them. The last thing I want to do is give a parent hope that we can find their baby and not come through. Everybody has already suffered enough, and we're not about to add to it."

Cruz lets out a deep breath and takes my waist, pulling me in tight against his body. "I just hate that I can't do more. I hate that we have Dynasty's red tape holding us back, and I hate that I'm not out there right fucking now, kicking down doors and saving these people. We need to do better."

"We will do better," I tell him. "We're going to win this. We're going to fuck up each of those monsters who bought these children. We're going to get every little piece of information out of them to find whatever connections we can, and we're going to save other children suffering through the same thing. Those sick bastards are going to wish they were never born. We've got this, Cruz. We're going to be unstoppable. Dynasty isn't about corruption and power anymore, and I'm going to see to it. We're going to use every little resource we've got. Dynasty is going to become an organization that's one hundred percent dedicated to fighting the evil in this world."

Cruz nods and gently presses his lips to my forehead, desperately needing that closeness. "And the bastards who bought from Sam Delacourt are going to be our first targets."

"You're damn right, they are," I agree, stepping out of his arms and looking back down at the ledger. "How can I help? I want to find these children, but I don't even know where to start looking."

Cruz shakes his head. "I wish I knew."

"What about that massive tech room that Dynasty has below ground? Could anything in there help?"

Cruz looks back at his laptop screen, staring at the image of Maddison Atwell. "Possibly," he says, his eyes going wider as the slightest bit of hope pulses through his veins again. "My dad was telling me that Dynasty was getting an updated facial recognition program, far beyond anything else on the market. If that's already been done, I can use the images from the missing person's site and do a scan, but if the victim hasn't been let out in public, then it's hopeless. Not to mention, running a scan for each child could take weeks."

"Fuck," I grunt. "Is that our only option?"

"At the moment, yeah. It's all we've got."

"But it's something," I remind him, looking up and meeting his broken stare. "Do it. I don't care who tells you that you can't be down there using that software. You have my direct approval and no one is going to stop you."

"It's not just going to happen overnight," he reminds me, making sure that I fully understand.

"I know, and quite frankly, I don't care if it takes us fifty years. We're finding every single one of them. Hell, create a team if you have to, but whatever you do, don't give up."

Cruz's eyes brighten by the second, and before I know it, he's diving into me and crushing his lips against mine in a bruising kiss. I don't even get a second to breathe before he's pulling away and grabbing his notebook and Sam's ledger. "I'll be back … fuck. I don't know when I'll be back. Don't wait up."

And just like that, Cruz storms back through the house, grabs Grayson, and all but launches himself out the front door.

11

My feet feel heavy as I drag myself up the grand staircase, my consciousness threatening to give out mid-step. It's been a long day, and as the boys took off one by one, I found myself alone with the broodiest asshole I've ever met. The minutes ticked by deathly slow. Though, I can't really complain. Carver's silence and my need to ignore his assholery gave me a chance to catch up on a little schoolwork, and I mean very little. There's still a tall stack of work I need to get through piled on the kitchen counter.

My brain is fried. All I want to do is find my bed and crash, though it's only seven in the evening. If I were to go to bed now, I'd probably be up at four in the morning, demanding attention. The boys would force themselves to wake up to give it to me, but I don't want to do that. They're under enough stress as it is and I don't need to add to that.

I miraculously make it to the top of the stairs and feel as though I get shorter with every step I take down the hallway. Until I walk past Carver's bedroom door and hear a soft, needy groan coming from inside.

My back straightens as something comes alive within me.

My, oh my. Carver with his dick in his hand would certainly be a sight that no woman would ever be able to forget.

I find myself backing up and coming to a stop outside his door, desperately trying to control myself. His door is open just a crack, but it's absolutely none of my business to be peeking through it.

I need to walk away.

I need to come to terms with the fact that Carver doesn't want to get on board the sharing train and leave him the fuck alone. Yet no matter how hard I try, I can't stop myself from wanting him. There's just something about Dante Carver that draws me in. He's intense in all the right ways and disturbingly gorgeous, but underneath all that broody assholery, he's got the kindest heart that I've ever had the pleasure of knowing, and I'm going to be absolutely wrecked when he finds another girl to share all that with.

When no other noises come from within, I somehow find the strength to step back from his door, but the second I do, a low, tormented groan sounds throughout the long hallway.

Fuck.

My fingers press against the hardwood of his door and I give it a gentle push. The door peels open before me, silently swinging wide into Carver's darkened room. I find him lying back on his bed, one arm popped behind his head, his bulging muscles on display as his other hand strokes his glorious cock.

My mouth drops.

He's as naked as the day he was born and it's even better than I thought it was going to be. Dante Carver is everything. His body is strong, ripped, and his cock is as veiny, thick, and delicious as they come. I know without a single doubt in my mind that I am not going to be able to walk away. Not now, not ever, but I always knew that. It's Carver who's always held back. I've been upfront about what I've wanted, but lately, things have been shifting. Emotions and feelings are being tested as we've been thrown into impossible situations and forced to admit things we never intended on sharing.

His room is bathed in a low, natural light from his bedroom window, casting long shadows across his room and over his body, making the sharp ridges of his abs look even deeper as it casts a glow across his warm, olive skin.

Carver just watches me, not flinching or bothering to stop. He has nothing to be ashamed of, and fuck, he knows it.

My thighs clench, and as his dark, stormy eyes rest on mine, need races through me faster than his bullet did. God, I've got to have him.

I step deeper into his room, my heart racing as my hands begin to shake. He doesn't stop moving, his hand slowly stroking up and down his throbbing cock as he watches me. Fire burns between us, fueled by the lust in his eyes and the desperate desire shining in my own.

Why am I so nervous? It's just Carver.

The door closes with a soft thud behind me, and I can't hear a damn thing over the rapid beat of my heart pulsing loudly in my ears. My breath comes in faster and I struggle to keep control. Fuck, who am I kidding? I lost control the second I heard that soft moan slipping from his warm lips.

I'd give anything to feel them on mine again. The last time he kissed me … no. I can't go there. All I know is that I miss his touch. I crave it every second of the day, and if I don't get to feel my nails digging into his back or his fingers tighten on my waist as I lose myself to his undeniable pleasure, I might just die.

I swallow hard and take a hesitant step forward. I'm terrified that he's going to turn me away, and that the rejection is going to create an inferno inside me, one that I'll never recover from.

All time is lost as I edge toward his bed, and as the sun dips below the horizon, the light in the room fades. But the darkness feels so much deeper than nightfall; it's as if the shadowy depths of Carver's eyes had seeped into the room around us, dragging me closer.

Pausing at the end of his bed, my heart races faster than I can keep up with, and the fear of rejection builds to impossible heights. My gaze sails over his body, and I bite down on my bottom lip, nibbling it as a rush of traitorous thoughts begin circling my mind.

I should go. This isn't what he wants.

I've already made it perfectly clear that I won't take him if it means losing the others, and he's made it clear that he won't take me if it's a package deal.

This isn't going to work. He and I… we're a train wreck waiting to happen.

What the hell is wrong with me? Since when have I ever been the girl to freak out over something like this? This isn't me. I'm not scared of putting myself out there; I'm not someone who backs down from a challenge, but Carver has my head in a mess.

My life is a million shades of fucked up right now, and despite how much I don't want to admit it, I desperately need stability. I need people I can trust, people who are going to stand by me and lift me up, and if I hear the word 'no' come out of Carver's mouth, it's going to kill me.

I start shaking my head and Carver instantly gets up from his bed, slinking across the soft carpet as he makes his way toward me.

The need to back up slams through me, and by the time my shoulder blades hit the door, Carver finally reaches me. His arm raises above my head and he props himself against the hardwood. His heavenly scent consumes me. He's just showered and there are still a few droplets of water sitting against his strong abs making my fingers flinch at my sides.

Carver leans into me, tempting me, teasing me with a good time, but I see it in his eyes, he's not ready to cave and neither am I.

He gets closer but doesn't dare touch me as my gaze travels over his body, scanning over his perfectly sculpted torso and dropping low to where his thick cock rests heavily in his hand.

Seeing what has my attention, he strokes his hand up and down, teasing his tip with his thumb and giving a firm squeeze.

A soft, desperate moan slips from between my lips as I clench my thighs harder, urgently needing to relieve the ache that builds between my legs. "What's the matter?" Carver murmurs, his head dipping low beside my face as his unruly hair brushes along the soft skin of my collarbone. His voice rumbles right through my chest, the vibrations hitting me like a wrecking ball. "Have you changed your mind?"

My eyes close as I breathe him in, tilting my head as the satisfaction of being this close to him rocks through me. I'm so tempted to throw it all away just for this night with him, but I won't dare. What I have with Cruz, King, and Grayson is too good. I'd be a fool to give that away.

No. I can't. If I'm going to go there with Carver, then I need to wait until I can do it right. There's too much to lose.

I shake my head, hating how the pain shoots through me at having to tell him no. All this time, it's been him rejecting me, but not this time. This time, it's his heart that's going to ache, and for some reason, that makes it so much worse. "I can't," I whisper. "I won't throw away what I have with them for a night with you."

The tip of his nose brushes along my skin and I sink into him, needing so much more as his warmth begins to wrap around me. "It's not just a night, Winter. Be with me. I need you." He breathes in, and as my heart continues to ache, he goes on. "Seeing you bleeding out … and knowing that I did that, it opened my eyes. I have to have you in my life. I can't lose you again. I won't."

"But you don't share."

He shakes his head. "I don't."

Tears threaten to well in my eyes, but I hold them back as my hand slips behind my back to grab hold of the door handle, far too stubborn to allow Carver to see me break right now. "Then you have no choice but to lose me," I tell him, my voice breaking as a lump grows in my throat and threatens the oxygen flowing in and out. "As much as I want that too, I won't give them up for anything."

Carver pulls back so his intense stare is locked on mine, and even in this darkened room, I can still make out every little speckle of brown, green, and gold deep within his eyes. Without a single word, he reaches around me and his hand finds mine over the door handle. He twists, and not a second later, the door pops open behind me. He takes a step back, allowing me space to open it properly and walk out.

I don't look at him, fearing what I might see in his eyes, and fearing that if I did, I would take it all back and run straight into his warm arms.

I step out of his room, the cool air in the hallway stealing my breath, and as the door slams shut, the finality cripples me. Standing out in the hallway, I struggle to put the distance between us—the distance we so desperately need. So, I just stand … stand here as my heart shatters into a million pieces.

A second passes, and then another, and after a minute, I finally feel as if I can maybe hold myself together. So without missing another beat, I storm down the hallway with my head an absolute mess and push through King's bedroom door.

The lights are on and his room is filled with steam from the open bathroom door. I hear his shower running and suck in a breath, knowing that being with one guy to ease the pain of another is no way to handle my feelings, but I need to. I need King to help take the pain away before I break.

I storm into King's bathroom to find him standing in the shower. His hand is propped against the tiles and his head hangs into the water, and judging by the steam rolling out in large clouds, I don't doubt that the water is scalding hot.

Perfect.

Hearing me race in, King's head whips up. He eyes me for less than a second before his brows furrow, leaving me wondering just how fucked up Carver must have left me to have King so instantly concerned about my well-being. "What did he do?" King demands, anger flickering over his expression.

I shake my head while grabbing the hem of my tank and pulling it up over my head. My jeans go next, and as I step into his boiling hot shower and his arms fall around me, my desperation shines as bright as a diamond. "No ... I can't," I say as the water rushes over me, the heat instantly helping. "Please ... just make me forget. Fuck me until the pain goes away."

"Babe ..."

"Please, King," I beg, looking up into his warm, ocean blue eyes. "I just ... I can't talk about it yet. Just take my mind off it for a moment and I promise, afterwards, I'll give you answers, but right now ... I just ... I need to ease the pain before it tears me to pieces."

King's lips press into a tight line, and it's clear he's not thrilled with using sex as a means to avoid my feelings, but he's not going to say no when seeing the desperation in my eyes. He'd do absolutely anything to ease my pain, even if it went against everything he believes in.

His knuckles sweep over the stitches just below my ribs. "You good?"

I nod. "I can handle it," I whisper as the water runs over my face. "I don't want you to be gentle."

King narrows his eyes, and before he's even said a word, I know he's reading me better than I could ever read myself, and for once, I'm not so fucking thrilled about it. "I'm not about to use sex as a way to punish you for whatever the fuck just went down between you and Carver. I'll fuck you and it'll be hard, but it's going to be on our terms, between you and me. Your shit with Carver stays out in the fucking hallway."

I go to pull out of his arms, knowing damn well that he's not about to give me what I need. There's no way that I'm able to leave my feelings for Carver out of this. The whole reason I'm standing in his fucking shower is because I can't process my goddamn feelings.

King latches onto the tops of my arms and pulls me back until I'm right where I was. "I'm not about to let you walk out of here because I'm not going to spend my night scouring the streets only to find you at the back of some sleazy bar beating the fucking shit out of some bastard. So, you have three fucking choices, and I suggest you choose wisely."

I clench my jaw and look up to meet his pissed-off stare. Most of the time, I love his forceful nature. I love his dominance and alpha bullshit. It's the sexiest thing I've ever seen, except when he uses it against me and keeps me from getting my way. Right now, I couldn't hate him more.

I just stare, too fucking stubborn to respond, but he doesn't let it faze him. "One, you can stay right the fuck here and let me fuck you up against the tiles. Two, you can start talking and tell me what the fuck just went down between you two. Or three, we can go down to the gym and you can take it all out on me. What's it going to be?"

Is he insane?

Fuck, feelings, or fight? Who in their right mind would have even bothered listening to the second or third option? But in all honesty, options two and three are just not things that I'm down with. It's one thing standing in that gym with Carver and beating on him until I reach exhaustion, but it's different with King. I don't take pleasure out of putting my hands on the guys. It makes me sick. What happened with Carver and that guy was out of pure desperation, not something that should be repeated. As for talking through my feelings, I'm nowhere near ready for that. That just sounds like a disaster waiting to happen.

I shake my head and try to pull out of his hold but he pulls me right back again. "Kiss me," he demands, his tone rough and filled with authority.

"No. It's not going to happen."

King grabs me tighter and pushes me up against the wall, being firm but not rough enough to wind me. "I said kiss me."

I meet his heated stare. His breath comes in short, sharp pants and it's clear that his emotions are just as messed up as mine. He doesn't know how to help me and that scares the crap out of him, but he's making it up as he goes, and fuck him, as he keeps his intense, gorgeous stare on mine, it starts to work.

"King …"

"Kiss. Me."

I let out a soft breath and slide my arms around his neck, and that one small touch is enough to send the need firing through me. My fingers knot into his hair, holding him close as I continue to stare into his eyes.

"Don't make me wait any longer."

I give in and push up, crushing my lips against his, and as his tongue slips inside my mouth, the thought of what happened in Carver's room instantly begins fading from my mind, allowing a subtle peace to settle over me.

King kisses me urgently. At first, he allows me to take control, but it doesn't last long until he's pressing harder, reminding me exactly why I love that dominance that lives inside him. It's raw, brutal, and addictive.

His body presses into mine, the familiar weight consuming me, drawing me in, and absorbing every ounce of pain I've tried so hard to hide. His lips are like the sweetest torture, and as his hands grip my waist, I run my fingers along the contours of his powerful chest. I have to have him.

King's hand drops to my ass, and in one smooth motion, he lifts me up and presses me harder against the cool tiles. Without missing a beat, he thrusts right into me, sending his thick, corded cock deep, hitting me right where I need to feel him.

I cry out, tipping my head back and groaning at the way his lips come down on the soft, sensitive skin of my neck. His fingers dig into my ass as the urgency builds between us. He draws back, and with a loud grunt, he slams back inside me.

"Oh, fuck. YES! King."

He's everything.

Hunter King is God's gift to women. Fuck, they all are.

Except Carver.

Fuck Carver.

I need to nut-punch Carver.

Why the fuck am I thinking about nut-punching Carver while King's are currently slamming against my pussy?

King picks up his pace, pushing into me over and over again as I cry out, losing myself in him. He works my pussy just the way I like it, hitting me in all the right spots, touching me the way I need, kissing me the way that drives me wild.

My body answers his every call, and it's only a minute before I feel that familiar pull drawing up inside of me, building rapidly with a fierce intensity, ready to tear me apart from the inside out.

I need this release like I need to breathe, and I'm sure that if he were to stop right now, I would die. He would take away everything good in the world and leave me with nothing but tragedy.

King's body rolls and moves with mine like a perfect match and it's everything I need. How am I ever supposed to live without him? I couldn't. I was right to turn Carver away. What I have with King is too important, too precious, and far too real. I wouldn't give that up for anything. A life without Hunter King is a life not worth living.

King keeps moving, thrusting and giving me everything he's got. My nails dig into the strong muscles of his back until I can't hold out any longer.

My orgasm tears through me like an explosion, clenching, squeezing, and convulsing around King's cock, and as I scream out his name and pull him in closer, he comes with me, sending hot spurts of cum shooting up inside me, making me feel like some kind of sexual goddess.

I collapse into him, my feet hitting the floor just as the exhaustion of my afternoon begins to catch up with me.

King pulls me straight back into the stream of hot water, holding me tight to his chest as his arms wrap around me like a cocoon. "Are you good?" he murmurs, pressing his lips to my temple and treating me like the most precious creature he's ever met.

I nod into his warm chest, closing my eyes as I focus on the stream of water slamming against my back. "I'm good."

"Did I take your pain away?"

I raise my chin and meet his lips with my own. "You did."

"Good, I'm glad," he murmurs against my lips, reaching around me to cut the water and instantly sending a wave of disappointment soaring over me. I wasn't even a little bit ready to finish in the shower. I would have happily stood under that warm stream of water for an hour. Though from now on, this is where I'll be showering. King's water pressure is absolutely perfect.

King shuffles us out of the shower, wrapping a soft, warm towel around my shoulders and scooping me into his arms. With my head against his chest, he walks across his room, turning out the lights as he goes. Within moments, I'm curled in his bed, his blankets practically up to my head. "Right," he murmurs, his hand slowly rubbing up and down my back. "You promised that once you were good, I'd get answers, so give it to me straight. What the fuck just went down between you and Carver?"

12

The loud, obnoxious bell seems to drone on as I drag myself out of my fourth period science class and trudge out into the hallway. It's been a long day, and as most people would have learned by now, I don't cope well with long days. I'd give anything to go home and lie out in the sun, soaking up the rays with one or more of my boys between my legs. I don't know what it is, but there's something about getting naked and fooling around in places where I can be caught that thrills me to no end.

My books weigh my arms down as I drag my feet toward my locker. I can't believe that school isn't even close to being over for the day. Though, I have an hour for lunch to spend with the boys and Ember and that's bound to make the rest of the day a little more bearable.

I feel a familiar hard stare from the opposite end of the hall, and as I look up, I find Carver watching me closely. His eyes bore into mine and I can't help but see the hurt that lives within him.

It's been nearly two weeks since I walked into Carver's bedroom and then walked away, and since then, he's been hurting. I freaking hate it. I can't look at him without remembering how I broke what little hope he had for a future between us.

He's hardly said a word to me. The only thing we've shared are these longing, painful glances that only remind me just how fucked up things are between us.

I let out a heavy sigh and tear my gaze away. I'm not making it any easier for myself by pining over a guy who's made it clear that he's not interested in the shit that I've got going on.

One foot drags after another as the familiar heaviness sinks back into my chest. I don't think I'm ever going to get used to this. It hurts in a way that I wasn't prepared for.

I'm just about to my locker when a body cuts in close beside me, bumping my shoulder and launching me into the row of lockers. A tall guy walks past, laughing as I catch myself and drop my books in the process.

The guy turns to watch me as he continues to pass. "Sup, dyke," he laughs, looking me up and down before slipping his hands together and rocking them back and forth in the universal sign for scissor sisters.

I clench my jaw, instantly stepping over my books and leaving them scattered across the hallway. "Hey," I yell, gaining the attention of everyone in the hallway and watching as the guy comes to a stop, thinking that his fun isn't nearly over yet.

I walk right up to him, my face not breaking and silently reminding him why the rest of the students like to stay away from me. Maybe he's forgotten what I did to Knox. Either way, he's about to get a reminder.

His face drops for just a second before he finds his bullshit bravado, and as he straightens his back to prepare for a threat, I feel four sets of eyes piercing into me, three from behind, and one coming from the opposite end of the hallway.

"You got an issue?" I ask, more than done with the 'dyke' comments that have been coming my way ever since I returned to school nearly two weeks ago, courtesy of Sara and her ability to spread rumors faster than she can spread her legs. Telling the whole school that she pity fucked me was low, but if she wanted to really burn me, she should have chosen something with a little more depth, something that isn't so easily defended.

The guy scoffs. "I don't have an issue at all. If you want to eat pussy, then I'm here for it," he starts. "I just think that you're confused."

I cross my arms over my chest and pop my hip. "Dare I ask why?"

Dickhead leans into me. "Because all you chicks are the same. You think you're into pussy, but really, you just don't know what it's like to have a fat cock buried deep inside of you."

"Really now?"

He grins, nodding his head as though I'm actually going to bend over for him and beg him to show me what I've been missing. He moves in even closer, brushing his fingers over my collarbone. "Let me fuck you. I'll take you right now and have you screaming. You'll never think about eating another pussy once I'm through with you."

I press my hand against his chest and push him back, stepping with him until he's pressed right up against a locker. "You really think you can change me?" I whisper, pushing myself closer into him and cringing at the feel of his fingers finding my waist.

"Positive."

A slow smile stretches across my face, and his eyes light up like Christmas morning. I feel his cock against my hip, hardening by the second. Without warning, I slam my hand against it and squeeze tight. "Let's get a few things straight," I tell him, smirking at the way he freezes under my hold. "I don't eat pussy, but what the fuck would it matter if I did? Pussy is fucking hot. It's strong, sexy, and it can do a hell of a lot more than any cock could. I didn't fuck Sara, but I'd prefer to fuck her than someone like you. But even if I did, how does that give you the right to question me on my sexuality?"

The guy swallows hard, his cheeks turning an angry shade of red as his breath comes in hard, pained pants. "Fucking let go, bitch."

"You know, I don't think I will. I bet I'm not the first girl you've accosted in a hallway that you already knew wasn't into you," I say before continuing on as though he's not about to pass out from the pain. "What is it about assholes like you thinking that you're God's gift to women? Let me tell you, you're not. I can feel your fucking cock in the palm of my hand and it's nothing to be boasting about. You have a pin dick, and I honestly feel sorry for any of the chicks that you've actually managed to get into bed. I can guarantee that with this little thing, they didn't get off. I bet they fucked themselves in the bathroom while you were still lying in bed thinking you were the fucking man."

Dickhead pushes back against me, but I refuse to release his junk as I feel a familiar body step in behind me. I breathe him in, recognizing King's heavenly scent, and when he doesn't make a move to stop me, I keep going, seeing it through to the end. "I don't know what it is about men who are so challenged and threatened by chicks who have no interest in them. Fucking hell. Just because a chick likes to eat pussy, doesn't mean that she's silently wishing for some asshole jock to come by and offer his pin dick on a silver platter. IT MEANS THAT SHE LIKES TO EAT PUSSY AND NOT CHOKE ON A FUCKING DICK. No questions asked. For fuck's sake. How is that so hard for men to understand?"

Feeling myself getting too worked up, I release his junk and the guy instantly relaxes, grabbing his dick and groaning in pain, but I'm not quite done. "Hey," I snap, watching his head raise back up to meet my irritated stare. "What's your name?"

His face twists in annoyance but seeing King standing right at my back, he lets out a defeated sigh. "Sam."

I laugh to myself. "Of course it is," I grumble under my breath before giving him a wide smile filled with a false innocence. "Well, Sam. I hope you rot in the deepest pits of hell." Then without even a second of warning, my hand curls into a tight fist and I throw it forward, feeling my brass knuckles slam against his jaw and rebound with a perfect arch.

King adjusts himself behind me to avoid getting my elbow to his face, but the way he moves so effortlessly tells me that he saw it coming a million miles away, and I kinda love that about him.

Sam crumbles to the ground as his friends laugh at him on the floor. I step over his foot and move back to start collecting all of my spilled textbooks when King drops down first, beating me to them and scooping them into his arms. "Are you good?" he asks, scanning over me and lingering on my fist, making sure I didn't break anything in the process.

"I'm fine," I tell him as he walks with me to my locker.

"You're not fine," he tells me, taking another few steps before pulling up short at my locker and entering my code—the code I was positive that no one knew. He shoves the books in and grabs my bag before handing it over. "You've been getting bullshit comments like that for two weeks, ever since Sara opened her big fucking mouth. Everyone knows it was a lie. Sara even admitted to it being a lie, so why the hell did you react?"

I let out a sigh and shrug my shoulders as I fall into his chest. "I don't know," I groan, hating how frustrated it's making me. "There was just something about his forcefulness. He was an ass. I haven't hit anything for weeks and I've been itching for that adrenaline. When I saw his stupid face, I couldn't help but think it would make a really great punching bag."

"Fuck, babe," he laughs, wrapping his arms around me and holding me tight. "We need to get you a punching bag stat."

I roll my eyes as my stomach growls for something to eat. "No. We need to get me a fucking burger, and a big one."

"Anything else, my queen?" he grumbles, giving me a dorky grin and ushering me toward the cafeteria with an exaggerated wave of his hand.

I follow his lead and bump his side with my hip, unable to help the twisted smirk that settles over my lips. "A four-way in the school parking lot wouldn't go astray," I comment, thinking about the failed one that was attempted last night, only for Lady Dante to come in and start humping Grayson's leg, thinking it was more of a group activity. Well, it was, but not the kinda group Lady Dante clearly had in mind.

A wicked grin cuts across King's face as he glances down at me to show off that gorgeous sparkle in his ocean eyes. "I can make that happen," he says before his gaze takes on a seriousness that has butterflies swarming in my stomach. "I ... uhhh."

My eyes narrow. "Spit it out. You're making me all anxious and nervous, and when I get nervous, I get sweaty. I'm in leather pants, King. I can't afford to get sweaty."

King's face scrunches up, hating to bring up whatever the hell is on his mind. He lets out a sigh and grabs my hand before pulling me into an empty classroom and closing the door behind him. My brows furrow and I watch him closely as he instantly begins pacing the room.

"I've been meaning to talk to you about this for a while, but every time I got the nerve, I chickened out like a little bitch."

My gaze narrows. "King," I warn, using my don't fuck with me voice. "You have three seconds to spit it out before I walk back into that hallway and tell everybody that you let Lady Dante fuck you."

His mouth drops. "What? No. You wouldn't do that. Besides, that was Grayson, not me, and she was only humping his leg. The poor dog didn't even get to finish before Gray kicked her off."

"King ..."

"Alright, fuck," he groans, looking like he's about to be sick. He takes a shaky breath and I can't help the grin that tears across my face. All this time, I thought Hunter King was superhuman. I didn't realize that he was capable of feeling nervous. He's always been so confident in what he wants, so forward, and able to throw himself headfirst into what he wants. He doesn't hesitate, but this guy right here—he looks as though talking to me now is the equivalent of getting his balls waxed.

I put myself right in front of him, getting a good idea of what this is about. I bring him to a stop, putting my hands on his shoulders and meeting his eyes. "King, it's just me. What is it?"

King's tongue rolls over his lips, and as he looks into my eyes, he relaxes, curling his arm around my waist. "I love you, Elodie Ravenwood," he whispers, letting out another shaky breath.

My brows furrow and he stares at me as though he just dropped one hell of a bomb. "What?" he rushes out, pulling out of my arms and instantly starting to pace again. "Fuck. You weren't ready for that. Shit. I'm sorry. I just ... ahhh FUCK. Just pretend I didn't say shit. We can just pretend that I didn't go and open my big fucking mouth."

I raise my chin, meeting his stare. "What the fuck are you talking about?" I laugh. "I already know."

King pulls back, stopping in his tracks and giving me a confused stare. "The fuck are you talking about? I've never said that I love you before."

"Does talking to your sister in the hospital ring any bells? I get it. You were pretty fucked up over losing your dad, but I'm not going crazy. Your sister laughed about you being in love with me and you said 'so what if I am.' I mean, you didn't exactly say the words, but you didn't have to. It was there."

King watches me for a second, his lips pressed into a tight line. "So, you picked up on that, huh?" he questions. "I was trying to say it without actually saying it because you weren't ready, but I guess it wasn't as discreet as I was hoping."

My eyes widen. "Oh, you were going for discreet? Yeah, you missed the boat on that one. You might as well have had it written in flashing lights. You couldn't have been more obvious."

"Well, shit. So, you've known all this time?"

The massive, cheesy-as-fuck grin that spreads across my face is response enough, and King just shakes his head and throws his arm over my shoulder. He pulls me into his chest, crushing me there as he wraps me in his warm arms. His fingers hit the bottom of my chin and he pushes it up until his lips are coming down on mine.

I welcome his kiss eagerly, happily ignoring the growling coming from my hungry stomach. His tongue sweeps into my mouth and I have to resist biting it, more so when his hand slips under the fabric of my tank and claims my skin as his own.

He pulls away and drops his forehead to mine. "I'm not looking for you to say anything back. I know you have an … unusual situation with all of us guys, but I promised you at the start that if something were to change that I'd let you know."

"Thank you," I whisper, pushing up and pressing a feather-soft kiss to his lips. "I appreciate that, but just so you know, while I'm not ready to go throwing that word around, I do really care for you. For all of you. I'm not just playing around with you guys. This, for me, is as real as it gets, and if I were to lose you—any of you—it would kill me."

"I know," he murmurs. "Which is part of the reason why I don't need to hear those words out of your mouth. I can see it in the way you look at me, in the way you seek me out in a crowded room. You might not be able to verbalize how you're feeling, but you practically scream it in your actions, and that's more than enough for me."

Despite my body being pressed right up against his, I somehow manage to sink into him further. "So, why now? You said you wanted to wait to tell me until I was ready, but what makes you think that I was ready?"

A soft laugh rumbles through his chest, and I pull back so I can look up at his perfect face, only to see a guilty cringe staring back at me. I narrow my gaze and watch him carefully and he lets out another heavy sigh. "Would you believe me if I said it was because my love for you was just too strong that I was compelled by my heart to let the words fly or some sappy bullshit like that?"

"King …" I warn.

He laughs. "Alright, so after Cruz dropped his 'I love you' bombshell and you didn't tear him a new asshole, I figured that I was in the clear."

"What?" I laugh. "But that was weeks ago."

"True, but Cruz is a proud man, and I didn't want to take away from the moment he had with you. I also didn't want you to think that I was telling you just because he did. I wanted this moment to be just between us."

My cold, dark heart thaws and my eyes soften as I watch him. "Thank you," I whisper, "but just so you know, I never would have thought you were telling me just because he did. I see it in both of you. I know it's true. I can feel it."

King dips his head to mine, and just as our lips finally meet in another bruising kiss, the classroom door flies open and Ember stares at me with a stupid grin on her face. "Well, well, if it isn't my favorite human pin cushion," she says. "Where the fuck have you been? I've been waiting for you for ages. I have to tell you about the graduation party."

"What graduation party?" I ask, pulling out of King's arms and feeling him right behind me as we make our way out of the classroom.

Ember's smile only widens as she meets my stare. "*My* graduation party," she tells me as we head toward the cafeteria. "It's going to be insane. My parents are going to be away for the weekend and we're all getting fucked up."

My brow raises as I narrow my gaze. "Just how fucked up?"

"Like I'm inviting the whole senior class kind of fucked up."

"No way."

"Yes way, but that's not even the best bit," she says, her tone raising an octave as she continues. "I just snuck out of fourth period History, met Corey in the student parking lot and fucked him in the back of his car."

I gape at her, shocked to my core. "What?"

"Yeah," she laughs. "That was after he ate me out on the hood and I sucked his dick like I was applying for the cock-sucking championship. And for the record, if I were, I would have won. This tongue is a bad freaking bitch. Got me out of my speeding ticket last Christmas."

My mouth drops and I just stare at her as King laughs from my other side. "I guess that means the parking lot is free now," he mutters under his breath, just loud enough for me to hear. "You still down for that four-way?"

13

Music blares from Ember's house as Cruz slings his arm over my shoulder and practically struts up the massive stairs leading to her front door. I smile up at him, loving the feel of his warm arm wrapped around me and the smile that always seems to accompany it.

Cruz has been a busy boy these past few weeks working hard on Sam's ledger and trying to find his victims, wherever they may be. Lately it's been rare that I get to see Cruz or Grayson, but not tonight—tonight they're all mine. Don't get me wrong, I understand more than most their need to spend hours slaving over that ledger, but the only thing that is more important is that they're looking after themselves as well, which is exactly what tonight is about. Besides, they wouldn't miss tonight for the world.

Tonight's graduation party is like a breath of fresh air. School is done and now every single one of us seniors are finally moving on to the next stages in our lives, whether that be a shitty desk job, college, or ruling over a billion-dollar secret society filled with corruption, murder, and secrets.

Yeah … when I moved to Ravenwood Heights and into Kurt and Irene's shitty little home, this really isn't where I expected my life to end up by graduation. Hell, for the most part, I figured that I would have been living under a bridge by now with my ankle chained to my bike as I slept, just so it wouldn't get stolen.

The door of Ember's gorgeous home has been left wide open, and though they don't show it, I know each of the boys are now second guessing whether we should even walk through it or not.

An open-door policy means that anyone could be inside. We could potentially be walking into a death trap, and I'm sure the guys will have something to say about it later, but for now, they're sucking it up and taking the risk, knowing this is the only graduation party I might ever have. Though, one thing is for sure, my night of reckless drinking and letting loose just turned into a night of watching my back and checking every dark corner.

Fun times.

Intent on having a good night, I put the invasive thoughts to the back of my mind, allowing Cruz to pull me through the front door. The music vibrates through my chest as I take in my surroundings. Ember's loving family home is now a full fucking rave. Colored spotlights shine over small stages. Girls I never got the chance to know are grinding against stripper poles, and a massive bar spans the length of Ember's living room.

I stare in shock.

How the fuck did she get this shit past her parents? Surely they have to know about this. It would have taken a week to set up, but she said they were only gone for the weekend.

Fuck me, she must have her parents wrapped around her little finger. There is no other explanation.

Bodies are everywhere, and as I look around to find Ember, I quickly realize that this is more than just the senior class from school. This must be every senior class from every fucking school in the area. And judging by the way Cruz remains right by my side and the way King, Grayson, and Carver seem to get even closer, they realize this too.

We weave our way through the bodies, and within seconds, random girls from school are rushing into my guys, desperate to get their attention one last time. A cocky smile spreads over my face as they make quick work of dismissing the girls on their heels. That's right, keep moving.

Random guys from across the room eye me up and down, but for the most part, they play it cool, keeping their distance and knowing all too well what would happen if they tried to make a move, especially with my guys by my side.

People dance around us, most of them already so drunk that they don't know which way is up or down. They bump into us, and before we even get halfway across Ember's living room, I've had three drinks spilled on me, my foot trampled, and a marriage proposal that quickly ended with Grayson's fist slamming into some guy's face.

We get across the room to the bar and Carver leans forward, resting his elbows against the table and ordering our drinks, saving the rest of us from having to yell just to be heard.

I turn beside Carver, leaning up against the bar while looking out at the hundreds of bodies crammed into Ember's home. It's insane, but honestly, what was I expecting? I should have known Ember would go all out for a party. I should have been better prepared.

The small bit of hope that I'd allowed myself to feel for tonight quickly begins to fade away as I look back at the boys. They create a tight, private circle around me as we wait for our drinks. "You guys are going to make me leave, aren't you?" I ask, scanning over their big shoulders and feeling the disappointment quickly filling me at the thought of not being able to stay and have a good time.

Grayson's lips pull into a tight line. "There's just too many people. If you got lost in this crowd, it'd be too hard to keep you safe."

"Besides," King adds, reaching between us and brushing his fingers over the back of my hand. "We don't know half of the fuckwits here. We have no way of telling if any of these people have any connections to Dynasty, and if they do, what side they are on. It's too risky."

I sigh heavily and lean into Carver's side, wishing it were one of the other boys standing the closest. Without question, his arm curls around my waist and he holds me against his chest. I pause for a moment, wondering if this is even happening. I was certain he would push me away or just stand there awkwardly, but the fact that he's even bothering to comfort me over something so trivial speaks volumes. Maybe he's not hurting so bad anymore, or maybe he's just gotten better at hiding it. Either way, I don't ever want to move. Even if it means standing here while the party goes on around us.

"There you are," a high, squeaky yell comes from behind King just moments before he's barged out of the way and Ember comes barreling through the small gap between King and Cruz. "I've been looking for you for ages. Where the hell have you been? It's already after ten."

"Sorry," I laugh, noticing the way King and Cruz both rub their elbows, wondering how the hell Ember managed to inflict harm on them. These boys are like tanks. "We um … We had some things to finish."

Ember's eyes bug out of her head as she gapes at me in surprise, which quickly turns into jealousy as she flicks her gaze around the boys. She steps in a little closer and whispers in my ear. "Were you in the middle of a Winter gang bang?" she asks, her whisper not as quiet as she hoped as the guys start snickering around us.

A wicked grin stretches across my face, and while we're late because I accidently passed out after eating too much pizza, the opportunity to mess with her is too good to pass up. "How many dicks technically make it a gang bang? I mean, two dicks plus me is a threesome and three dicks makes a foursome, so … what technically makes a gang bang? Is it like four or more … or is that just an orgy?"

Ember's face drops and she just stares at me, for once in her life, lost for words. "I … I can't … I don't even know how to deal with you."

"Trust me," I laugh. "Sometimes, neither do they, but they always work it out."

Proud grins rip across the guys faces as they all laugh. Carver silently glares as a soft growl rumbles through his chest, wordlessly letting me know that he's still jealous as fuck over our situation, but judging by the intense need that flickers through Ember's stare, Carver's not the only one.

"Uhhh," a strange voice says to my right, instantly cutting off the boys' laughs. "Why are we discussing orgies?"

I look up, and standing just behind Grayson's shoulder is a guy I've never met, but there's something oddly familiar about his voice. My eyes narrow as I watch him, taking in his beachy golden locks and strong frame, but that's nothing compared to the way the guys go rigid with their chests puffing out and their hands curling into strong fists, always ready to protect me against any threat.

"Whoaaaaaaa," Ember says, instantly throwing her hands up towards the guys. "Calm down, this is Corey, my new boyfriend."

"Oh," I laugh, discreetly stepping in front of Carver to hide the gun he just pulled out of the back of his jeans. "Forgive the guys. They're a little … jumpy."

"No problem," he says, quickly glancing around the circle of muscle and easily coming to the conclusion that he doesn't stand a chance against my guys. But when he looks back at Ember and a softness spreads through his eyes, I realize he doesn't care if they could kick his ass with their eyes closed, he's just happy to be where she is. "I'm glad my girl is surrounded by guys who would stand against a threat to keep her safe."

Carver scoffs and my elbow goes straight back into his stomach, knowing all too well that the guys' protection of Ember is only there because I made it so. If they had their way, they'd leave her to fend for herself. At least, that's how it was in the beginning. I hope by now her chatty ways have grown on them and they'd happily throw themselves in the line of danger to keep her safe, just as they would for me. Though, I guess the question is, would she do it for them in return? I know I would.

The guys nod while still sizing him up, but I just smile, seeing that same adoration shining through Ember's eyes. "So, you're the guy who's been stealing my best friend away and corrupting her in student parking lots?"

Corey grins back at me, proving that he's certainly no threat. "What can I say?" he chuckles as the bartender finally gets all our drinks and slides them across the table. "I think Ember is the one corrupting me."

Ember scoffs and has the audacity to look offended as Carver passes out drinks to the guys and saves me for last. "Excuse you, assface. Do I need to remind you that you video called me during my family dinner two nights ago and requested that I finger fuck myself under the table while you got to watch?"

I suck in a breath, looking at my best friend in shock. "You didn't."

Both Ember and Corey grin wide. "You bet your fucking ass she did," Corey says proudly as Ember's cheeks flush, though it's not from embarrassment. She's probably thinking about the exact moment she came for her boyfriend while her parents sat cluelessly across the table, discussing their weekend plans.

"Alright," Ember cuts in before any more of their dirty secrets can be spilled. She grabs hold of my arm and yanks me into her. "Let's go. We have about six drinks to catch up on, some ass shaking, and a whole shitload of grinding to do on those poles."

I laugh and let her drag me away before the guys remember that they're supposed to be keeping a close eye on me. Though something tells me that's not something they're bound to forget anytime soon. The fact they let Ember pull me away without trying to stop me speaks volumes.

Ember drags me onto the dancefloor and instantly pushes my drink to my lips. As I throw it back all at once, one of her hired waiters descends from nowhere in his white suit shirt and a tray filled with shots and champagne flutes.

Ember grins wide. "Drink up."

And just like that, we each take two shots, cringe and groan as they burn their way down our throats, then grab the champagne flutes, sipping them like fancy bitches.

I feel the guys' sharp gazes on me, but as the alcohol makes its way through my body, I start to forget just how overcrowded this party really is. I'm safe though. I have the guys' protection, and besides, what could really happen with so many people around? It's not like someone could get a clean shot at me while there are so many grinding bodies hanging around.

Within moments our champagne flutes are empty, and another guy shows up with more.

We drink, party, and celebrate knowing that it could be a while before we get the chance to do it again. Our lives are so crazy, and with everything Dynasty has been throwing at me, I have a feeling that once tonight is over, they're going to expect me to really take control of this organization. There are no excuses about being too young or still being in high school. All my excuses have run dry, and it's time to truly step up and lead the organization that my family founded.

With that in mind, I finish another drink and grin back at Ember as we both realize all too quickly that tonight is going to be one hell of a messy night.

T he guys come and go, always checking in on me, and apparently, giving me this night to let loose. I don't doubt that all of them are deathly sober. Those drinks Carver ordered when we first got here are probably still full in their hands, the ice long melted.

King shows up at my side when I climb up onto one of the many small platforms with the poles, and before I can even hook my leg around the pole and shimmy down it, I'm pulled back to the ground and shoved into the crowd, watching in disappointment as another girl quickly claims the pole and starts shaking her ass.

"Uh oh," I grumble, coming to a sudden standstill in the middle of the dancefloor and toppling forward when King crashes into my back, only just catching me in time.

"What's wrong?" he questions as I spin around and look up at him with fear in my eyes.

My hand shoots between my legs, tightly cupping my pussy as I feel the dread and horror starting to come over me. "I need to pee," I tell him, the urgency thick and heavy in my tone as I squeeze my legs together. "Actually, maybe I just did. I don't know. I think it's going to come out. I need to go. I ... I ... No. No. No."

King grabs me, throwing me over his shoulder and instantly squishing my bladder and making things so much worse. "NOOOOOO! PUT ME DOWN," I scream. "I'm going to pee down your back."

"You better fucking not," he roars as he barges his way through the crowd, knocking people clear on their asses just to get me to the bathroom, or hell, the back garden, or kitchen sink—which ever one we reach first. "MOVE."

King clears a passage through the crowd in no time, and before I know it, he's crashing through the door of one of Ember's many guest bathrooms. He all but throws me toward the toilet and as I'm busily trying to yank my pants down, I realize that he's locked himself inside with me. "The fuck do you think you're doing?" I demand, having to dance to stop myself from peeing all over the floor. "Get out."

"What? No. Just pee," he says, standing in front of the door as though he's some kind of bouncer. "Babe, I've fucked literally every hole in your body. I'm not going to be offended by a little bit of piss. Just do your thing so I can fuck you after."

My jaw clenches and my ability to squeeze my legs any tighter begins to fail. "OUT NOW BEFORE I BUST YOUR ASS WIDE OPEN, HUNTER KING. There are some things a girl just shouldn't have to share. If it's pee this week, what's next? Are you going to demand that I shit glitter in front of you? FUCK NO! OUT BEFORE IT STARTS RUNNING DOWN MY LEG."

King groans and rolls his eyes before scrunching up his face like a kid about to have a tantrum. "Fine," he snaps, grabbing the door handle and pulling it open, "but I'm not leaving this door."

He slips out a second later and I can't even wait until it's closed properly before dropping my ass down on the seat and letting sweet, sweet relief overcome me.

My eyes close and I tip my head back, instantly getting dizzy as I start to regret the last three shots that Ember and I so eagerly took when the boys weren't watching.

I laugh to myself and just sit there, despite having finished peeing long ago. I could do with a little nap. The darkness behind my eyes is welcoming and my body is exhausted from the constant dancing. Not to mention my feet—they're aching. Usually I'm good at parties like this from all my days walking around in my thigh high boots, but Ember and I went hard in a way that neither of us were expecting.

My head continues to spin but when I hear the loud thumping on the door from the bitches demanding that I hurry up, I decide it's probably best to get back to the party. I clean myself up and confirm that I didn't actually piss my pants earlier, but as I stand, my head spins more violently and the nausea begins to creep in.

"Oh, shit," I mutter, fumbling toward the sink before catching myself on the edge and turning on the taps. I quickly wash my hands and thank whoever lives above that King is just outside the door.

I splash some water on my face and let out a shaky breath. All I have to do is make it to the door and open it, then King can take my stupid ass home. Though, I'll have to apologize. There's no way I'm about to let him fuck me in here. I'll probably offer to suck his dick only to test my gag reflexes and throw up all over him. Fuck me, I know he loves me and will quickly forgive, but he'll never forget. I'll be teased and tormented about it for as long as I live.

I stumble across the bathroom, silently cursing Ember's parents for having such a lavish lifestyle. This bathroom is fucking huge, and usually I'd love that, but right now, the long walk to the door is killing me.

After what feels like a million pain-filled steps, my hand curls around the handle and I tear the door open into the busy hallway. There are people everywhere and I have to force myself to study each of their faces closely.

Someone laughs and the noise vibrates inside my head like a chainsaw. I instantly stumble back, slamming into the wall and desperately try to catch myself before I fall and drop to the ground.

What the fuck is wrong with me? I've been blind drunk a million times before and have never fumbled over myself like this before.

The nausea creeps up again and I slam my hand over my mouth, leaning back against the wall and taking slow, deep breaths to try and keep it down. The last thing I want is for my whole senior class to remember me as the chick who couldn't control herself at the graduation party and ruined it by throwing up all through the hallway.

"King?" I call out, briefly remembering that he was supposed to be here. "King?"

I study the faces of everyone, looking at them closely, but all their features begin to blur together. Where is King? He was supposed to be here.

I push myself off the wall and start making my way back down the hallway, but there are people everywhere, bumping into my shoulders and standing in my way. I run headfirst into a platinum blonde and spill her drink all over her dress, and as her head snaps up, I groan.

"What the fuck is wrong with you?" Sara snaps, looking down at her ruined dress before looking at me more closely, and for once in my life, I'm actually happy to see the bitch. "Like seriously? What the fuck is wrong with you? You look like shit."

Her friends laugh but she narrows her eyes, ignoring them. I shake my head. "I ... um ... King. Where's King?"

Sara watches me for a second, her eyes focused way too hard on mine before a smile pulls at her lips. "Come on," she says, looping her arm through mine and turning back the other way. "My phone is in a room back here. We can call him."

Relief rushes through me as Sara drags me away, holding me up and promising that she'll find the boys. With every step I take, my body gets heavier and harder to hold up, and when she finally finds the door to a secret room and pushes through it, I've never felt so happy.

The door closes behind us with a bang and Sara instantly switches on the light before helping me across the room. She lets go of me and I fall onto a hard bench, my ass hitting it with a heavy bang.

I groan, really having to fight to hold myself up. "Phone?" I mutter, my eyelids getting too heavy to keep open.

"Yeah, I'm finding it," Sara tells me, her voice coming like a soft whisper as she steps right up in front of me and reaches for my black leather jacket. "Are you hot? We should take this off."

I nod. How did she know? It really is hot in here. It must be all the bodies.

Sara draws my jacket down my arms and I tip my head back as I close my eyes, trying to block out all the dizziness. The darkness quickly spreads and I drop down, my back hitting the bench as my mind quickly fades, desperately needing to find the sweet silence of unconsciousness.

Something soft hits my neck and I tilt my head, opening up for more. Fuck that feels nice. Different, but nice. A soft groan pulls from deep within me as I get on board with this dream.

A hand takes my waist, slipping up under my tank, and if my limbs weren't so heavy, I'd be pulling him closer, needing him to touch me more and make me feel alive. The softness at my neck is there again, and a breathy sigh slips from my lips, wanting more. The hand on my waist pushes my tank up and starts exploring my body.

The hand is small and not as rough as I'm used to. It's almost sweet … sensual. I didn't know the boys had it in them, but I'm here for it. I bet it's Cruz. Only he can be this sweet.

Lips hit mine with a yummy cherry flavor and I open my mouth, wanting more of his sweetness as his tongue slips into my mouth.

I groan low. I want more. So much more.

I try to open my eyes. I want to see him. I want to watch him work my body, but it's too hard. My eyes are too heavy. My whole body is heavy, and I know that the second I open my eyes, the dizziness will return, and my whole world will implode.

My tank is pushed over my head and I try to help Cruz to take it off, but my arms won't work. I can't help him, but I don't need to. Cruz knows what he's doing. He knows what I like.

The hands continue to roam over my body as his lips drop back to my neck, going lower to my collarbone and then dropping to the curve of my breast. His hands slip around my back to release the hook of my bra, and the second it falls to the ground, his lips come down over my nipples.

I try to arch up into him but he holds me still, not letting me move and taking control just as he likes it. Most of the time, Cruz and I will fight for control, both of us needing that dominance in our lives, but right now, he can have it all. There's nothing I want more than to just lie here in bliss.

Cruz reaches for the button on my pants and starts undoing them as he continues his sensual torture over my nipples. My leather pants are dragged down my legs as the music from the party continues to thump and vibrate right through me.

He kisses his way down my body, and finally I feel him climbing over me, his head down between my legs. He parts my legs and I feel his breath against my wet pussy as his sweet fingers trail over my clit, taking his time and teasing me with what's to come.

His fingers push deep into me just as his warm mouth closes over my clit.

I suck in a needy breath, knowing that something is different but unable to figure out why. His tongue works my clit, and as his fingers massage deep inside of me, every last thought falls from my mind. Who cares why it's different? It's too good.

Everything deep inside me clenches as that familiar burning builds within me. I need that release and I need it now. My body is too exhausted to hold on. All I want is to fall into a deep unconsciousness, but I refuse to do it until I've felt that intense orgasm pulsing through my body and making every single one of my nerves scream from pure satisfaction and pleasure.

Cruz's tongue works over my clit making tight, pulsating circles as his fingers work in and out, building me higher and higher and when he sucks my clit into his warm mouth, everything explodes.

I come hard, my orgasm pulsing through my body as my pussy convulses around Cruz's fingers. I feel his smile against my pussy and if I had the energy right now, I'd be returning the favor, sucking his big, thick, veiny cock, choking on it until I feel his sweet cum hitting the back of my throat.

I guess I'll just owe him one.

Cruz pulls away from me and my body relaxes as the light is switched off and true darkness surrounds me. A blanket is draped over me and not a second later, my world fades away into the sweet blissfulness of sleep.

15

The bed creaks beneath me and my eyes peel open into the darkness to find Grayson sneaking out of my bed. He slinks across the room being way too obvious that he's sneaking out. Had he just gotten up and walked to the door, I wouldn't think much of it, but the way he's tiptoeing and being extra careful not to make a damn sound has my spidey-senses on high-alert.

My mind is still foggy from whatever the fuck I did last night, so I have to focus extra hard to make out his frame as he walks across the room, collecting his phone and wallet off the top of my dresser, but it's his smell that lingers on my body and pillow that tells me it's him. If it were a little muskier, it would have been King and add a hint of pine and you've got Cruz.

Grayson reaches the door and just as he pulls it open to the brightly lit hallway, he looks back at me and I quickly close my eyes, not wanting him to know that I'm onto him.

Satisfied that he hasn't woken me, he gently pulls the door closed behind him and I sit up a little straighter as I hear King's deep voice in the hallway. "She good?"

"Yeah, sleeping like the living dead," Grayson mutters, keeping his tone down and making it nearly impossible to make out what he's saying. "After the night she had, she'll probably sleep well into the afternoon, but she'll be fucking pissed so we probably won't hear from her."

A breathy laugh sounds through the door. "It's fine. She'll cave and text Cruz to let us know she's alive, but only to get him to leave her the fuck alone."

"Too right," Grayson murmurs. "Are we good to go?"

Good to go? What the fuck? Where do they think they're going? I push up onto my hand, hating the way that my head spins with the movement. Maybe I'm hearing them wrong. Glancing across the room, I focus on the digital clock that sits on my desk. It's only four in the morning. It doesn't make sense.

"Yeah," King grumbles, his words distorted by a loud yawn. "Carver's already downstairs packing the car and Cruz said some shit about writing a letter for Winter so she doesn't freak the fuck out if she were to wake and we were all gone."

All gone? Have I missed something? Why the fuck would Carver need to be packing the car?

I hear the guys move away from my bedroom door and anger instantly starts pulsing through me. These motherfuckers aren't going anywhere without me.

I throw my blanket back and swivel until my feet are finally on the floor. My head aches. I clearly partied way too hard at last night's graduation party. Fuck, I don't even remember how I got home and in bed, but I'm definitely going to be paying for it today.

I quickly hurry around my room, grabbing some clothes and pulling on a pair of sweatpants and a hoodie. I stuff a few things into a backpack and double check that I have my phone before slipping out of my room. I mean, if the boys are going somewhere, then so the fuck am I.

My eyes practically scream at the brightly lit hallway, and for a second, I curse the boys for leaving it on, but at the same time, if they hadn't, I probably would have walked into the hallway and fallen right down the stairs. Not only injuring myself but giving myself away. There's no way I would have been able to fall down the stairs while keeping my goddamn mouth shut.

I tiptoe down the hallway, being careful to step around all the creaks in the floor, and now that I've visualized falling down the stairs, I have no choice but to hold onto the railing and creep down them like a fucking cat. Besides, stairs and I have a love-hate relationship. I mean, I've been fucked on them, but I've also been fucked over on them.

I get halfway down when I hear the boys moving around downstairs. I crouch down and peer through the balustrades to find

Cruz leaning against the hallway table with a pen and paper. I watch him write, taking in the pained look on his face. My stomach twists. Something tells me that he doesn't want to go without me, or maybe doesn't want to go at all. Either way, I've got to get my hands on that letter.

King walks past with a bag and heads toward the internal door for the garage, and as he opens it, I hear the soft rumbling of the Escalade.

These assholes really are about to leave me here in the middle of the night.

Fuck that.

I hurry back upstairs and dart into my room to fill up Lady Dante's automatic feeder and make sure there's enough water in her bowl to last a few days. I grab my phone charger, my makeup, and a few more changes of clothes. I have no idea what was in the bag that King had packed, but it didn't look light and if we're going for a while, then I want to be prepared.

I start making my way back down the stairs to find Cruz gone and an envelope with my name resting on the table beside his pen. I grab the envelope and shove it into my bag despite how desperately I want to read what's in it. I can't risk getting caught just yet. I have to play it smart. If they find me, the game is over and I'll be fucked.

The light in the foyer is dimmed and I dart across to a massive vase and hide behind it while being able to see directly into the garage. Just as King said, Carver is in there, shoving bags into the back of his Escalade and looking pissed about it. Though, when does Carver ever not look pissed?

I watch him for a moment while listening to the boys rummaging around in the kitchen, and from the sound of it, they're packing snacks, but why the hell not? I just hope they remember my favorite little gummy bears. There's no such thing as a road trip without them.

Carver takes the last bag and tosses it into the back, being extra careful and making me wonder what the hell could be in there. He closes the back door and lets out a heavy sigh before coming right for me.

I suck in a breath and sink back behind the massive vase, hoping to whoever exists above that he didn't see me.

I hold my breath, listening to his nearly silent footsteps as he gets closer, and with every step, my heart races just a little bit faster. The hairs on my arms stand up, and as he passes, I shrink to my smallest possible self, while wondering if he's able to hear the rapid beat of my heart. Knowing Carver, he could probably smell me here.

He passes by and the second he disappears around the corner, I let out my breath and take a second to ease my heart, only now I have a clear path to the Escalade, and fuck it, I'm not stupid enough to miss an opportunity like this. I just wish that I'd peed first.

I dart out from behind the vase and sprint to the garage, racing through the foyer and all but bouncing off my toes to try and keep quiet. Carver's voice rings out and I come to a screeching standstill, certain that I've been sprung. "Yo, what the fuck is taking so long? Let's go."

"Shut the fuck up," Cruz calls back as relief thunders through my chest and I take off again. "You're going to wake up Winter and then we'll have a whole new shitstorm to deal with."

Yeah, fuck you too, Cruz Danforth. These boys aren't ready for the shitstorm that I'm going to rain down over them.

I reach the Escalade in no time and fly through the open side door just as I see the lights beginning to flick off, sending the inside of the house into darkness.

They're coming.

I glance around. What the fuck am I supposed to do now?

My heart refuses to ease up, but as I find a blanket in the front, the idea shoots through my mind. I grab it and just as I hear the boys coming through the foyer, I dive through to the trunk and curse myself as I land on a hard bag, my back slamming down against it.

I shimmy down between two bags and manage to spread the blanket out on top of me just as the boys start piling into the Escalade.

"You sure about this?" King questions as four doors slam shut.

Carver grunts. "Too fucking late now." And just like that, he hits the gas and the Escalade takes off like a rocket down his long driveway with every intention of leaving me behind.

Those motherfuckers.

"Who took my fucking blanket?" Cruz mutters from the front seat as soft music plays through the car to keep everyone awake.

"Dude, you'll be twenty next month," Grayson says from the seat right in front of me. "Why the fuck do you need a blanket?"

Cruz is going to be twenty? What the fuck? I thought he was the same age as me.

I don't get a chance to think about it before he mutters something inaudible under his breath then speaks a little louder. "Get fucked, man," he says in an oddly pissed-off tone, one that doesn't come out of his mouth very often, unless we're dealing with some dickhead who threatened my life. "It's four in the fucking morning and if I'm about to spend six hours in a fucking car with you assholes, you bet your ass that I'm going to sleep the whole way through it."

Six hours? Fuck. Maybe sneaking in here wasn't the best idea. My bladder is good, but it's not that good. Add a little alcohol to the mix and my bladder is practically non-existent.

"I'm with Cruz," King murmurs, another yawn tearing out of him as a hand is thrown over the back of the seat and starts feeling around. "I could use another few hours of sleep. That party last night fucking killed me."

"If I have to be up," Carver grumbles, stopping for the gate. "Then all you fuckers are up."

The hand in the back continues to feel around until it stops right over me and grabs hold of the blanket. I hold my breath, positive that I'm about to be sprung, but when nothing happens apart from the blanket flying across the car and into the front seat, I let out a breath and realize that I might just get away with this after all.

As the guys talk among themselves, I try to get comfortable by pulling my backpack behind my head when my fingers brush over the envelope that Cruz had left for me. I pull it out and as quietly as I can manage, I open the envelope and unfold the letter, only to feel devastation tear through me at the three lines he'd left for me.

> *Babe,*
>
> *We're heading out for a few days to deal with some shit. We've locked the house down and all the alarms are on. You have everything you need in the house so you shouldn't need to leave.*
>
> *Please don't fucking leave. You're safe here.*
>
> *Cruz.*
>
> *P.S. I fucking love you. This wasn't my idea so don't be pissed at me!*

That's it? That's his fucking letter? Screw him. That tells me absolutely nothing. I want to know where the fuck they're going and what they're going to do when they get there. Hell, I want to know everything and the asshole leaves me three lines and a plea not to be mad at him.

God. If I could climb into the front seat and pull his junk out through his throat without being seen, I would. Instead, I toss his stupid letter aside and stare up at the roof, feeling completely helpless.

The car keeps moving, and it's not until we're flying down the main road toward the highway that Carver finally speaks again. "Did you leave some water and painkillers for Winter? She's going to be feeling fucking sorry for herself when she wakes up."

"Yeah," Grayson says with a slight chuckle. "She completely wrote herself off. I've never seen her so bad. I know she just wanted to let loose after graduating, and it's not like life hasn't been throwing flaming piles of shit at her lately, but we can't let her get that bad again. She stripped down to her birthday suit in Ember's closet and fell asleep with nothing but her jacket covering her. What if someone had walked in and taken advantage of her? We should have been watching her better."

"Bullshit, really?" Cruz demands. "We should have left the second we got there. There were too many people. We put her in danger."

"So, now you fuckers want to listen to me," Carver grumbles. "She got you all hooked by the fucking balls. If Winter says she wants to fuck one of you on a bed of razors, all three of you would fight over who got to be the one to do it."

"We don't need the fucking 'I told you so' speech," Grayson mutters. "We know we fucked up, but so did you. You could have said no and we would have taken her straight home. You're just as guilty in all of this, if not worse. If she hadn't been shot and cooped up at home for weeks, she probably wouldn't have gone so hard."

"Really?" Carver grunts. "Twenty minutes into a six-hour drive and you want to bring that shit up now? Really, that's fucking great."

Grayson lets out a loud huff and the car falls into silence for a short minute before King speaks up, his tone broken and full of guilt. "Fucking hell," he mutters. "I swear, I put her in the fucking bathroom and she was completely fine and then I don't know what happened. One minute she was kicking me out, and two seconds later, she was gone. I was looking for her for ages. I just don't … I don't know how she could just disappear like that."

Gone? I wasn't gone. I was sitting on that toilet for like half an hour and then my head started to get dizzy which is pretty much where my memories of the night start to get a bit hazy. I remember getting up and washing my hands and face, and then stumbling out into the hallway, but why was I stumbling so much? I can be a sloppy drunk, but even when I'm throwing up my guts, I never get so clumsy.

Last night was different.

I was calling for him, searching every face, but he wasn't there. I couldn't find him when I needed his help.

A heaviness sinks into my stomach as I start to recall the weird feeling in my arms and legs and how my head wouldn't stop spinning, especially as I was calling his name. People were bumping into me, making it harder and I just wanted to scream but I couldn't. No one was coming to help me.

I felt like I was in one of those dreams where you're running as fast as you can from the monster chasing you. You're pushing yourself harder and faster, but you're not getting anywhere. You can't save yourself and the fear just keeps rising.

But that hallway. I feel like there's something I need to remember from that hallway.

My heart thunders as I desperately think back to last night, to what happened after I was practically dragging myself along the wall just to keep myself up. How did I get from the hallway outside the downstairs guest bedroom to Ember's closet all the way upstairs?

I could hardly walk. My head was spinning. My arms and legs felt like I had lead pulsing through my veins.

I was drugged. That's the only explanation for it.

Someone must have put something in my drink, and at some point, I blacked out. But ... Sara.

I bumped into Sara. I spilled her drink all over her dress and she was going to help me find the boys. I asked her to help me find King and she said that she'd take me to get her phone. She dragged me along, holding me up, and I thought I was safe.

She took me to a room and dropped me onto a hard bench and then … my jacket.

Tears fill my eyes as I come to the realization of what had happened last night. She took off my jacket and put her hands on my body. She kissed my neck and the drugs took over. I lost all sense of what was right and wrong.

I thought Cruz was touching me.

Sara stripped me naked and took advantage of me while I couldn't do a damn thing to stop her.

She took away my ability to consent, she stole my trust in womankind, and she abused my body for her own personal, disgusting gain.

She saw me.

She touched me.

She put her fingers inside me and closed her mouth over the most private, intimate part of my body.

She took the one thing I promised would only ever belong to the four men in my life. She stole from me and I will never forgive or forget it.

She left me there, alone and vulnerable in a house filled with hundreds of drunk teenagers. Anything could have happened to me. I should consider myself lucky that Grayson found me in Ember's closet, but luck is not what any sane person would call being drugged, sexually abused, and left vulnerable.

How am I supposed to tell the boys what she did? I don't … I don't even think I know what it is. What classifies as being raped? Is that even what happened or did I urge her on? Moaning and wanting more when I thought it was Cruz?

I was drunk. I know I didn't verbally consent to it, but did I allow it to happen in other ways?

Fuck. I don't know.

I stare up at the ceiling as the boys talk among themselves, completely oblivious to the mental trauma taking over me as I silently cry in the back of Carver's Escalade.

An hour passes and then another, and before I know it, the remaining drugs in my system quickly catch up to me. And as my mind tries to make sense of the night for the millionth time, my exhaustion takes over and I fall into a fretful sleep.

When a soft, chilly breeze hits my skin, I wake to find four pissed-off guys staring down at me with anger shining brightly in their eyes.

"Well, shit," I tell them, sitting up and stretching out my cramped body, deciding to keep my new horrors to myself. "About time you found me. Do you know how squished I was in there?"

I climb out of the back of the Escalade, grinning to myself as each of the guys just stare at me, completely dumbfounded. My feet hit the road and I step out from around the back of the Escalade to find nothing but rolling mountains. "So, where the hell are we?"

Carver is the first to regain control. "What the fuck do you think you're doing?"

16

I stare out at the beautiful manor home situated right in the middle of the most exotic mountains that I've ever seen. This was the home my parents built—well, the one that Carver's father burned down and Dynasty had rebuilt to pay their respects.

"Holy shit," I breathe, completely blown away by its beauty. "I've never seen anything like it. Did my father really build this?"

"Yep," Cruz says, laying his hand on my thigh as we all stare out the side windows of the Escalade, looking up the long driveway, past the iron gates to the home that sits at the top of the mountain. "Well, that's the story, at least. Apparently, your parents had designed every little aspect of the home. It took them years to complete."

"So, it's exactly the same as before it got burned down?"

King shrugs his shoulders beside me. "I'd assume so," he mutters, looking past me, out the window to the big house. Though something tells me the boys are looking at the mansion with very different intentions than I am. I just want to see the beauty of it and feel a fraction of what my parents must have felt when they got to see it for the first time. The boys just want to case the joint and figure out if my crazy mother is still living here or not. "The interior and furniture would be different than what your parents had. They mostly kept this place private, so it was probably styled for what was modern at the time it was rebuilt, which would have been slightly different to your parents' personal taste."

"Not really," Carver says. "If London has been living here all these years, then she's probably brought her own personal touch back into it."

"Yeah, I guess so."

Grayson groans and flops back into his seat. "Are we seriously just going to sit here and look at the house all day or are we actually going to go in and see if we can find the bitch, or if anything, a little bit of information on who the fuck she's been working with?"

"He has a point," Cruz mutters. "I've also been stinging to take a piss so I wouldn't mind if we could hurry this along."

"Get fucked," King says, looking back at Cruz. "We're not rushing into this just so you can take a piss. Get out and piss in the trees like the rest of us have, and while you're at it, do a perimeter check that there are no bears or mountain lions."

Sheridan Anne

"Fuck off," Cruz throws back at him. "I'm not about to get mauled by a fucking lion. You lost Winter last night, you should do the perimeter check."

"All of you fuck off," I tell them, not wanting the boys to get into an argument over the bullshit that went down last night. If anyone is to blame—it's me. I should have been more careful. Hell, watching your drink is the number one rule when at a party. I fucked up, not them, and they sure as hell aren't going to be punished for that. I start climbing over Cruz. "I'll do the fucking check."

"Like hell," Carver spits, reaching into the backseat, grabbing me by the back of my tank and throwing me right back into my seat. "You're not going anywhere by yourself. If London is here, and you're left by yourself, then all we're doing is offering you up on a silver platter. You might as well walk straight up to the door and ring the bell. Perhaps we could save her some time and cuff you before you go."

I roll my eyes. "Fuck me," I grumble. "Why are you so pissy today? Did someone accidentally misplace their dildo up your ass?"

Carver turns back to the front with a huff and Grayson turns around, deciding it's best that he runs the show. "Carver and I will do the perimeter check while you two fuckheads check over our weapons and scan the house for any heat signals. Do you think you can do that without losing our girl?" he snaps unfairly at King. "We'll be gone for fifteen minutes and then we're going in, and while we're gone, you two need to figure out who the fuck is staying back with Ellie."

I shake my head. "You can leave someone back here to babysit me all you want but no matter how this goes down, I'm going inside that

186

house, whether she's standing at the front door inviting me in or not. I'm not giving you any other warnings, so you might as well include me in your plan to save us all a little bit of time and effort."

"Jesus Fucking Christ," Grayson exclaims through a clenched jaw. "Why is it always so hard with you? Why can't you just stay here and do what you're told for once?"

I lean forward into the front, not appreciating the tone he's taking with me, and while I can easily use the 'leader of Dynasty' card, I take another direction. "Because this is my home. This is my mother, and this is my history. That house right there is the place where my father was murdered, and if I were to sit back here, twiddling my thumbs like a useless piece of shit, I'd go insane. I need to be in there. I need to see that house, and I need to put this bullshit to rest. So, the question isn't when will I start behaving like a good little soldier, it's when will you start believing that I'm not a fragile little princess who needs your constant supervision? I got by eighteen years on my own, and believe it or not, I don't need you guys always up my ass making sure I don't trip and fall."

King, Cruz, and Carver all scoff as Grayson watches me for a long, drawn-out moment, deep in thought before finally letting out a breath. "Fine, but you stay with one of us at all times."

Carver groans. "Seriously?" he mutters, glancing at Grayson. "She gives you one guilt-ridden speech about her feelings and you cave like a little bitch? You know just as well as the rest of us that she needs constant supervision, more so now than ever before."

"Hey," I snap, resenting his comments only to get ignored.

Sheridan Anne

Grayson glares back at Carver. "You don't think I know that?" he growls. "But consider our options. You know she's right. The second she gets a chance, she's going to make a break for it and storm through that house like a little fucking wrecking ball. It's better for us to control the damage than letting it run free and fuck up everything in the process. Besides, no matter how much you disagree, she deserves to see this home. Two birds. One fucking stone."

I resist rolling my eyes. I hate how they treat me with kid gloves, like I'm some wild caged bird who's desperate to fly. If they would just give me a little trust and a little freedom, they'd see I have my shit together. I can handle this.

Carver lets out a sigh, and without another word, hits the gas and drives his Escalade off the road and into the trees of the mountains, keeping his car concealed just in case London is inside. All it would take is one quick glance out the window and she would have seen us stopped outside the front gates. Who knows, maybe we've already fucked up the mission.

Carver instantly gets out and hurries around to the back before yanking open the door and grabbing a few things. Grayson meets him around back before looking through to Cruz and King. "Fifteen minutes," he reminds them.

They both nod, and I watch as not a second later, the boys disappear into the trees.

The minutes tick by painfully slow, and I find myself looking up at the ginormous house as King and Cruz get themselves organized while also checking the property for heat signatures.

"Nothing," Cruz says after a few minutes, looking slightly pissed about the outcome. "The house is empty. The only heat signals I'm getting are from Gray and Carver. We're good to go in."

King nods. "So, I guess that means Carver didn't get mauled by a mountain lion."

"Not today," Cruz mutters under his breath.

"So, what now?" I ask, jumping down from the open door of the Escalade and stepping out into the road.

Cruz comes to stand by me on the road before slipping a gun into the back of my jeans and pressing a knife into my hand just in case. "Now, we go in and hope we find a bit of information that tells us a little more about who she's been working with and how she got away with this for so long."

"Why do you sound so disappointed?"

Cruz's lips press into a hard line. "Because I was hoping this would be the end of it. I hoped she'd be home and that we'd get the drop on her. I hate not knowing when she might show back up in your life and attack. Who knows? She could come back to haunt you next week or it could be next year. No one knows, and that scares the shit out of me."

I take Cruz's hand, lacing my fingers through his. "We're going to get her," I promise him, "and when we do, it's going to be epic."

Cruz rolls his eyes. "Yeah … let's hope."

King's phone rings a second later and I glance back at him, watching as he slips his phone out of his pocket and glances down. "It's Grayson," he mutters, letting us know before accepting the call and pressing the phone to his ear. "Yeah," he says down the line. "It's clear. We'll meet you up there."

The call ends quicker than it started, and before I know it, King is walking toward us and nodding up at the big house. "So, you want to see the house your father created or what?"

Fuck yeah.

It takes well over ten minutes just to walk from the front gate up the long driveway, and for a slight moment, I'm left wondering why the fuck we didn't just drive up considering that she's not here. But the boys know best, and when I can, I follow their lead.

I might be stubborn as hell, but I'm not stupid. I've learned from my mistakes. I'm not looking to get shot again. That was a whole lot of bullshit that I don't plan on reliving anytime soon.

We make it to the house and I stare up at the grand entrance in awe. How is it that places like this have existed all my life while I've lived in shitty foster homes with no electricity, moldy food, and a bad smell? I still find it hard to believe that I belong in this world. It doesn't feel right, but somehow it is.

Just as Cruz enters the code for the house, we all hold our breath, waiting for an alarm to go off. Carver and Grayson show up and join us just as the door unlocks, and as a goofy, smug grin rips across Cruz's face, relief slams through my chest.

He pushes the door wide. "After you," he says, dramatically waving me through the big door.

I walk in and instantly stop, making the guys step around me as I stare up at all the beauty. There are high ceilings and everything is marble. It looks like something right out of a movie. It's insane. I feel as though I need to walk with my hands tied behind my back just in case I break something that I'll never be able to replace. Though … technically it's all mine. At least, I think it is.

"Let's make this quick," Carver says. "I'm going to start upstairs."

Just like that, the boys all go separate ways to look for information, and I'm left with Cruz dragging me through the lower portion of the house, showing off everything as we go. His fingers brush over every wall, and just when I'm about to ask why the fuck he's touching everything, I realize that he's searching for hidden walls or little secret rooms like my home back in Ravenwood Heights.

Cruz leads me into a study and it takes us no time to realize that this is the room we've been looking for, giving us all the proof we need to confirm that she has in fact been living here.

There are shelves filled with folders and paperwork, a desk scattered with random things, USB sticks, and a laptop which Cruz instantly takes and slides into a backpack. I drop down onto the desk chair and start pulling out drawers, looking for anything that ties her to any of the heads of Dynasty.

I get nothing and quickly move onto the drawers of the small table that sits behind the desk. The first drawer is locked and I jiggle it for a second, desperate to get it open. After a quick scan of the room, I realize that searching for a key in this massive house is going to be a whole new task that nobody has the time for. So instead, I bring my foot up in a sweeping kick, and slam that motherfucker right into next year.

The lock breaks and I dive for the drawer, yanking it out to find at least fifteen different passports and driver's licenses, all with London's face on them. Only in each one the names are different and her hairstyles are slightly changed.

They pull at something within me, memories that I'd long tried to forget. The woman who lived down the street when I was eight, the woman who worked at the grocery store when I was ten, my substitute teacher at twelve.

What the ever-loving fuck?

She's been following me my whole life. Every step of the way she's always been ahead of the game, always watching me, always keeping close by just waiting for her chance to strike.

Nausea drops into my stomach and I grab the passports and licenses off the desk and shove them into my back pocket before I race from the study, desperately searching for a bathroom to hurl.

I've been such a fool.

I make it to a bathroom just in time and slam the door before Cruz decides that it's a free for all and helps himself to an up-close view of the snacks I'd stolen in the car. "You good, babe?" he calls through the locked door.

I throw up a little more. "Get lost. You don't need to hear this," I call back. "I'm fine."

"You sure?"

"CRUZ," I snap.

"Jesus. Alright," he mutters. "I'm going. Just come back when you're done. The last thing we need is you falling down the laundry chute or accidentally getting stuck in some hidden secret dungeon."

Ha. Ha. Fuck, I hate him sometimes.

I get myself cleaned up and as I stare at myself in the mirror, the anger quickly sweeps through me. How could I have missed this? My mother has been stalking me my whole life. Add that on top of the shit Sara pulled on me last night and the fact that just up the stairs of this massive house lies the very spot that my father was betrayed and murdered ... I'm seeing red.

I've let these bitches walk all over me. They've gotten away with it, but not anymore.

How could I be so stupid?

I pace the small bathroom, my hands pulsing in and out of fists by my side. The anger is too much. I can't control it. I need to run. I need to be free. I need a release and it's not the kind that I'm going to get from any of the boys. It's the kind I get from beating the ever-loving shit out of a pervert behind a bar.

I need to get out of here.

Without thinking, I unlock the door and throw it open. Instead of doubling back to Cruz, or any of the guys for that matter, I find my way to the impressive garage. Just as I knew it would be, my father's stolen car sits idle, the front end still smashed from when my bitch of a mother drove it through my garage door less than two months ago.

I tear open the door, and finding the key still in the ignition, I drop down into the driver's seat. Despite never having a single driving lesson in my life, I kick over the engine and hit the gas.

The car jolts forward and a panicked squeal tears out of me as the muscle car tears straight through yet another garage door and flies down the long driveway, taking me away from the pain that resides in that house and giving me the freedom to take back my control.

17

My father's car races up the side of the curb as I bring it to a screeching halt outside the shitty bar just a few miles from my parents' mountain mansion. I have to make this quick. The guys would have all caught my grand exit, and considering my phone has been blaring in my pocket for the last ten minutes, I'd dare say that they're onto me.

They'd all be piled into Carver's Escalade right now, following the destruction I've left behind on the road. Either that or following the fucking tracker that they have on me. I wouldn't be surprised if those big bastards had a GPS tracker on my phone.

Assholes.

Fuck, they're going to hate me for this, but I have to do it. Besides, is it not better to beg for forgiveness than ask for permission?

I really shouldn't be driving. I have absolutely no idea what I'm doing behind the wheel of a car, all I know is to steer and hit the gas and somehow, I'll get myself from A to B. I've flown over speed limits, swerved past other cars, and taken out a small garden.

I'm a danger to myself and the other people on the road, but I couldn't just stand there in that bathroom going over everything that was happening. It was too much. I have too much rage boiling through my blood. I have to release it. I have to let it out. The desperation flooding my system is too much and they'll never understand. If I stayed there, they would have made me talk, they would have made me face it instead of allowing me to bury my problems in violence.

I need to hit something. I need to release the fury burning through me.

My door flies open and I storm toward the dodgy dive bar, knowing that the boys are going to be less than ten minutes behind me. It was a ten-minute walk from the Escalade up to the house, and the second I broke through that garage door, they would have run.

I need to make this quick.

As I make my way toward the bar, I glance back at my father's car. It's a pile of steaming shit now. I'm sure it used to be amazing, but the condition it's in now is nothing special. I bet he's looking down on both me and Mom so fucking ashamed.

The thought has the fury igniting all over again and I clench my jaw as I throw myself through the door of the bar.

It's just after midday and I'm not surprised to find a few men already here, telling me everything I need to know about them. Who in their right mind needs to be drinking at this time of the day anyway? Pathetic.

As I look around, searching out today's victim, I'm reminded of Kurt and his reckless alcohol addiction. He was a sloppy drunk and I hated him for it, though there's also a few other reasons why I hated him, but that's all in the past.

I walk through the bar slowly, taking my time while knowing that once I get my first hit in, it won't take long to finish the fucker off. I just hope that Carver and the boys don't get to me first.

A wolf whistle sounds across the bar and my gaze instantly snaps up.

Bingo.

I guess it won't be hard looking for today's punching bag after all. It seems that he's going to beg for it instead.

I zone in on the old fucker sitting across the bar with a sleazy smile across his dirty face. He's old and gives off a filthy Santa Claus vibe with his big belly, rosy cheeks, and need to please children. Dirt covers the front of his white, holey shirt, and I can see exactly where he's used it to wipe food from his mouth. He's the definition of filth. "Come here, sweetheart," he says through the three missing teeth at the front of his mouth, making me long to knock out a fourth. "Come and let Daddy buy you a drink."

Fuck. Maybe I didn't throw up everything in my stomach before because that shit makes me feel sicker than the thought of Sara and

London combined.

I strut around the bar, giving an extra sway to my hips as I go and getting longing glances from the other drunk assholes lingering around. "That's right, baby," Santa says. "Let me take care of you. You're a young thing, aren't ya?. Way too young to be in a place like this."

I make my way over to him, sneering at the way his eyes drop over my body as though he has the right. He pats his lap, inviting me to take a seat and my stomach churns at the thought of getting anywhere near this asshole, but luck isn't on my side because to actually beat the shit out of him, I'm going to have to get a shitload closer.

I take a deep breath, knowing that when I take that final step to close the distance, I'm going to smell that toxic stench that rolls off drunks as the alcohol comes out through his pores and sits clammy on his skin.

God, it's so gross.

My hand curls into a fist and the sweet feel of my brass knuckles tightening over my skin gives me the strength to keep going. "Why don't you stand up and let me see what I'm working with?"

"Oh, a lady of the night?" he slurs. "Trust me, I've got exactly what a girl like you needs."

"A girl like me?" I question, watching as he shakily gets to his feet and has to grab hold of the table just to keep from falling. "What's that supposed to mean, Santa?"

He laughs at the name, thinking it's something cute, but he couldn't be more wrong. "You're a dirty little slut," he says with a wink. "I haven't got any cash for ya, but I'll get you off real nice."

Ugh. Gag.

"Oh, yeah?" I ask, stepping right up into him with a flirtatious smile. He beams from ear to ear and before he gets another word out, my fist slams right into his nose. Blood spurts out and I hit him again and again. His jaw, his eye socket, his brow.

He falls to the ground, unable to hold himself up, but I just keep going, letting out all the rage as the bartender just watches on, making sure no one dies in his bar.

Blood spurts all over me, but I don't care. All that matters is getting that sweet, sweet release and burning out the fury and rage that lives inside me.

With every hit, I calm down a little bit more, until finally, the rage eases and I can breathe again.

I catch my breath and wipe the sheer layer of sweat off my brow as I get back to my feet. I glance down at my bloodied fists, making sure it's all his and not mine, and after shaking out my hands a few times, I step over Santa's unconscious body and casually make my way to the bar.

"Hit me with your strongest," I tell him.

The bartender just nods and fills up a shot glass before sliding it across the bar. I take it and throw it back, cringing with the burn before asking for a refill.

The liquor only just touches my tongue when the door flies open and the boys come barreling in. They storm toward me in their pissed off, alphahole glory, and the second I turn and lay my eyes on them, the tears stream down my face.

"What the fuck was that?" Grayson roars, staring straight at me and ignoring the passed-out body just behind me, though I know they see it. They're not stupid.

I stare up at the boys and as I swallow the shot, defeat filters through me. "I think Sara Benson raped me last night."

18

The Escalade speeds down the highway as King's fingers brush back the hair off my face. I lay across the backseat, my head in his lap and my feet in Grayson's. I keep my face turned in toward King's stomach, keeping myself hidden from the guys' lingering stares. Every time I meet their eyes, the tears start, and I have no choice but to berate myself for telling them what happened.

I wanted to keep it to myself. I should have kept it to myself because now every time they look at me, I see the fear in their eyes, wondering when I'll break. Though seeing fear is better than pity. If they were to look at me with pity, I'll have no choice but to bust their asses wide open.

One by one, they sat down beside me at the bar, and together, we took shot after shot as I explained exactly what happened last night at the party. I told them how I thought it was Cruz, how I wasn't sure if I consented. But they assured me, anyone in the state I was in last night wouldn't have the ability to consent. She took advantage of me. Which only led us all to take another shot.

We spent the day sitting at the bar, then slept it off in some shitty hotel while Grayson held me all night and let me cry into his shirt. But today is a new day, and I'm putting that shit behind me. Well, I'm putting it aside to deal with it on my own, where I won't have to bring the boys down. This is my mess to clean up, and while I know the boys would do anything to stand by my side and help me through it, that's not what I want.

Sara and I will be handling this privately, and I'm going to make sure that she understands just how badly she fucked up by putting her hands on me.

We've been locked in the Escalade for nearly four hours. The boys have tried to keep my mind occupied by going over everything we found yesterday. Our main goal was to find both London and the name of the asshole who she's been working with, and while we certainly failed there, we were able to get a few things that could help.

I showed the guys the passports and driver's licenses and explained why her voice was so familiar to me the night King and I overheard her organizing the attack on me. She has followed me through every home, always being ahead of the game.

We have to play this smart now. If she knew where I was all these years, then there's a good possibility that she knew where we were yesterday and knew to avoid the house at all costs.

We're fucked. How are we supposed to move forward from here? It's like the worst game of cat and mouse that I've ever played, only I'm the mouse and the cat has had me surrounded since day one.

Needing to keep my mind off it, I pull out my phone and after scrolling through social media and catching up on all the bullshit celebrity scandals, I pull up the audio book about some chick named Ocean who's been getting fucked over by a sexy billionaire dude. Though, everyone knows this bitch should have just gone home and fucked all the hot guys she left behind.

Not wanting to share this book with everyone in the car, I plug in my shitty earphones and press play, but have to quickly adjust as the sound blares through the little speakers and nearly shatters my eardrums.

There's another two hours before we get home, and if I'm going to make it all the way back without screaming, I need a distraction.

I close my eyes and try to lose myself in the story, and for a while I do, especially when the main chick starts getting fucked within an inch of her life. A wicked grin stretches over my face as I listen to all the dirty details of the fuck fest, taking notes and trying to figure out how I can make that work with three guys instead of just one. Though, there's no denying it. I've definitely got a much better deal than Oceania Munroe. The poor girl only gets to play with one dick where I get three, hopefully four if Carver would pull his finger out of his ass and get on board.

I listen to the words of Oceania getting everything she deserves, and just as she's about to come hard, the boys start cackling around me, completely ruining my moment, more so when my whole head starts bouncing on King's lap from his violent laughter.

"What gives?" I demand, pulling myself off his lap and sitting up to glare at the guys.

King continues shaking with laughter as Grayson desperately tries to hold his in. Cruz outright loses it, slapping his hand down on the dashboard while Carver sits in his stupid driver's seat with a cocky as fuck smirk stretched over his gorgeous face.

I pull my earphones out of my ears and glare at each one of the fuckers. "What did I miss?" I question, the fear of missing out rapidly burning up inside of me.

King simply grabs the cord of my earphones and windmills it around, showing that while I'd put one end into my ears, I'd completely forgotten to plug the other. "Who the fuck is Ocean and who gave her the right to be hitting it so hard?"

King's comment starts another round of laughter while all the blood drains from my face.

Well, shit. I guess the guys have been listening to my audiobook for the past hour and not one of them decided to tell me.

Just fucking great.

"So," Cruz says, twisting around in his seat and giving me a ridiculous little grin that has me groaning to myself, knowing exactly what's about to come out of his skilled mouth. "You read smut, huh? Is that where you learn all your little tricks?"

My hand shoots out and connects with his shoulder before I push him back into the front. "Would you prefer that I didn't read smut? I might have to watch porn to get all my ideas, and who knows what kind of shit I might see there. All those guys with all those dicks …"

"Books, huh? I can get down with books," Cruz says. "Do you need any more? I'm sure I can find you the good shit."

A grin tears across my face. "Oh, no worries," I tease. "Your mom came over and shared all her recommendations, and damn, now that woman knows where to find the good stuff. I mean, if that's what she's been reading then I don't doubt that your dad is one lucky man. I bet he's been getting it real hard for years, in every kind of position. BDSM, blood play, choking, all the good shit. Your mom is one filthy lady."

"STOP," Cruz rushes out, his fingers desperately clinging to the door handle as he looks across at Carver in a panic, his face turning a sickly shade of white. "Stop the fucking car, man."

Carver darts to the side of the road and comes to a screeching halt just as Cruz throws the passenger side door open. His head flies out just in time for the rest of us to hear as he violently throws up every last thing in the bottom of his stomach.

King just keeps laughing, and for a moment I wonder if the man is some kind of robot. Who can laugh so hard and for so long without their stomach aching and begging for sweet relief? Either way, I love the sound so there are no complaints from me.

Grayson grumbles beside me, slipping his hand into mine and lacing our fingers. He loops his arm over my head and pulls me into his side. "Now you've done it," he mutters, the smirk still playing on his lips as Carver watches Cruz with his lips pulled up in disgust.

"Really, man?" Carver grumbles. "You're splashing it all over the side of the car."

Cruz's hand flies back and Carver instantly shoves a water bottle into it as I try not to watch, but it's like seeing a horror movie. You know you should close your eyes, but you can't help it and end up paying the price.

Cruz gets cleaned up and lets out a heavy breath as he rights himself in his seat and closes the door. Knowing this isn't over, Carver doesn't bother hitting the gas and just waits as Cruz slowly turns around and gives me a hard stare, one that I've never had the displeasure of being on the opposite end of. "Never again, Elodie Ravenwood," he demands, using my real name just to prove a point. "Is that clear? I never want to hear about what my mom is or isn't doing in the sack with my father. From now on, I will source your reading material. Whatever book you want, you go through me. I will get it for you. Hardback, paperback, audio book or those digital ones. Me, not her. My mother will never again influence what filthy smut goes through your pretty head."

I bite down on my lip, forcing myself not to smile. "I, uhh … I was just joking," I tell him. "I've never actually spoken to your mom about books."

He gives me a hard stare, not believing me for one second. "How am I supposed to fuck you every night without wondering if each move you twist your sexy little body into was something you got from my mom?"

"Every night?" King sputters. "Ease up, tiger. You need to share her around a bit. I'll give you every second night."

"Fuck off," Grayson says. "That shit might have worked when there were only two of you, but there's more players in the game now, and I intend on making up for lost time."

The boys start fighting between themselves and I flop back against my seat, crossing my arms over my chest and glaring right out the front windshield as Carver laughs to himself and hits the gas, sending us soaring down the highway once again.

"Do I get a say in any of this?" I cut in when they refuse to give up. "Why can't I do you all every night?"

"Because you're not a human pin cushion," Grayson says. "And besides, after you've been with me, you'll be too exhausted to venture into their rooms."

Cruz scoffs. "Who says you're going first?"

"Fuck me," I mutter under my breath, though that's the whole reason we're in this mess in the first place. The boys continue arguing between themselves and I quickly lose interest, knowing all too well just how long this bullshit is going to go on for. Don't get me wrong, I'm kinda flattered that they're fighting over me, but after sitting in this car for five hours, it can be a bit much.

The boys don't do road trips well, and unfortunately for me, that's something I've had to learn the hard way. They're cooped up, frustrated, and have far too much energy. They've argued and bickered for hours on end and it doesn't look like there's an end in sight.

Though thankfully, Carver's idea of a good road trip is to stare out his windshield in silence with a broody as fuck glare across his face. As much as I'm starting to really care for the boys and adore the smooth, velvety tones of their deep voices, I'd be more than happy if they all took a page out of Carver's book.

It takes nearly twenty long, drawn-out minutes for the boys to stop bickering between themselves, and as I listen to each of them giving up and fading into silence, I try to work out how the hell they got from fighting over a fuck-fest schedule with me to arguing over who makes the shittiest Bolognese sauce. For the record, it's King. His cooking is a whole new level of fucked up but when he cooks, he's so damn proud that you just eat it with a smile on your face and tell him how fucking great it is.

Once silence fills the car, I rest back into Grayson's arm, and as his fingers unconsciously trail soft patterns over my skin, I find myself watching Carver through the rearview mirror, my odd angle only allowing me to see the darkness of his eyes and nothing more.

As if sensing my stare, he clenches his jaw, already knowing that something's on my mind. "What?" he demands, not bothering to look up into the mirror to check if his senses were right. He doesn't need to—he's right and he knows it.

Cocky fucker. His confidence knows no bounds.

My lips press into a hard line, more than just hesitating. Hell, I should be scrambling for the door handle, ducking and rolling my ass right out of here before bringing up old scars, but apparently, I'm a sucker for punishment.

"You know that day that we almost …"

I cut myself off, hating how awkward the words sound slipping from between my lips, but hating it even more when Carver's gaze snaps up to the mirror and narrows on mine. "You're going to have to be more specific," he tells me as he approaches the neighboring town of Ravenwood Heights, reminding me that I'm quickly running out of time. "There have been many times that we've almost."

I cringe and try to take comfort in the way that Grayson's fingers stop tracing patterns and grab hold of me instead, squeezing me tight and trying to ease my awkwardness, but I shouldn't need that. After everything we've all been through together, there's no reason at all for me to be nervous. "The day we were interrupted by Scardoni's ridiculous attempt at an escape. In the living room, we were inviting you to … play and you watch—"

"I don't need a recap, Winter," Carver says, his tone flat and void of all emotion. "I'm not fucking stupid. I was there. I know exactly what happened."

I resist rolling my eyes as I squeeze my hand into a tight fist and slip it under my thigh to keep from letting it fly toward the back of his head. After all, he's driving, and while Cruz has quick reflexes to grab the steering wheel, it's not exactly something I want to risk. "You know, I understand that it's a difficult concept for you to understand, but did you know that it's not actually a requirement for you to be an ass one hundred percent of the time?"

"Winter," he groans in warning, already frustrated after being cramped in the car for so long and having to endure the boys' bullshit.

I let out a breath and meet his stare through the mirror, and the closed off hesitation in his eyes tells me that he already knows what I'm about to ask. "You said that you'd make me a deal," I remind him, picturing the moment perfectly in my head, remembering the way his eyes were boring into mine as he walked deeper into the living room, preparing himself to finally take the leap and join in on our group ... project.

Not needing me to spell it out, he simply shakes his head and averts his stare back to the road. "The moment's gone Winter," he grumbles, his wavering tone telling me that it's complete bullshit. "There is no deal. It was a brief second of weakness that won't happen again. Move on. I have."

Well fuck. That stung like a motherfucking bitch.

I sink back into my seat, unable to stop watching him through the stupid little mirror.

He's lying.

He has to be because what I feel between us isn't something that you can just 'move on' from and he knows it. Fuck, everyone in this car knows it, and judging by the grim expressions on their faces, they're more than ready to throw down about it, but they won't. They'll sit back and take it just like I do because despite their relationships with me, this is just between Carver and me, and they know how damn important it is that we get there on our own.

My head drops against Grayson's shoulder as King's large hand takes over my knee and gives it a gentle squeeze.

I've never wanted to be out of a car so badly. The others don't know what happened in Carver's room apart from King, and only he knows just how deeply it cut.

We fall into an uncomfortable silence, and the last few minutes of our drive seem to go on forever. Hell, those few final moments seem to drag on longer than the past six hours have, so when Carver slows the Escalade and brings it to a stop by the main gate of our private residence, the relief quickly soars through me.

He makes fast work of hashing in the code, and as he does, a sinking feeling twists my gut. There's a deep silence in the car, and I can't help but wonder if the boys can feel it too.

The Escalade begins creeping down the road and I watch out the window, desperately trying to work out what's giving me this strange feeling. I sit up a little straighter, and as I do, the guys adjust themselves in their seats. Carver's fingers tighten on the steering wheel while King's hand falls from my knee and fiddles with the door handle.

They feel it just as strongly as I do, yet not one of us voices our concerns because we have absolutely nothing to go on.

I look up ahead through the wide windshield of the Escalade, finding the massive gates for my property intact and untouched. The sight seems to ease me, but the feeling doesn't go away.

The street is empty. I've gotten used to seeing the children playing in their yards and the wives coming and going for their mundane little chores, but today, there's nothing. It's a fucking ghost town.

"What's going on?" I murmur to myself, not waiting for a response because it's not like the guys actually know. "Where is everyone?"

Grayson just shakes his head, not ready to even attempt to piece the puzzle together.

We slowly continue down the private road, and as Cruz leans forward with his eyes widening in horror, my stomach drops. I follow his gaze to Carver's driveway and my heart sinks. His big iron gate has been rammed right off its hinges, but the size of it should have made that impossible.

"Explosives," King mutters, answering every single one of our thoughts.

My heart races like never before, terrified of what we might find if we continue, but how can we not? This is our home. This is the one place the boys trusted that I'd be safe.

Fear rattles me. This shouldn't be possible. The guys locked this place down like Fort Knox when they intended to leave me behind. The alarms should be blaring and Carver's phone should have been lighting up with calls from the security company letting us know that shit has been going down. Hell, we should have at least had calls from the neighbors telling us that someone was trying to fuck with our home.

Where's the fucking loyalty around here?

Carver stops by the fallen gate and we all stare out the window, looking down the long driveway at the house that sits at the very end. Even from here, it's clear to see that the front door is wide open. The hedges have all been hacked at with chainsaws, the garage door has been rammed, and there are tire marks all over Carver's manicured grass.

My heart races even faster. Someone has really come in here with the intention to fuck things up, but if it's this fucked up out here, I can only imagine what it's like inside.

I suck in a gasp, remembering that when I ran out of here just two mornings ago, I left something extremely important behind.

Lady Dante.

Carver's knuckles whiten as he grips the steering wheel with an iron like force, and without missing a beat, he hits the gas and we fly down the long driveway. He has to swerve to avoid fallen branches, sending us all fumbling to the side in the Escalade.

The moment his tires come to a screeching halt, I start to climb over Grayson's lap, aiming for the door handle, but King grabs the back of my tank and yanks me right back into my seat. "Stop," I screech, glaring back at him. "What are you doing? I have to check on her."

The guys ignore me, pulling guns and weapons from who the hell knows where, and not a second later, Carver is reaching over to the passenger side glove compartment and pulling out a small handgun. His arm stretches back and the gun is pressed into my chest as Carver looks back, his eyes boring into mine. "Whoever did this could still be in there," he tells me. "Shoot first. Ask questions later. Got it?"

I swallow hard and let out a shaky breath as the rapid pulsing in my ears makes it nearly impossible to hear. "Got it."

19

The boys share a quick glance, each of them meeting one another's hard stare with a million messages passing between them. Then as if on cue, they nod, and every door handle is pulled hard.

They dive out of the car, and before I can even think about trying to keep up with them, Grayson's fingers are curling around my wrist with a hard, impenetrable grip.

He pulls me hard and I fly out of the Escalade behind him, barely getting my feet under me before the boys start running toward the house. Carver goes straight for the front door, racing up the stairs three at a time and not even breaking a sweat while Cruz races around the back of the house, catapulting himself over the side gate.

King also heads for the side gate, but instead of jumping straight over it, he uses it to launch himself up to the second story of the house while Grayson pulls me around to the side of the garage and hoists me up through the window.

He comes down beside me, landing on his feet like a cat. He instantly grabs my wrist again, pulling me through Carver's massive garage and skimming his eyes over the ruined car collection. Whoever the fuck came in here threw buckets of acid over his cars, the paint dissolving before our eyes. The fumes are the worst part, coating our throats and burning our eyes as we forge forward.

The wreckage is heartbreaking, but I can't focus on material things right now. Houses and cars are replaceable; the lives we stand to lose today are not. God, even Lady Dante; if anything happens to my puppy, I can't fix that. Just the thought of her running around this house scared and alone sends my heart into overdrive.

Grayson moves through the garage with me on his heels, his tactical training apparent in the way he rounds each dark corner, letting the barrel of his gun sweep right to left as we move. When the garage is clear, we approach the internal door, my gun held down at the ground in a sweaty death grip.

We stop for a moment and Grayson silently pushes the door open and peers into the house. I doubt the assholes who did this are still here, but we're not taking any chances on this. The boys' lives are too precious.

He looks back at me and nods, silently telling me that it's all clear, and without a spoken word, we slip into the main part of the house, keeping to the walls and scanning every inch of the rooms as we go.

There's devastation everywhere. Broken windows, shattered vases, destroyed couches. Whoever the hell did this, did it with the intention to scare us, and something tells me that they were kinda hoping that I'd be here as well.

Within moments, we meet Carver and Cruz who both nod. "It's clear," Carver tells us, keeping the emotion out of his tone despite how broken he must be feeling at seeing his home like this.

"Lady Dante?" I question, keeping my voice as low as humanly possible.

Both Carver and Cruz shake their heads. "Nothing yet," Cruz murmurs before nodding toward the stairs.

We all walk as one, and I don't miss the way the boys create a protective circle around me as we start creeping up the stairs. With every step we take, heaviness sinks into my chest. Something is wrong. Every time I come home, Lady Dante meets me at the front door. I hear her yapping from inside and she jumps up and down until I scratch her belly.

"She's not here," I mutter to myself, shaking my head.

"You don't know that," Grayson says, keeping his stare focused on every little thing around him, but he's wrong. I do know it. I know it deep down in my heart. If she were here, she'd be at my feet, yelping and trying to tell me exactly what's been going on, but she's not. I can't hear her. *I can't feel her.*

We get to the top of the stairs just as King steps out of the private study. "Clear so far," he tells us. "It's just the bedrooms to go."

Carver nods as we all turn down the hallway that leads to our bedrooms. We pass Carver's on the left first while Cruz's door is a few steps down to the right, and at once, Carver and King storm through his bedroom while Grayson and Cruz search his, leaving me out in the hallway, staring down toward my door that's been left open just a sliver.

I know I should wait for the guys, but I can't stop myself from moving forward. One foot in front of the other and I have absolutely no control.

My eyes are wide as my heart thunders in my chest, and with every step, it just gets louder.

I creep closer, fearing what I might see, and as I reach my bedroom and raise my hand to nudge it open, I hear the boys in the hallway. "Winter," Cruz rushes out just as all four of them start storming toward me, but I can't wait.

I push the door open and step through to my room, and as the boys barrel in behind me, my whole world shatters.

Lady Dante lays lifelessly over my bed, her blood smeared across my destroyed room and seeping into my sheets. There's a slice right through her little body, starting at her throat and going straight down through her belly.

"Fuck," King spits as a loud, horrific scream tears out of me. I collapse to the ground, Cruz only just catching me before I make matters worse. My stare locks onto Lady Dante's glossy, dead eyes as tears quickly well in mine and run down my face. Who the hell would do this? She was just an innocent puppy who only just got her second chance in life. She was happy here with me. She was supposed to be safe.

Anger boils within me, but the rage is too much, too overwhelming that my usual need to go and beat the living shit out of someone is long gone. I'm left with nothing but pure devastation, grief, and exhaustion.

How could they take her away from me like this? Who could be so cruel?

The boys walk deeper into my room, more than aware that they still haven't cleared the room yet, but judging by the darkness of the blood seeping into my sheets, I'd say this happened yesterday or maybe even the day before, maybe right after I left her with nothing but a full bowl and a little scratch on her head.

She deserved so much better.

I cry in Cruz's arms as he desperately tries to soothe me, needing to take away my pain, but it's too much. It hurts too bad.

Big, painful sobs tear from my body as Cruz's arms tighten around me, but they relax as the boys turn to look back at us and stare at the wall opposite my bed. Their jaws drop, horror filtering through their eyes, and as I turn around to look up at the wall, that same horror pulses through me.

Smeared across the wall in Lady Dante's blood, making fear rattle my bones are the words 'YOU'RE NEXT.'

My eyes widen, terror racing through me, but I don't let it cripple me. Not anymore.

I got it before. It was about Dynasty. It was about keeping their bullshit corrupt world and refusing to let me rule over it. Attacks came at me, they hurt me, and they pushed me to my limits, but now it's personal.

They killed my dog, my best friend, and for that, I am going to tear every last one of them to shreds.

20

The vase shatters against the wall as I desperately try to release the anger that pulses through my veins. The boys sit around me, watching as I pace back and forth through Carver's living room—one of the only rooms in the house that's not completely destroyed.

I grab another vase—one of his mother's favorites—and launch it across the room with a loud, roaring yell. It shatters against the fireplace, and for just a second, I feel a little bit better. But then I remember the innocent dog lying upstairs on my bed and the rage comes pulsing back.

I continue pacing, my hands balling in and out of fists as I struggle to wrap my head around the fact that she's gone.

What kind of monster … FUCK. I can't handle this.

I go to grab another when Carver reaches out and grips my wrist. He gives it a hard tug and I instantly fall into his arms. He adjusts me on his lap and wraps his arm around me, holding me tight to his chest as his hand slides up to the back of my head.

My face buries into the curve of his neck and he holds me there like a weighted blanket, swallowing all my pain. "Just close your eyes and breathe," he murmurs. "In and out. You'll get past this. We're going to figure out who the fuck did this and then we're going to put him down like the bastard that he is."

I don't respond, just close my eyes and focus on breathing, and as I do, all I can smell is Carver. He wraps around me, he consumes me, and after a minute of silence, I find my control and relax into his hold, feeling right at home.

"All I know," King mutters, "is whoever did this knew we were going to be gone. They knew we were planning on leaving her unprotected."

"It has to be London," Cruz says. "She was gone from the mountain home. What are the chances of her being gone the same day we planned on going up there only to come back to find our place trashed? It has to be her."

I nod against Carver's neck, refusing to open my eyes and pull away from him just yet. Right now, he's the only thing keeping me calm, and though he can't stand his mother, I doubt he really wants me trashing all the remaining vases in his home.

"You have a point," Grayson says. "But it's too easy. Any of the fuckers who live on this street could have seen us driving away first thing in the morning. It could have been any of them. We can't rule them out just because London seems like the most likely culprit. I'll never forgive myself if we went after her and left the door wide open for someone else to swoop in and take Ellie away from us. I won't do it."

Cruz lets out a deep sigh. "You're right. Either way, whoever the fuck did this is not getting away with it. They've gone too far."

"So, what do we do?" I mutter against Carver's neck, my lips moving against his soft skin like a caress, though for the first time, being close like this is the furthest thing from my mind.

Carver's fingers knot into my hair as his other hand trails up and down my back. "We regroup," he tells me. "We find out who the fuck hacked my security system and move our asses back into your place. We don't do anything until we're certain that you're safe."

I nod, swallowing hard over the lump in my throat. "I'm sorry," I whisper. "If it wasn't for me, your home wouldn't be destroyed and all this bullshit wouldn't be coming down on you guys."

"This isn't my home," Carver whispers. "It's just a house that will be rebuilt, it's just possessions that will come back to us. Home is where you are. Home is where the guys are. As long as the five of us are together, we're okay."

I hold back the tears. I hate it when Carver gets sentimental and says sweet shit like that. I can't handle it. It messes with my heart and my head. If those words had come out of Cruz's mouth, I'd be fine.

I'm prepared for the sappy shit that comes from him. I've worked up to it and now embrace his sweet words, but Carver … it's like being hit with a curve ball. It shocks me right down to my core.

I pull back and meet his stare. "You really mean that?"

Carver nods and I feel the weighted stares from the guys on us. "I do," he says.

My brows furrow as I search his eyes. "But … in the car, you said …"

"I know what I said, Winter, and I stand by that. There is no deal between us. It's time we move on from whatever … thing is between us, but you're my family, and that will never change. Where you are, is home to me."

I watch him for a moment, hating how sweet and yet so devastating his words are. Hell, I don't even know how to respond to him, but if anything, they only make me want him more. I have to respect him though. I can't keep pushing a relationship between us when he's clearly told me time and time again that he doesn't want it. It's just confusing because he tells me no, and then he goes and does shit like this. He didn't want me in that way. He should have let King, Gray, or Cruz comfort me, but deep down, I know he needs me just as much as I need him.

I pull back a little further and look away, knowing that if I keep looking into his eyes, I'm going to end up kissing him and right now, that's the last thing any of us need.

I slide off his lap and drop down onto the couch beside him as Cruz stands across the room. "I'll go and pack your things," he tells me, not wanting me to go back into my bedroom upstairs. "Then we'll go down to your place and figure out where to go from there."

I nod, and just like that, the boys all get up and leave me sitting in the living room while they grab all of their belongings, preparing to leave the home that they've all lived in for the past few years.

The sorrow and grief quickly start to take over again. I shouldn't have been left alone, but I can't expect the guys to be on top of me every minute of every day. I'm the leader of the biggest secret society in the world. At some point, I'm going to have to learn how to handle my emotions.

Just as Carver had taught me, I close my eyes and take slow, deep breaths, trying to find that calm that I'd felt sitting on his lap.

My phone screeches through the silence and I jump, my eyes flying open as I look down to find Ember's name flashing across the screen. My lips press into a hard line. I haven't talked to her in a while and I messaged her in the car to tell her that I'd be home today, but I can't bring her into this right now. She was just as much in love with Lady Dante as I was. This would crush her, and after the bullshit she went through with Jacob, she shouldn't have to be exposed to this. Besides, she's doing well with Corey. I should leave her to bask in her happiness.

I hit ignore on her call and just as I put my phone back down, the boys come back with bags full of their things. "Come on," Grayson says, walking deeper into the living room and offering me his hand. "Let's get out of here."

My fingers curl into his and he pulls me up, wrapping his arm around my shoulder in the process. We start making our way to the door as I let out a sigh, thinking way too hard about our situation. "So, assuming it was London, how the hell did she know that you guys were planning on leaving? Did you tell anyone or talk about it publicly?"

All four of the boys come to a sudden stand still, meeting each other's horrified stares before rushing back through the house and into the living room. They start searching, looking everywhere as I watch in confusion. "What's going on?" I ask, standing at the entrance of the living room and watching the chaos around me. "What are you looking for?"

Cruz sweeps his fingers across the mantlepiece of the fireplace while Carver kicks over the couch and tears the fabric right off the frame. King pulls out the drawers of the coffee tables and dumps them out on the floor while Grayson starts pulling the priceless artworks off the walls.

"Got it," Cruz calls out, making the guys stop what they're doing and all rush into his side to look over a piece of … I actually don't know what the fuck it is. I start creeping into the living room, pushing myself between King and Grayson to get a good look at the little piece of technology in Cruz's hand. "What is that?" I question, looking over it closely but not being able to determine a damn thing about it.

"It's a bug," Carver says with a frustrated sigh. "Every fucking conversation we've ever had in here is no longer private. She's been listening in on us this whole time. The entire fucking estate is going to have to be swept."

Well, shit.

Carver groans and kicks the couch he just flipped over, sending it soaring across the room. "Your place too," he tells me. "If mine is bugged, it's more than likely yours is as well."

I nod, assuming that all our houses have to be checked.

Grayson takes the bug from Cruz and looks over it a little closer. "If we can run a trace on this and find out where all the information is leading back to …"

A grin pulls at my lips. "We'll know who the fuck to go after," I say before taking the bug from Grayson and bringing it right up to my face, speaking directly into it. "You better start running motherfuckers. We're coming for you. What you did to my dog is going to look like child's play compared to the shit I have planned for you."

The boys grin back at me, and just like that, we take our things and leave this hell house, more than ready to take down the bastard who dared to fuck with us.

Nothing bores me more than staring up at a dark ceiling in the middle of the night while not being able to sleep. Every time I get close, I'm reminded that there's supposed to be a little dog on the ground beside me, licking my fingers every time my hand falls off the bed.

I don't know why she always wanted to sleep down there. I made a whole bedroom just for her, complete with everything a dog could want and need, and yet, every single night, Lady Dante would prance into my bedroom and curl up in a ball on the ground beside me. It's as though she knew how much of a hard time I had importing her little bed and that was her way of laughing at me.

She was a bastard through and through, but in the best possible way. She was cheeky and so full of life, and while she was getting old, she was extremely happy, playful, and always ready for a snuggle. She had a hard life before coming to stay with me, and while I can't even pretend to know what goes through a dog's mind, I think she was grateful that King and I had stolen her away that night.

She loved me in her own doggy way, and for a short time, she got to be the best friend that I always wished to have, you know, apart from Ember. Growing up, having something so permanent such as a dog was always a ridiculous dream. Kids in foster care don't get to have dogs, they hardly get to have belongings, let alone a pet to call their own. But Lady Dante … she was proof that life was turning around for me. She was what gave me hope that I could truly have everything I ever wanted.

I let out a deep sigh and slip out from under Cruz's arm, trying not to wake him. "Where are you going?" he murmurs, attempting to peel open his tired eyes but failing. I guess the whole trying not to wake him thing was a bust.

"Just getting a drink of water," I tell him, pulling the blanket back up over him. "Go back to sleep. I'll be back in a minute."

"You sure?" he grumbles. "Just give me a minute and I can go and get it for you."

A soft smile spreads over my face. He's so damn thoughtful; I've never met anyone like him. Today was hard for him. He feels so deeply, and seeing me so broken and hurt was just as painful for him as it was for me, which is part of the reason why I asked him to be the one to hold me in bed tonight. He needs that comfort just as much as I do.

Cruz mumbles an "Mmmkay," and I don't waste another second, slipping out the door and gently closing it behind me.

I trudge down the hallway, bypassing Grayson's open door to see him wide awake and watching something on his phone, probably porn. He looks up as I pass. "You okay?"

"Go to sleep already," I tell him, walking straight past his door. "It's the middle of the night."

"Look who's talking," he mutters under his breath, though something tells me that I wasn't supposed to hear it.

Laughter bubbles up in my throat and I instantly feel guilty for it. I shouldn't be laughing today. If anything, I should be lying in bed with Cruz, crying my eyes out until the pain goes away. It's not fair to be here enjoying my life and enjoying the boys I share it with while something so horrible just happened.

I let out a sigh and continue down to the kitchen. I make myself a glass of ice water and lean against the counter as I sip it. If I were smart, I'd be drinking a glass of warm milk in the hopes of actually getting to sleep, but I can't stomach it, not tonight.

Once my ice water is long gone, I stare across the kitchen, not moving, just wishing I could do something to fix this. I feel so lost. I should be out there trying to figure out who the hell this was and how they pulled it off. I should be creating a list of all my enemies and working out a way to keep myself and the guys safe from them.

It's been months since I was pulled into this fucked-up little world. I should have my shit together by now. I should be soaring, but instead, I'm drowning. The current is pulling me down and the harder I swim, the more I seem to sink. There's no winning here. I'm a lost cause. The guys would be better off without me.

I let out a heavy sigh and push up from the counter. I have to do something. I can't just go and lie in bed for the rest of the night, staring up at the ceiling while wishing it could all go away. I need to fix this. I need to be proactive and claim back what's mine, and where better to start than inside my enemies' heads.

My feet drag down the hallway until I get to the big door that I constantly refuse to go in. My father's private office. I can only imagine the kind of shit that went down in here, though to be fair, when he was running Dynasty, I don't think he had to deal with the kind of shit that I've been dealing with. I had a warning of my bad luck, where his just showed up unannounced in the middle of the night and killed him before he even got a chance to fight.

I push through the big door and take a quick look around. It smells old and dusty in here, making it clear that this room very rarely has visitors. Moonlight streams through the window, and while it's enough to see where I'm going and ensure that I don't trip and fall, it's not enough to scour every piece of paper in the room without giving me an epic headache.

Walking deeper into the office, my eyes scan over the shelves of books as I remember a brief conversation that I had with Tobias King, telling me that if I wanted information on someone, perhaps here was the best place to start. And considering that there are sixteen folders, each with a family name sitting on my father's shelf, I'd assume that's the best place to start.

I step right up to the shelf and brush off the light layer of dust over the folders while trying to decide who to start with. Royston Carver's stands out to me, but considering that he's already dead and obviously not someone who can actively jump out of his grave and trash his own damn house, his name is clearly off the table.

I scan down the line of names. Beckett. Danforth. Luca. Rhodes. Scardoni. None of them jump out at me until my gaze sweeps over Harding.

Michael Harding.

He's a snake. There's simply no other way to describe him, and up until now, he's been flying underneath the radar. I don't know what he's involved in or who's side he's even really on, but something tells me that he's the kind of guy who could easily be paid off.

I pull the folder off the shelf and take a seat at my father's desk before turning on the small lamp.

My hand trails over the folder, brushing away dust that's built up over the last eighteen years, and the second I open the hard case, it's clear that these folders were used as often as possible by my father. There are papers falling out, small handwritten notes, receipts, and information.

I suck in a breath, and as I scan over the first few pieces of paper, I realize that this is every little bit of dirt that my father was able to put together on the Harding family.

My gaze quickly shifts back to the row of folders with excitement. If there's this much dirt in here, I can only imagine what else I'll find in the other folders. It's like hitting the jackpot.

Why the hell didn't I take Tobias' advice and come storming through here earlier?

Wanting to focus, I drop my gaze and start scanning through the papers, and within the first few minutes, I've determined that Michael Harding and his father before him were both pieces of shit. Michael has had many affairs, many overnight stays at hotel rooms with prostitutes, money laundering, and dirty deals. His father was just as bad.

I flick through the papers until I find an old image, and my face instantly scrunches up as I find Michael Harding staring back at me. He must only be in his early twenties here, but what stops me is the heavily pregnant woman standing right beside him and looking up at him as though he holds the whole world in his hands.

London Ravenwood. They were having an affair.

Oh fuck. If that's me she's pregnant with, could I technically be Harding's kid?

My heart starts to race as I pick up the old photograph and lean back in my father's chair, looking over the woman who looks so much like me. How is it possible that my mother is such an awful person? I should have known that I couldn't be so lucky.

It was luck finding out who my parents were but finding out that my mother is a psychotic murderer—that's just typical. Now finding out that she was screwing none other than Michael Harding … well, that just makes me sick. I guess it could be worse. She could have been screwing Matthew Montgomery, or Preston Scardoni.

Just as I go to put the image back down, the light from the small lamp hits the back of the image, and for a slight second, I see writing on the back.

I slam the photograph down and hastily flip it over, seeing my father's handwriting, something I've become accustomed to over the past few months.

I adjust the lamp, needing to see it clearer as I scan over the words. 'Paris Moustaff & Michael Harding affair.'

Paris Moustaff? Who the fuck is Paris?

I flip the photograph back over and look a little closer as I shake my head. This is my mother. This is London, not some woman named Paris.

My heart begins to race, hating the confusion that circles my mind.

I grab the photo frame of my mother and father with me cradled in my mother's arms from beside the old computer and put the photos side by side.

They look exactly the same, but when I look a little closer, there's a small freckle on the woman who cradles me, which isn't on the woman smiling at Michael. Their teeth are different, the shape of their faces, the way they part their hair.

Holy fuck.

They're twins.

How the hell didn't I know this?

Michael Harding was having an affair with my mother's twin sister, which means there's a possibility that the woman who's been coming after me now, the woman living in my parents' mountain escape, and the woman who held a knife to my throat, isn't my mother at all, but her sister, and thank fuck, I'm not Harding's secret love child.

We've been going after the wrong woman all this time. Perhaps there's a chance that my mother isn't actually a psychotic killer after all.

My mind races with questions, and without even thinking, I grab the photo and walk right out my father's office and fly through the front door.

21

The midnight chill seeps into my bones, but I push myself forward, too many questions desperate for answers that I can't possibly stop now.

My mother has a twin.

Paris and London Moustaff.

Fuck me, I don't think I've ever heard of anyone ever wishing their aunty was a murderer, but damnnnnn, I do. Because if Paris is a murderer, then that means that my mother isn't. Well, technically I guess I don't know if my mother was or wasn't. I have no way of knowing what she did while she was alive, but assuming that she was as great as everyone else around here believes, then yeah, I'd say she's as clean as they come.

With every step I take, my head whirls with untold truths, mysteries, and possibilities, while also sinking with fear. What if I'm wrong? What if Paris really is out there somewhere and London is too? What if it's been my mother all along and she really does hate me enough to kill me. What if they're working together?

Fucking hell. I just can't take any more bad news.

My feet slam against the pavement as I wrap my arms tighter around my body, desperately needing my own warmth, each step taking me faster and faster. If I were smart, I would have jumped on my Ducati and rode my ass down here, but apparently when my mind is a mess, I have issues thinking straight.

After nearly fifteen minutes, I pull myself up over a thick fence and scrape my legs in the process. I cringe with the pain but push past it. I've come this far and I'm not about to let a few scrapes and bruises stop me.

I hear my name called in the distance and let out a sigh. I should have known they'd come for me, and really, I should have run my ass upstairs and woken them all up. They'd want to know what I know, and they'd want to be the ones running the show. I bet every shitty scenario is currently going through their minds, but they'll find me eventually, and when they do, I don't know what kind of state I'm going to be in.

I jump down from the fence, making it quick before I allow myself to think about all the bullshit that comes along with heights. I land in a mess of bushes and grunt and groan as my skin gets all cut up while trying to find my way out in the darkness.

I probably should have found another way over, but I think I've made it perfectly clear that absolutely no thought has gone into this. Especially when I get out of the bushes and look up to see just how far back the house is from the gate.

Just fucking great.

I start moving again, more determined than ever.

By the time I reach the grand stairs leading up to his home, the voices from the road are getting louder. "Winter, baby? Where the fuck are you?"

It goes against everything that I am not to call out to Cruz and let him know just how close he is, but calling out now would tip off the asshole living inside this house, and I'm not ready for that yet. I still have the element of surprise and I'm not about to waste it.

My fingers curl around the door handle and I suck in a deep breath, knowing that the second I turn it, the alarm is going to squeal to life with a blazing, obnoxious sound that's going to wake every bastard living on this street.

I let out my breath and slowly count to three.

One. Breathe in.

Two. Breathe out.

Three. Fucking go for it.

The handle twists freely, and I swing the door open with an exaggerated force, letting it bang against the adjoining wall. The alarm screeches, just as I knew it would, but there's no going back now.

I slide straight through the door, leaving it open because … why the hell not? If the asshole knows something and has been lying about it for twenty years then he deserves to have the breezy, cool night flowing through his house.

I turn the light on and look around, knowing that right now, he's probably falling out of bed with his wife fretting beside him. If he was the one who destroyed Carver's home and killed Lady Dante, I don't doubt he's shitting his pants right now.

I stroll through his home and stop when I get to his office, trying to be quick. He's bound to come running down here any second, and when he does, I want to be ready.

Taking a seat at his desk, I switch on his lamp just as I had at my father's desk, and as I lean back to make myself comfortable, I hear the tell-tale signs of someone running through the house.

I wait patiently, knowing it won't be long.

The boys are surely sprinting down his driveway right now, and I have no doubt that Michael Harding is just about to show his pissed-off face in the doorway.

One second passes and quickly turns into two, and before I know it, thirty seconds have slowly ticked by before he finally creeps into the doorway of his office looking suspicious as fuck.

I let out a sigh. Perhaps I've been expecting too much from the heads of Dynasty. The boys are always so quick to jump into action. Had this been one of the boys' homes, they would have been down here in nanoseconds, but Harding took forever. Maybe the boys have given me an unrealistic expectation for everyone else.

Besides, this is a big house. I'm sure he wanted to sweep every room, though had it been me, I would have started with the room that had the light turned on.

Michael steps fully into the doorway of his office and I don't miss the way that the light from the desk lamp shimmers against the knife wielded in his hands.

Michael lets out a deep sigh of relief, seeing that all this commotion has been caused by little ole me, and as he steps into the office, I keep my gaze trained heavily on his knife. I don't trust him one bit. The guy is as shady as they come.

Michael turns on the main light in the office, and as he walks through the room to the little alarm keypad on the wall, he keeps his gaze trained on me. He turns his back as he enters the alarm code, proving that he doesn't see me as a threat, but why should he? I'm just some stupid eighteen-year-old girl who doesn't know shit about the world she was just dragged into. He could take me down in seconds.

He walks toward me and I nod to the chair opposite his desk. "Take a seat."

"Unlikely," he spits, leaning onto it while keeping the knife tightly in his grip. "What the hell do you think you're doing breaking into my home in the middle of the night? My wife is in a panic and my children are scared. You should be arrested for this."

I shrug my shoulders and slam the photograph of Michael and Paris down for him to see. "I think your wife and children are the least of your problems right now," I tell him. "Sit your ass down and start talking."

Michael's eyes bug out of his head as his hand flinches around the knife. He scrambles for the picture, quickly looking over his shoulder at the door, making sure there isn't anyone here to overhear our conversation. He shoves the old photograph into the pocket of his pants. "Where did you get this?" he hisses.

I laugh knowing my father wouldn't be stupid enough to not make copies. "I think the question is how long have you been having an affair with Paris Moustaff, and how long has she been claiming the identity of her twin sister?"

His eyes bug out again, telling me that I'm right. The woman in the picture really is Paris, and the woman who showed up at my house and put a knife to my throat wasn't my mother at all.

A massive relief settles through me, but I do my best to mask it. He doesn't need to know where my head has taken me or just how messed up I've been at the thought of my mother wanting me dead.

Michael straightens and takes a step to his right, and I instantly stand and step in the opposite direction, circling the desk. "I wouldn't do that if I were you."

A twisted grin cuts across his face, thinking he has this in the bag. "And why the hell not?"

"Because the boys have this place surrounded."

Michael pauses for a moment, his eyes flicking around the room as though he's mentally trying to map where on the property the boys would be, though if I'm completely honest, they're probably still sprinting down the long ass driveway, cursing me for going out alone. Though, once they understand why, they'll get it. They won't like it, but they'll understand … I hope.

Ahh, shit. Who am I kidding? I'm going to get my ass rammed for this, and not in a good way.

Michael looks back at me, his gaze shifting over my pajamas, and after a short moment, a cockiness seeps into his gaze. "Really?" he questions. "They have my home surrounded? Because to me, it looks like you've just rolled out of bed and walked your ass over here without a second thought. Typical Elodie Ravenwood, act first, think later. You're trying to tell me that those boys allowed the great Ravenwood heir to break into my home and stand in a room with me while I hold a knife, and they're not busting down my doors? You're lying, Elodie. You're all alone. There's no one here to save you, not this time."

Well, shit. He's got me there, but I'm not about to go and admit it.

"The picture, Harding. You have two seconds to start explaining yourself."

Michael shakes his head, taking another step around the desk. "You're not in a position to be demanding answers, Elodie," he says, spitting my name like it's poison in his mouth.

"I am your leader," I remind him. "You took a vow to follow me."

"That I did," he says, spinning the knife in his hand to intimidate me. "I vowed to follow you. I said nothing about liking you, and that I don't. You're not cut out for this world. Do yourself a favor and step aside before someone makes you."

"And you think that you're that someone?" I laugh, realizing that not only is he having an affair with the woman who's been trying to kill me and concealing her identity from Dynasty, but he's in Preston Scardoni and Royston Carver's pocket ... at least, he was when they were alive. So, who's his leader now? "I've been watching you. I've been watching you all, and let me tell you, you haven't got what it takes. You're weak. You're a follower, a sheep. You couldn't make me do anything. Which begs the question—who's pulling your strings now that Carver and Scardoni are dead?"

His jaw clenches. "I was not working with them. I had nothing to do with their crimes."

I laugh, not believing him for a second. "Who else is in on this shit? What about Montgomery? Nah," I continue, answering my own question. "Montgomery is even more of a sheep than you are."

Anger bubbles in his eyes, and I stop walking, watching as he continues his way around the desk until he's standing right in front of me, his eyes blazing with the cold, hard truth. "I'd kill you myself if I—"

"If what?" I question, grinning wide as I take his comment as a confession. "If I could just give you a second to get your puppeteer on the phone to give you a little guidance? Who is that by the way? All the other assholes are dead, so that only leaves Paris. Does she have your balls hanging by a thread? What does she have on you, Michael?"

The cockiness in his eyes quickly fades, and within seconds, he's left with nothing but panic, scrambling and unsure of what to say. "Nothing … I … I didn't do anything. I have nothing to do with Paris Moustaff. She's working on her own. Her, Carver, and Scardoni. They were all in it together."

I step into him, the low growl in the back of my throat evidence enough of just how pissed I'm getting. "Stop being such a little bitch, Harding," I demand, my hand pulsing at my side as the need to beat the living shit out of him rages heavily through my body. "I'm no fool. I know you're in on it. You know how I work, and you know I won't stop until I get what I need out of you, just like with Scardoni. I killed Carver for crossing me, so what's it going to be, Harding? Are you a fucking bitch or a man?"

His eyes burn with rage, and in an instant, his hand snaps around my throat and he throws me across the room until my back is slammed right up against the wall and the tip of his knife pressed hard against the healing bullet wound on my abdomen, his panicked façade quickly fading away to reveal the real Michael Harding, the one I didn't know existed.

I suck in a gasp. I guess he's not as much of a bitch as I'd always thought.

"Call me a bitch one more time and I will take this knife and fuck up your pretty little face," he growls.

I narrow my eyes. "You're not going to kill me," I say, knowing that I'm wrong. "You don't have what it takes."

"Don't get me wrong, Elodie," he says, leaning into the knife and piercing through my skin as a sick grin stretches over his too-confident face. "I've been wanting you dead since the moment your bitch of a mother pushed out a baby girl, and if I hadn't promised Paris that she could do the honor, you'd already be bleeding out on my floor."

"You've been pretending for all these years?"

He grins down at me. "Eighteen fucking years of sitting in silence, plotting and planning to move against you. Royston moved too fast. He was too cocky and proud. He wanted it all for himself when I told him to sit back and wait it out. Scardoni though, he gave his kid power that he wasn't ready for, and because of that, they fucked up their chances."

"You've been working with them this whole time?"

Harding scoffs and pushes the knife just a little deeper, making me suck in a sharp breath as I will the tears not to fall. "Working with them?" he laughs. "Those little assholes were working for me. I'm running this show."

Oh, fuck.

"You have no idea what you're getting yourself involved in here," he tells me, taunting me as he slowly pushes the knife a little deeper. "Breaking into my house was the worst possible move you could have made."

I take slow breaths, trying to keep myself calm despite the pain tearing through my abdomen, though it's only going to get worse. He's only got the tip in and something tells me that he won't hesitate to sink it right in, slamming it deep inside me until the hilt is pressed firmly against my stomach. Kinda like the way Grayson likes to fuck—tease me with the tip and then slam it deep inside me until I feel his balls smacking against my ass.

"You're making a mistake," I tell him, playing any angle that I can, knowing there's only a slim chance of me getting out of this. "Let me guess, her endgame is to take over leadership while claiming the identity of my mother, and she's prepared to kill me to do it— her own flesh and blood. So, tell me, do you really think you're that special to her? Do you really think she's going to take you along for the ride? You're just as fucked as I am. You're a pawn to her. Nothing more. Eighteen years of playing her game and she'll slit your throat the second you deliver me and she won't think twice about it."

"You're wrong," he says. "I don't make mistakes."

"You're making one right now," a deep, chilling voice says from the door of the office.

Relief settles through me knowing that I won't be dying today, but that doesn't mean that I'm getting out of this unscathed.

Grayson cautiously steps into the office with Cruz, King, and Carver coming in behind him, and while I feel their gazes hitting my face, I refuse to look away from Harding's haunting stare. The guys stand around us, not making any sudden movements, knowing that just the slightest pressure on the knife could have it sinking deeper into my abdomen.

In a flash, Harding winks and slams the knife deep inside of me, and as I crumble to the ground, clutching at my stomach, Harding sprints to the window and throws himself through the thin glass.

"Don't let him get away," I cry as Carver dives down to catch me. "He's behind it all."

Without another word needed, Cruz, King, and Grayson race after him. Grayson launches himself through the broken window while King and Cruz race out the door they just came through.

Carver adjusts me in his arms and reaches across to the desk. He grabs the landline phone and dials 911 as I groan in pain, desperately holding onto my stomach, though one thing is for sure, this doesn't hurt nearly as much as getting shot did, or maybe it just didn't go as deep.

Carver lays me down and puts pressure against the wound as he holds the phone between his ear and shoulder. Within seconds, an ambulance is dispatched and Carver is looking down at me with wide, fearful eyes.

"We're not doing this again," he spits, the panic in his eyes breaking my heart. "I'm not going to lose you like this."

"I'm fine," I groan through my clenched jaw, desperately wishing that he'd just hold my hand and tell me that everything is going to be alright. "It just hurts like a motherfucker."

Carver looks over me, focusing on my hard stare. "Are you sure?" he demands, not ready to take my word for it.

"Yes," I snap back at him, positive that I'm not about to bleed out all over the floor. "Just don't let go and we won't have any issues."

"Then talk to me, babe. What the fuck just went down in here?"

I cringe as he presses down a little harder, getting a good hold on the wound and judging from the look in his eye, he's calling on every little piece of control inside his body to not berate me for slipping out of the house by myself. "Harding and Paris Moustaff," I tell him. "They've been working against us since the very beginning. Your dad and Scardoni were just pawns in their game."

"Who the fuck is Paris?"

"My mother's twin sister," I pant before slowly sucking in a breath and trying to think of anything but the pain. "It's been her all along. She wants to take me out and claim my mother's identity so she can have it all for herself."

"Fucking hell," Carver mutters, shaking his head. "How the fuck did we miss a twin sister?"

I shake my head, wishing I knew.

"We're not going to let them win," Carver tells me just as King strides back through the office door.

"He didn't get far. The boys are taking him back to Winter's place and we'll 'talk' to him there," he explains before dropping down beside me and cradling my head. "But the real mystery is how the fuck do you keep getting yourself in this situation?"

I shrug my shoulder, cringing at the pain the movement causes. "Beats me," I say. "But if someone doesn't get some epic doses of morphine in me soon, you're all going to be feeling it."

22

The sunrise peeks out over the horizon as I lay across the back of Carver's Escalade. Technically, I should be lying in a hospital bed right now, but considering everything, the guys thought it'd be safer to break my ass out and take me home.

I can only imagine what the doctors and nurses must be thinking right now, but Grayson has enough medical training to take care of me. Don't ask me how though. I thought he'd only just finished school like the rest of us. So it came as a shock when he explained, not only had all the boys been trained in weaponry skills, combat, and martial arts, but Grayson was trained as a field medic. He won't be performing heart surgery anytime soon, but he could keep us alive until help arrived.

To be honest, I shouldn't be so surprised. I don't know why every time the boys open their mouths and give me just a snippet of new information about themselves, it surprises the ever-loving shit out of me. Anyone would think that I'd be used to it by now. When I was bleeding out on my parents' garage floor, he remained cool, calm, and collected as he fought to keep me alive.

It's been a long-ass night. After waiting for what felt like forever for the ambulance to arrive at Harding's place and having to deal with his confused and panicked wife, I ended up in yet another surgery. It was nothing like the first one though. The stab wound wasn't nearly as bad as the gunshot wound, but the doctors wanted to be thorough and make sure that everything that's inside my body was still where it was supposed to be. The doctor stitched me back up, forced some pain meds into my system and whacked a few bandages on me.

I was technically all good to go, but the doctor required me to wait a few days just to make sure I was healing properly. After all, if I were to get up and start moving around, I would risk opening my stitches, and nobody wants that—apart from the guys, apparently.

When Cruz mentioned the hospital policy that states the cops must be called when patients come in with stab or gunshot wounds, the boys all shared a look. So, now we're here, flying down the highway.

Carver drives over a bump and I groan, gripping onto my stomach and glaring into the front seat. "Jesus Christ. I know you've been dying to get me bouncing around in the backseat of your car, but fuckkkkkk," I groan, spitting the words through my clenched jaw, "the goal is to avoid all the fucking potholes. Is it really that hard to drive in a straight fucking line?"

Carver takes a moment, slowly breathing in and out, calming himself before tightening his grip on the steering wheel and purposefully hitting another bump. "It's not too fucking late," he murmurs. "We can still ditch her on the side of the road. She's on enough pain meds. She'll just fall asleep and forget about it till morning."

Grayson smothers a laugh and turns around in his seat to meet my hard stare. "Carver's driving isn't what's important right now. The real question is why the fuck you thought it was a good idea to walk out of the house in the middle of the night, the same fucking day we get home to find our place ransacked and your dog dead on your bed."

I groan. "Here comes the 'I told you so.' "

He continues as though I didn't say a damn word. "At any point did that little messed up voice inside your head suggest that maybe, just maybe, it was a stupid fucking idea? I was awake all fucking night. At any time you could have come and told me what you'd found out. We could have worked out what to do as a group and your ass wouldn't have ended up in the hospital again."

I look Grayson dead in the eye, holding his questioning stare for a moment too long. "You know, I think the real question is if you think that little voice inside my head is so messed up, then why the hell did you think it was a good idea to fuck me until all I could think about was your monster cock? Actually, better yet, at what point did you think it was a good idea to get that monster cock pierced? I mean, what has to run through a guy's head to wanna shove a thick as fuck needle through their junk? Jesus, and you think the voice inside my head is messed up."

King laughs as his hand rests on my thigh, his other hand entwined with mine. "You can't deny it, bro. The girl is right."

Grayson scoffs. "The girl is high on fucking pain meds."

I scoff right back at him. "You're just jealous."

"Jealous of what?"

I grin, knowing damn well that I'm not making any sense, but screw it. I feel good, and if I want to talk shit after being stabbed by a deranged, crazy dude, then fuck it, I will. "Jealous of my pierceless pussy."

Grayson turns back around, staring at me with a straight face, his usual cocky smirk well hidden. "Really?"

"You're damn right."

"Ellie, having that fat as fuck needle sliding through my cock was one of the best things that ever happened to me because despite how fucking bad it hurt, it means that every night after tasting your sweet little pierceless pussy, I get to fuck it and listen to you scream as that tiny piece of metal slides in and out of your tight cunt."

Well, damn. Monster cock's got me there.

Everything inside of me clenches but it's short lived as Carver hits another bump and then swerves, throwing Grayson back into his seat. Though, something tells me that hitting that bump wasn't as accidental as his stupid innocent face is letting on.

"Hey, Monster Cock." Grayson slowly turns back around, meeting my stare with an impatient silence. "Speaking of tasting my sweet little pierceless pussy, why don't you sneak into my bedroom after these asholes have finished fussing over me and really make me feel better?"

Grayson's brows arch as Cruz scoffs from beside me. "Don't even fucking think about it. If anyone is tasting you today, it's me."

"Don't get feisty," I laugh, looking up at him with a wide grin and melting as he meets my gaze with a heated one of his own. "You can all have a turn, but Monster Cock first. Watching him Superman out that broken window got me all shades of hot."

Carver grumbles from the front seat. "No one is fucking when we get home. Winter is going to her damn bed and staying there until we can be certain that she can walk around without her stitches tearing open."

I roll my eyes. "Ugh, fun police," I mutter, reaching forward and nudging his elbow that rests on the center console. "You should try fucking one of these days. It'll do wonders for that attitude that's always shoved right up your ass."

Carver ignores me as King and Cruz silently shake with laughter on either side of me, probably enjoying me being high on pain meds more than they should. "Maybe you've forgotten, but there's a crazy, psychotic killer after you who will stop at nothing to end you, and as of five hours ago, was exposed. With Harding out of the game, she's got no one now. No inside information, no one getting her the codes, and no one telling her where the fuck you're going to be. I give her twenty-four hours until she figures out that Harding is out, and after that, she's going to be desperate. She's un-fucking-hinged and will be coming at you full force with bullshit attacks that haven't been thought out. It's going to be messy and brutal, the kind of shit that you don't want to get caught up in. Is that clear?"

I clench my jaw, hating his tone. I know all of this. It's the only thing that has circled my mind for the past five hours, but sometimes to get through something, you need to laugh, and right now, I need these boys to keep my mind occupied with anything but Paris Moustaff and her insane obsession with ending my life. I need the boys to distract me with the promise of a good time because my only other option is to focus on the pain shooting through my abdomen. And if I do that, I'm going to break, and something tells me that isn't going to be a pretty sight.

"Geez," I mutter under my breath, grabbing hold of Cruz's thigh and using it to push myself back up into a sitting position to each of the boys' dismay. "You really are the fun police."

Carver meets my stare in the rearview mirror, watching me for a long moment, surprised by my audacity to not take him seriously right now, but he doesn't need to know that I actually do. I take him more seriously than I ever have before. "This isn't a joke, Winter. You can't be going around playing these stupid little games anymore. Call me the fun police all you like, but from now on, until we take this bitch out, you're playing by my rules. We have to set up a meeting with the heads of Dynasty to figure out how to proceed with Harding, and then after that, you're staying in bed until you're healed. There won't be any more sneaking out in the middle of the night to beat the shit out of someone, and you're going to have one of us watching your ass everywhere you go, even if it's to take a piss. I am not taking any chances. With us all knowing her real identity now, we all have targets on our backs. Her game just got four times bigger. The stakes have risen, and now it's not just about protecting you, it's about protecting us all."

"You don't think I know that?" I demand. "You don't think the thought of something happening to one of you guys has been circling my mind since the second Harding first mentioned it? I know the stakes have risen. I know this affects us all now, but I'm not going to go running scared. I'm not going to hole up in my room, terrified that she's about to come barging out of my closet with a chainsaw and a death wish. I get it, I'm injured and I'm not helping anyone while I'm like this, but the second I can, I'm going to be out there with you guys, doing everything I can to end this, and there's not a damn thing you can do to stop me. Dynasty is mine, and I'm not about to let some identity stealing bitch take it away from me."

Carver's stare doesn't waver despite being the one in control of a vehicle currently speeding down the highway. He watches me for a second, his stare hard and as lethal as they come. The moment seems to go on forever, and when he finally rips his gaze away, the breath is knocked right out of me.

Silence fills the car, and for a while, I'm grateful. But all it does is allow the train wreck of thoughts to come steamrolling back inside my head.

"You good?" Cruz asks as we travel down the road, closing in on the massive gate at the front of my property.

I nod as he squeezes my hand. "Yeah. My head is foggy from the pain meds," I say, knowing damn well that he's not asking about my physical wellbeing but more so the mess that's going on inside my head. "I just want to get upstairs and sleep for a week."

"No problem," he tells me. "I'll help you up the stairs."

"Thanks," I say, and not a minute later, the Escalade comes to a stop outside my home. Cruz helps me out and carries me right up the stairs as King enters the code for the automatic lock on the door.

We get inside and I rest my head against Cruz's chest, the exhaustion of the day quickly creeping up and reminding me that I didn't sleep all night. No, instead of curling up in my bed like a good little girl, I went out and decided to get stabbed by the asshole who's been plotting against me this whole time. Where the fuck were my survival instincts when I decided to do that shit?

Fucking hell. Let's hope I gain a few extra brain cells after having a sleep. After all, while every ounce of my body is telling me to be a stubborn asshole and ignore everything Carver says purely because he decided to deliver it with an attitude, he's never been so right.

Paris is going to be scrambling. She'll be feeling everything that she's worked for slipping away, and she's going to get desperate. Now isn't the time to fuck up. I need to be on my A game all the damn time.

Cruz makes his way up the grand stairs, ready to hand-deliver me to my bedroom. I don't doubt that he has every intention of staying with me until I fall asleep, but his stomach has been making an angry 'feed me' noise for the past two hours. Taking care of himself is definitely more important than watching me sleep, but something tells me he's not going to see it that way.

We make it to the top of the stairs, and as he trudges down the hall with both Carver and Grayson trailing behind him, he gives me a goofy as fuck grin. "You've got to stop scaring us like this."

"Sorry," I say, a guilty cringe spreading across my face. "How else am I supposed to keep you on your toes?"

Cruz rolls his eyes and gently shakes his head, trying to mask the grin that threatens the corners of his mouth. "Literally any other way would do."

Carver walks into his bedroom as I laugh, but it's quickly cut off when Cruz turns and steps into my bedroom, coming to a standstill in the middle of the doorway. "Ughhh … guys?" he says, making a cold shiver trail down my spine. "You're going to want to see this."

My head whips back to look deeper into my room, and before my mouth can even drop, Carver and King are barreling in behind Cruz.

Sara Benson lays butt-freaking-naked in my bed, her ass up in the air, her back arched, and her head squished against my pillow with her blonde hair neatly laid out. Her head is positioned looking back at the door with her fingers gently massaging her clit, and I can't help but feel as though she's waiting for me, spread out like some kind of happy surprise, but not for long.

She comes to a sudden stop, her eyes widening as she takes in the boys barging through my bedroom door.

"Holy shit," I breathe, staring at the horrendous sight before me as the memory of what she did to me during Ember's graduation party comes flooding back to me. "The whole bed needs to be burned."

Cruz smirks as Sara quickly scrambles, collecting the blanket in her arms and desperately trying to cover up, the embarrassment far too great. "Just give me a minute to commit this to memory," Cruz murmurs, wanting to soak this up before stepping in to fix it.

I ram my elbow back into his ribs as he releases his hold on me and helps me to my feet. "The fuck do you think you're doing?" Carver demands, beating us all to the punch.

Sara acts as though he didn't say a damn word as she hurries off my bed and focuses her wide stare on me. "I ... ummm."

"I ... ummm?" I repeat, mocking her tone and staring at her in shock. Is she kidding me right now? She's just going to stand there and scramble over her words rather than give me a damn explanation. "What the fuck is wrong with you? Are you insane? Breaking into my home and getting off in my bed? Fucking hell."

"Call it a celebration. You're supposed to be dead. Though, for a while there, I guess it could have been mourning my shot at killing you myself."

The fuck?

"I ... I don't even know how to respond to that," I tell her, searching her face for any sign that this is some kind of twisted joke. "Are you fucking serious right now or are you just epically unhinged?"

"You have some fucking nerve speaking to me like that," she growls, stepping forward and dragging the blanket along with her—a blanket that I hope she takes with her when her bitch ass is kicked out the door. Otherwise, I'm going to have to burn it. "You've put me through hell. You publicly humiliated me, you rejected and then assaulted me."

Cruz laughs, knowing exactly where this is about to go as Carver seems to silently shake in rage on my other side.

"I assaulted you?" I spit, skipping right over the whole 'you're supposed to be dead' thing. I have priorities, and right now, this one takes the cake. But don't be fooled, unless one of the guys beats me to it, I'll be circling right back to that shit. "You got a little fucking punch to the face, I got fucking raped by an unhinged psychopath in the back of a closet during a fucking party."

Sara's eyes widen just a fraction. "I …"

I scoff, shaking my head, unable to mask the irritation and disgust pulsing through me. "What's the matter? Shocked that I remember, or shitting your pants because I know what you did to me?"

She shakes her head. "You're a liar, Winter. Always have been. I didn't do anything that you weren't begging me for."

Cruz flinches at my side, more than ready to take this bitch out, but I place my hand against his strong arm, silently urging him to find control. There's still so much ground for us to cover and I don't want him scaring her away before we have the chance to really fuck her up.

I take a deep breath, and as I exhale, I attempt to regain my control. I step around King, putting myself right in front of Sara and hating the way the boys step with me, not trusting me or not trusting her, either way, it doesn't sit well with me. When dealing with a guy who can easily overpower me, I get it, but this? This bullshit is all mine. "How the fuck did you get into my house?"

Sara's eyes widen, and as I continue toward her, she starts to back up, realizing that right now, she's not the only crazy, unhinged bitch in the room. "I … I … I just know it. The code … It's been the same every time that I've come here."

"That's impossible. It's been changed a million times over the past few months. You're lying."

She shakes her head violently, her gaze snapping back to the boys as if she has even the slightest chance in hell that they're about to help her. "I swear," she insists. "Your birthday—0225. Go and try it if you don't believe me."

I glance back at Carver who watches Sara with apprehension, his eyes narrowed in suspicion. "What do you mean every time you've come in here?"

My head whips back to Sara. I was so caught up on the code not changing that I'd completely missed that little piece of information.

Sara swallows hard, her guilty expression turning back to me as horror twists across her face, realizing that the more she opens her mouth, the bigger the hole she's digging becomes. "I didn't … that's not what I meant."

I step into her, and in a flash, throw my hand up and twist it into her hair. I rip her head back and force her stare to mine, letting her see just how quickly my patience is running out. "You have two goddamn seconds to spit it out before I make you."

"I … fuck. Okay, I come here all the goddamn time. Ever since you humiliated me. I've been watching you, keeping tabs on you, just waiting until the moment I can finally strike. Lucky for you, I thought the bastard that stabbed you last night took my shot. Turns out, I'm going to get my chance after all."

I stumble back a step, sucking in a sharp breath as I release her so quickly that she has to catch herself on the edge of the bed.

King races in, stepping past me and gripping Sara by her chin. He forces her chin up with a quick snap and her eyes widen in fear—not the 'I just fucked up' type of fear, but the real, gut-wrenching 'I'm about to die' fear. "How the fuck do you know she got stabbed? No one knows that."

Irritation spreads across Sara's face. "Do you not listen? All beauty and no fucking brains. How wasteful," she spits, having the nerve to push his buttons despite his hand wrapped around her chin. "I just told you that I watch her. I watch her all the fucking time. She snuck out of her bed and left Cruz all alone, had a glass of water then sat in her daddy's office, and when she walked out of the house, I followed her right up the goddamn street. I'm surprised you didn't see me. You and Cruz ran straight past me when you were chasing that guy."

I push past King, slamming my hand into Sara's shoulder and throwing her back against my bed. She stumbles, falling back as the blanket tears away from her body. Her leg hits the back of my bed and she only just manages to stay on her feet. "Why? Hoping for the chance to get me alone? You already did that, but leaving me there alive was a mistake. You should have killed me when you had the chance."

"I'll get my chance," she promises, "But not before I humiliate you just like you humiliated me."

"You're fucking insane," I tell her, shocked that not a single one of us caught onto just how fucking unhinged she really is.

I gape at her, and just before I go to tell her for the millionth time how fucking crazy she is, Grayson walks past my bedroom door and quickly backtracks to shove his head right through it. "Oh, whoa," he laughs, stepping through the doorway to join the party. "No one told me we were roasting bitches today."

Grayson's easy comment has something settling within me, and I take a breath before calming myself and looking back at Sara. She stays still, the bed behind her making it impossible for her to back up any further, but seeing that my control is slipping, her survival instinct starts kicking in. "Let me go and I won't show anyone the footage of what happened in that closet."

Grayson laughs behind me. "Holy fuck. I've been missing out," he says before focusing his attention on the guys. "Please, for the love of all that's sweet in the world, tell me she was fucking herself on Ellie's bed."

No one says a thing, but one of the boys, probably Cruz, must have silently nodded as Grayson's laugh only gets louder, but I tune it out, keeping my focus on the crazy bitch standing before me.

I get nice and close, my body pressing right up against Sara's as a sinister smile twists across my face, showing her just how fucking crazy I can be. "I hope you've said all your goodbyes," I tell her. "Because you're done."

Without another word to Sara, I turn and face Carver knowing that out of the four guys, he's the one who knows exactly what I want done and how I want it done. He doesn't say a single word, just nods and not a second later, Grayson and Carver step around me.

She instantly starts screaming, fearing for her life, and the sound is like music to my ears. I don't doubt that she thinks she's about to die. That's what I want her to think. I want her shitty little life to flash before her eyes, for her to think she's never going to see her family again or get the chance to accomplish anything she's dreamed of. I want her to know the kind of fear that I fall asleep with every fucking night because of people like her. I want her to be terrified and regret all the fucked-up decisions she's made, but where she's going, all she's going to have is time to think about those regrets. Besides, she'll be around her kind of people. She should feel right at home in that straight jacket, the white clinical rooms, and group meetings to remind her that she's fucked in the head.

Ease settles through me, knowing that I made the right call. I could have so easily had her life ended right here in my bedroom, but I like to think that I've grown. If I kill every asshole who steps against me, it'd be a lonely world.

I walk out of my bedroom and across the hall to Carver's room, silently closing the door behind me, knowing this is the one room where I won't be disturbed.

I crash down into Carver's bed, groaning as the pain tears through my abdomen. Sure, what's another two weeks of bed rest while the whole world plots against me? Sounds great.

The exhaustion crashes through me, and the second my head hits the pillow, I breathe in Carver's delicious scent. As I think of all the ways that Sara Benson and Michael Harding can go fuck themselves, a deep sleep finally claims me. By the time I wake, I know Sara will be gone, and my life will be that much easier.

23

It's well past six in the evening when I wake to find my ass back in my own damn room. A bottle of water and painkillers are on my bedside table next to a plate filled with chicken schnitzel, fries, and gravy waiting for me to annihilate.

My stomach grumbles, but as I sit up and start to feel nauseous from the pain, I realize that the bed I've been sleeping in is no longer my own. I let out a heavy sigh. The boys got me a new bed though that doesn't change the fact that this room is now tainted with Sara and her naked pussy. I bet she rubbed that shit over every single one of my belongings. Ugh, I can't be in here.

My stomach churns at the thought and I push the schnitzel away despite how badly I want it.

I get myself sorted out and take the painkillers, knowing that while I get ready for the stupid Dynasty meeting to figure out what to do with Harding, it's going to start hurting more than I can bear. But there's nothing I can do about it. This meeting has to take place, and it has to be today. I'm not letting that asshole get away. We're dealing with this, and we're dealing with it now.

I throw my blanket back and groan. This really does suck, but I keep telling myself over and over again that it could be worse. After getting shot, there's no way I would have been able to get up and walk around so soon. I should be grateful that a small stab wound is all I suffered, considering who Harding is in all this bullshit. I very well could have been lying on the ground taking my final breaths.

I guess sneaking out of the house in the middle of the night really was a stupid idea.

Sucking in a deep breath, I get to my feet and try not to groan too loudly. If the boys knew that I was trying to get up by myself, all hell would break loose, and I really don't need their help going to the bathroom. I have boundaries that not even they can cross.

"Who the hell put me back in this room?" I call out as I creep across my bedroom and step into the bathroom. My favorite black tank and leather pants lay across the counter, paired with the skimpiest thong and bra imaginable. I guess Cruz was in charge of helping me today, and the very thought has a grin stretching across my face. I'm glad that even when hell is raining down over us, some things just don't change.

"You were drooling all over my pillow," Carver calls back from his room. "If you want to be gross, do it in your own space."

"The whole house is my space," I remind him. "You're more than welcome to take your ass back to your place if you don't want me drooling over everything."

"Shut up and eat your dinner," King calls from somewhere down the hall. "The council meeting starts in less than an hour and you need to be ready."

I roll my eyes and drop my ass down onto the toilet, and as I take care of business, I pull off the gross clothes that I've been in since last night and look down at my stomach. Deep bruising peeks out from under my bloodied bandages and I let out a sigh. I'm going to have to take a shower.

I get myself up, and within moments, I'm standing under the warm rush of water. I try to go fast, wanting to beat the boys to the punch, but before I can even get the shampoo out of my hair, Grayson is standing at the door of my shower with new bandages in his hand and a warm towel ready to wrap around me.

I give him a small smile, and after turning off the taps, I allow him to wrap me up. Once I'm thoroughly dried, Grayson sits me up on the counter and wordlessly looks over my wound before bandaging me up and helping me to get my new tank over my head.

"Did you take the painkillers?" he asks. "If they're not enough, I could probably find you something a little stronger."

I shake my head. "It's fine," I say, stopping his hands when he insists on helping me get into my pants, starting to cross that boundary line. "I want a clear head for this meeting. I can't risk fucking it up. You can drug me up as much as you want once we get back."

"You sure?" I nod and he helps me down off the counter. "Did you eat?"

"Couldn't," I grumble, gripping onto his strong arm as I bend down to try and pull my thong and pants up my legs. "The thought of being in this room with what Sara has been doing ... ugh. I'm going to move my bedroom down the hall. There's probably pussy juice spread all over my room."

"Pussy juice?" he questions.

I nod, as serious as can be. "Would it be weird if I moved into my parents' room? I mean, it's the biggest with an awesome walk-in closet and the bathroom is just ... it's beautiful, but ... you know, it was their room."

Grayson shakes his head, grabbing hold of my pants and yanking them up my legs and over my ass when he decides that I'm taking too long. "I think it's fine. It's not like they're coming back to claim it. Besides, I think they'd want you to be comfortable in your own home. The boys and I can pack up all their stuff and put it in storage so it wouldn't feel like you're intruding on their space. You can make it your own."

"Are you sure? You don't have to do that. I can move everything. I don't expect you guys to always be running around after me. I just wanted to know what you thought."

"It's fine. Besides, I think Carver could use the physical labor to work out some of that bullshit energy he's been bottling up. He's bound to snap at some point, and when he does, it's best if he's not so … energetic."

"If you're going to talk shit about me," Carver calls from his bedroom, "at least have the decency to do it to my face."

Grayson smirks, looking down at me with his eyes sparkling like twinkling stars in a dark sky. "See what I mean?"

I can't help but laugh, and after turning around to take in my reflection and fixing up the bird's nest that sits on top of my head, I look back at Grayson. "Let's get this shit over and done with so we can focus on finding Paris."

"I've never heard such sweet words."

Twenty minutes later, the boys and I sit around the massive round table, the first ones to arrive. We weren't exactly thrilled with the idea of all the big guns around here watching me hobble in with another injury, so we got here early and hid me behind the table. I was the first to walk in and I'll be the last to leave.

Cruz and Grayson sit across the table, taking up the spaces usually reserved for their fathers, but King stands. He has every right to claim the seat, but he looks uncomfortable and awkward about actually sitting in it. It's not been long since his father was poisoned, and I can only imagine that it's still messing with his head.

Carver though, he has absolutely no reservations about taking what was his father's. He leans back in his seat, his arm casually thrown back over the chair with his feet propped up on the massive table. He looks across the room at Grayson. "What happened with those bugs? Did you run the tracking on them?"

"Yeah," Grayson says, leaning forward and propping his elbows against the table. "Took fucking hours and came back with nothing, so we're back at square one. The fucking thing took me on a wild goose chase and I ended up with nothing but a bullshit fake account. Whoever did this must have bought them out of the back of some dodgy semi on the side of the highway. It's a dead end."

"Fucking great," King mutters, hanging his head as he lets out a deep breath.

"What's the point of trying to track them? Isn't it obvious that they were put there by Harding or Scardoni? It makes sense. They've been feeding the information back to Paris. Hell, maybe she was the one who bugged the place. She's probably been there a million times by now. Who knows what she could have done."

Carver shakes his head. "While it's the most obvious answer, what if it wasn't them? What if we're wrong and there's another threat out there? It could have been Sara. The crazy bitch just admitted to stalking you for the past few weeks, or maybe it was someone that we don't even have on our shit list."

"Okay, okay. I get it," I say just as the door to the big room opens and Cruz's father steps through with Harlen Beckett and Matthew Montgomery.

Both Grayson and Cruz instantly get out of their fathers' seats, and before their asses have even hit their chairs, Earnest Brooks and three others are making their way through the door.

Within the space of three minutes, every single seat is taken except for two—the space reserved for the head of the Harding family and the space that will never again seat a Scardoni.

"Shall we get started?" I ask, glancing around the table at the questionable men surrounding me, wondering who the hell are allies in this twisted game and who's waiting for their turn to shove a knife deep into my back … or abdomen.

Harlen Beckett scoffs in a tone so similar to his son, that for a brief moment, I have to look up and double check who's talking. "I hardly think so," Harlen says. "You have been here long enough to know the rules. We wait until every member is present at the table. Harding is a prompt man, he will be here shortly. Waiting two minutes isn't going to kill you."

I bite my tongue. Clearly Harlen has been living in a fantasy world because over the past few months I've come to learn that two minutes is more than enough time to kill me. Hell, the explosion during the ball happened in less than a second and killed countless people, something we still haven't gotten to the bottom of.

I glance across the big room and meet Cruz's stare. I nod and without a single word, Cruz walks around the table with the eye of every man in the room on him. He pushes through to an adjoining room and when he walks back out with Michael Harding bound and barely able to keep on his feet, the outrage begins.

"What the hell is this?" Matthew Montgomery roars as Cruz drags Michael across the room and violently shoves him into his seat.

A pleasant smile stretches across my face as I turn to face the men at the table, as innocent as can be. "There," I smile at Harlen. "Every member is now present. I am assuming you now have no issues with me commencing tonight's meeting?"

Seeing that I'm clearly a little unhinged and should probably have joined Sara in the institution, Harlen silently nods and flicks his gaze between me and Michael, unsure of what the hell is about to go down. Though one thing is for sure, the confusion on his face makes it clear that he's been left out of the loop. And while I can't necessarily trust him, I can trust that he's innocent in this.

"Why don't we start with the elephant in the room?" I suggest as everyone nervously looks toward Michael.

I slam the photo of Michael and Paris down on the table and slide it toward Earnest Brooks beside me. His eyes go wide, and as he flips it over to read the writing on the back, he gasps. "No, this isn't possible."

The photograph is passed around the table, and by the time it gets halfway, I know I have their attention. Being guilty of stepping against the leader is one thing, but concealing the fact that London had a twin sister for the past however many years is like throwing acid over an already gaping wound to these men.

"'Last night, I discovered this photograph in my father's files," I tell them, watching as the photo continues to make its rounds. "What you are seeing is the start of an affair between Michael Harding and my mother's identical twin sister, Paris Moustaff. Michael has concealed Paris' existence from Dynasty for all these years as their affair has continued. Over the past eighteen hours, Grayson Beckett and Dante Carver have been responsible for leading an investigation into this relationship, and the information which has been uncovered … Michael must be held accountable for his actions."

Mr. Danforth straightens, looking at Michael with a hard stare. "What actions are you referring to? The affair in itself is grounds for dismissal. Do vows mean nothing anymore?"

Carver adjusts himself slightly, and I look toward him to find his eyes on mine, silently asking for permission to take it from here. I nod and he doesn't miss a beat. "As you all know, a few weeks ago, Elodie was attacked in her home. We believed it was London Ravenwood, however it has come to light that the woman who attacked Win—Elodie is in fact her aunt, Paris Moustaff. After speaking with Michael Harding, we have discovered that together with Paris, the two of them have been organizing attacks on Elodie in an attempt to claim Dynasty for themselves."

"That doesn't make sense," Earnest says to my right. "How will she claim Dynasty?"

Grayson steps forward moving into the space beside his father's seat. "Paris plans to murder our leader and claim the identity of her dead sister, London Ravenwood."

Gasps sound around the table as horrified stares come back to Michael. "She will never sit where London and Andrew once sat," he spits, his disgust for Michael shining through loud and clear. "I won't allow it."

"The other attacks?" Harlen questions. "The assassins in the woods, the hitman in the pool, the ball? That was all you?"

Michael's head snaps up. "I HAD NOTHING TO DO WITH THAT EXPLOSION," he roars. "I lost my brother that night. How dare you."

"I thought Scardoni was responsible for the attack in the woods," Cruz's father asks, sailing straight over Michael's hurt feelings about the ball comment.

"He was," I say. "However it has come to light that both Preston Scardoni and Royston Carver were working under Michael and Paris. They all wanted Dynasty for themselves. They wanted control and power over the rest of you and the world, and they worked together to make it happen. Though who knows what would have happened had they been successful. It would have been a shitstorm of power struggles that would have ended with them and the rest of us dead."

Carver stands. "My father and Preston have been held accountable for their part in all of this, and now it's Michael's turn."

"Wait," I say, my sharp glare focusing on Harding. "Tobias King?"

Michael's jaw clenches as he shakes his head. "I had nothing to do with that and neither did Paris."

I hold his glare for a moment and for some damn reason, I believe him. He's been forthcoming with everything else and at this point, there's no reason to lie. He knows he's done for. There's no way in hell he's going to walk out of here alive and he knows it.

Heads nod all around the table as Sebastian Whitman slams his hands down against the hardwood. "Let's vote and get this over with. Our families have been fretting for weeks, absolutely terrified. I'm tired of telling my children that they can't go out and play in their own damn yard in fear of a random shootout." His hand raises high above his head. "I vote for immediate execution. Who is with me?"

Hands begin rising all around the table as Harding watches on with wide eyes, shaking his head in fear. "No," he rushes out as the final hand raises, making it a unanimous decision. "I will do time. I don't want to die. Please, I beg of you. My children need me. My wife ..."

Cruz's father scoffs. "Your wife is better off without you," he says, looking at me with a sharp nod to get this underway.

I look back at Michael with disgust. "He's right. Your wife is better off without you and no matter how much you beg, plead, or pray, you will be dying by my hand today."

Michael slams his bound hands on the table, attempting to make a scene. "No. This is insane. Are we heathens? Barbarians? Fuck that. A court of law would sentence me to prison. Who are you to determine whether I live or die?"

"I'm your leader," I growl, "and this is Dynasty, not a court of law. So don't sit there looking at me like I'm committing some heinous crime against you. You stole my freedom, you stole my safety, and you took it upon yourself to determine whether I was to live or die. An eye for an eye, Harding, and today, the game just turned in my favor."

"NO, I ..."

I look to Grayson, standing ever so still behind his father. "Get him out of here. I will follow in a minute."

Grayson nods and instantly starts moving toward Michael, and as he does, Cruz moves too, reading the situation probably better than us all and knowing that Michael isn't going to go easily.

Michael stands and the men on either side of him grip his arms, holding him still as the boys move around the big table to grab him. He flicks his gaze around the room in a panic, desperately searching for a way out of this, looking for freedom or at the very least an ally, but he won't find one here, not anymore.

Grayson and Cruz finally reach him, and as they start dragging him from the room, Michael looks back at me. "Wait. Wait. Please. The bylaws state that I am entitled to the chance to say goodbye to my family ... my wife. Please."

Grayson pulls on his arm as I look across at Earnest Brooks beside me. "Is that true? Do I have to allow him that?"

Earnest nods and I let out a sigh. "Fine. Your wife will be brought down to your holding cell where she will determine whether she would like the chance to say goodbye after the full situation has been explained to her in exact detail."

Michael's face breaks, making it clear that he hasn't shared any of this bullshit with his wife, but I'm not surprised. How is that conversation even supposed to go? 'Honey, after you pass the butter, do let me share with you how I've been fucking a psychotic bitch for the past twenty years and plotting to overtake the whole organization.'

Yeah, right. What a load of horse shit.

Michael is removed from the room, leaving me with only the heads of Dynasty, and as I look back at them, I let out a deep breath, hating just how hard that was. But with Carver and King's eyes on me, I feel as though I can keep going. "While I have you all here, there are a few more matters that need to be discussed."

"We're all ears, Elodie," Mr. Danforth says with a subtle nod of his head.

I glance around the room, meeting the eyes of every man who sits at my table. "At our last meeting following the death of Tobias King, it was discussed that the local law enforcement was sniffing around places they weren't welcome. I need an update."

Matthew Montgomery stands and meets my stare. "Harding was following this. However, I will assume the responsibility." He pauses and I quickly realize that he's searching for my approval and not having anyone else to dump the shitty jobs on, I nod, just wanting this meeting to be over with so I can go and deal with Harding and put an end to his betrayals. Montgomery continues. "As far as I am aware, the cops are still looking into us. However, there have been no more public nuisances that they can connect back to Dynasty. Their trails are beginning to go cold. Though our inside sources have mentioned whispers of the FBI, so this may not be over yet."

Matthew sits, letting me know that's all he's got on the topic so far.

"Thank you," I say with a small nod, pleasantly surprised that Matthew and I have the ability to exchange words without hostility and a bullshit argument. "Keep me updated on the situation. I want to know every single time one of those cops takes a shit."

"Yes, ma'am."

Ma'am? What the fuck is that bullshit about?

I put it to the back of my head. It's not exactly something I want to decode right now, hell, ever. When men start sucking up, it's either because they want to fuck you or because they want a false sense of trust, and neither of those options are great.

Moving on, I glance at Carver, needing to keep myself focused. "I am sure by now many of you would have noticed both Cruz Danforth and Grayson Beckett in the technology room—"

"They don't have authorization to be down there," Sebastian Whitman calls out, cutting me off.

My gaze snaps to his. "They do now," I spit, not liking his tone one bit. "They have been given my authority to use Dynasty technology to search and locate the many victims that were listed in Sam Delacourt's ledger. They will be putting in the hours to find them and using our resources to perform rescue missions to save them and bring them back home to their families where they belong."

Mr. Danforth shakes his head. "I'm sorry, Elodie. I understand that this means a great deal to you considering your own experiences, and I really do wish that there was a way that we could all help. It is a great cause and I stand by that mentality, but Dynasty doesn't operate like that. We cannot approve that reckless use of our resources. What comes next? Where does it end? Are we busting local teen drug dealers and breaking up wild parties with noise complaints? We have police and FBI for a reason. Let them do their job and we will do ours."

I lean back in my seat, watching Cruz's father, and only now realize just how far the apple fell from the tree. "I'm sorry," I say, not looking away for even a second. "I wasn't looking for approval. Filling you in on our plans was a courtesy, not a question. Dynasty is going to be on the right side of history, and I suggest that you all get on board with that."

His eyes narrow, and it's more than clear that he doesn't approve of my authority on this, but he doesn't have a leg to stand on, nor is he willing to speak up about it again and risk ending up on my shit list. After all, people on my shit list have a way of ending up in shallow graves.

Harlen Beckett shifts in his seat. "Was that all for tonight?"

I let out a sigh. I had wanted to discuss the empty seats at the table and what's going to happen to them, but after everything else that's gone down today, I just want to go and get back in my bed ... or at least one of the guys' beds seeing as though my room needs to be torched after Sara destroyed it.

With the eyes of every man in the room on me, I nod. "Yes, that is all," I tell them. "We will schedule another meeting once we know a little more on the Paris situation. You may all be excused."

And just like that, the meeting is over and the heads of Dynasty quickly make their way out of the room, leaving me with King and Carver, both staring at me with a heaviness that quickly weighs down on my shoulders.

I've played the role of judge and jury tonight and now all that's left is to become the executioner.

24

B rynn Harding's hand slaps across her husband's face with such ferocity that his head whips back under the pressure. She spits at his feet and growls, her heart breaking before my eyes. "Don't be fooled, you sick son of a bitch. I will not mourn you, I will spit on your lonely grave, and my children will never remember your name. You're nothing to me, not anymore. It was all a lie. Fifteen years of marriage and this is how you repay me."

"Brynn—"

"Don't," she growls, holding her hand up to cut him off. "Everything we worked for, everything we built is all gone. Dynasty owns me, my home, our money. It's all theirs, and without you as the head of our family, I have nothing. You've destroyed me. Our children won't be able to afford to eat, won't have clothes on their backs. You did this. You took from me and you stole from your children. I hate you, Michael Harding, and I hope you rot in the deepest pits of hell."

"Dynasty will provide for you. The children will be okay. You can't run. You have to stay and keep fighting for what we believe in. You're all I've got in this world. Stand with Paris," Michael urges her. "She will be generous to my family for everything I have done for her."

Brynn's eyes bug out of her head, horrified by the suggestion of having anything to do with her husband's mistress. "Do you honestly think I can stay here after what you have done? You have disgraced my name. You have embarrassed me. What am I supposed to do now?"

"I have money hidden in the safe. You can have that."

Brynn steps up to her husband, tears fresh in her eyes. "I will make it on my own without your dirty money. I don't want it." She holds up her hand and rips her wedding rings right off her fingers before throwing them at him, though if it was me, I would have kept them to pawn for cash. "Screw you and screw this marriage."

Brynn turns and steps toward the door with her head held high, and as I watch her move, I see nothing but pure embarrassment, pain, and devastation in her eyes. She was completely blindsided by this. She had absolutely no idea and now she's left with nothing.

I didn't realize that each family's wealth is dependent upon Dynasty and the urge to look out for her pulses through me, but I can't think about that yet. I have a job to do.

I stand beside the open door, leaning against the wall and watching as Michael hangs by his cuffs above his head. He looks broken. His wife's words have cut him deeper than I ever could and that's all the satisfaction I need.

Brynn approaches the door, and in the final seconds before walking out of Michael's cell, her gaze flicks to mine. "Make it hurt," she begs, and then with one final step, she's out the door and released from the hold of her husband. Though something tells me that he's not the only one who will never see her again. As far as I can tell, Brynn Harding is taking her children and fucking right off out of here, away from her husband's stain and embarrassment.

I wait a moment, just staring at the man who has had a hand in numerous attacks against me over the few short months since my eighteenth birthday. The gun weighs heavily in my hand, but even heavier on my mind knowing what it is that I have to do.

At one stage, I thought ending a man's life was getting easier, but I was wrong. How could this ever be easy? No matter how many times I have to pull a trigger, and how great the relief is afterward, it will never be something that I can do without feeling it deep in my chest.

I'm a murderer. I'm something I never thought I would be. Dynasty has taken my innocence and corrupted it until it's something that I don't even recognize anymore, but this is me, and this is who I am, who I will forever be.

A hand falls to my shoulder and squeezes and I suck in a surprised gasp. "Let me," Carver says, his other hand twining around mine as he attempts to take the gun from me.

I look up and meet his heavy stare, knowing that he'd do anything to take the burden off my shoulders, but I have to do this. The burden is mine.

I tighten my grip on the gun and shake my head. "No. I will do it."

"Are you sure?"

I take a shaky breath and position myself in front of Michael who instantly bucks against his binds, pulling and pushing, desperately trying to get free and save himself. I raise my hand, the gun pointing right between his eyes.

My hand is steady despite the fear that rattles deep inside me.

As if sensing my unease, Carver steps in behind me, and just as he did with Sam Delacourt, he positions my aim, making sure I won't miss.

With his chest pressed against my back and his other hand on my hip, I let out another breath. Then with fire burning in my stomach and determination pulsing through my veins, I pull the trigger and send a bullet square between Harding's eyes, evening the score.

Come and get me, Paris. I'm ready.

25

Grayson's fingers trail up and down my back soothing every nerve within my body as I stare up at my bedroom ceiling. Apparently having both Cruz and Grayson lying in my bed is enough to mask the taint that Sara left in my room, because damn, lying here between them both with their hands grazing along my body has me forgetting that she even exists.

Well … with the pills the psych ward is giving her, I bet she doesn't even remember that she exists.

"Do you think they're alright?" I ask the boys, referring to King and Carver, who elected to stay behind in the cells and clean up the mess created by my bullet shooting through the center of Michael Harding's brain.

"They're fine," Cruz says, tightening his grip on my hip. "It's not the first time they've had to clean brains off the back wall of a holding cell, and it won't be the last."

"Do I even want to know?"

Grayson laughs. "Most chicks would say no, but you'd probably get turned on."

My brows furrow and I raise my head off his chest to meet his eyes. "Umm … what?"

Cruz laughs, moving his hand from my hip to gently smack my ass as Grayson continues. "Carver slammed some fuckwit against the wall so hard that he shattered his skull and smeared brains all over it."

My brows instantly fly back up. "You're fucking with me," I say, watching him through a wide, shocked stare.

"Wish I was," Grayson says, his lips pulling into a sexy as fuck smirk.

Cruz pulls me back, pressing himself up against me. "In Carver's defense, the dude was really fucked in the head, even more so than you," he teases.

I laugh. "Not possible. No one is more fucked in the head than me."

Grayson grabs me right back and rolls right on top of me, bracing himself against his elbows so he doesn't crush me or touch my abdomen. "Ain't that the truth," he murmurs, his eyes sparkling with laughter.

"Get off her," Cruz grumbles, shoving his hand into Grayson's shoulder and all but throwing him off me, making him land beside me on the bed with a heavy thump.

I look back at Cruz with a wicked grin stretching across my face. "What's the matter?" I tease. "Jealous?"

Cruz just laughs, scooping me back into his arms and pulling me in against his chest once again. "You're damn right, I am."

He nuzzles his face into my neck and presses the softest kisses along my skin, making warmth and happiness spread through me like wildfire. I glance up to find Grayson watching me with nothing but adoration on his face, and I can't help but grab him and pull him in.

He's far too heavy for me to be able to drag him across the bed in the same way that the guys are constantly doing to me, but he reads my body language as easily as he reads a book. He shuffles in, sandwiching me in between both of their strong chests. I don't waste a single second and raise my chin, bringing my lips to his in a hungry, sensual kiss.

He melts into me, and even though we've done this plenty of times, I will never get used to just how good it feels. Grayson kisses me back, treating me as though I'm an angel sent from heaven just for him … and all of his friends.

Cruz picks up on the energy I'm putting down, and his hands instantly move over my body again, sending me into a world of blissful, erotic happiness. How could life ever get better? You know, apart from the healing stab wound below my last rib and the crazy psycho killer that wears my mother's face and wants me dead.

I feel Grayson's monster cock waking up and hardening against my thigh and I grin. The boys have vowed to take it easy with me while I'm healing, but I don't think that either of them are going to be able to resist right now. When it's one on one, that's about sharing a private, intimate moment together with all the feels, growing as a couple, but when there's three of us, that's a party, and who can resist a party?

Cruz's hand slips over my hip and trails down to my pussy just as my ass presses back against him, feeling him there. He groans low and I let out a needy sigh, the sound of his desperation enough to have my core drenched with readiness.

His hand slips into the front of my sweatpants and I feel his grin against my neck as he realizes that I'm not wearing any panties. He doesn't waste any time.

Cruz's fingers instantly find my clit, trailing over it and teasing me with everything they can do. They keep traveling down, mixing with my wetness and spreading it around, making my eyes roll into the back of my head.

I groan into Grayson's mouth and as I pull back to breathe, his fingers find my hip and slip under my tank, brushing ever so softly over my skin and sending goosebumps soaring over my body. He drags my tank up until it's completely gone.

Grayson ducks his head, sucking my nipple into his mouth and tormenting me as his tongue flicks over the tight bud. "Oh, fuck," I breathe, turning my head back and begging Cruz to kiss me as the need becomes almost too much.

He doesn't disappoint, and within seconds, his tongue is battling with mine for dominance.

Needing them to feel as alive as I do, I slip my hands into the front of both of their pants, curling my fingers around their impressive cocks. Grayson groans and as my thumb brushes over his tip and feels his metal piercing, his whole body flinches, wanting so much more.

"Fuck, babe," Cruz murmurs against my lips as his fingers press against my clit, making everything inside of me burn with a fierce desperation. "I gotta feel that tight pussy squeezing my cock."

Fucking hell. Yes, please.

I smile against his lips. "Only if you promise not to hold back."

Cruz groans, knowing that he could possibly hurt me, but I'm sturdy. I've survived against all odds, so at this point, I doubt that I'm going to suffer death by cock. Though if I had to choose a way to go, that's definitely at the top of my list.

His eyes sparkle with excitement as he pulls his hand out from my sweatpants, grips the waistband, and shuffles it down my legs.

Within moments, I'm lying between two of my favorite people in the world, more than ready for them to rock my world.

I pull my knee up over Grayson's hip and Cruz reaches in behind me. I feel his cock right at my entrance, and as he slowly pushes into me, I suck in a breath. He fills me completely, stretching my walls and making me feel more alive than ever.

"Fuck," I breathe, my pussy clenching around him and making him groan low in my ear. "You need to start moving."

He doesn't hesitate, pulling back out, painfully slow and making my eyes flutter with the overwhelming pleasure. He pushes back into me, faster this time, sending himself even deeper. "Oh, shit. Yes, give it to me, Cruz. Right there."

Cruz's lips come back to my neck as he starts to really work my pussy, and without missing a beat, my hand curls tighter around Grayson's monster cock.

He pulls back just a little and looks down at my weeping pussy, watching as his friend pushes deep inside of me, his cock glistening with my wetness and making me feel more desired than ever before.

Grayson's cock flinches in my hand as his eyes burn with need, loving what he's seeing. His hand comes down over mine, squeezing even tighter as he becomes mesmerized by watching his best friend fuck his girl.

"Grayson," I beg, desperately needing his eyes on mine. He reluctantly pulls his gaze away from my pussy, and as he meets my stare, my tongue rolls over my bottom lip. "I need you to fuck my mouth."

I feel the vibration through his chest as he growls his appreciation. He instantly adjusts himself on my bed and I raise myself up onto my elbow until his beautiful, pierced cock is right there, ready for the taking.

I lick my lips, the hunger showing brightly in my eyes.

Grayson curls his hand around the back of my head, collecting my hair in his tight grip until he's holding me close with complete control of my head. "Open up, Ellie."

Fuck, yes.

I open wide for him and swallow a gasp as my lips close around his giant cock. I instantly feel his piercing at the back of my throat and I take him deeper, because fuck, why the hell not? A guy like Grayson deserves the best a girl can give. Shit, all the guys do, even Carver.

With his cock being so big, I have no choice but to grip it and work him with my hand at the same time. My tongue roams over his tip and each time I feel him at the back of my throat, I push myself further, prepared to choke on his dick if that's what this bitch has to do.

Grayson's grip tightens in my hair, moving me up and down and taking control of just how fast I take him. Cruz grips my hips, holding the rest of me still so he can plow into me over and over again, and with my other hand free, I slip it between my legs and show them exactly how I like to touch myself. Though, by this point, I'm pretty damn sure that they know exactly how I like to be touched. Hell, they do it better than I could ever do it myself.

Grayson's other hand trails down my body and pinches my nipple, sending an electric current pulsing through me and making my pussy clench, which only has Cruz groaning behind me. He leans into me and gently bites my shoulder as I drown in the feel of him moving in and out of me, giving me everything he's got. He pushes deeper, hitting the places deep inside of me that only King, Grayson and Cruz know exist.

Grayson's cock flinches in my mouth and I look up and meet his eyes only to see the pure desperation burning beneath the surface. He needs to come, but not yet. We've only just got started.

Just to tease him, I flick my tongue over his tip and watch as he groans. Every muscle in his body clenches as he holds onto it, probably thinking of old grannies on their back just to keep from blowing his load.

I grin as he shakes his head, gripping my hair even tighter, stopping my movements. Instead, he fucks my mouth, moving into me and making my eyes begin to water as he hits the back of my throat, but damn it, that look in his eyes … holy hell.

My fingers move faster over my clit and I clench down around Cruz, feeling that familiar sensation building deep within me. Maybe Grayson was right. Maybe we're not just getting started. Maybe they're going to make me come hard and fast. Fuck, either way it'll be worth it.

"Aww fuck, Winter," Cruz grumbles against my skin, his fingers digging into my hip. "Squeeze me any tighter and you're going to make me come."

Oooh, I like the sound of that.

I press my ass back into him, taking him at a new angle and squeezing as fucking tight as I possibly can, moaning against Grayson's cock and making the both of them growl deep in the back of their throats as my fingers work tirelessly over my clit.

Grayson clenches his jaw. "I'm going to come in that pretty little mouth," he warns me through his teeth, and if my mouth wasn't so full, I'd be begging him to hurry up. I'd give anything to feel him come in my mouth and taste him as his warm cum travels down my throat.

I put my tongue to work, pushing back against Cruz and taking everything they've got. They both speed up. Grayson goes deeper down my throat as Cruz picks up his pace, slamming into me over and over with brutal precision.

My pussy clenches and screams for more.

I moan around Grayson's cock, feeling him holding on and waiting for me to go first, but he doesn't need to worry, I'm almost there.

Just a little while longer.

It builds and builds, the pressure almost becoming too much as my fingers furiously rub tight little circles over my needy clit. "Fuck,

Winter," Cruz pants, his tone dominant and full of authority. "Give it to me. Let me feel you come."

His words shatter me and my orgasm takes over, exploding around me until I'm seeing stars. I'd give anything to scream out, to cry, or to curse. But Grayson is there, fucking my mouth until he comes hard, shooting that delicious seed right into the back of my throat and groaning loudly, the satisfaction clear in his tone.

"Oh, fuck," Cruz roars, his fingers digging into my hip as he comes undone inside of me. His fingers are bruising but in the best damn way, and when his hand comes down and spanks my ass, everything clenches again, keeping me going.

My orgasm rapidly pulses through me, reaching every little nerve ending in my body. My eyes clench, my head tips back, my toes curl, and my pussy convulses like never before. "Holy shit," I breathe after Grayson pulls out of my mouth, slowly coming down from my high, only to feel it continuing when Cruz's hand slips around my body and lightly brushes over my clit.

"Yeah," King grunts from the doorway with Carver standing right beside him, both of them looking in with interest. "It seems we missed the fun."

Carver rolls his eyes, pretending that he isn't at least a little bit curious about what just went down in here. "I'm out."

"No," I call out, a slight hint of hysteria in my tone that doesn't just surprise me but surprises us all. "Just … wait. There's something that's been bugging me the last few days."

Carver stops and returns to King's side, narrowing his eyes at me as

Cruz and Grayson pull their pants back on. "Like what?" he grumbles, watching me closely, keeping his eyes on mine and skillfully avoiding the rest of my naked body as I adjust myself on my bed, trying to sit up and pull the blanket up to cover my tits without showing them how much it actually hurts.

I instantly feel gravity doing its thing as Cruz starts leaking out of me and judging by the wicked grin that settles across his face, he knows exactly what's happening. I ignore his stupid grin and glance around at the boys narrowing my gaze, particularly on Grayson. "You guys have been lying to me."

King straightens, pushing himself off the doorframe and glaring right back at me. "Bullshit. What have we lied about?"

"I ... I don't exactly know," I say with a slight cringe. "But something isn't adding up."

"Like what?" Cruz asks.

My tongue rolls over my lips and I still taste Grayson there. "You guys aren't eighteen," I accuse. "All this time I thought we were all the same age because we were seniors together, but we're not, are we? You're all older."

All of their eyes start doing the weird shifty thing where they look at one another, having a silent conversation and trying to work out who the fuck is going to straighten this one out, and today, it's Grayson who draws the short straw. "Why do you say that?"

I give him a hard stare, hating that he wants to try to play the field first instead of coming out with a straight answer. "Because no eighteen-year-old has medical training, and when I was cramped in the back of

Carver's Escalade going to my parents' mountain property, Cruz was whining about his stupid blanket and you made a comment about him being nearly twenty ... so, what am I supposed to say? Gotcha?"

The boys keep going with their shifty eyes, each of them looking a little more guilty than before. "Okay, yeah," Grayson says slowly, a slight cringe playing on his lips as he realizes there is no way around this. "We're all a little older. I'm twenty-two. I did a year of medical training after I graduated high school, Carver was twenty-one the month before you got here, King is twenty and Cruz ... well, clearly you know Cruz will be twenty soon."

King scoffs shaking his head as he looks at Grayson. "Really, man? After all these years, you're still forgetting my birthday?" He looks across my room, meeting my hard stare. "Just for the record, my birthday was a month before Carver's. I'm twenty-one."

I shake my head. "I don't care how old you guys are. I want to know why the hell you've lied about it for so long."

Cruz shrugs his shoulders. "Technically, we haven't lied about it. You never specifically asked how old we were. If you wanted to know, we would have told you at any time."

I adjust my blanket, pulling it tighter around my body. "You let me think you were all graduating high school with me. You might not have technically lied, but you did when you let me believe that you were in school with me. Like what the fuck was that? Were you just in school to keep an eye on me?"

Carver nods. "Pretty much," he says with a bored shrug. "We started 'school' at the beginning of the year so we could learn the layout and get familiar with everything for security reasons. To all the other students we just looked like four new transfers at the start of senior year. We knew every inch of that school. Fuck, I bet these guys even know that school better than they know every inch of your body."

My cheeks flush the brightest shade of red as Cruz smirks. "Nah, fuck the school. I don't know anything better than your body."

Holy shit. These guys.

I give myself a second to cool down before getting back on track. "You guys went to graduation and even had the principal reward you with a certificate, like come on."

King just laughs. "It was far too late in the game to give up the act. All the other students thought we were graduating. It would be fishy as fuck if we showed up to watch you graduate and not get a certificate ourselves, and with the entire Ravenwood Heights police department sniffing around, we couldn't afford that kind of attention."

King's comment pulls at a memory of Ember standing before me on my first day at Ravenwood Heights Academy, telling me how she has been crushing on them for years, how she's been watching them around the school since she was a freshman, and how the whole school has been trying to decode the secrets of Dynasty. But that doesn't add up. How could she have been crushing on them for years if they only showed up at the school a few months ago? And since being here, Ember is the only person who's even whispered the name Dynasty to me ... apart from the boys of course.

Someone's lying to me and I don't think it's the boys, but why?

I let out a heavy sigh and stare at them all, my mind beginning to whirl. I'm not ready to question them about Ember, that's too raw and I want to be sure before I go accusing her of anything, but what am I even accusing her of? I don't know.

Not wanting the guys to see that something is bugging me, I force a smile. "So, I've been screwing a bunch of old fuckers."

Cruz laughs and scoops my tank off the floor. "Get dressed and go to sleep. It's been a long as fuck day. Besides, you're never going to heal if you keep letting us assholes fuck you into oblivion."

I roll my eyes and go to pull my tank over my head, but as the blanket falls to my waist, I don't miss the way that Carver's gaze drops to my tits with a need that nearly knocks me the fuck away.

"Well what are you waiting for? Get out of here and give a girl some privacy," I grumble to all four of them, sliding down in my bed and letting my head crash onto the pillow. "If you need help with your hearing aids just let me know."

The guys walk away, scoffing and laughing to themselves, and when a soft "Night, Winter," sounds through the room, I raise my head off the pillow and look back toward the door to find King standing there with his fingers resting over the light switch. "Love you."

Warmth fills my chest, and as I look back at him, taking in the adoration shining through his ocean eyes, I realize just how right this is. It's pure, unrelenting, and absolutely everything. I will never find this kind of deep, unfiltered connection with anyone.

I love him.

I love him so deeply, and honestly, I'm not just in love with him— I'm in love with all of them, even Carver. And that realization has something waking up inside of me. I've been fighting it this whole time, but right from the start it's been there, building and building until I couldn't possibly deny it anymore, and now that I know, all I want to do is scream it from every damn rooftop, but for now, I'll settle with just telling King because he deserves to know what's in my heart.

"You know what?" I murmur, watching as his eyes fill with curiosity. "I love you too."

A soft smile spreads across his face and before he gets a chance to get all emotional about it, he flips the switch for the light, sending the room into darkness. There's silence for a second before I feel his lips pressing against mine and his warm body sliding into bed beside me.

His arms wrap around my body, and as he pulls me in against his chest, I feel his soft breath hitting my skin. "It's about damn time you figured it out."

26

Cardi B's *'Bodak Yellow'* blasts through my bathroom as I shake my ass under the hot stream of water that shoots from my shower. My hairbrush rests in my hand, my grip firm around the handle as I recite every damn lyric, spewing the words like they're gospel, and fuck it, they are. I don't think I've ever heard a song that speaks so directly to my soul.

I finished all the important showering things nearly an hour ago, but I'm still here rocking out, because why the hell not? I'm feeling good. It's been a shitty few months, but last night's realization of being in love with the boys has overshadowed all the bullshit and is shining so much brighter than anything else ever could. Even realizing that

Ember, the girl who's supposed to be my best friend has been lying to me about the boys. It doesn't make sense and I'm determined to get to the bottom of it, but not now. Right now, it's time to shake my ass and pretend that outside of these shower doors the world isn't falling apart around me.

My fingers went pruney ages ago, but I don't care. I'm content here in my little box of hot water and steam, though, it would be better if one of the guys would come and join me. I bet they'll be down for my dance moves, and if they're not, I'm sure I can figure out something else to do that might be a little more their speed.

Actually, scrap that, I'll accept a visit from King, Cruz, and Grayson, but not Carver. We're not there yet, not even close. He would just stand there and judge me with his brows furrowed and his lips all scrunched up, trying to make out that I was the weird one in the room.

As the days go by and we get past death threats and close calls, Carver and I become closer and closer as the hostility between us begins to fade. It's as though we're standing in an empty room, each of us at opposite ends, standing as far away from each other as possible with the walls slowly caving in, forcing us together. It's scary as hell, but I think I like it.

Carver and I would be electrifying. Just having his fingers inside of me down in his father's little dungeon after ending Sam Delacourt was more than mind blowing. Would it be better than what it is with the others? I don't know but I'm more than willing to find out.

The thought of all the different ways that Carver could get me off start swirling through my mind, and before I know it, that familiar desperation is building within me. My pussy clenches with need, and not being one to skip out on a good opportunity, my gaze shifts up toward the showerhead.

Damnnnn… it would be so easy.

The boys haven't come to check on me in over an hour, so they're either busy or just trying to give me a little bit of privacy to shower. Who am I kidding? The boys don't understand the word privacy. Though, even if I was going to town on myself with the showerhead and they walked in, who cares? It's not like they've never seen me getting off before. If anything, they'd probably sit back and watch. Well, Grayson would. He appreciates art, whereas King and Cruz are all about getting in on the action.

A grin rips across my face. Decision made.

I reach up and unhook the showerhead from its little holder and look over it, seeing that it has a few different settings. I glance over the one labelled as 'massage' and quickly push the little button. The water shoots out in a narrow stream and I swear, it even looks as though it's pulsating.

Well, damn.

My gaze nervously flicks toward the door, making sure that I'm not about to have one of the boys barge in on me. I'm no prude, my bedside drawer is proof of that, but if I'm experimenting with something new, then I like to make sure that I have the hang of it before inviting friends to play.

I turn down the heat, not wanting to burn my kitty and slowly lower the showerhead down my body as an excited thrill shoots through me.

I bite my bottom lip, the anticipation almost too much.

It trails over my ribs, down past my belly button, and then BAM, it hits my clit with a firm, relentless pulsation. I suck in a gasp, my eyes widening in surprise. "Holy fuck."

Wowza. How have I never tried this before?

I get myself in a better position and instantly start laughing at just how good this is. My eyes roll into the back of my head and my pussy quickly starts begging for a release. It's so fast and strong. Every nerve in my body is telling me to pull away, to ease up and take my time while my pussy is begging for it hard and fast.

I don't think I've ever experienced something like this. It's like going from zero to one hundred in a flick of a finger. Hell, screw hiding this from the boys. This thing is a party trick. I need to get them up here stat and show them just how magical this thing is.

Who would have ever known that I'd become instant best friends with a showerhead?

The water pulsates over my clit, relentlessly forcing my pussy into submission. I fall back against the wall, unable to hold myself up as I spread my legs as far as I possibly can. My orgasm builds and I know that it will only be a matter of time before it tears through me and shatters me from the inside out.

Hell, I'm going to need a few hours of sleep after this.

The music cuts off and a chilling voice echoes through my bathroom. "Fucking hell. I knew you were a whore, but I never expected this."

The showerhead drops from my hand, spraying up the side of the shower as my head snaps up, my heart racing for a whole new reason.

Paris Moustaff stands in my bathroom doorway, a knife in her hand and disgust stretched across her face.

I gape, unable to think of what to do. I'm standing here naked as the day I was born with my legs spread, my pussy wound up and right on the edge while the spray from the showerhead is pointed up towards the ceiling and is currently redecorating my bathroom.

What do I do?

My only option is to run, but I can't get through the door without passing her. I'm going to have to beat her ass, but how? I have no weapons, no formal training, and an abdomen full of stitches, while she comes fully prepared. I don't even have my brass knuckles. I took the fucking things off thinking that I'd be safe in the shower.

Where the fuck are the boys? A second ago, I was more than happy that they hadn't been up here to check on me, but I take it all back. An hour is a long time for them not to at least walk by. Something has to be wrong.

I have to make a break for it.

Seeing the resolve in my eyes, Paris straightens in the doorway, her hand gripping the knife even tighter. She takes a step deeper into the bathroom and my chance at getting out of here quickly begins to dwindle.

I run.

I barge out of the shower, throwing the door open so hard that it shatters against the wall and breaks into a million pieces. My feet slam down against the broken glass, flying out of here with a desperation that makes me feel as though I'm running much slower than I need to be going.

Paris' eyes shimmer with excitement, and I can't help but wonder if this is what she wanted. Does she get off on the chase? Does she like being the one in control who gets to sit back and watch everyone around her shitting themselves out of fear?

She's fucking deranged.

I throw my hands up and try to shove her out of my way. The only shot I've got at freedom is getting through this bathroom door and out of my bedroom. From there, she's got nothing. I might have a stab wound in my abdomen, but youth is on my side. I might not be a great fighter or clever enough to outsmart her, but I've been running my whole life. Running from predators, running from foster homes, running from assholes with bad intentions. If I can outrun them, I can outrun this bitch.

My hands slam against her chest and narrowly miss the sharp tip of her blade before her hands fist in my hair and she pulls hard. My feet fall out from under me and she quickly drags me through the glass. "Not today, bitch. We're seeing this through once and for all."

I scream as she threatens to tear my hair right from my scalp. Hell, I wouldn't put it past her. She's that fucking crazy. "CARVER," I yell, knowing that he'd be the first one up the stairs, not because the others don't care enough but because he's simply the fastest. "CARVER. HELP!"

I fight against Paris' hold on my hair as she shamelessly drags me through the bathroom and back into my bedroom. A deep, howling laugh tears out of her as I scramble on the floor, desperate for freedom. "Scream all you want, but they're not coming. It's just you and me, Princess."

I kick my legs and my right foot slams right into the center of her back but she doesn't let up, only laughs louder. "What did you do?" I growl, grabbing hold of her hand over my hair and trying to pry it free. "Where are the boys?"

"What does it matter?" she says, dragging me toward a chair that's been placed in the center of my bedroom. She pulls with everything she's got, hauling me across the carpet like a sack of shit and burning my skin. "You'll be dead by the time I'm through with you."

Like hell. I kick harder, ignoring the pain in my abdomen and the burning from where she pulls my hair. "WHERE ARE THEY?" My growl is deep and authoritative. It instantly burns my throat, but I push through it, determined not to give up. I will not be dying here today. I need to make sure the boys are okay.

Paris just laughs and adjusts her hold on me until the knife is at my throat. "On the chair, now."

"Fuck you."

The blade presses harder and despite my need to fight her every step of the way, if she gets bored of her little, twisted game and slices through my throat, I'm done for and I'll never get the chance to make sure the guys are alright.

I pull myself up off the ground and slam my naked ass back into the chair with a deep scowl. I watch her every movement as she grabs a belt and fastens it around my arms, chest, and the back of the chair.

She pulls it tight—too fucking tight that it squishes my tits and is bound to leave a mark.

I suck in a shallow breath, unable to take anything deeper as I try to reach for her, desperately wishing that I could rip that smirk right off her face.

How am I related to this bitch? I know I have my moments of insanity, but fuck. Is this chick for real? She takes crazy to a whole new level. It's as though she saw how fucked Sara was in the head and saw it as a challenge rather than a warning.

Once I'm completely bound and unable to move, Paris takes a step back and surveys her handiwork with a sick, twisted grin. She holds the knife in one hand and presses her finger to the tip, spinning it like it's some kind of cheap toy rather than a deadly weapon that she intends to stab right through my chest.

"You've been more trouble than you're worth, girl," she spits, looking at me as though I'm nothing but trash that got stuck to the bottom of her foot. "But don't worry, momma is going to take real good care of you."

I pull at the belt and she flinches. "Drop the fucking act, Paris. I know you're not my mother. Everyone fucking knows. You're done. Kill me all you want but you will never get Dynasty. Your bitch ass plan to take me out and claim my mother's identity is never going to work. Your game is over. They all know. Everyone fucking knows. You're done."

Her eyes widen and they start flickering round the room in a panic. Silence overtakes her and she starts pacing back and forth in front of me, clearly trying to figure out her next move.

"Just tell me what you did to the boys and I'll let you walk out of here unscathed."

Her glare shoots back to me as though only just remembering that I'm in the room. "UNSCATHED?" she wails, jumping at me with her knife outstretched, dragging it in a shallow arc across to the top of my shoulder. "You're in no position to make demands, especially because you're lying. If everyone knew, I would know."

I laugh, desperately attempting to mask the sharp stinging coming from my shoulder. "How? Because you've got Michael Harding wrapped around your crazy little finger?" Her eyes go wide and she gapes at me. "Yeah, that's right. We know all about your little affair with Harding, and so does his wife, but don't worry, we took care of those loose strings for you."

Her face reddens with anger and she rushes into me, throwing the knife down and grabbing my throat with both hands, squeezing it tight. "What did you do? Where's Michael?"

Her grip on my throat is bruising and I don't even bother trying to respond knowing that any attempt to talk is only going to make it hurt more and waste what little oxygen I have left, so instead, I just smile, loving the way her eyes go wild with irritation.

She shakes me. "ANSWER ME. WHERE'S MICHAEL? WHAT DID YOU DO TO HIM, YOU LITTLE BITCH?" Realizing that I'm not about to answer with her hands wrapped around my throat she releases me and scrambles for her knife.

I suck in a deep breath, hating that although she's released me, I can still feel her fingers wrapped around my throat, bruising and squeezing, and instead of crying about it, I just smile up at her, knowing that no matter how I spin it from here, I'm fucked. The boys aren't coming and she's far too unhinged to see reason.

"Your little game is unravelling faster than my bullet tore through his brain."

Fury ripples in her gaze and her breath comes in short, fast gasps that get louder and louder by the second. She's only moments away from losing her shit, but I'm not nearly done. I'm only just getting started.

"You should have seen how quickly Dynasty voted for his death, how quickly his wife abandoned him, and how quickly he fell. You have no one to blame but yourself, Paris. You're a joke. You're just a jealous bitch who wished that she had what my mother had. Are you so pathetic that instead of making a name for yourself, you need to steal hers? I didn't even get a chance to know her, but without question, I know that she's twice the woman you always wanted to be and more. You're nothing, and although I know you won't leave this house without ending my life, just know that the boys will never stop hunting you. They will make you wish that you never even heard the name Elodie Ravenwood."

Paris just stares at me, her eyes as wide as saucers and her short shallow breaths almost terrifying, and like a switch being flipped, she loses it.

Paris runs at me, her high-pitched battle cry deafening me as she races toward me with her knife. It slams down, impaling the chair right beside my thigh, her crazed, messed up head fucking with her aim. She yanks it out hard. "London Ravenwood was a bitch," she squeals, attempting to stab me again, but as she comes down at me, I push off the ground and send the chair toppling to the side, crashing down with a hard thump.

The leg of the chair catches her right in the center of her chest and she screams out in pain, but I don't dare miss my shot. I kick out as hard as I can, catching her in the chest again and sending her crashing back against my dresser.

The whole dresser rocks under her weight and she rights herself, but I don't doubt that she's in pain. The little knobs on the dresser would have slammed right into her back, and the shrieking squeal is proof of that—music to my ears.

Paris stares at me as though I'm just as crazy as she is, but in reality, I'm crazier. Only today, I'm doing a better job of concealing it, but if she keeps fucking with me and trying to hurt my people, then she's going to see just how fucking crazy I can be. Consider me a selfless person because right now, I'm sharing the spotlight and allowing this bitch the chance to shine.

She makes her way toward me, and the determination in her eyes tells me that this is it. She won't miss her next swing. She's going to make it count, for herself, for Harding, and for her bullshit plan that died and crumbled the second I discovered who she was.

She wants to send me right to the deepest pits of hell to burn and rot with the likes of those I've sent before me. But I won't allow it to happen, not yet. I've been building a list of enemies and one by one,

I've been crossing them off my list and proving to the bastards around me that I'm not someone they want to fuck with, and soon enough, Paris Moustaff is going to learn that lesson the hard way.

Paris takes another step just as a low, ferocious growl comes from the doorway. "Get the fuck away from her." While the tone is filled with rage, guilt, and a definite lethality, it's the sweetest sound I've ever heard.

Paris whips around to find Grayson looming toward her and the fury in his eyes even has my bones shaking with fear, though something isn't right. With each step he takes, he wobbles. His feet don't want to move and when they do, they don't take him in a straight line—he zig zags.

But his eyes ... fuck.

Paris instantly inches back, her wide gaze locked on Grayson's. But as she backs up, she puts herself closer to me, which only serves to piss Grayson off more. Though right now, the way his eyes are glazed over and the way he trips over his own damn feet, I'd prefer her closer to me with that knife. If he gets hurt trying to save me ...

He stumbles and catches himself against the dresser that Paris had only just stepped away from, and the fear that rattles me is like nothing I've ever felt before. I'm not going to lie, when it was just me and her, I was scared, but now that Grayson's involved in this vulnerable state—I'm terrified.

"GRAYSON," I call, realizing that he's either severely concussed or fighting the effects of some hard drugs and in desperate need of motivation to keep himself going, to keep fighting the effects of whatever the hell she did to him.

His eyes flick to mine and the second they move off course, he tumbles again, having to catch himself against the bed.

Paris keeps backing up, but she adjusts the knife in her hand. "You can't save her," she spits, making Grayson's eyes fly back to hers as she raises her chin, trying to act as though she's in control. "Look at yourself. You can't even walk in a straight line."

"Straight lines are overrated."

And just like that, he jumps at her.

Grayson all but flies across the room, rapidly closing the gap between them. Paris squeals. She may have a knife but that's nothing compared to the strength and weight that Grayson packs. She tries to scramble as his arms close around her and as they lose their balance, they begin to fall toward me.

Paris pushes hard and Grayson goes crashing down over my legs, crushing the wooden chair and my legs beneath his weight as he desperately tries to cling onto her. The chair breaks into little pieces, freeing my arms, but with Grayson's chest weighing down my legs, I'm still trapped.

Paris lands right beside me, slamming down on her ass and she instantly starts using her feet to push him away. The knife is nowhere to be seen, and as I try to reach for her, she gets herself out from under him and scrambles back until she's against the wall.

Paris flies to her feet and I watch as panic surges through her wild stare, trying to figure out if she should take Grayson out and kill me, or if she should bail and try again another day. Resolve flickers through her eyes and she curses before grabbing the windowsill and launching herself out onto the second story roof.

"NOOOO," I cry out, trying to wriggle free from under Grayson, knowing it could be ages before we get another chance at her again.

Grayson groans just as I get my feet out from under him, cutting my leg against the splintered wood of the chair. I scramble to my feet and fly to the window, looking out just in time to watch Paris jumping down from the second story of my home and dropping into the manicured lawn below.

Every bone in my body tells me to throw myself out the window and chase after her, but with the boys unaccounted for and possibly hurt, I won't be going anywhere. Not until I know they're okay.

"You're a piece of shit, Paris Moustaff," I yell after her, gripping the windowsill as anger bubbles within me. "Don't be fooled, I will find you, and when I do, you're going to wish that you were already dead."

Paris looks back at me with a wicked smirk, knowing that with the boys unaccounted for, I won't be going after her. "We'll see about that," she calls back, and just like that, she disappears into the bushes, leaving me in a furious rage.

"FUCK," I yell, swiping my hand out over the top of my desk and watching as everything goes flying off and crashing to the ground.

"We'll get her," Grayson promises, his face all scrunched up in pain as he tries to get to his knees.

I rush in beside him and try to help him up onto my bed where he instantly crashes back down, his eyes drooping closed as the effects of whatever she did to him still overwhelm his senses. "Where are the guys?" I ask, shaking his shoulder, needing him to stay awake. "Are they okay?"

"Will be," he grunts. "They're just passed out. She gassed us."

"What? How?"

Grayson shrugs his shoulder, too out of it to think about the little ins and outs of Paris' twisted plan.

I start moving. "I need to check on them."

Grayson grips my wrist, pulling me back until my ass is crashing down on the bed beside his head. "No," he demands, the authoritative growl in his tone keeping me seated. "It's not safe. I opened a window, but we have to wait until the gas clears, otherwise we're both fucked too."

"But—"

"No. They'll be alright. They'll just have wicked headaches when they wake."

I let out a sigh and look down to find him staring back up at me, fighting the need to close his eyes just to make sure that I'll be alright. "Thank you," I whisper, trailing my fingers over the side of his face. "I really thought I was done for."

Grayson shakes his head, his eyes growing heavy again as he reaches out and pulls me into his arms. "Not as long as you've got us in your corner. We will always find a way to get to you, even in the most impossible situations. I'll never let her hurt you."

I roll in his arms and press my lips to his as he closes his eyes. "I love you, Grayson."

"I know," he murmurs, not needing to say it back because I already know exactly how he feels. "Now let me sleep this off so I can work out how the fuck I'm going to kill this bitch."

A soft smile spreads across my lips, but it doesn't last long as the worry for the guys downstairs pulses through my veins. "Okay," I tell him, snuggling into his warm arms, grateful to still be alive. "Sleep. I'll be right here when you wake."

27

My heart breaks as I sit down beside Cruz, brushing my fingers over his forehead. "Are you alright? Can I get you anything?"

He shakes his head and as he opens his eyes, I see just how much pain he's in. "A strip tease would be good," he murmurs, his tone low and rumbly.

His hand slips into mine and I lean forward to brush my lips over his. "I'm being serious."

I feel his lips pull into a smile against mine. "So am I."

I groan and start to pull away, determined to get him some painkillers and a glass of water anyway. The boys woke up twenty minutes ago, and so far, they're all being stubborn assholes, too tough to admit that they need help when I know their heads are pounding and their bodies are aching.

"If he's getting a strip tease, then I want one too," King grumbles from the couch opposite the fireplace.

I look back over my shoulder and roll my eyes as I meet his, but seeing the wicked grin across his face, I can't help but laugh. "You're an idiot," I tell him, seeing Carver from the corner of my eye sitting up and hanging his head into his hands. "No one is getting a strip tease. You guys all need to rest. Besides, you never let me do anything fun when I'm hurt."

"That's bullshit and you know it," Cruz murmurs, squeezing my hand to draw my attention back to him. "I seem to remember tag teaming you last night while your stitches were staring right at me. Try and tell me that wasn't fun."

I groan, feeling my ability to keep this situation under control slipping right out of my fingers. "Fine, I'll flash you one tit, and that's it," I say, getting up and looking between King and Cruz before quickly glancing at Carver. "And that's only if you let me force some painkillers down your throats—and that includes Carver."

King lets out a loud, defeated sigh. "Fuck, man," he says, glancing toward Cruz. "We've got no chance."

Carver just scoffs, and before another word gets said, I hurry out of the room, more than ready to force some painkillers into their tough bodies. I rush into the kitchen, grabbing a glass of water for each of them before scrambling through the cupboards, searching for something to help their heads.

I've already got Grayson sorted upstairs and after finally letting me help him, he crashed all over again, more than happy to sleep it off, but these guys … this could be a challenge.

After taking far too long to find what I'm looking for, I walk back into the living room, trying my hardest not to drop anything, only when I get there, I find two patients, not three. "Where's Carver?" I ask, placing the three glasses of water down on the coffee table and handing out pills like a shady dealer at a festival.

Cruz scrunches his face as he sits up and allows me to put the painkillers into his hand. "He got up the second you waltzed out of here," he says, looking up and meeting my concerned stare with one of his own. "Don't go after him, babe. He looked pretty fucked up. He's going to need a minute to wrap his head around all of this."

"Wrap his head around what?"

"That we couldn't protect you. We all got fooled, and because of that, you were left defenseless. She could have done anything to you. Fuck, we could have all woken up to find you gone or fucking dead."

King sits up and leans forward onto his elbows, much like Carver had been earlier. "We let you down, Winter. We got lucky today, but next time … fuck, babe. I don't even want to think about what could happen next time, especially now. She's getting even more desperate by the second, and now that Harding is dead, she's got no one. She's getting far too unpredictable."

"What about that kid?" Cruz grumbles, making my head whip back to him, my brows furrowed in confusion.

"Kid? What kid?"

"Are you serious?" Cruz questions. "In that photograph you found in your father's office. Wasn't that bitch pregnant? How long ago was that taken anyway? Fifteen, twenty years ago?"

Shit, he's right. She was pregnant which means she has a kid wandering around here somewhere and I've been wasting all my time searching for Paris when I could have been finding something to use against her. I stand and start pacing, trying to figure out what little bits of information I have. "Well, my father died eighteen years ago and for that photograph to be filed in his office, assuming no one planted it in there after the fact, the picture had to be taken at least over eighteen years ago."

"So, you have a cousin about your age," King says. "And I'd assume, seeing as though both your moms are identical twins, that he or she would look kinda similar to you."

I drop down on the end of Cruz's couch, staring ahead at the fireplace but not really seeing anything. They're right. I have a cousin, which means that all of this shit is so much bigger than just me, Paris, and Dynasty.

Fuck, I've always wanted family, but the simple fact that Paris is his or her mother means that trusting this new cousin is going to be hard.

I have to find this person.

I shoot straight back up off the couch. "Take your pills," I call to the guys, running straight back out of the living room and racing down the hall to my father's office. If there were details on Harding's affair with Paris, then surely my father must have had something more on her. I don't care if I have to go through every single file on his shelf. I'm certain that there's something there. There has to be.

Tobias King was the one who told me that my father's office would always bring me answers and I'm trusting him now. That little piece of information has proven useful before, and now I need it to come through for me again.

I hook my fingers around the door frame of my father's office and slingshot myself into the room. I come to a screeching halt as I find Carver rummaging through the shelves, tearing files off and flicking them over his shoulder, trashing the room. "What the fuck do you think you're doing?" I demand.

He doesn't even flinch at my tone, almost as though he already knew that I was standing right here. "I've let you down for the last fucking time, Elodie," he growls, grabbing the next file and flicking through it. "She could have fucking killed you and I just passed out on the goddamn floor. FUCK. I should be better. I was trained better."

"Carver," I say, instantly getting ignored.

"She was in your fucking room with a goddamn knife. How the fuck did I miss this?" He throws another file. "I can't lose you. I won't fucking lose you."

"CARVER."

He still ignores me, getting more and more frustrated. He pulls out the last file, flicks through it and throws it over his shoulder to join the rest of the mess he's created until he turns around and wipes everything off my father's desk with a ferocious growl. "FUCKING HELL."

He props his hands against the desk, leaning into it and breathing heavily as he desperately searches for control, but it's gone. The broody, controlled, and precise Carver that I'm so used to is completely gone, leaving me with this reckless, unsure version of himself, one that has my heart racing in all the wrong kinds of ways.

I walk around the big mahogany desk, approaching him with caution, like one would do to a wild animal. "Carver," I whisper, bringing my hand up and placing it over his big shoulder, the thoughts and urgency of finding this long-lost cousin completely gone and replaced with nothing but pure concern for the man before me, a man who I'm madly in love with.

When he hurts, I hurt.

Carver flinches at my touch and as his head whips around and his wild, erratic gaze falls upon mine, I see nothing but devastation and failure. "Don't," he rumbles, the lone word echoing through the room and bouncing off every wall. "Don't come over here and try to convince me that it's all going to be alright. That was our shot, our one chance at ending this, and we fucked it up. *I fucked it up.*"

I shake my head and he looks away, sending a wave of anger pulsing through me. I give his shoulder a hard shove and grip his chin with everything that I have, forcing his stare back to mine, knowing that he can take it. "You didn't," I growl, the frustration running through my veins like electricity reacting to water. "She fucked up. We did nothing wrong. We didn't fail. You're better than this Dante Carver. You're stronger."

He rips his chin out of my grip, the fury bubbling behind his eyes and if I were a weaker woman, I'd be running, fearing the worst, but despite how out of control he is right now, he'd never hurt me, not in the ways that count.

Carver grabs me and with one big stride, slams me up against the wall, pinning me with his big body. "What don't you get?" he growls, the fire in his eyes completely burning him up. "I FAILED. You could have died by her hand and I was lying on the fucking floor, unable to move. Do you have any fucking idea how that feels? How fucking helpless I felt fighting the fucking gas while knowing she was upstairs trying to take your life?" He pushes harder against me, making it nearly impossible to breathe. His rock-hard body presses against the stab wound on my abdomen but I remain still, knowing how desperately he needs to get the words out. "The thoughts that went through my head, knowing that I was going to pass out and not be able to do anything about it, knowing what was about to happen to you. Never again. I will never let that happen again."

Carver's jaw clenches and he drops his head forward, his forehead resting against mine as he tries to catch his breath and then without warning, he tears away from me, dropping me to my feet and turning his back. He starts pacing the length of my father's office, swiping a vase right off the side table as he passes.

It crashes to the ground with a loud bang, but I keep my focus on him.

I balance myself, taking a deep breath as I watch the hard muscles in his back roll with unease and conflict. I've tried rationalizing with him, I've tried letting him talk it out, but nothing is working. It's time to fight fire with fire. We'll collide to create an inferno and hope to fucking God that we both survive the flames.

I bury the fear within me, take a deep breath, and go for it.

My feet fly back toward the desk and I reach him just as he turns to start pacing back toward me. "Cut the bullshit, Dante Carver," I yell, the anger bubbling out of me in waves. "You're better than this. You're stronger. You're stronger than anyone I know. You are not allowed to break. You're the only one holding me and the guys together. We need you, so snap the fuck out of it and instead of feeling sorry for yourself, help me figure out what the fuck we're going to do to put this bitch in a grave."

His eyes burn like never before, and while every bone in my body is telling me to retreat, I don't move a single muscle. He's more than okay with the idea of throwing me around, but I stand by what I said, he won't hurt me. He'll never hurt me.

"Do you have any idea what it's like being the one who's not allowed to break? Who always has to stay strong for the sake of his friends, just so that they can keep going?"

I raise my chin. At any other moment, my heart would break for him. I know he's under worlds of pressure to be this big, top-dog, alpha guy that never shows a hint of weakness, but now is not his time to break. Now is his time to rise above and prove to everyone that he's the real MVP. That he's at the top of his game, that no one can touch what's his, especially petty bitches like Paris Moustaff.

"Like I said," I rumble, the words pulling from deep within me as I focus my heated stare right on his. "Cut the bullshit. The Dante Carver that I know would be horrified by this little 'poor me' act that you've got going on. Pull it together and be the man that I know you can be. You can break down after. I'm not about to stand by and watch you fall apart over some petty bullshit like Paris sneaking in and gassing you all. It could have happened to anyone, and believe it or not, you're human."

"STOP."

"NO," I roar, shoving my hands against his chest and hating how he doesn't move an inch. Tears well in my eyes and the anger instantly intensifies at how weak I am, making Carver not the only one who's losing control. "You're larger than life, Carver. You don't get to fall apart."

"I'm weak," he growls, stepping right into me. "I'm no good to you like this. I'm a liability. You have three guys who would move the fucking universe just to get to you, but I couldn't do that. You're better off without me."

I shake my head, my jaw clenching as his words hurt more than the bullet he shot through my abdomen, then before I can even think about how to respond to that, a gun is pressed into my hand. I suck in a gasp as he raises it to his chin and stares me right in the eye, that usual bravado shining brightly. "Pull the fucking trigger, Elodie," he demands. "I can't keep you safe, not like this. You're a losing battle. Every fucking odd is against you, and I can't be here to watch you die. It will destroy me. *Pull the fucking trigger.*"

Fuck this. If he wants to play dirty, then we'll play dirty.

Without hesitation, I shoot, giving him exactly what he fucking wants.

28

The bullet flies right over his shoulder, the silencer keeping my outburst private as the bullet lodges into the wall behind him, neither one of us flinching, but then I turn the gun on myself, not taking my hard stare from his for even a second. The barrel sits against my temple, the hot metal a stark reminder that it's there, though I better get used to it. Something tells me that in this life, having a gun pointed at my head is going to be a common occurrence.

Carver's eyes widen with fear.

"Don't fucking move," I growl at him, knowing him all too well. "Who the fuck do you think you are shoving a gun in my hand and begging me to take your life? You're such a goddamn asshole, Carver.

Do you honestly think that I'd be able to go on if you weren't here? What do you think would happen? I'd pull the fucking trigger and then walk away? Fuck no. I'd turn the goddamn gun on myself. I can't live in a world where you don't exist, and I especially can't live in a world knowing that I was responsible for ending your life."

"Give me the fucking gun."

I shake my head, the desperation pulsing through my veins like a rocket as a single tear falls from my eye and rolls down my cheek. "Don't you fucking see? You made me love you, Carver. I fucking love you and because of that, I hate you. All my goddamn life, I've had to run. I've taken myself away and made it impossible to fall for someone, but I can't anymore. I hate you so fucking bad because loving you means that for the first time in my life, I have something to lose and I can't bear the thought of losing you."

He just stares at me, his chest rising and falling with rapid movements as realization dawns in his eyes.

"If you die, Carver," I whisper, hating the raw and honest vulnerability in my tone, "then I die too."

His heart falls out on his sleeve and without warning, he steps into me, pushing my hand away that holds the gun and fusing his lips to mine.

I melt into him, the instant satisfaction coursing through my veins and filling every inch of my body with warmth. His kiss is desperate, as are his hands on my body.

I throw my arms around his neck, dropping the gun and listening as it clatters to the ground at our feet. He holds me so damn tight, the fear of truly losing me today rattling us both.

Carver presses his body against mine and I feel his raw need, so hard and demanding as his tongue slips into my mouth. We fight for dominance, just like I do with the other guys, but with Carver, it's a real power struggle, one that we will never get to the bottom of. We'll forever clash and fight over who wears the crown.

His rough fingers slide under my tank and tear the fabric up over my head and before it's even hit the ground, his hands are back on my body. I groan into him, needing his touch more than I need the air I breathe.

He's so forceful, so dominant, so … everything.

I need so much more.

I grab his shirt and start tugging it over his head, and not wanting to waste a single second, Carver takes over and shrugs out of it, giving me exactly what I want. My hands drop to his warm chest, feeling his strong, ripped muscles beneath his tanned skin.

He's simply stunning. He's cut from stone in every possible way—mind, body, and soul.

He groans with my touch, and the sound is filled with such fire that it feels as though he's been waiting a lifetime for this exact moment.

Every movement is filled with desperation, urgency, and passion. We've spent an eternity pushing each other away, letting our circumstances drive us apart, but we can't hold on any longer.

Our height difference makes it nearly impossible to keep going like this, so I'm not surprised when his strong arm winds around my body and he lifts me off the ground. My legs wrap around his narrow waist and as a soft moan slips from between my lips, his mouth drops to the sensitive skin below my ear.

"Oh, fuck," I breathe, unable to find the words to describe just how badly I need him. I want him inside of me, I want his hands all over me, I want everything that he is to wrap around me and to never let go.

My nails dig into the soft skin of his shoulders, holding on as he steps back toward the massive mahogany desk and sets me down. He instantly leans into me, and I fall back against the desk, letting his weight settle over me. I refuse to unwind my legs from his waist or give him enough space for doubt to creep in between us. And just as well because like this, I can feel his rock-hard cock grinding against my pussy, needing me in the same intense, reckless way that I need him.

His hands roam over my skin as though he's been dying to feel the soft curves beneath his fingertips all his life, and as he pulls back and looks down at me, his hand slowly trails down my body and slips into the front of my sweatpants.

I'm soaking wet for him.

His fingers graze over my needy clit, and I suck in a sharp gasp, my whole body flinching from the touch. The overwhelming need for more is almost too much to bear. I don't dare look away from his intense eyes, especially as he finds my center and pushes two thick fingers deep inside of me.

Oh shit, oh shit, oh shit, oh shit.

"Yes, Carver," I breathe, knowing that in this very moment, I would do absolutely anything that he asked of me.

His eyes soften and I watch with a needy awe as his tongue rolls over his bottom lip. "I fucking love you, Elodie," he murmurs just as his thumb presses against my clit and makes my body ache for more.

Emotion swells in my chest, and for just a second, I can't say a damn word, too afraid that if I open my mouth to even breathe, the floodgates will open and this whole moment would be destroyed. But when he pushes his fingers even deeper and a sick, twisted smile plays on his delicious lips, I realize that I don't need to say a damn word because he already knows. He knows how I feel, and now that he's finally said what he's been holding back for so damn long, nothing can stop him from having his wicked way with me.

And fuck it, I'd give him just about anything he asked for because I really do love him, and I'd give anything to feel this connection with him, to have his thick cock sliding up inside of me and stretching me wide, to feel his body pressed against mine, to turn our fucked up little relationship into something real. But with Carver, sex isn't just about getting hot and heavy or coming hard enough to make me scream. It's about the raw connection that comes with it. It's about giving in to our most basic urges and admitting that this pull between us is real, that it means something, and that no matter what, I'm in it for the long haul.

Carver takes a small step back, forcing my legs to unwind from around his waist. He looks over my body, watching the way my fingertips trail over my breasts, watching the way my chest rises and falls with my quick, needy breaths, and watching my eyes to see nothing but pure need, love, and commitment pulsing deep within them.

Not wanting to waste a single moment, he grabs my sweatpants and tears them down my legs, leaving me completely bare. I watch as his heated gaze swivels down my body, over my tits and stomach, all the way down to my weeping pussy, that not two seconds ago, his thick fingers were buried deep inside of.

He bites his bottom lip, almost as though he can't believe his luck. "Fuck," he breaths, unable to tear his gaze away. "I've been wanting to eat your sweet little cunt since the second I met you."

Anticipation burns within me and I grin back at him. "Then what are you waiting for? It's all yours."

Carver groans as his eyes become hooded, the excitement nearly too much as he's forced to adjust his cock in the front of his pants. He takes my knees and slowly spreads them, opening me wide and putting me on display just for him.

He licks his lips and I shudder, feeling my wetness beginning to soak me. His arms are hooked under my knees and in one quick pull, he drags me to the edge of the desk so that my ass is barely hanging on.

Carver drops to his knees, and I groan as I feel his warm breath against my pussy. But before I can even make a sound, his lips are against my clit and I'm crying out, his warm tongue proving way too much for me.

He holds me still, refusing to let me move as his tongue rolls over my clit. I have no choice but to push up and watch the show, because why the fuck not? My fingers knot into his hair as his tongue flicks against my center, teasing me as he slowly moves back and forth, an orgasm already building deep within me. "Oh, Fuck, Carver. Yes."

His tongue is relentless and his lips are pure evil, but it's the fingers that push up into me at the same time that has me screaming his name. "DANTE, FUCK."

My grip tightens in his hair and his tongue only moves faster, his lips sucking harder and his fingers pushing deeper. My legs wrap around his head, my orgasm quickly building to levels I've never felt before, and if he's not careful, I'm going to come all over his face.

His fingers scissor, and I suck in a gasp as his tongue rolls over my clit in a tight circle. My back straightens, my head tips back, and as I feel him smile against my clit, my orgasm tears through me like a tornado, destroying everything in its path.

My pussy clenches down on his big fingers, convulsing and holding him hostage as his tongue keeps working my sensitive clit, letting me ride it out. But fuck, I see no end in sight. It just keeps pulsing through me and wrecking me until I have nothing left to give.

I breathe hard, finding it nearly impossible to bring myself back to earth, and as my orgasm finally eases and my grip on his hair relaxes, Carver stands, bringing us eye to eye. His hand doesn't leave my pussy, always playing, always teasing.

"That was …"

His lips pull up into one of those dorky half grins as his eyes focus heavily on mine. "Yeah," he agrees just moments before leaning into me and kissing me deeply, letting me taste my arousal on his lips.

Not nearly done with him, my legs curl around his hips once again and I pull him in closer, not breaking our kiss. My fingers hook into the waistband of his low-riding sweatpants, and I slowly peel them down his hips until his cock springs free and points right at me, daring me to grab hold.

What can I say? I'm not one to skip out on a good opportunity.

I pull away, breaking our kiss, and as my gaze drops, I know the next hour is going to be one of the best of my life. I suck in a breath. I've felt his hard cock pressed against me many times before, but nothing compares to this. I feel him watching me as I take in his thickness, the angry, protruding veins leading up to his cut tip. Fierce and demanding, just like Carver.

Fuck. A cock like this needs a name. No, it needs a fucking title. But its title will have to wait because right now, I need him to fuck me until we're both seeing stars.

I can't possibly wait a second longer.

I curl my fingers around his hefty length, knowing that if I don't feel him inside me soon, I might just die. My fingers barely close, and as I slowly move my fist right up to his tip, he shudders beneath me, both of us needing this more than we ever knew.

I get to work teasing him, my thumb roaming over his tip as his eyelids flutter and close, the satisfaction all too much. His head drops to my shoulder, breathing me in, as my other hand raises to his defined back, trailing my nails up and down his spine, and loving the way his skin pebbles with goosebumps from my touch.

Carver's face turns into my neck and he kisses me there. I tilt my head, opening for more and he doesn't disappoint. "Fuck, Elodie. I can't wait any longer."

My hand circles until my fingers are lightly pressing under his chin and I raise it up, needing his dark eyes on mine. "Then take me."

His tongue rolls over his bottom lip and everything clenches inside of me. I tighten my hand as I work it up and down his cock and his responding groan is enough to put me right back on the edge.

Carver presses into me, his body firmly up against mine and his hand twining around the back of my neck. I feel him right at my entrance and it takes everything inside myself not to tighten my legs around him and pull him in. "Condom?" he murmurs, his nose trailing over my cheek and making me lean into him, desperately wanting his lips on mine again.

I shake my head. I need him bare. "Not unless there's a bunch of girls you've been fucking that I don't know about."

I feel his grin against my cheek. "You mean like the bunch of dudes you've been fucking?"

I raise my chin and meet his lips with my own. "Shut up and fuck me," I tell him. "You know they're clean. Rubber or not, the call is yours."

He groans low in his chest and I feel the vibrations right through my own, and then in a moment of pure ecstasy, Carver hooks his strong arm under my leg, tears it right up toward his shoulder and as I fall back to catch myself on my hands, he slams that delicious, thick cock deep inside me.

"Oh, fuck," I groan, my eyes instantly rolling to the back of my head.

Carver's arm slips around my back, holding me tight as he rams up into me, giving me exactly what we've both been needing for so damn long, hitting me in that one spot that he hears me loving every time his friends fuck me like a goddamn queen.

He draws back and slams up into me again. As I cry out, a low groan slips from his throat. I clench my pussy, squeezing his cock as he moves in and out of me. "Fucking hell," he groans, bringing his lips back to mine and kissing me deeply.

His tongue moves with mine, so in sync and so perfect. His body was made for me—only me.

Needing that closeness, I draw my hand around his strong shoulders and hold myself up against him as he hits a whole new spot deep inside me. I know I only came a minute ago, but with Carver, I can guarantee that it'll be happening all over again, especially if he keeps going like this.

"You're fucking perfect," he murmurs into my ear, his words sending a welcomed shiver sailing over my skin. He grabs my chin and forces my stare back to his, and as he pushes up into me with his breath coming in short, sharp pants, he surrenders. "You've got me. All of me. I'll fucking share. I'll do whatever the fuck you want, just don't walk away. I can't. Not now."

I try to catch my breath as I feel my orgasm quickly building deep inside of me. "You'll share?" I ask, staring deeply into those dark, intense eyes. "No jealousy, no arguments, just free for all, down right sharing?"

He nods, bringing his lips back to mine. "Yes," he breathes. "I'll fucking share. I'll do anything if it means getting to have you too. I can't push you away anymore. Fuck Dynasty and their rules. I want you and only you."

I kiss him deeply and curl my arm tighter around his neck before laying back on the desk and pulling him down with me. "About fucking time," I murmur against his lips, and just like that, he swallows any of the words that are desperate to come flying out of my mouth as he kisses me like he might just die without me.

His hand slips down between us and he finds my clit as though it was screaming his name. He rubs tight, firm circles over it, drawing my orgasm to the forefront and making it the main attraction. "Come on, baby," he rumbles, his voice thick with desire. "I want to feel this tight little cunt shatter around me."

He pulls back and I catch him with a quick nibble to his lower lip. "Then fuck me like you mean it and it'll be yours."

Carver's brow raises and I grin back at him. He's already fucking me like a queen and I know that it doesn't get much better than this, but what can I say? Carver's the kind of man who likes to rise to a challenge—and rise he does.

He pulls back and grabs both my wrists in his strong hand and pins them above my head making the adrenaline burn within me. He takes my leg and hooks it right over his shoulder and as he draws his hips back, he has a shitload more room to move. "Are you ready?" he asks, that wicked sparkle lighting his eyes up like Christmas morning.

"Do it."

His body rolls like a fine piece of art and then in one, perfect thrust he slams back inside of me, his thick cock stretching me wide as his fingers relentlessly keep working my clit. I cry out, tilting my head back as I feel my soul leave my body. "Fuck, Carver. Again."

I look back at him as his gaze drops to my pussy, watching as he fucks me, and damn, I don't think I've ever seen anything so erotic. His body rolls again and he thrusts back into me.

A loud, strangled cry comes flying out of my mouth and I don't even care that I sound like a cat getting tortured. I need more and I need it now.

He gives it to me again and again, each time working me faster and deeper until my body is wound so tight that I can't possibly take it anymore. "I'm going to come," I cry out, twisting my hand in his tight grip and threading my fingers through his.

"Then give it to me," he growls, dipping down low and sucking my nipple into his mouth, grazing it with his tongue. My whole body jumps, and as his fingers come up and flick over my clit, I completely come undone.

My orgasm tears through me like a freight train and I clench down on his cock, feeling my whole body shaking with pleasure. My pussy convulses and I meet his stare, watching as the pleasure completely overwhelms him and he comes hard, shooting his warm seed deep inside of me as he keeps his body moving, letting me ride out my high.

The second my body finally begins to ease, Carver releases his hold on my wrists and I instantly reach up and pull him back down to me, but he flips us so I'm resting against his chest, listening to the rapid beat of his heart.

We lay still with his fingers gently tracing circles over my left ass cheek for a few minutes, both of us just needing a second to mentally go over everything that just went down in this room.

When my heart finally settles, I climb up and straddle his hips, looking down at his gorgeous face. "So, we're really doing this?" I whisper, terrified that he might take it all back now that the moment has passed.

Carver brings his hand up and trails his knuckles down the side of my body, gently brushing over the curve of my breast, taking it all in as though he's looking at a Greek goddess. "We're doing this," he murmurs. "I'm not going to lie, it's going to be an adjustment. But, every time I walk in a room to see you fucking one of my friends, it gets a little easier."

"So, what you're telling me is that I need to fuck them more, and in places where I'm sure you're bound to see us and after maybe a few hundred times, you might just be cool with it?"

Carver rolls his eyes and, in a flash, his hand is spanking down on my ass. "I'm not that opposed to it. I've gotten used to it over the past couple of months. It's easier knowing that they're in love with you too."

"They'll never hurt me," I promise him. "Just like I know you won't."

Carver nods, his eyes softening. "I know," he whispers. "But does this mean that you're finally going to come back to my bed? I've fucking hated not having you there."

A smug as fuck grin twists across my face. "Then you shouldn't have been such an asshole," I remind him. "But you know that I don't have those nightmares anymore?"

"I know. I used to sneak into your room at night and sit by the end of your bed, just to make sure they were gone," he tells me, making my brow arch right up into my hairline. "But … fuck. You're not the only one who struggles to sleep when the darkness seeps in. Maybe I need you too."

A wide smile stretches across my face and I put that little nugget of information away, saving it for later. "We'll see," I tell him. "But now you have three other guys who all want me in their bed too. It's not so simple anymore. You might just have to get in my bed and prepare yourself for Cruz to accidentally spoon you in the middle of the night."

Carver grins back at me. "You think you can scare me off with a little bit of man spooning?" he laughs. "It's not the first time I would have woken in the middle of the night to find Cruz moaning in my ear. That kid needs to work on his boundaries."

My hand drops to feel the tight ridges of his abs. "Speaking of boundaries," I grumble, nerves flooding through my veins. "If I was riding you right now and the boys walked in and wanted to join, are you going to send them away or are you down?"

Carver reaches up and pulls my bottom lip out from between my teeth. "As long as I get to see your pretty face when you come, I'm down for just about anything."

A grin tears across my face and I rock my hips against him, feeling him hardening beneath me. I raise up onto my knees and take his big cock in my hands as I feel his seed dripping from within me, mixing with my arousal. "Well then," I say, lowering myself down onto him.

Sheridan Anne

"Why don't we test that theory then?"

Carver grins and just as I'm about to yell out to the boys, his hand comes down over my mouth. "Don't even think about it," he grins. "I know I promised to share, but that doesn't mean that I'm ready to share right now."

And just like that, he lifts us both up off the desk and moves across the room, kicking the gun out of the way and not stopping until my back is pressed hard against the wall of my father's office, and only then does he fuck me into submission.

29

King stands between my legs, his face nuzzled into my neck as I sit up on the kitchen counter. His lips tickle, but they're so damn warm that the thought of pushing him away physically pains me. Besides, what woman in her right mind would ever push such a beautiful specimen away?

His lips move up to that little space below my ear and my whole shoulder and head squish together, trying to control just how sensitive it is as a ridiculous, girly giggle tears out of me. What is it about this spot on my neck? Had he touched me like that while his cock was also buried deep inside of me, I'd welcome it proudly, but right now, it tickles like a goddamn bitch.

My hands slip up the front of King's shirt, feeling his strong muscles as he grinds between my legs. A soft moan rumbles through my chest and as my legs wrap around his waist to pull him even closer, an irritated sigh sounds across the kitchen.

"Knock it off," King grumbles, his words muffled by my neck.

"I didn't do shit," Carver says from his perch in front of the fridge. He's been staring at the contents for the last five minutes and I'm starting to wonder if he's attempting to manifest whatever the fuck he's looking for because I can guarantee that whatever it is, it's not there.

"You didn't need to do shit, ya jealous fuck," King says, his tone flat, but the hidden smile against my neck evidence enough that he's amused by the whole situation. "Your thoughts are screaming loud enough, and no, I wouldn't fancy you ramming that fucking cucumber up my ass, but if you ask nicely, *our girl* might enjoy it."

Carver slams the fridge door and the way he groans tells me that he had in fact thought about ramming King with the cucumber, which has a laugh bubbling up my throat. I glance up and meet Carver's stare and the amusement on my face has the hostility and jealousy quickly fading out of his.

It's been a week since he railed me in my father's office, and while it's been incredible having him on board, there's been a steep learning curve involved. He's not as open to sharing as the others, but he's still down to try. We haven't had a chance to really share together and I don't doubt that when we do, he'll see the brighter side of things. He's definitely getting used to it though, but for now, we just have to put up with these sudden jealous outbursts that always have him begging for forgiveness with his tail tucked between his legs—or at least, his cock buried between mine. Both are a win-win situation for me.

Having Carver on board and watching as he got used to our new little dynamic was the only thing that has kept me sane over the past few days. Grayson and Cruz went out of town a few days ago, chasing a lead on one of the victims from the ledger, and while I love what they're doing and truly hope that they find what they're looking for, I miss them, and I can't wait for them to be home. Not only to screw me until I can't breathe, but because having Carver and King on guard duty twenty-four seven is putting us all on edge.

Not one of us have said it out loud, but we're all petrified that we won't be ready when Paris comes back. We haven't had any more spontaneous visits from her and we sure as fuck haven't found out a damn thing about this long-lost child of hers. I feel like we've been getting nowhere. She's like a ghost, just showing up when she's ready to say boo. This constant state of unknown has made my anxiety skyrocket, and I don't like it.

It's like spinning the handle on a Jack In The Box, only my version is creepy as hell and when it pops up, it's a psychotic, deranged killer, not just a weird little puppet. I don't know when she's going to appear next and that scares me, especially now that I know she's willing to use the boys to get to me. I can handle me getting hurt, but them? No. They're off limits, and if she ever comes for them again, I'm going to tear her apart with my teeth like a rabid dog. Then she'll see who the real bitch around here is. Spoiler alert—it's me.

Carver grabs a frying pan from the cupboard and walks over to the stove beside us. He places it down and as he sets the temperature, my phone on the counter starts ringing. All three of us glance down beside my thigh to find Ember's name flashing on the screen.

"Ugh," I groan, before dismissing the call with a quick swipe of my finger.

"Trouble in paradise?" King questions, pulling back just a little to meet my gaze.

I pause, only now just realizing what I've done. Since first realizing that Ember was lying to me, I haven't told the boys about it. Even though I'm not ready to face the music, dismissing her call like that makes it pretty damn obvious that something is wrong.

"Oh, umm … it's nothing," I tell them, hating the white lie, but knowing that if I told them what I knew, they'd be throwing me in the Escalade and not stopping until we were parked outside Ember's home, demanding answers. And damn it, the extremes they would go through to get the answers isn't pretty. I'm not sure if I'm willing to put her through that. I mean, what if I'm wrong? What if I'm remembering it differently or if I just misunderstood what she said? Damn it. "It's just girl stuff."

"Huh? Girl stuff?" Carver grunts, knowing me far too well to know that 'girl stuff' is a load of shit. In fact, it's probably the worst lie I could have possibly come up with. "What's that supposed to mean? Did she steal your vibrator or something?"

I roll my eyes just as King's hand punches out, aimed straight for the soft spot between Carver's ribs, but Carver is too fast. His hand snaps out and catches King's fist with a solid grip. The two of them share a look, their eyes narrowed, waiting for the other to give in, but it'll never happen. "So … are we just going to sit here with you two holding hands all night or are we going to order dinner?"

Carver's mouth drops, clearly annoyed that I'm prepared to order in when he was about to start cooking, but he doesn't get a word in when a voice hollers, "WHERE'S THAT SEXY AS FUCK ASS?"

My eyes widen in excitement and I throw myself off the counter, breaking the boys hold on each other in the process.

I dart around the corner and run when I see Cruz's gorgeous face. My feet slam against the marble tiles and his whole face lights up in excitement when he sees me.

My heart thunders in my chest for all the best reasons, and before I can think too much about it and focus on the fact that I'm still healing from the stab wound, I throw myself in the air, my arms and legs out, ready for Cruz to catch me and wrap me in his warm arms.

Without hesitation, Cruz runs at me, throwing his arms out and catching me with ease. I cling to him like a koala as he spins me around, his good mood quickly becoming infectious. He stops spinning and my body rocks from the momentum, and before I even get the chance to say hello, his lips are crushing down on mine.

"Get a room," Grayson mutters, walking in behind him but there's a smile in his tone, one that tells me he's happy to be home and patiently waiting for his turn to shove his tongue down my throat.

When Cruz pulls away, he meets my stare and a huge grin cuts across his face.

"Tell me you found her," I beg.

"We got her," Cruz says, his chin raised and his shoulders back with pride. "It wasn't easy, but we fucking got her."

My eyes bug out of my head as I look over Cruz's shoulder at Grayson who nods, silently telling me that my guys really are the heroes I knew they could be. "No freaking way. That's amazing," I squeal, crushing my lips back against Cruz's in a bruising kiss. "How was she? Was she hurt? Is she okay? Did you reunite her with her family? HOLY FUCK. I have so many questions. I don't even know where to start."

Cruz laughs, holding me tighter as his eyes shimmer with happiness. "She was malnourished and had been through a lot. She was pretty fucking scared, and we really had to gain her trust to get her to come with us. But we got her out and took her down to the hospital. Her parents were waiting and the look in their eyes when they saw their baby girl ... Fuck, Winter," he says, proving in the tone of his voice just how fucking happy he is. "We really saved her. We did it."

"I knew you would," I murmur, the pride filling me like nothing before. "What about her purchaser? Tell me that you dealt with him too."

Grayson scoffs, walking past us and stopping to press a gentle kiss to my cheek. "We didn't just deal with him," Grayson mutters, a wicked grin stretching across his face. "We fucked with him until he begged for death and then we killed him so fucking slowly, that even now, hours after he's long gone, he'd still be feeling it."

A twisted grin pulls at my lips. "Fuck, I love it when you talk dirty to me." Grayson laughs and keeps walking to dump all his things at the bottom of the grand staircase as I turn back to Cruz. "So, what now?"

He shrugs his shoulders and walks with me back through to the kitchen. "I don't know. I guess that's the parents' and doctor's decision, but I'd assume Maddison will be going into therapy for a while. Physically she's fi—"

"Maddison?" I ask, cutting him off. "Wait. Is this the same girl that you were telling me about just a few weeks ago?"

Cruz nods and I instantly crush my lips back to his. Little Maddison Atwell. The girl Cruz was agonizing over. She was so little, maybe five in her picture, and the boys stuck it out, put in the work, and persisted. And now because of them, this little girl has the chance to get her life back, to live in a world where she doesn't have to be scared, to get to feel the loving arms of her mother and father around her every night, singing her to sleep. To think what life she would have had if Grayson and Cruz had given up or if we hadn't found the ledger ... fuck. I can't even go there.

"You're amazing," I tell him, glancing back at Grayson. "You both are. What you're doing with this ledger is incredible. You're saving so many lives and I ... I can't even tell you how proud I am of you guys."

"You don't have to," Cruz says. "We know, but what we do have to do is go out and celebrate. Just one night where we can let loose, fuck around and have fun. Then I swear, come tomorrow, we'll be back to locking your ass up like Fort Knox."

I let out a sigh and pull back to meet his gaze. He's so excited and truly deserves this, and while I desperately want to go, there are two guys standing under this roof who are going to whip their big dicks around and remind me that they're massive alphaholes, but I understand their reasoning. Hell, I understand it more than they do. Though ... it couldn't hurt to ask.

I untangle my legs from around Cruz's waist and slide down his body until my feet are planted firmly on the ground. His hand remains on my back, steadying me until I turn in his arms to face the major alphahole behind me.

Carver shakes his head. "No. Fuck no. It's not going to happen."

I groan and walk across the room until I'm standing right in his arms. "Oh, come on," I grumble. "Don't be such a party pooper."

Carver's hands fall to my waist and as his eyes soften, I know that in the next twenty minutes, we'll all be heading out of here, ready for one hell of a good night.

Carver leans into me, his lips brushing past my jawline, and just as they fall to my neck, his soft words rumble through his chest. "Absolutely not," he tells me. "You've got a snowball's chance in hell of getting out of here tonight."

Fuck. How did I get that so wrong?

Cruz's fingers weave through mine as we all but race out through the front door with a begrudged Carver following behind. King steps out with us, laughing as he shakes his head. It's been twenty minutes since I stood in the foyer with Carver telling me that there was no way on this green earth that we were going out tonight, and he still can't figure out how the hell I got both him and Grayson to agree to this, let alone come with us and pretend to be happy about it.

What can I say? I have a way with words … or a magical pussy. Yeah, my words aren't that great. It's got to be the pussy.

Cruz pulls me and we go tumbling down the front stairs of my home, barely catching our feet beneath us and somehow remaining upright the whole way down. Carver stays behind with Grayson, checking over the brand-new security system, making sure that my home remains secure and safe while we're out.

Cruz and I reach the bottom with King only a few steps behind, and as I walk toward the Escalade, Cruz pulls on my hand again. I look across at him and my brows furrow as he indicates for me to follow him.

I don't hesitate.

He leads me out around the Escalade, and as I finally figure out his intentions, a wide grin stretches across my face.

"Really?" I squeal, releasing his hand and racing toward the two bikes waiting for us. It feels like it's been a lifetime since I've been able to ride my Ducati. It's always made me feel so free and independent, and I've really missed that over the last few months. This couldn't have come at a better time.

Cruz laughs, moving forward to place a hand on the side of his Harley. "Yeah, I thought we could ride together, but don't get ahead of yourself. You know Carver's going to be riding your ass the whole time in the Escalade."

I roll my eyes. "I wouldn't expect anything else from the King of assholes."

Cruz's phone rings and he sighs as he pulls it out. "Hey, Mom," he murmurs, winking at me as I step up to my bike and take my helmet off the handlebar. Cruz chats away with his mother, telling her all about his trip to save Maddison. No matter how many times I hear the story, I love it more and more because the pride and joy that comes spewing out of his mouth is like nothing I've ever heard before.

A smile sits across my face as I throw my leg over my bike and look back at the house to see Carver and Grayson making their way down the stairs.

God, it's going to be a good night. I need this more than I need my next breath.

I listen as Cruz tells his mother that we're going out to celebrate and laugh as he groans. "Yes, Mom. I'll open the doors for her and keep her safe."

Cruz grins and rolls his eyes, then after a short pause, raises his brows in interest. "You know," he says through his phone. "That's not a bad idea. Let's do it. I'll warn the guys so they can get all their overprotective bullshit out of the way."

There's a loud, screechiness coming through the line and it's clear that his mother is scolding him about his language. Cruz cringes before murmuring a forced apology. He wraps up his call and as he slips his phone back into his pocket, he looks up at me with a wide smile stretching across his handsome face. "How do you feel about fancy-as-fuck dinner parties?"

King groans, clearly overhearing, and his response is even more reason for me to grin back at Cruz. "You know what?" I laugh, turning the key in the ignition and feeling the familiar rumble beneath me. "I fucking love dinner parties."

Cruz straddles his Harley and I instantly take off, speeding around the massive fountain in the center of my drive. The second the Escalade rumbles to life, I hear Cruz moving in beside me, and together, we race down my long driveway, stopping at the gate to enter the code.

The gate opens and we ride out slowly with the guys following behind us in the Escalade. The second the massive gate closes, I glance across at Cruz and watch as he looks back at the guys.

A grin stretches across his face, and as if reading my mind, we both take off, racing down the private road and leaving the boys behind in a cloud of dust. They'll catch up ... eventually.

I laugh to myself, imagining the bullshit thoughts and grunts coming out of Carver's mouth while Grayson and King desperately try to smother their laughs, but when we reach the main gates of our private estate, our fun comes to an end. Once we ride out of here, it's business as usual.

Cruz pulls over to enter the gate's code, and as I wait, I glance back over my shoulder to see the Escalade pulling up right behind me, so close that my back tire is practically in Carver's lap.

Even through the darkened tint, I can still see his hard glare, and despite my helmet, I know he can see my wide grin. Some things will never change, and fuck, I absolutely love that about our relationship. Though, while I like to mess with him, he knows that once I pull out onto the main road, I'll behave. I may have a wild heart and a reckless soul, but I'm not about putting my guys in danger, and I sure as hell know when to ease up on my bullshit.

The wide gate slides open and I hit the gas before Carver has a chance to make an imprint on my ass from the front bumper of his car. Cruz waits for me to catch up to him and as a group, we start making our way through Ravenwood Heights.

I take a deep breath. There's nothing quite like feeling the wind whipping through my hair and getting back to my roots. My time in Ravenwood Heights has been insane, but right now, riding my Ducati, I finally feel free again. There's just something about feeling the soft hum of the bike between my legs and flying down a freeway that takes me back to a time where life wasn't quite so crazy.

If only I had known what kind of bullshit was coming my way back then. Maybe I would have just kept driving through town and right out the other end, but then I wouldn't have met the boys, and I sure as fuck wouldn't have fallen for each of them and given my whole heart away in one quick swoop.

God, when I think about it like that, it's pretty damn reckless. What am I supposed to do if they decide they don't want me anymore? I'd be left with nothing.

I can't think like that. The boys aren't going anywhere. I feel it in the way they love me. This shit is as real as it gets. There's no faking those kinds of emotions.

We cut right through the center of town, and as we pass through a big intersection, I can't help but look across at Cruz. He loves riding just as much as I do, and fuck me in the ass, he looks good doing it. His shirt flows in the wind as his hair is swept back, making him look like an all you can eat buffet. Someone should have really reminded him to put a helmet on. Hell, if I had even thought about going out without mine, the guys would have stapled it right to my head, but I guess Cruz is too cool for a helmet.

As if reading my mind, he pulls a face and instantly gets hit with a bug to the forehead.

I laugh to myself and as I turn back to focus on the road, my heart stops, finding an old beat-up car flying over the median and careening right for me. My eyes widen in fear. "OH, FUCK," I screech.

Carver slams on his horn, trying to warn me, but the other driver picks up his speed, his foot to the floor, determined to make roadkill out of me. My heart thunders as I try to think of what to do, but it's too late, he's going to hit me no matter what I do. Carver is too close behind and Cruz is to my side.

I'm fucked.

My face scrunches, preparing for impact and just as I swerve, Cruz's bike cuts in front of me, taking the full force of impact. My front tire slams into the back tire of his bike and I go flying over my handlebars just as the car rams right into the side of Cruz's Harley.

Cruz is launched through the air, his back slamming down against the windshield of the Escalade as Carver's tires squeal against the road, coming to an immediate stop. Both of our bikes are shattered into a million pieces, skidding across the pavement with sparks flying up around them, not stopping until they slam against a thick tree.

My body rolls and tumbles over the hot road, tearing my skin and burning like a motherfucker, a loud bang echoing through my mind.

I groan, unable to move as the pain rocks through my body. Cars stop around me and people start rushing in. "Miss, Miss," someone yells in my ear as a firm hand comes down on my shoulder and shakes me. "Miss, are you alright?"

Stars blur my vision as I try to open my eyes, desperate to figure out what the fuck just happened. I take a mental note of my body, feeling myself out to be sure that I have all my body parts intact. I try to roll, pushing myself up onto my hands and knees.

I glance up just in time to see Carver racing toward me, but behind him, I find Cruz lying motionless on the hood of the Escalade that's rammed right into the front of the other car. "Cruz," I murmur, my voice barely a whisper as I force my feet underneath myself.

"Babe, stop," Carver demands, crashing into me and gripping my arms with a steel force. "Are you hurt?"

"Cruz," I demand, somehow pushing past Carver and desperately trying to peel my helmet over my head. My steps are wobbly and forced but each one comes a little easier as my head stops spinning. "CRUZ."

I fall into the Escalade and catch myself on the hood just as King and Grayson lift Cruz off the car and safely lay him down on the ground, clearing away any glass. Grayson instantly starts checking over him as I fall to my knees beside Cruz, grabbing hold of his hand and squeezing it as tight as possible, making damn sure that he knows I'm here. "Cruz, please," I cry, fat tears forming in my eyes and instantly falling down my cheeks, splashing onto his warm skin. "I'm right here.

Please don't die. I need you, you freaking idiot. Why did you do that?"

Cruz squeezes my hand back and a little ray of hope flutters inside my broken heart. "I … I."

I lean down into him, prepared and ready to give him anything he needs. "What is it?" I whisper, barely getting the words out over the lump building in my throat.

"I … I'm not going to make it," he forces out, looking up at me through narrowed slits, as his eyes roll into the back of his head from the amount of effort that took him. "Please, I just need to …"

"To what?" I rush out, the tears flowing freely. "What do you need? Please, Cruz. You're going to make it. Don't give up on me. I can't do this without you."

He squeezes my hand again and I search his face. "Say it," he murmurs, his tone filled with pain. "I need to know if you love me."

"I … fuck. Cruz, you know I fucking love you. I love you so badly that it hurts, but if you die … I …" A loud sob takes over and my head drops, unable to take the pain of what losing him would do to me. "I won't be able to go on. Cruz, please. I need you to be okay."

His eyes spring open as a wide grin stretches across his beautiful face. "Really?" he asks, trying to push up onto his elbow and groaning in pain. "You love me?"

I stare in confusion, looking over him and realizing all too late that the moronic fucker was just screwing with me. "What the fuck?" I screech, my gaze snapping up to Grayson's to find his lips pressed into a tight line. "He's not dying?"

Grayson shakes his head and smacks Cruz up the back of his.

"Unfortunately, not today," Grayson mutters. "He's just got a few broken ribs, and once I'm through with him, I'm guessing a nasty as fuck concussion."

Cruz's grin stretches wider but the relief coursing through my veins is too great to even pretend to be mad at him. "You're an asshole," I tell him, dropping my head to his and capturing his lips in a gentle kiss.

"Yeah," he laughs. "But you love me."

I roll my eyes and sink into him, loving the way he ignores his pain to hold me back. "Not anymore," I grumble, just as a loud screeching noise comes from behind us.

I twist around, sucking in a sharp breath as the road rash along my thigh screams for medical attention.

Carver's attempting to tear the door right off the other car, and for a moment, I'd completely forgotten that the car was even there. King gets up to help him, and we watch on as an unconscious body is pulled from the driver's seat.

I suck in a breath as Cruz whispers, "What the fuck," from right behind me.

I stare in shock, unable to believe what I'm seeing, not just because the person is someone that I know, but because that person was blown up into a million pieces only a few short months ago.

That person is supposed to be dead.

30

Knox Fucking Delacourt.

If I looked up his name in a dictionary, it would come up with worthless piece of shit, only put on earth to prove to everyone around him just how much of a sheep he is. Probably can't satisfy a woman. Has no original thoughts and is easily bought. Sucks the cocks of low-life sex traffickers just to avoid a bullet between the eyes.

Well, I guess today is his unlucky day. No amount of cock sucking is going to get him out of the bullet I have planned for him. Though, I should probably do the right thing and allow Cruz to take the lead on this one. After all, I've already beaten his ass and attempted to have him blown up for his crimes committed against me, but today, Cruz is the one who got hurt. He deserves to be the one to pull the trigger—or gut, burn, and torture him. Whatever floats his boat.

The onlookers flurry around us, moving in to check on Cruz and me, while others rush in to watch the mayhem. We hear sirens in the distance and Carver instantly meets my stare, giving a quick nod in the direction of the bushes.

We can't get caught by the cops. That'll only bring more unwanted attention our way, especially when they're going to discover that the other driver who was pulled out of the car has mysteriously gone missing. My bike and the Escalade are both registered in Carver's name so the cops already know we were involved, plus the way that Knox's beat-up car has rammed right into us at an incredible speed—it doesn't look good. I don't want to be here to see what happens next. Besides, I know I'm innocent in this particular incident, but something tells me that they will find something to pin on me and I'll be in for another night behind bars. I'm just not down for that.

Grayson holds out a hand to Cruz and the crowd gasps and rushes in, insisting that an ambulance is on the way. But one sharp look from Grayson has each of them backing up, and I don't blame them. Grayson is scary as hell on a good day, but when he's actually giving it a bit of effort, he looks like your worst nightmare.

Grayson carefully helps Cruz to his feet and my heart breaks as a cringe settles across his face, but seeing that I'm watching, Cruz slaps on a fake smile and pretends that all is good in the world. I roll my eyes. Boys and their stupid pride. It's ridiculous. Do they realize that girls know they're human just like us?

Fuck me in the ass sideways.

I keep my mouth shut. I can give him shit about it when he's not hurting so bad, as for now, I have a thick set of bushes to disappear into.

I'm more than aware of the people watching us and just how easily one of them could point the cops in our direction, so we make it as quick as possible. King stands at the edge of the bushes and waits for us all to pass before making sure that we're not being followed.

We walk for a few minutes, heading deeper into the bushes, twisting and turning, making it hard for anyone to find us. Once we are completely surrounded by brush and trees, the sounds of the sirens fade to a distant hum. Carver slows ahead, letting Knox's heavy body fall to the ground with a satisfying thump.

Who the fuck does he think he is trying to turn me into roadkill? Though the bigger question is, who the fuck does Cruz think he is putting himself in direct danger to save my life? That selfless asshole. I know he loves me, but damnnnn. He really raised the bar today.

All eyes fall to Cruz, wondering how this will play out, but as we look his way, Knox's eyes spring open, and fear slams through him as he takes in the five imposing bodies surrounding him.

Knox instantly scrambles. "Oh, fuck," he breathes, pushing up to his ass and using his hands to drag himself backward. We don't bother moving as he gets only a few inches before his back presses up against a wide tree, backing himself into a corner.

The panic surges through his gaze as his eyes flick around our circle, knowing that without a doubt, he will die today, and considering what he just did to Cruz, and what he had intended for me, he knows that it's going to be brutal.

Cruz takes a step toward him and crouches down. He doesn't show that he's in pain, but I know he is, and I know it must be horrendous. "You look pretty good for a dead guy," he rumbles, his voice low and deadly.

Knox keeps looking around the circle, silently begging each of us for help that he knows isn't going to come. He attempts to back up further, though it's not as though he can magically go right through the tree. He's fucked and not in a good way.

Cruz clicks in his face, forcing his stare back to his and demanding answers. "How are you alive?" Cruz questions. "You were left in your uncle's house to rot."

"Window," Knox spits before his gaze flicks back to me with a sick grin twisting across his face. "But it seems that I'm not the only one capable of surviving an explosion."

My blood runs cold. I race forward and my hand shoots out, my fingers instantly curling around his throat and squeezing tight. "What the fuck is that supposed to mean?" I growl, my stomach churning as the dread quickly sinks in.

Knox laughs and I squeeze tighter. He looks up at me and his eyes sparkle, and although not a sound has come out of his mouth, I know he's laughing at me, at all of us. "That staircase certainly went BOOM, didn't it?" he mutters, his voice low and strained from the hold I have on his throat. "You practically flew like a bird."

"Fucking hell," King mutters behind me, the anger in his tone fueling my own.

I clench my jaw, struggling to control myself as I pull my hand back, pulsing it at my side. "All those people," I spit through my teeth, my head taking me back to that night, staring out at all the people that I couldn't help, who were screaming in agony while I stood paralyzed, wishing so desperately that I could save them. "They were innocent. They had nothing to do with this."

Knox just grins, taunting me, silently daring me to lose control. "What's that bullshit you used to say? An eye for an eye?" he laughs. "You killed all of my men, so I returned the favor. All those lives lost, they're on you. Their blood is on your shoulders."

Fuck, no. I shake my head, the rage boiling quickly inside of me.

My fingers curl into a tight fist, and without warning, my arm rears back and flies forward. My brass knuckles slam against his face, letting him feel the complete force of my rage. I hit him over and over again, one for each of my people who lost their lives to this sick bastard.

The boys stand protectively around me, and although I know that I should back off and let Cruz have his moment, I can't seem to stop. My control has completely slipped and there's no way in hell to rein in my fury.

I keep fighting through the pain, from my sore muscles that slammed down against the hard road, to my head that rocked furiously inside my helmet.

Knox's face splits with every punch, blood splattering all over me, but when his eyes start to roll, Carver steps in behind me and drags me back with incredible strength. "We still need him," Carver murmurs in my ear, desperately trying to help me see reason. "You can't kill him. Not yet."

I pull against his hold, unable to see anything past the faces of Dynasty's dead swarming through my mind. Carver pulls me right back against his solid chest, slipping his arm through both of mine behind my back like a tight vice and making it impossible for me to get away. "Breathe," he murmurs, brushing his fingers up and down my arm. "Focus on my touch."

I listen to his words, replaying them over and over in my mind, knowing just how important it is to find myself. What kind of leader loses control like this? I need to be able to rein in my emotions. I need to be able to take situations like this and keep my cool. I need to be better.

I sink against Carver's chest and focus on my breathing, but seeing Knox's face grinning back at me makes it harder than it should ever have to be. I close my eyes and feel the steady rhythm of Carver's heart beating strongly against my back, and it's just what I need to find myself.

My control comes back with the full force of my twisted mind, and feeling that change, Carver eases up on his hold, but he doesn't dare let go.

I meet Cruz's stare, letting him know that I'm good and that he's free to do whatever he needs to do, but Knox keeps his stupid stare locked on me. As I look back at him to see his eyes still sparkling with laughter, my stomach twists all over again.

There's more.

"What?" Cruz growls, seeing exactly what I'm seeing as Carver discreetly tightens his hold on me again.

Knox's grin widens and turns into a ferocious sneer, and just as he goes to gloat about whatever the fuck he did, a voice calls out in the bushes, a voice that's way too close for my liking. "R.H.P.D. Is anyone there?"

Dread sinks into my stomach like a lead weight as my gaze flashes around to the boys. "Keep quiet," Carver says in my ear as all eyes turn back to Knox who slowly pushes himself up the tree until his feet are under him, more than ready to run.

Cruz looks back at Carver and shakes his head. "They're too close."

"Then make it fast."

Cruz nods and as his hand reaches around his back to take his gun out of the back of his pants, I shake my head and slam my elbow back into Carver's stomach. His hold eases just enough for me to break free and I rush forward, gripping Knox tight.

"What did you do?" I spit, trying to keep my voice low as I hear the soft crunch of the twigs and branches breaking under the cop's feet, getting closer and closer.

"Move, Winter," Cruz hisses and sure enough as I look back over my shoulder, there's a gun pointed right at my head. "We don't have time. We need to end him and get the fuck out of here."

I clench my jaw, the clock ticking all too quickly. My heart breaks as I look at him. "I'm sorry. I have to know. I … I can't."

Cruz groans and I see the agony written across his face as I look back at Knox. "Speak."

"Hello? Ravenwood Heights Police Department. Is anyone out here?"

Fuck.

I push into Knox as the boys grow fidgety around me. "Now," I growl, the word coming out so low that it hurts the back of my throat.

Knox just grins. "Was Sara good?"

The fuck? "What's that supposed to mean?"

"She fucked you, didn't she?" he says. "Did you like it? Did you like her fingers inside your body? Her tongue on your dirty little cunt? I bet you did."

The branches break and the leaves rustle as bodies push through the bushes, searching for us. "Winter. NOW. We have to go."

My jaw clenches, ignoring the boys. "Explain yourself."

"Who do you think supplied her the drugs to fuck you up? She got you good, didn't she?" Knox winks, and as the words get caught in my throat, he roars loudly, shoving me hard and making me stumble back into Cruz. Knox darts around the back of the tree and takes off at a sprint. "HELP. THEY'RE GOING TO KILL ME."

"Fuck." Carver darts toward me and grips my arm and before I even know what's going on, we're tearing through the bushes at speeds my feet can't even begin to keep up with.

"NO," I demand, pulling back on Carver's tight grip as the boys come up behind us, Cruz struggling with the pain that rocks through his body. "He's getting away. We have to go back."

Grayson pulls up on my other side, shoving a hand against my back and making me go faster. "It's too fucking late. He's gone. We missed our shot."

"NO."

"Get moving," King snaps, barely dodging a branch that threatens to slice his face right open. "We'll get him next time. He's a fucking idiot. Finding him won't be hard."

"I—"

"No," Carver cuts me off with a ferocious growl, tightening his grip on my wrist and pulling me faster. "He's gone. Move the fuck on and run. We're not getting locked up today."

And just like that, I give up on the chase, and focus on saving myself, knowing that without a doubt, the boys will find him, and when they do, they're going to make it right for all the people who were killed during the explosion and all their grieving families.

31

I ce clinks into the bottom of my glass as Grayson refills my drink, doing everything he can to try and keep my mind off the shitty night we just endured.

A fucking car accident? Cruz was launched through the air and crash-landed against Carver's Escalade. This shit just doesn't happen. Not to mention that now Carver, Cruz, and I are all out of a ride.

The boys shrugged it off. They have insurance for this kind of shit and can get replacements at the drop of a hat, but losing my Ducati is a big freaking deal. Though, I know it's technically not mine. Carver purchased it for me a lifetime ago and let me think I'd won it in some ridiculous bet. But that doesn't change the fact that, for so long, my

Ducati was one of my only lifelines. I was attached, and now it's just … gone.

Don't get me wrong, I can buy myself a new one now or Carver will have it replaced through his insurance, but it's not the same. That bike suffered with me through some of the worst times of my life, and no matter what, was always right by my side, ready to take me away into a new world.

What's worse than losing my bike? Losing Knox.

I fucked up.

The hot water of the Jacuzzi bubbles around my chest as I rest back against the side, the heaviness of the day weighing on my mind. "It's all my fault," I murmur, sipping at my drink.

Carver scoffs from across the courtyard, placing his phone down on the table and glancing up at me, the anger from my comment clear in his eyes. "It's not your fucking fault."

"Had I not fought so hard to destroy everything that Sam created, all those people from the ball would still be alive," I argue, knowing just how fucked up that sounds.

Carver stands and leans onto the table, glaring at me. "Are you hearing yourself?" he spits. "Had we not gone and fucked up Sam's operation, those four girls would still be there or fucking worse, and we sure as fuck wouldn't have found that ledger. Because of what we did, victims like Maddison Atwell are free. So lose the freaking pity party. It is not your fault that assholes like Knox Delacourt can't determine the difference between good and bad.

"Besides," King adds, standing beside Carver. "I know it's a fucked

Sheridan Anne

up way of looking at it, but I knew every single one of those people who lost their lives that night, and I can guarantee that every last one of them would have gladly given their lives to save the victims in that ledger."

I give King a hard stare. "Seriously?" I grumble. "You're going to look at this as a win-win situation."

King groans and grabs his glass off the table. "You're fucked in the head if you think that I look at any of this as a win," he says while making his way toward the back door of my home. "No one in this situation is winning, not even the victims who are being saved because they're going to have years of trauma ahead of them. All I'm saying is that sometimes you have to fight fire with fire, evil with evil, and sometimes, you have to make a sacrifice for the greater good."

I stare after him, watching as he stops by the back door to look back at me. "You need anything?" he asks. "I'm going to check on Cruz and crash. I'm fucking exhausted. I can't keep my eyes open a second longer."

I shake my head. "I'm all good," I tell him, watching as he narrows his gaze, double checking and making sure that I'm being completely honest—I'm not. I'm so far from good that it's not even funny.

I know he sees the lie, but with both Grayson and Carver out here, he knows that I'll be alright.

King slips in through the back door and I sink against the side of the Jacuzzi, sipping on my drink as I look up at Grayson, standing just above me. "I let him get away," I murmur, my head so full of this bullshit that I can't even think straight. "I should have let Cruz take his shot. He deserved to take his shot."

Grayson nods as his fingers fall to the buttons on his shirt and slowly pops them open, letting the breeze catch the sides of his open shirt and blow them back to show off his sculpted body. "True," he mutters, his eyes on mine as he moves to the button of his pants. "But you needed your answers just as much as Cruz needed to destroy him. Cruz will get his chance. We just need to be patient."

"Patience isn't something that comes easily to me."

Carver scoffs behind Grayson but I pay him no attention, far too distracted by the way Grayson's pants fall from his hips. I watch as he stands before me in the most brilliant birthday suit I've ever seen. I gape for just a second. There's something about the way the moonlight hits his flawless skin that has my mouth watering and the disastrous thoughts from the day fading from my mind.

He steps down into the Jacuzzi, his eyes still heavily on mine and darkening by the second. "You think too much."

Ain't that the truth.

I watch him, unable to take my eyes off his deep stare as he moves through the water to get to me. One hand falls to my waist as his other finds mine. He pulls me to my feet, and as I stand in the deepest part of the Jacuzzi, he lifts me into his arms. My legs curl around his waist and I breathe him in, loving how quickly my tortured mind begins to ease.

"Let me help you relax," Grayson murmurs, his lips hovering a breath away. Not wasting a single moment, they press down against mine and instantly take control.

When a man kisses me, I'm usually that girl who likes to be in control. I like to be the big man in charge with my balls of steel and domineering alpha bullshit, but sometimes, a girl just needs a broody asshole to throw her down and tell her how it's going to be. Times like this.

Grayson's tongue forces its way inside my mouth, and I open wide for him, needing him to toss me around like a ragdoll and fuck me until I can't remember that today even happened. Hell, right now, I'd be happy to forget the past few months had even happened.

I curl my arms around his strong neck, holding onto him tightly as just our chests peek out from the water. A soft moan slips from between my lips and he swallows the sound just as he pulls away and drops his forceful lips to my neck, kissing and sucking while making the rest of my body silently beg for his touch.

I feel his monster cock hardening against the thin material of my bikini bottoms, his piercing pressing against my clit, so when I grind against him, I see my whole life flashing before my eyes as an electric current pulses through my body.

I tilt my head, opening my neck for more, and as I do, I look over Grayson's shoulder to find Carver still standing in the moonlight by the table with his eyes focused heavily on me in his best friend's arms.

The interest pulses through his hooded eyes, and while I know that this is a big step for him, I can't resist lifting my hand off Grayson's shoulder and with my pointer finger, slowly indicating for him to join.

Carver bites down on his bottom lip and my pussy clenches with just the thought of him keeping his eyes on me. He takes in the way that Grayson's fingers dig into my skin, tight enough to leave bruises, and he sees the way my body responds to it, and just like that, he knows I'll be getting fucked hard and rough with or without him.

I roll my tongue over my lips, letting him know just how badly I want him to take the bait and give me what I want, and just as Grayson's tongue rolls up to the sensitive space below my ear and I suck in a sharp gasp, Carver pushes away from the table.

He walks toward the Jacuzzi, not once taking his eyes off me and Grayson, even when he reaches over the back of his neck and grips the top of his shirt. He shrugs out of it and I groan, knowing that nothing will change his mind now.

Hook. Line. Sinker.

His fingers fall to the top of his pants and as he gets close, he pushes them down over his narrow hips and quickly steps out of them, letting his thick cock spring free. He instantly takes it in his hand, lightly curling his fingers around it and slowly stroking up and down. I've never been so jealous in my life. I'd give anything to trade places with his hand right now.

As Carver steps down into the hot Jacuzzi, a thrill shoots through me. I've had plenty of threesomes over the past few months, but with Carver, this is a first. The butterflies storm through my stomach, making me nervous even though I have absolutely no reason to be, but I push them down because not a damn thing is about to stop me from enjoying every second of this.

Carver steps in behind me and Grayson raises his lips from my neck, only now just noticing Carver. As they meet each other's stare over my shoulder, a wicked excitement pulses through their eyes, sending an intense shiver sailing right down my spine.

This is going to be good.

Carver's hand falls to my waist as I feel his ready cock against my ass. Grayson doesn't skip a beat, dropping his lips back to my neck and driving me wild with need. I look back over my shoulder and meet Carver's stare, while reaching behind me and curling my arm around the back of his neck. "You sure?" I murmur.

His only response is to grind his cock against my ass before his lips come down on mine, kissing me deeply and letting me know to prepare myself.

King and Cruz are my soft and sweet guys, and usually, they even out Grayson's darkness. But tonight, the soft and sweet are nowhere to be seen, and balancing out Grayson's darkness is another that's just as dark and wild.

This is bound to be a night that I don't forget, and this time, for the right reasons.

Carver's hand curls around my waist and travels up over my ribs, leaving a wake of goosebumps. His hand keeps going until it's cupped around my tit, and as his tongue slips inside my mouth and Grayson grinds that sweet piercing against my clit, Carver gently pinches my nipple.

I suck in a breath and he smiles against my lips, instantly doing it again.

Grayson's thumbs work their way into the waistband of my string bikini bottoms and I uncurl my legs from around his waist. The second my feet hit the bottom of the Jacuzzi, he tears my bikini over my ass and I feel the bubbly water rushing over my bare pussy.

"Oh, fuck," I whisper, unable to reel in my excitement.

Carver chuckles against my lips and my patience runs thin. I untangle my arm from around his neck and reach down below the water, curling my fingers around his thick cock as Grayson brushes past my clit and dives straight up into my waiting pussy.

"Oh, shit," I gasp as Grayson's foot hits my instep and kicks it out, spreading my legs wider for him. My grip tightens on Carver's cock as my hand works up and down, listening to his soft groans in my ear. I don't know how long I can handle this foreplay before it becomes too much.

Grayson's finger fucks me, pushing up into me while curling his fingers and massaging deep inside of me. My eyes roll. "Fuck, that's good," I murmur, turning back to capture his lips in mine as Carver's hand curls around my long ponytail and tears my head to the side, gaining access to the side of my neck. He takes instant advantage as Grayson's tongue fights for dominance inside my mouth.

Carver releases my tit and a wave of disappointment filters through me, but not a second later, Grayson's chest is pushing up against it and filling the void. I feel Carver's hand on my ass and I suck in a breath as his fingers work their way toward my hole, teasing me and silently asking for permission, but if he feels that he needs to ask permission, then he clearly doesn't know me as well as he thinks he does. I appreciate the gesture though.

I push my ass back against him and without hesitation, he takes what he wants.

He starts slowly, not having explored this with me, pushing a finger inside of me as his lips move down to my shoulder, gently biting me. I groan, pushing back again, wanting more, and for just a second, I wonder if the boys can feel each other's fingers working inside of me.

The thought sends an excited thrill through me and I reach down in front of me, curling my other hand around Grayson's monster cock and grinding his piercing against my clit.

"Mmmmmm," Grayson groans. "Are you ready, Ellie?"

Usually, this would be the point where I would give in and tell them both to replace their fingers with their cocks and fuck me until I come, but I want this moment to last as long as possible and I'm not nearly ready for the main performance.

I shake my head and kiss him gently before turning in his arms. The move forces both their hands away, but I don't doubt that within seconds, the issue will be rectified.

I press my hands against Carver's chest and push him back, and he instantly walks with me, stepping up onto the ledge in the Jacuzzi. I go with him, and when I nudge him again, he sits down on the edge.

I look down at him, feeling Grayson moving in behind me. Carver sits with his cock in his hand, slowly stroking it as he watches the water rushing off my skin and leaving it pebbled from the cool air around me.

My nipples harden, but as I push his legs wider and step in between them, I suddenly couldn't care about the cold.

Carver's tongue rolls over his bottom lip and he leans back, seeing the intention in my eyes and without skipping a beat, I drop down to my knees and take his thick cock into my mouth. His hand curls around my hair, controlling how fast I move and I groan deeply. I haven't had a chance to taste him on my tongue yet, and I can't freaking wait.

Grayson stands on the lower level behind me and excitement pulses through me, not knowing what he might do, but whatever he's down for, so am I.

He takes my hips and raises my ass out of the water, forcing me to rest my weight against Carver's thighs, but with his cock deep in my throat, something tells me that he doesn't mind.

My legs are pushed wide and I feel that same chill against my cunt, but in the next second, I also feel Grayson's warm breath. His mouth closes around my pussy and my eyes roll to the back of my head, the pleasure almost too much to handle.

His tongue licks over my clit and I instantly start working Carver's cock faster, desperately needing his cum in the back of my throat. "Oh, fuck," I mutter around Carver's cock, my words muffled.

Carver's grip tightens in my hair and he raises his hips up off the edge of the Jacuzzi, helping me to take him deeper.

My pussy clenches as Grayson's lips and tongue work me like never before. I shift my weight, freeing up my hand and reaching through my legs to find Grayson's cock completely neglected. I curl my fingers around it and from this position all I can reach is his tip, but damnnnn, it's more than enough for what he wants right now.

He fucks me harder with his tongue, sucking my clit into his mouth and grazing it with his teeth as Carver's thumb and pointer finger close around my pebbled nipple, rolling it between his fingers and making those electrical currents surge to life once again. It pulses right through to my pussy and I feel my orgasm quickly building. I clench the inner walls of my pussy, preparing myself because this one is going to be good.

I moan against Carver's cock, and as I force him deeper, his hand tightens in my hair and he comes hard in my mouth, shooting his warm seed into the back of my throat. I swallow him down, feeling like the perfect little whore as Grayson continues eating my pussy, but as his tongue flicks over my clit again, my orgasm erupts through me and I come hard on Grayson's tongue.

My cunt convulses and I cry out as I pull myself free from Carver's cock. "Ahh, fuck," I curse, feeling it tearing through my body, curling my toes and clenching my eyes. Grayson grips my hips, holding me still and refusing to let me move as he works my pussy even harder, intensifying my orgasm until a deep, guttural growl is pulled from within me.

Carver holds me up as my body crashes down against him. My knees give out and he slips down onto the step of the Jacuzzi, pulling me close until I'm straddled over him. His lips instantly come back to my neck, and despite the wicked orgasm that just tore through me, my hips rock back and forth against his growing cock.

I look back over my shoulder and meet Grayson's stare with a sparkle in my eye.

He knows what's up, and as he moves in closer, fusing his lips to mine, I feel his cock at my back.

Carver scoots forward on the step and leans back against the cool edge as I adjust myself on his lap. I raise myself up and reach down between us, feeling his thick, hard cock, more than ready to go again.

Lowering myself down over him, my eyes close and a soft groan rumbles through my chest. I lean forward and kiss him as I feel him stretching my walls, and just when I'm seated completely over him and feel him at his deepest, I arch my back, thrusting my ass back and preparing myself for more.

I slowly rock my hips back and forth as Grayson lowers himself down, placing his knee beside my leg as his hand steadies my hip. I feel that little metal piercing right at my ass and I feel myself flooding with need. I push back against Grayson, and as his fingers tighten on my hips, he pushes into me, going slow so I can get comfortable with his big size.

The deeper he goes, the more my eyes seem to roll. He curls his hand around me and gently rubs my clit, and as I look back over my shoulder and meet his stare, he knows I'm ready.

Grayson raises me high on my knees and holds me still, and just like that, Carver takes my hips and the two of them start to move, finding a rhythm that works for all three of us. Carver sucks my nipple into his mouth and flicks it with his tongue as Grayson continues working my clit, the two of them together making me see stars.

"Are you good?" Carver murmurs in that low, rumbly tone that speaks right to my cunt.

I meet his hooded, dark eyes and nod.

"Good," he mutters as his fingers flinch on my hips. "You ready for more?"

I stretch my knees wider and drop lower over him, taking him deeper as I lean right into him, opening myself to Grayson for easier access. My lips hit Carver's neck and I tilt my head, whispering right into his ear. "It's you who's not ready, Dante Carver," I promise him. "Now, fuck me."

Grayson pauses for a slight moment behind me, and I sense the boys looking at each other, and when Grayson applies more pressure on my clit, I realize that the fun is only just getting started.

They both fuck me hard, slamming into me and stretching me in ways I didn't know were possible. Water splashes up around us as a chorus of grunts, curses, and cries echo through my backyard.

My nails dig into Carver's back, holding on for dear life as they completely rock my world, and as I feel that familiar burning deep in my core, building and growing with each thrust, I know that tonight, I'm not just going to come, but I'm going to shatter into a million well-fucked pieces.

Carver's fingers dig into my hips, holding me tighter as he fucks my pussy, slamming into me and hitting me deep inside. "Fuck, babe. This tight little pussy is gonna be the death of me," he growls through a clenched jaw.

Grayson growls his agreement and presses into my back, flattening me down against Carver's strong chest, exactly where I want to be. I capture his lips in mine, kissing him deeply, and as Grayson's hand comes down with a soft smack over my clit, I see stars.

My orgasm tears through me, lighting up my body and burning me from the inside out. "Ahhhh, FUCK," I cry out, digging my nails right into Carver's back and drawing blood as I throw my head back.

Carver and Grayson both come with me, Grayson freezing inside my ass as he pours his seed into me, while Carver just keeps going like a fucking stallion making my pussy convulse and shatter around his thick cock. He tips his head forward and gently bites down on the soft skin of my shoulder, emptying himself into my pussy.

I revel in the pain of his fingers on my hips, only making my orgasm pulse through me that much longer.

As my body comes down from its high, Grayson's arm curls around my waist and he pulls me back with him, stepping back and dropping down onto the seat beside Carver. "Holy fuck, Ellie," Grayson pants in my ear, struggling to catch his breath before he trails soft kisses up the side of my neck. "That ass … fuck. Any day, babe. Any fucking day."

I smile as Carver reaches across the seat and captures my hand in his. His thumb roams over the top of my knuckles, and as I meet his heated stare, the emotion in his eyes stands out like a shooting star on the darkest night.

As I watch him, I realize that he finally gets it. He understands why I couldn't leave the guys to be only with him, and not only does he truly accept it, but he's going to thrive on it, just like we do. We'll each be as strong as the next, our bond unbreakable, and our love everlasting.

My chest swells with happiness. Not a word is said between us but there are none needed. He reads me just as well as I read him, and while sometimes that can come up and bite me in the ass in the worst kind of way, right now, it's nothing short of perfect.

"Come here," Carver says, raising our joined hands out of the water and hooking them over my head. He pulls me in and I fall into the small space between the boys, keeping them both as close as possible, knowing that at any point in this world, this happiness could all be taken away from me.

32

"**M**iss Ravenwood," Earnest Brooks says through the phone, dragging me away from Cruz's bedside and making him groan. After all, I was just two seconds away from giving him a complete rub-down. "A full council meeting has been called."

"Called?" I question, stepping out into the hallway to find King standing in Carver's doorway with his phone in his hand, looking just as confused as I feel. "Called by who?"

"That's the thing," Earnest continues. "The meeting was requested by an anonymous caller whom we are still struggling to track. I need your instruction on how you would like to proceed."

Carver steps out into the hallway with us, staring intently as if he could hear what Earnest has to say just by looking at me. As I meet his heavy stare, he shakes his head. "Absolutely not. What if this is Paris attempting to make a move and take out the whole council in one swoop? It's too dangerous."

"But what if it's not?" I argue. "What if this is something detrimental to Dynasty's well-being? Am I just supposed to shrug off every little thing that comes our way because we're paranoid as fuck that Paris is trying to make a move? At what point am I allowed to do my job?"

"When she's in a fucking shallow grave," King mutters.

I let out a sigh. "Give me a moment," I say, pressing the phone against my chest and looking back at the boys. "What are my options?"

Carver runs a hand over his face, giving it thought as King straightens from his perch against the doorframe. "Tell him no. It's as simple as that."

I shake my head. "Not an option," I say, looking to Carver, knowing that his suggestions probably won't be any better.

He presses his lips into a tight line, looking deeper in thought than I've ever seen him. He curses before letting out a defeated sigh. "Okay, here's what we're going to do," he starts. "At the very last moment, we will reschedule the meeting to be held here in the formal dining room where both Cruz and Gray can be present. That way if Paris has got something planned for the council chambers, she will be scrambling. Everyone must enter through the front door and will all be checked for explosives, guns, weapons … that kind of stuff. Give me an hour to check over the security system and call in backup for an emergency."

My brows furrow. "Do we really need to go to those extremes?"

"Do you want to live to see tomorrow?" he throws back at me.

I let out a sigh and bring the phone back to my ear, knowing that in order to hold a meeting today, I have no choice but to follow Carver's plan. "Alright, Earnest," I say, not looking away from Carver's intense stare. "Schedule the meeting for the council chambers in an hour. I want security in place and in the meantime, continue looking into the caller. I want to know who this anonymous caller is before they step foot into my council chambers."

"Yes, Miss Ravenwood," Earnest says before promptly ending the call.

My hand falls from my ears and I meet the boys' hard stares. "Okay," I mutter, feeling the nerves slowly begin to seep through my chest, knowing that I could very well be setting us up to fail. "Let's do this."

The boys nod and just like that, they disappear down the hall. Cruz dashes out of his room, his injuries long forgotten as Grayson flies past me, making sure to spank my ass as he goes. Not one of them waste a single second telling me how I can help and feeling as useless as a chick in a gay porn movie, I slink back to my room and get ready, making sure I look like the kind of bitch who shouldn't be fucked with.

Ten minutes out from the meeting, I put in the call to relocate today's adventure to my formal dining room and make my way down there, wanting to be the first in the room.

I sit down at the head of the table, drumming my fingers against the hardwood as the nerves pulse through my body. I hope Carver was just overreacting about this. Don't get me wrong, an anonymous caller making a council meeting is about as shady as it gets, but after the bullshit yesterday and Paris' attack in my bedroom last week, I'm not down for any more surprises—especially considering that I haven't heard anything from Earnest about this anonymous caller's identity.

Cruz is the first to join me in the formal dining room, taking his position to the right just behind me. I don't doubt that he'd prefer to be sitting through all of this. He's still incredibly sore after being thrown around like a ragdoll yesterday, but he's not the head of his family and something tells me that standing right at my back is his number one priority.

Carver comes in next with King right on his heels. They take their seats around the table, confident with the security they've pulled together, and make sure that no uninvited visitors barge their way onto the property.

The anonymous caller was given a code number to display at the door so we'd know it was the right person, but even still, I'm nervous as fuck.

Grayson is the last to enter. He gives me a tight smile and steps into position behind me, on the opposite side to Cruz. With an incredible force of muscle at my back, the first few heads of Dynasty begin to file in.

I meet the nervous eyes of every man that enters, even the assholes I don't like. This is out of the ordinary for us, and as the gentlemen quietly talk among themselves, it becomes clear that this isn't just out of the ordinary, that it's actually unheard of. The heads of Dynasty are the only ones who call meetings, and it has every single one of us off our game.

Harlen Beckett glances across the table and meets my stare. "Have you got any idea what this is about?"

His question has the rest of the table falling silent and looking my way, desperate for the answers that I also seek. I shake my head. "None," I tell the men sitting in my home. "I'm in the dark on this one, just like you all."

"Then why did you agree to take the meeting?" Matthew Montgomery asks, his tone full of curiosity and not disdain.

I meet his stare across the table. "Because if someone not only went to the effort to call a meeting like this but also has the balls to follow through on it, it must be important. Plus, I don't want to risk skipping out on information that could be detrimental to who we are because I was too scared or nervous to take the meeting. That's not who I am, and I sure hope it's not who any of you are either."

Heads nod all around the table and before another word can be said, the big double doors are pushed open and Ember Michaelson strides through, her head held high with a folder of papers shoved under her arm.

I throw myself to my feet, my eyes wide. "Ember," I hiss, drawing her attention to me and not the suits sitting around me. "What the hell are you doing? You can't be here. We're about to have a council meeting."

Ember just stares as she continues walking deeper into the room, making her way around the massive table and only stopping when she hits the spot that Michael Harding would have been seated had he still been alive.

"What are you doing?" I repeat a little more forceful as my stomach begins to twist and turn.

"Babe," Cruz mutters from behind me. "Get her the fuck out of here. This is not the time for her to be fucking around and throwing a hissy-fit because you've been dodging her calls."

My jaw clenches, feeling that this is so much more than just a hissy-fit. What's about to happen here is a knife stabbed right through my back.

Ember stands behind Michael's chair, her hand propped on the high back as I slowly lower myself back into my seat. "What is the meaning of this?" Harlen Beckett roars across the table. "This is a closed meeting. See yourself out at once."

Ember's sharp glare slices to Harlen with an icy stare before she leans around the chair and slides her folder of papers onto the table. She meets my stare and with a blank expression, says whatever the fuck it is that she needs to say. "Let me introduce myself," she says, her voice loud and clear. "My name is Ember Michaelson, formerly Ember Harding, the estranged daughter of Michael Harding and Paris Moustaff. I am your anonymous caller who requested this meeting today. I am the true Harding heir, and this," she says, pulling out Michael's chair and dropping her ass into it, "is officially my seat at the table."

"The fuck?" I grunt, flying back to my feet and gaping at the girl who sits almost directly opposite me, a girl who in the space of two seconds has become a complete stranger to me. A flurry of noise sounds around me, loud objections and gasps of outrage from the heads of Dynasty, yet my voice travels over it all. "You're fucking lying. Why are you doing this?"

"Don't believe me, *cousin*?" she says, leaning forward and giving the folder a hard shove so that it sails right across the table to me. "See for yourself."

Cousin? Fuck that.

My hand slams down on the papers as men come at me from all angles, wanting to see the papers for themselves. It's fucking chaos, and the closer the other men move in, the faster Cruz and Grayson move behind me.

I sit down, allowing space for people to see over my shoulder, and flip open the folder to find a birth certificate with Ember's name on it. Every single detail checks out, and as I pick it up to look even closer, Harlen snatches it right out of my hand. "It's doctored," he spits, instantly throwing the paper back down and disregarding it as trash. "Michael didn't have a kid with that whore. You're a liar."

Ember raises her brow, glaring at Harlen again. "That's the way you want to play this? Name-calling my birth mother?" she scoffs in disgust, almost as though she was expecting a mature response from the men at this table, but if that's the case, she clearly hasn't been paying attention. "Don't get me wrong, I'm more than happy to play along and let you know that your mother was a cheap farmer's daughter and a fraud who should never have been accepted into a Dynasty marriage all those years ago, but I'm sure you knew that."

Harlen's face glows with anger but Grayson steps into him, gripping his arm and forcing him back to his seat while I keep my hard stare on Ember. "I'm going to need a little more proof than a piece of shitty paper," I tell her with a fake grin. "You understand, don't you? After all, you've been lying to me since the day I met you."

Ember scoffs. "It's not my fault that you missed all the signs," she mutters before holding her arm out. "And for the record, I'd be more than happy to supply a blood sample."

Every word that comes out of her mouth grinds against my nerves. How the fuck could she lie to me like this? Knowing what her mother has been doing to me all these months … fuck, years. She's been following me from home to home, keeping a close eye on me and waiting for the right time to strike.

This whole thing is a fucking joke.

"Was any of it real?" I question. "Months of friendship, or were you just keeping me close to get information to feed back to Paris?"

Ember just smiles and my blood runs cold. "At first maybe," she tells me, "but your endless whining and tough girl act quickly got boring. Don't get me wrong, out of respect I attempted to tell you a few times, but you've been screening my calls and not giving me the chance to talk. I didn't want to blindside you like this, but you gave me no choice. I was able to get past you killing Jacob, but then you had my father killed and I decided that I just didn't give a shit anymore."

Grayson and Cruz shuffle in closer to my sides, ready to catch me when I inevitably launch myself across the table to strangle the bitch. "You're working with her," I accuse, now realizing that her relationship with Jacob Scardoni was never bullshit after all. They were truly together the whole time, and the bullshit Jacob said about being with her just to get information out of me was his way of taking the spotlight off her, covering their tracks, and making sure their bullshit plans could go on. Well, fuck them. Fuck them all.

My comment gets the attention of every last person at the table, and their heads snap up to Ember, waiting impatiently for her response as I watch Carver out of the corner of my eye, silently shaking with anger and clutching onto the side of the table to keep himself from marching over to Ember and kicking her bitch ass.

"No," Ember says, completely unaware of Carver sitting way too close. "I am innocent in all of this. I haven't done a damn thing against you, but that doesn't mean that I don't enjoy building a relationship with my mother, and if she just happened to tell me about her less than thrilling experiences with her niece, then I am all ears."

"You're a piece of shit," I spit, the anger and betrayal washing over me in waves. "Don't be fooled, every single person at this table knows your mother is a fraud. They know who she is and she will never get her hands on Dynasty. Do you really think that the men who sit around this table are going to give it up for anything? You haven't got a chance in hell. Every time that you claim your father's name to get a foot inside Dynasty, I'm just going to push you right back again."

"Try all you like, Elodie Ravenwood," she tells me, the grin settling across her face only making it hurt that much more. "But you won't be getting away from me that fast. I'm the head of the Harding family now. I am Michael Harding's firstborn daughter. I am eighteen years old and entitled to take his seat at the table, and as I'm sure you know, that means that I am also entitled to his home. I guess we'll be seeing plenty of each other now."

I shake my head, not trusting myself to lose control and smack her into next week. Little things all start making sense. Every time Cruz set me up with new security codes, they were always found out and taken advantage of. How Paris knew not to be home when we raided my parents' mountain home. Ember always seemed to know more about Dynasty than anyone else in town. It was all her. The girl I called my best friend.

"The bugs," I mutter to myself, looking over my shoulder and meeting Cruz's stare who nods, coming to the same conclusion as I had. Both mine and Carver's home were bugged and at the time, we didn't think to pin it on Ember because we trusted her with our lives ... but now. Fuck. I feel like such an idiot. All this time I was letting her in just so she could repeatedly stab me in my back.

I wonder if she had anything to do with trashing Carver's home and Lady Dante ...

Shit. I can't even go there right now. I can't stand to see her face a second longer, and if I find out that she hurt Lady Dante, I'm going to break, and that can't happen, not at this table.

I know she said that she had nothing to do with the shit her mother has done against me, but she lied about everything else. Why not that too? Besides, it's not like she's going to sit there in front of a group of self-made executioners and admit to something like that.

All I know is that from here on out, Ember Michaelson … or Harding, whatever the fuck she wants to go by, is no longer someone I can trust.

From here on out, she's dead to me.

"Grayson," I demand, my tone filled with authority. "This meeting is done. See Miss Harding out of my home and make sure that she never steps foot in here again."

Grayson nods and as he starts making his way around the table, Ember stands. "I don't need an escort," she says with a sickly-sweet smile. "This meeting is boring anyway. I'll be seeing you, Elodie."

And just like that, she turns and walks out of the room with both Grayson and Cruz following behind her, leaving nothing but a mess of chaos behind as the remaining fourteen heads of Dynasty scramble to figure out what the fuck we're going to do about this.

33

My thigh-high boots slip into place as I turn in the mirror, checking out the way my ass sits in my new leather pants. It's fucking perfect. Leather pants have always been tricky for me. They never fit me just right, but when I find a pair that does, I cherish it until it falls to pieces.

I search through my closet until I find the perfect tank to go with my outfit. Tonight is kinda big and I'm not about to fuck it up. Cruz's mom has been slaving over this dinner party, wanting to make it perfect for not only her son, but for everyone who's going to be there, which apparently is going to be everyone. All the main families with their children and wives—all the hoity-toity bitches who are going to judge her if she puts even a foot wrong.

There are going to be eyes on me all night, and probably from people who I don't even expect. I'll have all the heads of Dynasty making sure I don't fuck up and embarrass the whole organization, the wives silently judging me and reminding me that I wasn't raised to the same standard and class as they were, while the children watch closely, hoping they have something to gossip about to their friends tomorrow.

Did I mention Ember is going to be there? Just fucking great.

It's going to be swell.

Hell, and I thought tonight was supposed to be about celebrating Cruz and Grayson finding Maddison Atwell and making their first big save.

I pull a black tank over my head, the word Queen scrawled across my tits, and knot it at my waist, showing off my toned stomach just how I like. My tank is pretty old and ratty, but it's also comfy as hell. I've had it for years after I stole it off some dick who I shared a foster home with. Before that, I didn't even listen to Queen, but for the sake of the situation, I forced myself to and have been a fan ever since. Besides, it shows off just the right amount of side-boob and with it tied up like this, you can't even see the holes in it.

I grab my favorite choker and lean into the mirror as I fasten it around my throat, my eyes quickly darting to the faded love bites Grayson left at the base of my neck in the Jacuzzi. The thought of it sends a wicked thrill through me but I put it to the back of my mind. Party first, and then I can fuck the boys, and if they're in the 'organized sports' kinda mood, I'll see how they feel about all four of them taking me on at once. Though, where the hell is everything supposed to go? I'd be like a cream-filled donut with white stuff oozing out of every little hole. I can't wait.

Black liner circles my eyes, and just to get a kick out of Cruz, I add an extra two layers of mascara. Though for Carver, I put my hair up into a high pony, knowing how every time he sees it like this, he can't help but dream about the way he'd wrap his hand around it and yank my head back until my eyes were only on his. Sometimes his inability to share is a pain in the ass, but I can't deny that sometimes his jealous tendencies definitely have their advantages.

"Babe, you ready?" Cruz's lazy question comes from the doorway of my new bedroom—the very room that my parents once called their own.

I roll my tongue over my lips as I step away from the mirror. "Damn right, I am," I tell him, walking out of the massive closet and turning out the light as I go.

My gaze instantly sweeps over Cruz, leaning up against my door frame in a three-piece suit that has him looking like a Beckham at a royal wedding while also looking like he's about to step through the doors of a BDSM dungeon and fuck me until I scream a safe word.

"Well, shit," I say, my eyes greedily travelling over his perfectly sculpted body. "You're making me feel underdressed."

Cruz grins and shakes his head. "You look fucking perfect. No one else is going to be this formal, but mom would whoop my ass if I wore anything different. Tonight is her night, and I'm not about to fuck it up for her."

"Funny," I grumble, stepping into his warm arms and brushing my lips over his. "I could have sworn that tonight was supposed to be your night."

His hand comes down over my ass with a sharp slap, the tight leather making the sound bounce off every wall in the room. "Tonight is my night," he promises, meaning so much more than just the dinner party. "And don't you forget it."

"Promise," I tell him. "Tonight I'm all yours."

"Hurry the fuck up," King hollers from the foyer directly below us.

I groan and grab my phone off my dresser before looking down at my pants and trying to figure out where the fuck to put it. After all, I know I'm in leather pants, thigh-high boots, and an old Queen tank, but I have to be somewhat classy. It's not like I can just shove it down my bra like I would usually do.

Cruz laughs and holds out his hand. "Here," he murmurs, waiting patiently.

I let out a deep sigh and hand it over before watching as he slips my phone into his pocket. It's not fair, why do guys get all the pockets in their clothes? Even in a suit, he gets exactly what he needs and more, but for me? Nothing. It's just assumed that we'll all be carrying purses, and I don't know if these clothes designers have figured it out yet, but some of us prefer Ducatis over limos and would like a fucking pocket or two.

Cruz offers me his arm and I take it with a forced smile, hating that he can see right through it. Tonight is supposed to be about him. I can't spend the night sulking about Ember's betrayal. I need to fake it better because Cruz deserves this. Both he and Grayson do. They worked their asses off for this and it will hopefully motivate them to push even harder to find the next victim. Though, something tells me that the boys won't need any extra motivation. That's just the kind of guys they are.

Cruz helps me down the stairs and I hold onto him tightly. I can only imagine the smirks I'd get from the guys standing at the bottom if I were to trip and fall. They're such gentlemen. I'm sure they'd help me up, you know, once they're finished laughing.

We take it slowly, and while Cruz would insist that it's because he doesn't want me to fall, it's actually because his body is still incredibly sore and stiff from the accident. He has three broken ribs and the concussion lasted a few days. I was lucky though. Cruz literally saved my life. I came out with just a bit of stiffness and road rash over my thighs, but after massaging some balm into my thighs each night, it's starting to feel a million times better. My favorite ripped jeans weren't so lucky though. They were completely shredded and gave a whole new meaning to the term 'ripped jeans.'

Cruz and I reach the bottom of the massive staircase to find the rest of the guys waiting by the door, ready to go and get this dinner party over and done with. The guys have been to a million of these in their lifetimes, so they know exactly how it's going to go, which I'm assuming is why they've all put a little extra effort into their appearance, and damn, they look great, but not as delicious as Cruz.

"Ready to go?" Cruz questions, looking up at the guys.

Grayson nods and reaches for the door handle, swinging it wide open. "Yeah, let's get going. We didn't think ahead and forgot to get a ride for the night," he says, eyeing Carver, whose Escalade is currently in the shop getting fixed. "We have to walk."

"Ahh, fuck," Cruz mutters, completely capable of walking, but hating the thought of just how uncomfortable it's going to be.

"Surely my father would have had something we could use in the garage," I suggest, following the boys out the front door.

"Tried that," King mutters, a hint of anger in his tone. "Don't know when, but apparently someone thought it'd be a good idea to fuck with all your dad's cars. None of them are working. We're going to have to get a mechanic in to look at them."

"Fucking hell," I grumble under my breath, irritation deep in my gut. I mean, sure, fuck with me all you want, but not my parents. They were good people. Leave them out of it. "Ember?"

"That's my guess," Carver growls. "She's a fucking snake."

I let out a heavy sigh and start the whole process of hating myself again, before remembering that I'm supposed to be pretending to be happy for Cruz's big night. We make our way down the long driveway and make quick work of getting through the gate.

The boys stop to double check the codes and security. Ember was true to her word and yesterday, I sat out on my bedroom balcony, watching up the street as Ember moved into her father's house. No one is safe now. No matter how many times we change the codes or do a security sweep, our enemies are inside the border and I have to assume that Ember is feeding Paris information. Hell, she could very well move her mother into her big ass mansion in the middle of the night and none of us would have any idea.

With my head so far up my ass, I don't even realize when we reach Cruz's driveway. I keep walking and Carver curls his arm through mine and yanks me aside, facing me in the right direction. Otherwise, I would have ended up God knows where.

By the time we reach the front door, my feet are already aching and my excitement for the night is quickly plummeting. Cruz opens the door and welcomes us all in and I instantly look around. His mom really has gone all out. There are decorations, soft music, and champagne waiting for new guests. Though, what else would be expected of a wife who belongs to one of the sexiest organizations I've ever come across. It is her job to please, host, and succeed, and luckily for her, I think she truly loves this aspect of her life.

"Whoa," I breathe, taking it all in.

"You ain't seen nothing yet," Cruz murmurs, taking my hand and leading me deeper into his home.

The further we walk, the louder the chatter becomes, and as we round the corner to see the room completely packed with bodies, I realize that this is so much more than just a dinner party. This is a fucking party.

People are everywhere, dressed in their formal attire and I quickly glance down at my ripped shirt and thigh-high boots. I'm definitely underdressed, but a part of me just doesn't care. At the end of the night, I'll be the one prancing around in comfort while all the other women look as though they're strapped into corsets from the twentieth century.

"What the ever-loving fuck?"

Cruz laughs. "My mom knows how to throw a party, right?"

"She sure as hell does."

I find Cruz's mom a moment later, barging her way through the crowded bodies with at least six wine bottles piled up in her arms, looking nothing short of flustered, and without giving it a second thought, I grab the tray off the closest waitress and start helping.

The boys scatter behind me, each going their own way to talk to people they know or try to find a window to throw themselves out of, either way, tonight I'm free to mingle knowing that they will always be close.

I make my way around the party, helping guests with whatever they need before emptying my tray and hurrying back into the kitchen for more. I pass Cruz's mom a few times and she gives me a grateful smile that breaks my heart. Something must have gone wrong in her planning or someone canceled last minute, because any other time, she would have chastised me for helping and demanded that I go and enjoy the party.

My next tray is filled with a mixed array of drinks and as I take my first few steps back into the chaos of the party, I realize that in order to not have this whole thing tipped all over me, I'm going to have to concentrate.

I make my way around, passing King who stops me to discreetly grab my ass. I look up at him, more than ready to drop kick him when he nods into the crowd.

I follow his gaze and my night instantly comes crashing down around me. "I should have known she'd be here," I mutter, taking in Ember who stands around all the Stepford Wives acting like she truly belongs here and playing the 'woe is me' card. I can only imagine what kind of bullshit is coming out of her mouth right now.

King grumbles something before glancing down at the tray. "See if you can get closer without anyone realizing. We need to know if she's talking shit."

"I can already guarantee that she's talking shit."

King rolls his eyes and smacks his hand down against my ass. "Just go."

I grin up at him, narrowing my eyes and letting him know that the second we're out of here, he's going to be getting hell for that, but nonetheless, I put my head down and start weaving my way through the bodies, stopping to help guests with a fresh glass of champagne.

As I creep my way closer and closer to Ember, her high-pitched squeaky voice begins to stand out louder and louder. Perhaps after months of listening to her rambling on about stupid shit, I've become attuned to it.

"My mom had a hard life," she sighs, bringing out the puppy dog eyes. "She didn't mean to have an affair. They started seeing each other before my father had even met Brynn. It's not her fault. She promises that she didn't know he was married, but she just fell in love, and we've all been there, right? When you're in love, nothing else matters."

The women around her sigh, their hearts melting for her as some place their hands on her shoulders, lending her support while others nod their heads in understanding.

"I was adopted by the Michaelson family when I was six and they raised me all these years, but I never forgot her or the few brief moments I got to spend with my father before he was so abruptly taken away."

"Of course, dear," Mrs. Beckett says, tilting her head as the bullshit Ember is spewing pulls on her heart strings. "I can't imagine how that must have felt for you."

Ember nods and I try not to gag as I continue making an arc around them, listening from every angle and taking in each of the faces of the women that I'm now going to have to watch out for. "My mom … my real mom, Paris, she was struggling, especially after London passed. It was such a tragedy. I don't know how she would have gotten through it. Losing someone like that is awful, but they were twin sisters …"

Nope. Just no.

She doesn't get to use my mother in her bullshit sob story. It's not going to happen.

My jaw clenches and just as I'm finding somewhere to throw this tray, a high-pitched, joyful squeal comes tearing through the party. "DANTE!"

Dante? What the fuck? Who the hell around here has the nerve to call him by his first name?

Carver's head whips around so fast and I follow the voice, instantly seeking out who would have the power to gain Carver's attention so fast. A small body crashes into his arms, jumping up into the air and holding as tight as possible. Hell, she's holding him so tight that I'm even a little bit jealous.

Before Carver gets a chance to recover, a second body comes barreling into him, clutching onto his legs and holding on for dear life, and as he pulls his head back, I see nothing but pure joy. It's the same look in his eyes as when he's looking at me, only this one is filled with years of fondness and unconditional love.

It's clear as day that these girls are his little sisters and that's made even more obvious when his mother walks in and my blood runs cold. The last time I saw her … well, shit. It didn't go down so well, particularly because my hands were still dripping with the blood of her dead husband.

I find myself shrinking back into the crowd, not ready to face that unhinged cow when her gaze sweeps through the room and lands on me. Her expression darkens and I realize that no matter what, dealing with her is going to be a war, so I raise my chin and make a point that I am not afraid of her. If anything, she should be the one scared about returning to a town that's run under my leadership.

I plaster a bored expression over my face and slice my gaze back to Carver, letting her know that she's not worth my attention and watch as Carver starts talking to the girls. He's too far away to make out his conversation, but I wouldn't want to anyway. This is private between him and his little sisters.

I try to focus on what I'm doing, even more certain that tonight is going to go down in the record books. After all, with both Ember and Ida Carver here now, I can guarantee that either one of them is going to pull some ridiculous little attention-seeking stunt. Hell, Ember is in the middle of hers right now.

I slink back into the crowd and when the tray is emptied of fresh drinks and replaced with used glasses, I hurry back into the kitchen.

Tonight is supposed to be about Cruz and Grayson, yet I've been walking around this party for over an hour and I haven't even had a single thought about them. My hands slam down on the kitchen counter and all the busy wait staff pause to glance my way before going about their business.

"Are you alright, dear?" a soft, familiar voice asks from beside me.

I glance over at Cruz's mom and let out a sigh. "Yeah, I'll be fine," I tell her. "I just …"

"Wasn't expecting to see Ida Carver so soon?" she suggests, grabbing a glass of champagne and throwing the whole thing back in one go. "Me too."

My brows fly up and she shakes her head. "That's a story for another time," she tells me. "Now why don't you give this tray up and go and enjoy the party?"

I shake my head. "I … not yet. I just need ten minutes to hide out and then I'll be good. I mean, unless I'm in your way. I could help out here if you need. I'm good at scrubbing dishes, or maybe there's something you need out back?"

Her lips press into a hard line, clearly able to see that I'm rambling and desperate for a short escape. When she lets out a sigh and takes pity on me, my world finally feels right again. "We're running low on champagne," she tells me, despite the countless bottles on the counter. "You could make a trip down to the cellar and grab a few more."

"Oh, thank God," I rush out, relief pouring through my veins.

She laughs. "I don't think I've ever seen someone so happy to be given a chore. My boys would have whined and complained the whole time."

"Well," I tease, stepping away from her and looking back over my shoulder. "Your boys certainly are very … special."

"Indeed they are," she laughs, grabbing another flute of champagne and throwing it back.

I leave her be with her champagne and start winding my way through Cruz's massive house, searching out the cellar and trying to make sense of this ridiculous layout. Whoever built this house has issues.

I come by a door and hear a soft murmured conversation, far away from the party. I go to knock against the door. Obviously whoever is in here isn't part of the party and would know their way around the house, but just before my knuckles hit the door, I recognize Mr. Danforth's soft tone and something has me pausing.

My fingers gently push against the door and I peer in to find Cruz's father in a deep, hushed conversation with Harlen Beckett. My brows furrow as I try to make out their muffled conversation. Though one thing is for sure, it makes my skin crawl with unease.

What the hell could they be talking about in there?

My mind whirls with endless possibilities, but not wanting to believe a single one of them, I step back from the door and call out. "Hello, is anyone down here?"

There's a shuffle from inside the room and I take a few steps back from the door and put on an act as though I'm searching for something. The door is pulled wide and Cruz's father stands before me, showing off the wide expanse of his office with Harlen nowhere to be seen. "Elodie," he says in a gruff tone. "Is there something I can help you with? What are you doing down here?"

"Mr. Danforth," I say in a pleasant tone, making it sound as though I'm thrilled to see him. "Your wife sent me down to get more champagne from the cellar, but I seem to be a little lost. Could you point me in the right direction?"

His eyes narrow for a moment before waving his hand to the right. "You were close," he tells me. "Three more doors down and you would have had it. There is a light just inside the door and a steep staircase. Watch your step as you go down."

I give him a polite smile and start making my way past his office, sensing that he doesn't take his eyes off me until I've completely passed, and only then does he close the door firmly behind him.

Unease travels through me as my mind replays what I just saw on an endless loop. I reach the cellar in no time, and just as Mr. Danforth had said, there's a light just inside with a steep staircase and I do my best to concentrate. The light isn't great but it's enough for what I need to do.

I hit the bottom and stare up at the array of bottles in the room. It's insane. I don't think I've ever seen so much wine and champagne. Not wanting to keep Cruz's mom waiting, I start searching through the cellar, glancing over the labels while having absolutely no idea what I'm looking for. I'm so out of my depth here. I mean, what's the difference between a million-dollar bottle of wine and a cheap one from the liquor store up the road?

My mind agonizes over which bottles to select. I look high and low when I finally decide that random selection is the way to go. If *The Hunger Games* got to choose their participants at random, then so can I.

My hand hovers over the bottles and without giving it another thought, I just grab one. I pull it out of its slot, only a soft clinking sound has me pausing, terrified that the whole thing is about to come down on me. I step in closer, peering through the gap and give the bottle another pull to hear the sound of glass moving against glass.

What the fuck is that? Please don't tell me that I've somehow broken the bottle.

I pull the bottle out to find it in perfect condition, yet I can still hear the sound of a glass deep within the hole.

Without thinking, I reach in and feel around.

My fingers curl round a small, glass bottle with a cork-stopper on top and a smile spreads across my face. It feels like a miniature wine bottle. Only as I pull it out and glance over the little brown bottle, reading what's printed on the label, my heart stops.

Cyanide.

The same fucking chemical that killed Tobias King and it's hidden deep within the Danforth cellar.

I fucking run.

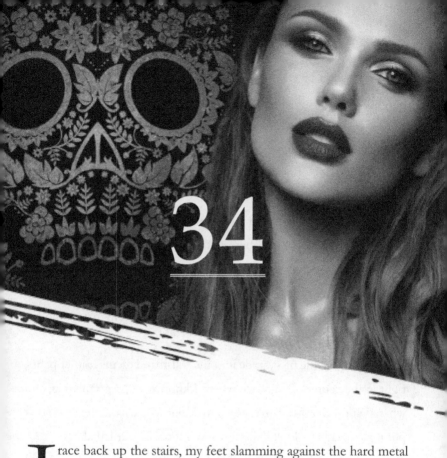

34

I race back up the stairs, my feet slamming against the hard metal as my heart races a million miles per hour.

This couldn't be right. I have to be missing something because right now, the idea that Cruz's father was responsible for killing Tobias King is rushing through my mind and really doesn't sit well with me. There has to be more to the story. There has to be something that I'm missing.

Mr. Danforth can really be an ass at times, but he's one of the good guys. Apart from my boys, he is one of the only guys who sits around my council table that I can actually trust.

No. This isn't right.

This is a mistake. Someone must have planted it there.

I have to find the boys.

I pull the cellar door open and just as I step up and raise my head from the metal stairs, I come to a startling halt, finding Ida Carver standing before me with a key in her hand and a guilty as fuck expression stretched across her face.

She sucks in a gasp and I push my way out of the cellar, seeing her intention to lock me in there shining brightly in her eyes, and fuck, she doesn't even look sorry about getting sprung. "What the hell do you think you're doing?" I snap, way too fucked in the head to even consider being polite right now, besides, I don't really have time for her bullshit.

I slip the bottle of cyanide into the waistband of my leather pants, right in the center of my back where I know it won't go missing, and where I know that Ida won't see it and decide to use it on me. I wouldn't put it past her. The look in her eyes right now is near lethal.

Ida scoffs. "I think we both know exactly what intentions I had coming down here."

I groan and turn my back. "I don't have time for this shit right now."

I start walking away when her voice roars out behind me and all but bounces off the walls of the hallway. "Do not walk away from me, young lady. You murdered my husband and now you're going to show me just a fraction of respect. You owe me a conversation."

Ahhhhh, fuck.

Sorry, Carver, for I am about to sin.

I turn back around and storm toward the cold-hearted bitch, knowing that I'll probably regret this later. "I don't owe you anything. Your husband stood before me and boasted about how he murdered my parents. He told me how my mother screamed while he slit my father's throat and once he was done with him, he did the same to her. The man you married was a pig, a cockroach. He was vile and deserved the worst kind of death. The fact that I was the one that got to hand it to him and avenge my parents makes me the happiest goddamn bitch who ever lived."

"Don't you dare speak ill of my husband like that," she shrieks, her face reddening with anger. "You didn't know him. You weren't around."

"Yeah, thanks to him," I scoff.

"You don't think I've heard about you while I've been away? You don't think that everyone knows you're a filthy little slut who has been sleeping her way around Dynasty? You're trash, Elodie Ravenwood. My husband was right to take your parents. They were nothing, powerless, and failing this amazing organization, but my husband would have ruled it all. He would have made it great again, but you failed him."

I choke back a laugh. "Excuse me? *I failed him?* Fucking hell. What is this? Comedy hour? Your husband would have turned Dynasty into a fucking dictatorship. He would have used it to gain power over the rest of the world and wreak havoc over the entire goddamn planet. He needed to be stopped, and you, do you really think he would have stood by you once that happened? Do you really think a man like that would have shared the spotlight? You've got to be fucking kidding me."

Ida steps into me, her face full of fury. "Don't you dare stand in front of me and pretend to know what my husband would have done. You didn't know him. You're just some forgotten kid with a habit of throwing nasty hissy-fits and losing control. You're an embarrassment to Dynasty and a joke of a leader. Don't be a fool, Miss Ravenwood. I will continue what my husband started and I will see it through, even if it means slaughtering you like the animal you are."

The fuck does she think she's talking to? I wonder if this bitch knows that her husband was in Paris' back pocket. Why the fuck did she even come back here? She would have been better off staying away and giving her children a proper life, but she's a greedy bitch. I bet she missed the money and lavish lifestyle.

"You should know," she continues, her face somehow even redder and now shaking. "I will do whatever it takes to protect what is mine. Dante was raised in his father's image and I will not let you take him from me."

I scoff. "He couldn't mean that much to you," I comment, my face twisting in irritation. "You left him behind. You gave him an ultimatum and when you didn't like what he wanted, you punished him by taking his sisters. You're an awful person and he sees right through you."

"You will cease this absurd relationship you have with my son immediately. I demand it."

I step in closer to her and raise my chin, silently reminding her that she's currently addressing her leader and that no matter what, I will not back down. She does not intimidate me, never has and sure as hell never will. "Wouldn't it be a shame," I murmur, lowering my voice to a near whisper just to fuck with her, "if I was already pregnant with his child."

Ida's face drops and she sucks in a dramatic gasp. "No. You're lying."

A wicked grin stretches across my face. "Wouldn't it be great? You're going to be the grandmother of the new Ravenwood heir. Oooh, I hope it's a little girl." My eyes widen as I meet her stare. "Shit, that would cease the Carver line, wouldn't it? What a shame."

Ida pushes into me, slamming her hands against my shoulders and giving me a hard shove. I rock back two steps and she keeps coming for me. "You're the descendant of the devil," she spits, disgust stretching over her face. "If you dare have a child with my son, I will take your life and the bastard child's."

I laugh. "Right, I can't wait to hear what he has to say about his own mother threatening the life of his unborn child. I'm sure he's going to love that. It's bound to give him all those warm fuzzies."

"I swear to God, Elodie Ravenwood, if you speak even a word of this conversation to my son, I will slit his throat and make you watch, just as your mother watched the blood drain out of your disgrace of a father."

I step back into her, the emotions welling up inside of me like never before. "Careful, Ida. Your true colors are showing."

"Is something the matter, Miss Ravenwood?" Mr. Danforth's voice sounds through the long hallway.

I turn and give him a pleasant smile, more aware than anything of the bottle of cyanide sitting in the back of my pants. "All is well," I tell him with a stupid innocence that seems so fake on my lips. "Mrs. Carver was just leaving. Please see to it that she finds her way out."

Cruz's father clenches his jaw and nods. He's not stupid. He knows that a whole lot of shit was going on here, but he's also a smart man and will pick his battles, and this simply isn't one of them. He walks forward and indicates to Ida to follow him. "Mrs. Carver," he mutters, "allow me to show you to the door."

Ida refuses to leave and after a pause, her elbow is taken and she's forcefully removed from Cruz's home, leaving me in the long hallway with my heart racing.

What the fuck is going on tonight? What ever happened to the easy life? I should be chilling on a beach somewhere with a goddamn margarita in my hand, not trying to determine the difference between someone who kills for fun and someone who kills just to be a heartless, power-hungry asshole.

Fuck me in the ass sideways. I can't take this world anymore.

My head spins with everything that's just gone down over the past twenty minutes and something inside my brain reminds me that I should be racing upstairs to tell the boys what I know.

I put one foot in front of the other, my heart racing so fast that I struggle to concentrate on just one thing. I pass by Cruz's mom who says something about champagne but I fly straight past her without a single glance, needing to free my mind from this mental torture.

Did that bitch really just tell me that she'll kill her own flesh and blood just to keep me quiet? No. I must have heard that wrong because the very thing she said before that was about protecting him from me. What the ever-loving fuck? I don't understand what just happened. Though one thing is clear, having her son's child would be the end of her world as she knows it.

I break into the party and instantly start searching the room. My eyes flick from one corner to the next in a complete panic, searching for the guys, but my head is too messed up to even see straight.

"Winter?" King rushes out, appearing right in front of me. "Where the fuck have you been? What's wrong?"

I shake my head, searching his eyes as I grip onto his arms with everything that I have. King holds me tightly and the way he looks at me is as though he's staring at a wild animal. Knowing that I can trust him completely, I attempt to string a sentence together but it all comes out in a jumbled mess of mixed-up words. "I... she said ... and then he ... I—"

"Fuck," King grunts, sliding his hands down my arms and gripping my hand. "Come on."

He pulls me along and as he does, he glances across the room. I follow his gaze, watching as he looks to Grayson, then Cruz, and finally Carver.

He doesn't nod or murmur a damn word, but just like that, the boys start moving, cutting across the room and following us out of the party.

King drags me through Cruz's home until he steps into the family's private living area and closes the door behind us. I instantly start pacing. "What the fuck is going on?" King demands, starting his interrogation before the others get here.

I shake my head. "The cellar ... I was picking wine, or champagne, or whatever. Why don't I know the difference between this shit?"

"Stay on track," King tells me. "What happened?"

"Cruz's dad," I say, my head spinning and making me feel dizzy. "Ida ... Carver's mom ... I told her I was pregnant with his kid and I—"

King's mouth drops as a booming "The fuck?" sounds through the room. Carver barges through the door with Cruz and Grayson on his heels, his stare focused heavily on mine and somehow helping me to see straight. "You're pregnant?"

"What?" I grunt. "No. I was just fucking with her."

"With my mom?" Carver clarifies.

"Yes."

"Why?"

I stare at him blankly, wondering why the hell can't he just read my mind and figure it all out for himself. "Because she's a stuck-up bitch who demanded that I don't see you anymore," I explain. "She was trying to lock me in the cellar, but I beat her to it."

Cruz moves across the room, his eyes narrowed. "You were in the cellar?"

I groan, feeling like I've already been over this part, but maybe I haven't. I don't know anymore. "Yes," I grumble. "I was in the cellar and Ida was trying to lock me in, but I got out just before she could. Then she was all like 'you owe me a conversation' so I let her have it, but she started talking shit about how I'm trash, and how she's going to kill mine and Carver's unborn baby."

"The fuck are you talking about?" Carver demands. "Are you feeling alright?"

"Just shut up and listen," I snap, sick of being interrupted. I let out a big breath and take a second to try and focus. "She said that she stands by what Royston did and that she intends to follow through on their plan."

I look back at Carver, feeling myself finally beginning to think straight, the more of the story that comes out. "I'm sorry," I tell him. "But when I threatened that I was going to tell you this, she said that she'd slit your throat and make me watch just like your father did to my parents."

Carver's mouth drops and he just stares, watching me as though I've completely lost my mind, either that, or he's in shock. Knowing my luck, it's probably the first option.

"You're fucking with us," Grayson says, stepping forward and bringing my full attention back to him.

"You don't know how badly I wish that I was," I tell him. "I can't even think straight from everything that just went down over the past twenty minutes, and to think that wasn't even the worst part."

"The worst part?" Cruz asks. "How could it possibly get worse than that?"

I reach behind me and pull out the little bottle of cyanide and meet Cruz's heavy stare. "I found this hidden behind a bottle of wine," I tell him. "I'm sorry, but I think your dad is responsible for killing Tobias King."

Each of the boys freeze and my gaze slices across to King, waiting for his reaction to what I just said and I watch as unease filters through his gaze and his jaw clenches. He looks across at Cruz and they stare at each other for a silent moment before Grayson starts looking around too.

Carver though, he just stares at me.

He lets out a heavy sigh before walking toward me and taking the bottle of cyanide out of my hands and gazing down at it. Resignation flashes over his face and as he looks back up at me, I know that whatever he's about to say is something that's going to shatter every little piece of my soul.

"There's something you need to know," Carver says as the boys step in line with him, showing their support for whatever they need to tell me. I keep my stare on Carver's, silently begging him not to break my heart. "I killed Tobias King."

35

No, no, no.

I shake my head and start backing away from them, but they match me with every step I take, keeping right up with me. It can't be true. "Tell me you didn't," I demand, tears welling in my eyes as I stare back at Carver, someone I thought I knew. "Tobias was my father's best friend. He was the closest thing I had to my father and you took him away. Please. Please, no …"

Carver looks shattered, but it's clear that it's only because he hates hurting me, not because he feels remorse for taking Tobias' life. "I'm sorry, Winter," he whispers, reaching out to take my hand, but I pull it far out of reach.

"Don't," I snap. "Don't touch me."

"Winter, I swear. It wasn't my intention to hurt you, but I had to. I had to do it for you."

"What?" I cry. "For me? What the hell is that supposed to mean? I never asked for this. Tobias was a good man. He was the only one I trusted at the table, the only one who took the time to teach me what I needed to know and taught me more about my father than I've ever been able to learn on my own. How the hell was this for me?"

Carver just stares at me, his heart out on his sleeve, completely broken. "Babe," Cruz says, moving forward. "Please, just give us a chance to explain. I swear, you'll understand when we're through."

I shake my head, glancing at King and wondering why the fuck he hasn't got Carver on his knees with a gun shoved right up against his temple. "I was there," I remind him. "I saw it. Tobias was a good man. How … how can you just stand there and be okay with this? He was your father, the man who raised you. Why aren't you doing something about this? Why are you just letting him get away with it?"

King lets out a breath, blowing his cheeks out and looking at me as though he's preparing to break my heart all over again "He's not getting away with anything. *We're all getting away with it,*" King tells me, making my breath come in sharp, painful gasps.

"You were in on this?" I question, the betrayal hitting me like a freight train.

King nods. "You need to understand, Winter. We did it to protect you. My father … he wasn't the man that you believed him to be. He had us all fooled, even me."

My gaze narrows and I quickly flick my stare to Carver, making sure that he's not about to try anything. "What's that supposed to mean?" I demand, my head hurting and my heart lying in a million, shattered pieces at my feet.

King drops down on the armrest of the couch behind him, his head drooped, but his eyes still on mine. "My father let you see the pieces of him he needed so he could win you over, just as he did with your father. Keep your friends close and your enemies closer. It's what he used to always say to me. It was all a game. He … fuck, Winter. He was working against us the whole time."

I shake my head. "No, I don't believe that for one second. He was like the father that I never got the chance to have. He … he took me in when I was a baby. I lived in your home. He said he was devastated when I was sent to live in foster care. He wanted me to stay."

"I'm sorry," King murmurs. "We confronted him a few nights before the ball and he admitted to working with Royston and Scardoni, but we knew how much you valued and trusted him. He was going to die anyway so we decided not to put you through the pain of learning that he couldn't be trusted. You'd already gone through so much, we couldn't bear to see you in pain over him."

"So, you just poisoned him in the living room and hoped that I'd never find out and instead, have me shit-scared of being alone with all the other heads of Dynasty, fearing that they're about to kill me too. You had no right to keep me in the dark, and absolutely no right to kill a member of my organization without my approval. You crossed a line."

Grayson shakes his head. "Listen to yourself, Ellie. Are you seriously going to stand against us on this? Tobias was a dangerous man. He had you believing that he was some kind of substitute father to you, when in reality, he was the one who had access to your whereabouts all these years. He was the one who was telling Paris where to find you, and he was the bastard who told Royston where your parents were staying that night. For eighteen years, he built a sob story around you being a long-lost daughter to him, that he even had his own son believing it. Don't be fooled, babe. The second everyone else was out of the picture, he would have worked his way right up beside you, and the second you looked away, he would have stabbed you right in the back."

I back up again, not liking what I'm hearing, but there's too much evidence. I've never had a reason not to trust these guys and while my head is screaming that they are wrong, this is just too big to lie about.

Are they really telling me that the man I trusted was the one responsible for giving up my parents' location to the man who ended their lives?

Fuck no. How could I have been such a fool. I trusted blindly. "He took me in as a baby," I remind them. "How could he do that?"

King stands, taking my hands and this time, I let him. "He didn't," he whispers. "You never stayed with my family as a baby. It was all a story that my mother went along with. Hell, they even had me fooled too."

"Then ... who did take me in after my parents were killed?"

King shakes his head, having absolutely no idea, just like the rest of us. "That's a good question," he says. "But I promise, we will find out. I want you to know who you are and where you come from, even if that means digging through eighteen years of bullshit just to figure it out."

"Thank you," I whisper, feeling completely broken and alone, despite the four boys standing around me.

Cruz steps in beside me, placing his hand on my lower back. "We told you from the start that you couldn't trust anyone in this world," he reminds me. "We just never realized just how far that was supposed to run."

I tip my head to meet King's stare as the tears begin to run from my eyes. "He really was working against us?"

King nods and pulls me in against his chest. "He really was," he murmurs, holding me tight. "I'm sorry. We didn't intend on you finding out like this. We were planning on telling you when this had settled down. We just wanted to find a way to explain it all without hurting you, but I guess that plan is all shades of fucked up."

I wipe my face against King's chest as the smell of Carver's cologne strengthens in the air and I pull back to find Carver standing right at my side. "Please don't hate me," he murmurs. "The thought of not being able to touch you kills me. Don't push me away."

I meet his dark gaze and stare right into his eyes, hating the wall that's sliding in between us. "Why did you have to do it? Why not King?"

Carver gently shakes his head. "I couldn't let King go through the pain of killing his own father. After all, he was still the man who raised him. Cruz … no, and Gray … he could have done it, but it would have weighed on his shoulders. It had to be me and I had to do it then. He was getting too close to you, and I swear to you, Winter, I fucking hate that we decided to keep it quiet from you, but you're the most important person in all of our lives and the thought of you hurting over this ..." he shakes his head. "I'm sorry, I couldn't risk it any longer. I spiked his drink with cyanide and stood back to watch him die."

I release my hold on King and turn to face Carver directly. I bite the inside of my cheek, feeling the awkwardness between us and desperately wishing that I could take it all away, but at the end of the day, he did it because he loves me and I'm the one who has the issue. I'm the one who's hurt when I should be thanking him for taking the burden on his own shoulders instead of sitting back and letting me get played.

I step into him and let him curl his arms around me, and the second he pulls me into his chest, the floodgates open. "I'm sorry," I cry, hating how weak and vulnerable I feel, but know that if at any time in my life that I have to be vulnerable, I'm glad that it's with them and not someone who would take advantage of me.

Carver's hand roams up and down my back as Grayson's low voice sounds through the big room. "Are we cool?"

I nod against Carver's chest, feeling like I'm snotting all over his suit. "I really want to hate you all, but I can't."

"Need some time?" Carver murmurs, knowing me better than I know myself.

I nod again and focus on breathing in and out, desperately trying to calm myself. "Time would be great," I grumble. "But so would ditching the party and getting drunk on the beach."

Cruz laughs, grabbing my arm and yanking me out of Carver's. "There's my girl," he booms, pulling me in hard against his chest and crushing me under the strength of his impressive arm. "I thought we lost you for a second."

"You'll have to try harder than that."

Cruz passes me off to Grayson who wraps his arm around my waist and pulls me into his side. "Give me ten," Cruz says with a wicked grin stretching across his too handsome face. "I've got to break the news to Mom that I'm bailing. She'll cry on my shoulder for a bit, then kick me out for making her cry in the first place."

"Shit," I say, biting down on my bottom lip, slightly horrified by how okay he is with that. "Then maybe we should stay. I don't want to upset her."

"Don't even think about it," he hollers through the room, making his way to the door. "Mom will understand."

Just as Cruz's fingers curl around the door handle, five phones begin screeching to life. "The fuck is that?" I mutter, feeling my thighs and remembering that Cruz has my phone.

The boys yank their phones out of their suit pockets faster than lightning. Cruz races back over and as he does, I'm forced to look over Grayson's thick arm to see his phone.

I suck in a gasp, my heart racing all over again as King's voice cuts through the noise of the five notifications hitting our phones at exactly the same time. "It's the new security system," King rushes out, speaking mainly to himself because we can all see exactly what he's seeing. "What the fuck is going on?"

The boys press buttons, trying to get into the system to bring up the camera feed. "It's probably just a squirrel or something like that," Cruz murmurs, waiting impatiently as the feed loads while trying to keep me calm. "Something would have tripped it. It'll be fine."

Grayson looks up at Carver. "You set it, right?"

"Fuck off, man. Of course I fucking—"

His words cut off as the feeds load onto everyone's phones to show us at least fifteen masked men breaking in through my gates and surrounding my home with big guns and weapons. Men are scattered all over the property, some climbing over fences and some getting up onto the second-floor roof.

"No, no, no, no, no," I breathe, clutching onto Grayson's arm with fear pounding through my chest.

My mouth goes dry, watching as each of them crouch down, trying to keep themselves hidden while clearly unaware of the new security system the boys had installed. Grayson zooms in, taking in the gear and noticing how they're all connected and able to speak to one another. "S.W.A.T. raid?" he questions.

Carver shakes his head. "No. The uniform is all wrong. This is another attack."

Then all at once, someone gives an order and the masked men make their move.

Windows are broken while doors are kicked in. Gas bottles are thrown in, and not a second later, the men rush into my home, their guns prepared to take out any threat.

"Fuck," Carver says, latching onto my arm and tugging me toward the door with the guys instantly following behind. "It won't take them long to realize we're not there. We have to get you out of here."

"But they'll come here," I demand, trying to put on the brakes, but Carver's grip is way too strong. "Your little sisters are here. Everyone's siblings are here. We can't risk them like that. Your families ..." I look up at Cruz. "Your mom. We can't leave them unprotected."

Cruz's face twists with the decision. "Fuck. She's right."

The boys break out through the doors and instantly break apart. Carver looks back at me. "Don't fucking move," he roars, gaining attention from everyone around us. "I swear to fucking God, Elodie, if you move ..."

"I won't," I promise, nodding. I may be reckless, but I'm not fucking stupid and I know a life-or-death situation when I see one.

Carver holds my stare for a moment longer before finally rushing away, and within seconds, the whole house is put on lockdown. Steel shutters slam down over each of the windows, an iron gate comes down in front of the main doors of the house, and the music is completely shut off.

Cruz fires one single bullet into the ceiling and everyone drops to the ground, his impatience getting the best of him as silence floods the room, all eyes on him. "Listen up," he roars, his voice loud enough to be heard right through to the kitchen staff as Grayson and Carver come back to my sides. "There's an organized attack currently taking place in the Ravenwood mansion. All women and children need to make their way down to the storm cellar below the house while everyone else is to protect what's ours."

"What the hell is going on in here?" Mr. Danforth demands, racing back in with Harlen Beckett.

Grayson steps up in front of his father, slamming a hand against his chest to stop him from getting too close to me. "There's another attack," he explains, which gets the mens' immediate attention. "We're taking Winter somewhere she can be safe. Put calls into the other families who aren't here. Have them lock down their homes. It won't be long until they realize Winter isn't there. Keep everyone safe."

Both Danforth and Beckett nod, more than onboard with the plan, and just like that, Carver grips my arm again and I go flying out of the room, my feet pounding against the hard marble tiles for the second time tonight.

We break through to the impressive garage and before I even know what's happening, I'm shoved into the back and pushed down into the floor space of the Danforth family SUV. Carver claims the driver's seat while Grayson and King launch themselves into the trunk, guns already in their hands. Cruz climbs across the backseat, kneeling as he drags a bag of ammunition and weapons up onto the chair above my head, and the second the door closes behind him, Carver hits the gas and the car goes screeching out of the garage.

36

T|he SUV races down the long driveway and it takes all of two seconds to gain the attention of the men at the end of the street.

"Oh, fuck, fuck, fuck, fuck," I chant over and over again, my stomach practically in my ass and feeling like I'm about to hurl all through the back of the car, though I'm sure it wouldn't be the first time that happened in here.

"You're going to be fine," Cruz calls down to me as he loads up a bunch of guns with expert hands and passes them to the boys in preparation. "Just whatever you do, keep down. Carver will lose them before we get the chance to kill them. This is all just … precautionary."

I groan, knowing he's just making it sound better than what it actually is. This is going to be a shit show and something tells me that the men currently racing to their trucks have been promised something really nice if they were to bring my head back on a stake.

Carver pushes the SUV to its limits, only to have to skid to a stop to enter the code for the gate which only serves to piss him off. He barely waits for the gates to peel back, clipping the front bumper of the car as he goes.

The second he hits the road, he takes off like a bat out of hell as I rock around in the back, my head slamming against the side door. "Fuck," I curse. "I know you're trying to save my ass and I swear, I'm not being an ungrateful bitch, but could you watch yourself on the corners? You drive like a fucking madman."

Carver just grunts, concentrating on the road as not a minute later, he's forced to another stop as we reach the main gate into the Ravenwood estate. He enters the code as quickly as he can while glancing up in his rearview mirror, getting a good look at how many trucks are currently speeding to catch us.

"We've got six on our tail," Grayson says, practically reading Carver's mind.

"Yep."

We get through the gate and Carver even takes the extra second to stop on the other side to make sure the gate closes properly before taking off again. He races out into the traffic on the main road and even though the men behind us are currently trapped behind a slow gate, it won't be long before they catch us.

There are too many cars to get a real head start, but the second we're out on a freeway or an empty road, Carver will kick their ass, assuming they haven't kicked ours first.

I close my eyes, pretending that the rocky drive is just a bumpy ride at a fair, but when a gun is shoved into my hand for 'just in case' it's not so easy to pretend.

I roll onto my back and stare up at the roof as I hold the gun to my chest, my fingers curled around it, prepared and ready if I have to use it.

Cruz looks down at me. "You good?"

I shrug my shoulders. "Just a usual Saturday night," I tell him. "You'd think I'd be used to this shit by now."

"No one ever gets used to this shit," Carver says from the front seat, swerving past something that I can't see and instantly getting a slew of curses screamed from the guy in the next car, prompting Carver to put his window back up. "You just get better at not dying."

I let out a shaky breath. "Wow. Great advice. You really have a gift for this."

Carver doesn't respond but the soft chuckle from King in the trunk is enough to give me what I need to keep going. "So," I say to the silent car, bracing my hand against the door behind my head as Carver swerves and cuts through traffic like a pro. "You guys do this often?"

"Third time this month," Grayson tells me and while his tone sounds like he's joking, it's hard to be sure.

"Show time," King says, cutting off our conversation and making my anxiety rear its ugly head. I clutch on tighter to the gun, hating that

I can't see out the window and instead, look through to the front seat, watching Carver drive.

His concentration and determination to save my ass calms me, and I know that no matter what, they won't let me get hurt. We might come out with a few bumps and bruises though, but what really scares me is just how far the guys will go to keep me safe. Cruz especially, he's still healing after the last time he saved me.

Carver's hands grip the steering wheel and I watch as he pulls it sharply to the left, his eyes continuously flicking up to the rearview mirror, watching as the men gain on us.

Horns blast with every turn we take and I don't doubt that in the space of a few seconds, we're going to have cops on our tail too. Though, they sure as hell wouldn't be able to keep up with the speeds Carver's set for this little outing.

"Right on our six," Grayson grunts, giving Carver the warning that he needs and making me fear for our lives. We got a good head start, but this SUV wasn't built for driving like this … their trucks were though. They're well equipped with what they need to take us down, while we're just flailing around, trying to not get bullets through our asses.

"Oh, dear God," I pray, my anxiety skyrocketing. I've never been religious but this sure seems like a good place to start. "I swear, if you let us get out of this alive, I'll … *pretend* to not love pre-marital fucking so much."

King scoffs before going serious. "We've got guns."

The guys adjust themselves in the trunk just as the first bullet shatters the back window of the SUV. They instantly return fire as Carver roars back to me. "KEEP DOWN."

Cruz leans back, putting his weight down on me to keep me still while feeding the guys more ammunition. Bullets rain down over the SUV, and within seconds, King is kicking out the glass to get clearer shots on the trucks behind us.

"On your left," Cruz calls out just moments before a bullet slices through the side of the car, just millimeters from my head.

"OH FUCK," I yell, my eyes wide with fear, my heart racing a million miles an hour as I scramble away from the side, somehow pushing Cruz's weight off me and curling into a ball right in the center of the floor space.

"SHIT." Carver swerves hard to the left, ramming the back of the SUV against the front end of the truck. I peek up just in time to watch the truck lose its traction and go slamming straight into a concrete barricade, taking them out of the game. Anger swarms through Carver's gaze. "This is the exact fucking reason why I had the Escalade bulletproofed."

No one responds. There's no point, especially because the boys are so focused on the fire power coming at them through the back of the car. Bullets whiz past my face and the boys do well to stay down but how soon until their luck runs out?

"Driver of the third truck is out," Grayson says, just as Carver takes a sharp right-hand turn onto an empty, deserted road, flinging me across the floor space of the ruined SUV.

"We'll lose the rest down here," Carver grunts.

I adjust myself on the backseat, holding my gun tightly as we lose another truck, leaving just three behind us. The flood of bullets coming our way begins to ease.

The panic settles in my chest and I find myself raising up on my knees, my curiosity getting the best of me. My head peeks out over the back of the seat and I get a look at the three angry trucks bearing down on us. Masked men hang out the windows, their guns aimed right for us, wildly shooting as Grayson and King lay across the trunk, shooting right back with skilled precision.

Cruz glances my way. "The fuck do you think you're doing?" he demands, shoving his hand right in my face and throwing me back down into the floor space. "Are you feeling a bullet through the head today?"

I push his hand away and climb back to my knees. "Let me up," I snap. "I can help."

"No offense, babe. But you can't."

Frustration pulses through me. "I can."

"How?" he throws back. "Are you going to shoot through the back seat, hope like fuck that you don't hit one of the guys and then somehow manage to land a shot? I don't think so, babe. I'll teach you to shoot once I know your ass is safe."

I push his hand off me and he lets it fall to his bag of goodies, grabbing a grenade and passing it back to the guys. Grayson takes it without hesitation, yanking the little thing off the top with his teeth, and launching it out the back window.

The grenade flies free and I watch with my mouth hanging open as it lands right through the sunroof of the middle truck and instantly explodes, taking another truck out of the race. But not a second later, a bullet pierces through Carver's window and shatters the glass all over his lap.

"Holy shit," I breathe, knowing that Cruz has a point. I'm so far out of my league, it's not funny.

Carver glances back to see my head peeking out again and he groans low, his frustration quickly getting the best of him. He slams hard on the brakes and I go flying right through to the front of the SUV.

Carver's hand snaps out and catches me before my back slams against the hard dashboard, and before I can even call him an asshole, I'm pushed down into the footwell under the dash.

The sudden stop has the trucks instantly catching up. Carver slams his foot back down on the gas and swerves the SUV to the right, shoving the guy beside us right off the road and down into a deep ditch.

Cruz laughs. "YES. Four down, two to go."

I try to peer through the middle to see out the back but Carver quickly pushes me back, his hold nowhere near as easy to break as Cruz's was. "Fucking hell," I grumble. "This is getting old fast."

"Tough shit," Carver grunts. "Being cramped beats a fucking bullet to the head any day."

I roll my eyes. He's right. This is definitely better than the alternative.

The shooting gets more insistent, but with the two remaining trucks so much closer, the boys are able to get cleaner shots. King shoots out the tires of the truck on the right and despite not being able to see it, I hear as it goes screeching into a tailspin behind us before the truck flips and rolls.

"Fuck yeah," King howls with laughter. "Did you see that?"

"No," I mutter under my breath.

With only one truck left, the boys throw everything they have at it, working together as a team as Carver watches closely through the rearview mirror, dodging and swerving every shot they take.

I hear sirens in the distance and I stare up at Carver with wide eyes. "Cops," I panic.

He shakes his head, keeping his eyes on the road. "They won't catch us," he says, the conviction in his tone immediately easing my fears.

I put my head against my knees, feeling safer under the dash than I had in the back. Perhaps it's the smaller space, who knows, but up here, I'm able to breathe. Don't get me wrong, if Carver accidentally rams headfirst into a tree and crushes me in here, I'm going to be pissed.

The boys work tirelessly in the back of the SUV exchanging gunfire and absolutely dominating. "Come on," Carver encourages. "Our turn is coming up."

The boys groan and grunt from the trunk, giving everything they've got to save our lives, and as the tension rises and the seconds tick by, I find myself peering up and watching again. Grayson's muscles bulge with every shot he takes as King leans back against the side of the SUV, getting the best angle possible.

There's a man hanging out the window with his mask pulled up to his forehead, clearly irritated with his lack of visibility. His gun is pointed right for the car, countering every shot the guys take. As the driver watches the boys carefully, he dodges and swerves just as well as Carver does.

"This asshole just won't give in," Cruz grunts, leaning onto the backrest with his gun out and helping the guys as best he can. "They're too good."

A string of curses comes flying out of Carver's mouth as he tries to put some distance between us, but nothing works, they keep up with us at every turn.

I need to help them, but how? We can't keep going on like this. There are too many people in our car and soon enough, one of us is bound to get hit.

I need to distract them. I need to do something to draw their attention away from the boys so that we can get our hit on them and finally take them out.

But what?

My mind whirls with ridiculous possibilities, each one as moronic as the last when I remember the gun in my hand, and without a second of hesitation or thought, I scramble across the front seat, launching myself across Carver's lap until my head is thrown out of the window.

I see the truck just as Carver's hand curls around my thigh, preparing to yank me back. The driver of the truck spots me immediately and it's all I need to pull my gun, aim and shoot before Carver yanks me back in through the shattered window.

My shot goes wide, just as Cruz had expected. But the small distraction is enough for Grayson to take the shot he needs. A sense of relief fills me as the last truck flies over the guard rail and soars off the small cliff into the thick trees below.

The boys breathe heavily as Carver tosses me back into the front passenger seat, my back slamming against the door as I stare at him in shock. His stare rests heavily on mine, his brows furrowed in shock, not believing for even a second that I actually just did that. Hell, I kinda don't either.

The guys make themselves comfortable, checking over themselves and making sure everyone is alright as Carver takes a turn down a familiar road. "We're going to King's cabin?" I ask, my eyes widening in surprise.

Carver just looks back at me, his brows still furrowed. "My mother really said that she'd kill my unborn child?"

"Umm … what?" I grumble. "We're back on that? I thought we already cleared this up?"

"I wasn't focused before. I am now," he says. "I need to know what she said."

I let out a deep breath, getting comfortable in my seat and curling my arms around my body, the cool air flowing in through the shattered windows freezing me from the inside out. "That's exactly what she said. If we were to have a kid, which I really don't intend on having any time soon, for the record, but if you knocked me up, she'd kill it and me before it had the chance to even see life."

"Dude," Cruz mutters darkly from the backseat, leaving the

single word hanging in the air, the weight of it resting on each of our shoulders.

Carver sits in silence for a second, rubbing his hand over his face before looking back at me again. "And she said that if you were to speak a word of your conversation to me, that she'd slit my throat and make you watch, just like my father did to your parents?"

I nod. "She's a great role model, isn't she? Perhaps we'll only visit on big holidays."

"Fucking hell."

The silence that follows is way too thick for me to stand and I let out a low breath. "Sooo ..." I start. "The cabin, huh?"

King nods in the backseat and I look around to find all three big guys squished in side by side. "It's our backup plan," King explains. "No one but us knows that's where you'll be. It's our safe house."

"So, we're just going to chill out there for a few days until everything dies down?"

Cruz shrugs his shoulders. "Honestly, we're just playing it day by day," he says before a stupid grin stretches across his face. "Think of it as a vacation."

I roll my eyes and sink back into my seat, making myself comfortable.

We drive for another fifteen minutes before we pull down the long dirt road leading to the cabin, and the closer we get, the more memories of the last time I was here surface through my mind. It was a great eighteenth birthday party until it wasn't, but this time is going to be different.

We pull up a minute later and the guys pile out of the car. "Wait here," Carver says, walking toward the cabin with Grayson. "We're just going to check that it's all clear."

I hang back with Cruz and King, talking shit as we wait for the all-clear call from the boys. When Carver gives us the wave, I rush from the car to find the bathroom in desperation. I get myself all fixed up and spend a minute or two hanging over the sink, splashing water on my face and telling myself that this was all a dream. If I allow myself to think it was real, I might just scream.

"Babe?" Cruz calls out.

"What?" I yell back, stepping out of the bathroom to find all four guys waiting by the front door, looking at me with hunger in their eyes.

"We're going to do a perimeter check, make sure there's nothing hiding out in the woods. Why don't you figure out which room you want to take and when we get back, we'll cook you dinner."

I look over them, knowing exactly what I want for dinner. "Sounds good to me," I murmur. "Hurry back."

The boys grin and file back out the door, but before the door can close behind them, I call out again. "Hey, Cruz."

He stops in the middle of the doorway and looks back at me. "What's up, babe?"

"Just reminding you that I promised that I'd be all yours tonight."

He grins wide, that adorable little sparkle hitting his eyes as he winks and makes everything melt inside of me. "Trust me," he murmurs, his voice low and full of seduction. "I haven't forgotten."

Something darkens in his eyes, and just like that, the door closes behind him.

I laugh to myself and dive toward the door to flick the lock. After all, it's better to be safe than sorry around here, and seeing as though they haven't cleared the woods yet, I'm not down for testing my luck tonight.

I turn and face the massive cabin, wondering where the hell to even start. When I was here for my birthday, I saw the living room, one of the many bathrooms, and the epic kitchen before seeing way too much of the woods.

I start exploring, taking myself up the stairs and glancing into each of the bedrooms. They're modest and not quite as grand as the ones back home, but what was I supposed to expect? It's a vacation cabin, not a main residence. The main bedroom though, that's where it's at.

I instantly claim it as my own with a cheeky as fuck grin settling across my face. The boys can fight it out for the other rooms … or they can just join me and finally let me live out my fantasy of taking them all on at once.

I make my way back down the stairs and as I hit the bottom step, I hear the familiar engine to the SUV coming to life.

The fuck? Are they going somewhere? Did they find something in the woods?

I rush over to the window and watch as the boys stand around the SUV, grim expressions on their faces, deep in conversation. I drum my fists against the window. "Hey," I call out. "Where are you going?"

They don't hear me and I bang again, this time more insistent. "HEY. CARVER. KING. WHAT ARE YOU DOING? CRUZ?"

All at once, each of them look back at the cabin with broken expressions and I watch as they start sliding back into the SUV. King first, followed by Grayson.

The fuck are they doing? Where are they going?

Are they leaving me here?

I watch Cruz get in and I don't wait a second longer. I rush through the cabin, making my way back to the front door. I have to stop to unlatch the lock and just as I swing the door wide and run out onto the deck, I look up to find the SUV speeding back down the long dirt driveway, not one of the boys in sight.

"HEY," I yell out, waving my arms over my head. "COME BACK. WHERE ARE Y—"

BOOM!

The cabin explodes behind me, the deck tearing up under my feet and launching me high into the air as the wood splinters into a million pieces, destroying what was once an incredible cabin.

I'm thrown far across the property, my body slamming down against the hard dirt with a loud thump, my head instantly spinning as a ball of fire explodes around me, the heat burning against my back and getting hotter by the second.

I suck in a shaky breath, pushing myself up off the hard, cold ground and rolling onto my back to see the inferno of flames that was once the Kings' cabin.

I just stare, tears welling in my eyes.

The boys ... no.

No, they couldn't have done this.

I twist around, looking back toward the dirt driveway to watch as the SUV continues speeding away, the dirt kicking up beneath the tires and leaving a cloud in their wake.

I just stare, my chest aching as I breathe heavily, my lungs instantly filling with thick smoke from the cabin.

No. I can't believe it, but I have to trust what I see with my own two eyes.

The boys did this. All this time, I trusted them with everything that I had. They promised to keep me safe. They promised to love me and give their lives to save mine, and when I was at my most vulnerable, they took that trust away.

They did this.

They blew up the cabin. They tried to kill me. I feel it deep in my gut.

I trusted the wrong people.

The tears fall from my eyes, blurring the inferno before me. I scramble back, my feet pushing against the hard dirt to gain leverage, the blaze getting too hot to withstand and only when my back slams against the trunk of a tree, I achingly push myself to my feet.

My heart breaks, the boys' betrayal riding heavily on my shoulders as the SUV disappears out of sight, leaving me stranded with nowhere to go and not a damn soul to trust.

All I know is that I can't stay here.

I turn and without a backward glance, I take off into the darkened woods, my feet pounding against the cold ground, stumbling and tripping, knowing that this has to be the last time that I will ever see the Kings of Ravenwood Heights again.

From here on out, I'm on my own.

<u>Boys of Winter Series Playlist</u>

Blood // Water - Grandson
Evil - 8 Graves
11 Minutes - Yungblud Ft. Halsey & Travis Barker
Hate The Way - G-Eazy Feat Blackbear
Control - Halsey
Play With Fire - Sam Tinnesz
You Should See Me In A Crown - Billie Eilish
Everybody Wants To Rule The World - Lorde
Courage To Change - Sia
You Broke Me First - Tate McRae
Yellow Flicker Beat - Lorde
Sweet Dreams - Marilyn Manson
Wicked Game - Daisy Gray
Nobody's Home - Avril Lavigne
Stand By Me - Ki: Theory
Paparazzi - Kim Dracula
Bringing Me Down - Ki: Theory (feat. Ruelle)
Therefore I am - Billie Eilish
I see Red - Everybody Love An Outlaw
In The Air Tonight - Nonpoint
Tainted Love - Marilyn Manson
Saviour - Daisy Gray
I Put A Spell On You - Annie Lennox
Heaven Julia Michaels
Heart Attack - Demi Lovato
Dynasty - Mia
Weak - AJR
Redemption - Besomorph & Coopex & RIELL
Legends Never Die - League of Legends & Against the Current
Time - NF
Rumors - NEFFEX

Thanks for reading!

If you enjoyed reading this book as much as I enjoyed writing it, please leave an Amazon review to let me know.

https://www.amazon.com/gp/product/B08WWQYLBB

For more information on Boys of Winter, stalk me online –

Facebook Page - www.facebook.com/SheridanAnneAuthor

FacebookReaderGroup–www.facebook.com/SheridansBookishBabes

Instagram – www.instagram.com/Sheridan.Anne.Author

Sheridan Anne

<u>Other Series by Sheridan Anne</u>

www.amazon.com/Sheridan-Anne/e/B079TLXN6K

<u>YOUNG ADULT / NEW ADULT DARK ROMANCE</u>

The Broken Hill High Series (5 Book Series + Novella)

Haven Falls (7 Book Series + Novella)

Broken Hill Boys (5 Book Novella Series)

Aston Creek High (4 Book Series)

Rejects Paradise (4 Book Series)

Black Widow (A Rejects Paradise Novella)

Boys of Winter (4 Book Series)

<u>NEW ADULT SPORTS ROMANCE</u>

Kings of Denver (4 Book Series)

Denver Royalty (3 Book Series)

Rebels Advocate (4 Book Series)

<u>CONTEMPORARY ROMANCE</u>

Men of Fire Rescue One (4 Book Series)

Until Autumn – Happily Eva Alpha World

<u>URBAN FANTASY - PEN NAME: CASSIDY SUMMERS</u>

Slayer Academy (3 Book Series)

Made in United States
Orlando, FL
16 April 2024

45868726R00275